Janet Evanovich's novels are:

"Suspenseful."—*Los Angeles Times*

"Terrific."—*San Francisco Chronicle*

"Irresistible."—*Kirkus Reviews*

"Thrilling."—*The Midwest Book Review*

"Hilariously funny."—*USA Today*

"A blast of fresh air."—*The Washington Post*

"Inventive and fast-paced."—*San Diego Union-Tribune*

"Superb."—*Detroit Free Press*

BY JANET EVANOVICH

ONE FOR THE MONEY
TWO FOR THE DOUGH
THREE TO GET DEADLY
FOUR TO SCORE
HIGH FIVE
HOT SIX
SEVEN UP
HARD EIGHT
TO THE NINES
TEN BIG ONES
ELEVEN ON TOP
TWELVE SHARP
LEAN MEAN THIRTEEN
FEARLESS FOURTEEN
FINGER LICKIN' FIFTEEN
SIZZLING SIXTEEN

VISIONS OF SUGAR PLUMS
PLUM LOVIN'
PLUM LUCKY
PLUM SPOOKY

WICKED APPETITE

FULL HOUSE

WITH DORIEN KELLY

LOVE IN A NUTSHELL
THE HUSBAND LIST

WITH CHARLOTTE HUGHES

FULL TILT
FULL SPEED
FULL BLAST
FULL BLOOM
FULL SCOOP

WITH LEANNE BANKS

HOT STUFF

WITH INA YALOF

HOW I WRITE

AVAILABLE FROM HARPERCOLLINS

HERO AT LARGE
MOTOR MOUTH
METRO GIRL

TWELVE SHARP

&

LEAN MEAN THIRTEEN

TWO NOVELS IN ONE

JANET EVANOVICH

St. Martin's Paperbacks

This is a work of fiction. All of the characters, organizations, and events portrayed in this novel are either products of the author's imagination or are used fictitiously.

Published in the United States by St. Martin's Paperbacks, an imprint of St. Martin's Publishing Group.

For information, address St. Martin's Publishing Group, 120 Broadway, New York, NY 10271.

www.stmartins.com

ISBN: 978-1-250-62078-1

Printed in the United States of America

St. Martin's Paperbacks edition 2020

10 9 8 7 6 5 4 3 2 1

TWELVE SHARP

This book was gloriously edited by
Super Jen Enderlin.

Thanks to Deanne Waller
for suggesting the title for this book.

Chapter ONE

When I was twelve years old I accidentally substituted salt for sugar in a cake recipe. I baked the cake, iced the cake, and served it up. It looked like a cake, but as soon as you cut into it and took a taste, you knew something else was going on. People are like that, too. Sometimes you just can't tell what's on the inside from looking at the outside. Sometimes people are a big surprise, just like the salt cake. Sometimes the surprise turns out to be good. And sometimes the surprise turns out to be bad. And sometimes the surprise is just friggin' confusing.

Joe Morelli is one of those good surprises. He's two years older than I am, and for most of my school years, spending time with Morelli was like a visit to the dark side, alluring and frightening. He's a Trenton cop now, and he's my off-again, on-again boyfriend. He used to be the hair-raising part of my life, but my life has had a lot of changes, and now he's the normal part. He has a dog named Bob, and a nice little house, and a toaster. On the outside Morelli is still street tough and dangerously alluring. On the inside Morelli is now the sexy guy with the toaster. Go figure.

I have a hamster named Rex, a utilitarian apartment, and my toaster is broken. My name is Stephanie Plum, and I work as a bond enforcement agent, also known as a bounty hunter, for my cousin Vinnie. It's not a great job, but it has its moments, and if I mooch food off my parents the job almost pays enough to get me through the month. It would pay a lot more but the truth is, I'm not all that good at it.

Sometimes I moonlight for a guy named Ranger who's extremely bad in an incredibly good way. He's a security expert, and a bounty hunter, and he moves like smoke. Ranger is milk chocolate on the outside . . . a delicious, tempting, forbidden pleasure. And no one knows what's on the inside. Ranger keeps his own counsel.

I work with two women I like a lot. Connie Rosolli is Vinnie's office manager and junkyard dog. She's a little older than I am. A little smarter. A little tougher. A little more Italian. She's got a lot more chest, and she dresses like Betty Boop.

The other woman is my sometimes-partner Lula. Lula was at this moment parading around in the bail bonds office, showing Connie and me her new outfit. Lula is a way-beyond-voluptuous black woman who was currently squashed into four-inch spike heels and a sparkly gold spandex dress that had been constructed for a *much* smaller woman. The neckline was low, and the only thing keeping Lula's big boobs from popping out was the fact that the material was snagged on her nipples. The skirt was stretched tight across her ass and hung two inches below the full moon.

With Connie and Lula you get what you see.

Lula bent to take a look at the heel on her shoe, and Connie was treated to a view of the night sky.

"Crikey," Connie said. "You need to put some underwear on."

"I got underwear on," Lula said. "I'm wearing my best thong. Just 'cause I used to be a 'ho don't mean I'm cheap. Problem is that little thong stringy gets lost in all my derriere."

"Tell me again what you're doing in this getup," Connie said.

"I'm gonna be a rock-and-roll singer. I got a gig singing with Sally Sweet's new band. You heard of the *Who*? Well, we're gonna be the *What*."

"You can't sing," Connie said. "I've heard you sing. You can't hold a tune to 'Happy Birthday.'"

"The hell I can't," Lula said. "I could sing your ass off. Besides, half those rock stars can't sing. They just open their big oversize mouths and yell. And you gotta admit, I look good in this here dress. Nobody gonna be paying attention to my singing when I'm wearing this dress."

"She's got a point," I said to Connie.

"No argument," Connie said.

"I'm underrealized," Lula said. "I gotta lot of untapped potential. Yesterday my horoscope said I gotta expand my horizons."

"You expand any more in that dress, and you'll get yourself arrested," Connie said.

The bonds office is on Hamilton Avenue, a couple blocks from Saint Francis Hospital. Handy for bonding out guys who've been shot. It's a small storefront office sandwiched between a beauty parlor and a used bookstore. There's an outer room with a scarred imitation leather couch, a couple folding chairs, Connie's desk and computer, and a bank of files. Vinnie's office is located in a room behind Connie's desk.

When I started working for Vinnie he used his office to talk to his bookie and set up nooners with barnyard animals, but Vinnie has recently discovered the Internet, and now Vinnie uses his office to surf porn sites and online casinos. Behind the bank of file cabinets is a storeroom filled with the nuts and bolts of the bail bonds business. Confiscated televisions, DVD players, iPods, computers, a velvet painting of Elvis, a set of cookware, blenders, kids' bikes, engagement rings, a tricked-out Hog, a bunch of George Foreman grills, and God knows what else. Vinnie had some guns and ammo back there too. Plus a box of cuffs that he got on eBay. There's a small bathroom that Connie keeps spotless and a back door in case there's a need to sneak off.

"I hate to be a party pooper," Connie said, "but we're going to have to put the fashion show on hold because we have a problem." She slid a stack of folders across her desk at me. "These are all unresolved skips. If we don't find some of these guys, we're going belly-up."

Here's the way bail bonds works. If you're accused of a crime and you don't want to sit and rot in jail while you're waiting for your trial to come up, you can give the court a wad of money. The court takes the money and lets you walk, and you get the money back when you show up on your trial date. If you don't have that money stashed under your mattress, a bail bondsman can give the court the money on your behalf. He'll charge you a percentage of the money, maybe ten percent, and he'll keep that percentage whether you're proven guilty or not. If the accused shows up for court, the court gives the bail bondsman his money back. If the accused doesn't show up, the court keeps the money until the bondsman finds the accused and drags his sorry butt back to jail.

So you see the problem, right? Too much money going out and not enough money going in, and Vinnie might have to refinance his house. Or worse, the insurance company that backs Vinnie could yank the plug.

"Lula and I can't keep up with the skips," I said to Connie. "There are too many of them."

"Yeah, and I'll tell you the problem," Lula said. "It used to be Ranger worked full time for you, but anymore he's got his own security business going, and he's not doing skip tracing. It's just Stephanie and me catching the bad guys these days."

It was true. Ranger had moved most of his business toward the security side and only went into tracking mode when something came in that was over my head. There are some who might argue *everything* is over my head, but for practical purposes we've had to ignore that argument.

"I hate to say this," I told Connie, "but you need to hire another bond enforcement person."

"It's not that easy," Connie said. "Remember when we had Joyce Barnhardt working here? That was a disaster. She screwed up all her busts doing her *big bad bounty hunter* routine. And then she stole everyone's skips. It's not like she's a team player."

Joyce Barnhardt is my archenemy. I went all through school with her, and she was a misery. And before the ink was dry on my marriage license she was in bed with my husband, who is now my ex-husband. Thank you, Joyce.

"We could put an ad in the paper," Lula said. "That's how I got my filing job here. Look at how good that turned out."

Connie and I did eye rolls.

Lula was about the worst file clerk ever. Lula kept her job because no one else would tolerate Vinnie. The first time Vinnie made a grab at Lula she clocked him on the side of the head with a five-pound phone book and told him she'd staple his nuts to the wall if he didn't show respect. And that was the end of sexual harassment in the bail bonds office.

Connie read the names off the files on her desk. "Lonnie Johnson, Kevin Gallager, Leon James, Dooby Biagi, Caroline Scarzolli, Melvin Pickle, Charles Chin, Bernard Brown, Mary Lee Truk, Luis Queen, John Santos. These are all current. You already have half of them. The rest came in last night. Plus we have nine outstanding that we've relegated to the *temporarily lost cause* file. Vinnie's writing a lot of bond these days. Probably taking risks he shouldn't. The result is more than the normal FTAs."

When someone doesn't show up for a court appearance we call them FTA. Failure to Appear. People fail to appear for a bunch of reasons. Hookers and pushers can make more money on the street than they can in jail so they only show up in court when you finally stop bonding them out. All other people just don't want to go to jail.

Connie gave me the new files, and it was like an elephant was sitting on my chest. Lonnie Johnson was wanted for armed robbery. Leon James was suspected of arson and attempted murder. Kevin Gallager was wanted for grand theft auto. Mary Lee Truk had inserted a carving knife into her husband's left buttock during a domestic disturbance. And Melvin Pickle was caught with his pants down in the third row of the multiplex.

Lula was looking over my shoulder, reading along with me.

"Melvin Pickle sounds like fun," she said. "I think we should start with Melvin."

"Maybe a bond enforcement agent wanted ad in the paper isn't such a bad idea," I said to Connie.

"Yeah," Lula said, "just be careful how you word it. You probably want to fib a little. Like you *don't* want to say we're looking for some gun-happy lunatic to take down a bunch of scumbags."

"I'll keep that in mind when I write it up," Connie said.

"I'm going down the street," I told Lula. "I need something to make me happy. We'll go to work when I get back."

"You going to the drugstore?" Lula wanted to know.

"No. The bakery."

"I wouldn't mind if you brought me back one of them cream-filled doughnuts with the chocolate frosting," Lula said. "I need to get happy, too."

At mid-morning the Garden State was heating up. Pavement was steaming under a cloudless sky, petrochemical plants were spewing to the north, and cars were emitting hydrocarbons statewide. By mid-afternoon I'd feel the toxic stew catch in the back of my throat, and I'd know it was truly summer in Jersey. For me, the stew is part of the Jersey experience. The stew has attitude. And it enhances the pull of Point Pleasant. How can you completely appreciate the Jersey shore if the air is safe to breathe in the interior parts of the state?

I swung into the bakery and went straight to the doughnut case. Marjorie Lando was behind the counter, filling cannoli for a customer. Fine by me. I could wait my turn. The bakery was always a soothing experience. My heart rate slowed in the presence of massive quantities of sugar and lard. My mind floated over the acres of cookies and cakes and doughnuts and cream pies topped with rainbow sprinkles, chocolate frosting, whipped cream, and meringue.

I was patiently contemplating my doughnut selection when I sensed a familiar presence behind me. A hand brushed my hair back, and Ranger leaned in to me and kissed me on the nape of my neck.

"I could get you to look at *me* like that if I had five minutes alone with you," Ranger said.

"I'll give you five minutes alone with me if you'll take over half my skips."

"Tempting," Ranger said, "but I'm on my way to the airport, and I'm not sure when I'll be back. Tank is in charge. Call him if you need help. And let him know if you decide to move into my apartment."

Not that long ago I needed a safe place to stay, and sort of commandeered Ranger's apartment when he was out of town. Ranger had come home and found me sleeping in his bed like Goldilocks. He'd very graciously not thrown me out the seventh-floor window. And in fact he'd allowed me to stay with a minimum of sexual harassment. Okay, maybe minimum isn't entirely accurate. Maybe it was a seven on a scale of ten, but he hadn't forced the issue.

"How did you know I was here?" I asked him.

"I stopped at the bonds office, and Lula told me you were on a doughnut mission."

"Where are you going?"

"Miami."

"Is this business or pleasure?"

"It's bad business."

Marjorie finished with her customer and made her way over to me. "What'll it be?" she wanted to know.

"A dozen Boston Cream doughnuts."

"Babe," Ranger said.

"They're not all for me."

Ranger doesn't often smile. Mostly he thinks about smiling, and this was one of those thinking-smile times. He wrapped his hand around my wrist, pulled me to him, and kissed me. The kiss was warm and short. No tongue in front of the bakery lady, thank God. He turned and walked away. Tank was idling at the curb in a black SUV. Ranger got in and they drove off.

Marjorie was behind the counter with a cardboard box in her hand and her mouth dropped open. "Wow," she said.

That dragged a sigh out of me because she was right. Ranger was definitely a *wow*. He stood half a head taller than me. He was perfectly toned muscle, and he had classic Latino good looks. He always smelled great. He dressed only in black. His skin was dark. His eyes were dark. His hair was dark. His life was dark. Ranger had lots of secrets.

"It's a work relationship," I told Marjorie.

"If he was in here any longer, the chocolate would have melted off the eclairs."

"I don't like this," Lula said. "I wanted to go after the pervert. I personally think it's a bad choice to go after the guy who likes guns."

"He's got the highest bond. The fastest way to dig Vinnie out of the hole is to get the guy with the highest bond."

We were in Lula's red Firebird, sitting across the street from Lonnie Johnson's last known address. It was a small clapboard bungalow in a depressed neighborhood that backed up to the hockey arena. It was close to noon and not a great time to roust a bad guy. If he's still in bed, it's because he's drunk and mean. If he's not in bed, it's most likely because he's at a bar getting drunk and mean.

"What's the plan?" Lula wanted to know. "We gonna just bust in like gangsta bounty hunters and kick his ass?"

I looked at Lula. "Have we *ever* done that?"

"Don't mean we can't."

"We'd look like idiots. We're incompetent."

"That's harsh," Lula said. "And I don't think we're *completely* incompetent. I think we're closer to eighty percent incompetent. Remember the time you wrestled that naked greased-up fat guy? You did a good job with that one."

"Too early in the day to do the pizza delivery routine," I said.

"Can't do the flower delivery either. Nobody believe someone sending flowers to this dope."

"If you hadn't changed clothes you could do the

hooker delivery routine," I said to Lula. "He would have opened the door to you in that gold thing."

"Maybe we pretend we're selling cookies. Like Girl Scouts. All we gotta do is go back to the 7-Eleven and get some cookies."

I looked Johnson's phone number up on the bond sheet and called him from my cell.

"Yeah?" a man said.

"Lonnie Johnson?"

"What the fuck you want? Fuckin' bitch calling me at this hour. You think I got nothin' better to do than answer this phone?" And he hung up.

"Well?" Lula asked.

"He didn't feel like talking. And he's angry."

A shiny black Hummer with tinted windows and bling wheel covers rolled down the street and stopped in front of Johnson's house.

"Uh-oh," Lula said. "Company."

The Hummer sat there for a moment and then opened fire on Johnson's house. Multiple weapons. At least one was automatic, firing continuous rounds. Windows blew out and the house was drilled with shots. Gunfire was returned from the house, and I saw the nose of a rocket launcher poke out a front window. Obviously the Hummer saw it too because it laid rubber taking off.

"Maybe this isn't a good time," I said to Lula.

"I *told* you to go for the pervert."

Melvin Pickle worked in a shoe store. The store was part of the mall that attached to the multiplex where he'd been caught shaking hands with the devil. I didn't have a lot of enthusiasm for this capture, since I had some sympathetic feelings for Pickle. If I had to work in a shoe store all day, I might go to the multiplex to whack off once in a while too.

"Not only is this going to be an easy catch," Lula

said, parking at the food court entrance, "but we can get pizza and go shopping."

A half hour later, we were full of pizza and had taken a couple new perfumes out for a test drive. We'd moseyed down the mall and were standing in front of Pickle's shoe store, scoping out the employees. I had a photo of Pickle that had come with his bond agreement.

"That's him," Lula said, looking into the store. "That's him on his knees, trying to sell that dumb woman those ugly-ass shoes."

According to Pickle's paperwork he'd just turned forty. He had sandy-colored hair that looked like it had been cut in boot camp. His skin was pale, his eyes hidden behind round-rimmed glasses, his mouth accented by a big herpes sore. He was five-foot-seven and had an average build gone soft. His slacks and dress shirt were just short of shabby. He didn't look like he cared a whole lot if the woman bought the shoes.

I moved my cuffs from my shoulder bag to my jeans pocket. "I can manage this," I said to Lula. "You stay here in case he bolts."

"I don't think he looks like a bolter," Lula said. "I think he looks more like the walking dead."

I agreed with Lula. Pickle looked like he was two steps away from putting a bullet in his brain. I moved behind him and waited for him to stand.

"I love this shoe," the woman said. "But I need a size nine."

"I don't have a size nine," Pickle said.

"Are you sure?"

"Yeah."

"Maybe you should go back and look again."

Pickle sucked air for a couple beats and nodded. "Sure," he said.

He stood and turned and bumped into me.

"You're going to leave, aren't you?" I said. "I bet you're going to go out the back door and go home and never come back."

"It's a recurring fantasy," he said.

I glanced at my watch. It was twelve-thirty. "Have you had lunch?" I asked him.

"No."

"Take your lunch now and come with me, and I'll buy you a piece of pizza."

"There's something wrong with this picture," Pickle said. "Are you one of those religious nuts who wants to save me?"

"No. I'm not a religious nut." I held my hand out. "Stephanie Plum."

He automatically shook my hand. "Melvin Pickle."

"I work for Vincent Plum Bail Bonds," I said. "You missed a court date, and you need to reschedule."

"Sure," he said.

"Now."

"I can't go now. I gotta work."

"You can take your lunch break."

"I had plans for lunch."

Probably going to see a movie. I was still holding his hand, and with my other hand I clapped a bracelet on him.

He looked down at the cuff. "What's this? You can't do this. People will ask questions. And then what will I tell them? I'll have to tell them I'm a pervert!"

Two women looked over at him and raised their eyebrows.

"No one will care," I said. I turned to the women. "You don't care, right?"

"Right," they murmured and hurried out of the store.

"Just walk out into the mall quietly with me," I said. "I'll take you to court and get you rebonded."

Actually, Vinnie would rebond him. Vinnie and

Connie could write bond. Lula and I did the capture thing.

"Darn," Pickle said. "Darn it all."

And he took off with the cuff dangling from his wrist. Lula stepped in front of him, but he had momentum and knocked her on her ass. He faltered for a moment, got his footing, and ran off into the mall. I was ten steps behind him. I stumbled over Lula, scrambled to my feet, and kept going. I chased him through the mall and up an escalator.

A hotel with an open atrium was attached to one end of the mall. Pickle ran into the hotel and barreled through the fire door into the stairwell. I chased him up five flights of stairs and thought my lungs were going to explode. He exited the stairwell, and I dragged myself, gasping, to the door.

There were seven floors in the hotel. All rooms opened to a hallway that overlooked the hotel atrium. We were on the sixth floor. I staggered out of the stairwell and saw that Pickle had made it halfway around the atrium and was straddling the balcony railing.

"Don't come near me," he yelled. "I'll jump."

"Fine with me," I said. "I get my money dead or alive."

Pickle looked depressed at that fact. Or maybe Pickle just *always* looked depressed.

"You're in pretty good shape," I said, still winded. "How do you stay in such good shape?"

"My car got repossessed. I walk everywhere. And all day long I'm up and down with the shoes. At the end of the day my knees are killing me."

I was talking to him, creeping closer. "Why don't you get a different job? One that's easier on your knees."

"Are you kidding me? I'm lucky to have *this* job. Look at me. I'm a loser. And now everybody's going to know I'm a pervert. I'm a pervert loser. And I have a big herpes. I'm a pervert loser with a herpes!"

"You need to get a grip. You don't have to be a pervert loser if you don't want to be."

He sat on the railing and swung both legs over. "Easy for you to say. You aren't named Melvin Pickle. And I bet you were a baton twirler in high school. You probably had friends. You probably date."

"I don't exactly date, but I sort of have a boyfriend."

"What does *sort of* mean?"

"It means that he looks like my boyfriend, but I don't say it out loud."

"Why not?" Pickle wanted to know.

"It feels weird. I'm not sure why." Okay, I knew *why*, but I wasn't going to say *that* out loud either. I had feelings for two men, and I didn't know how to choose between them. "And I wish you wouldn't sit like that. It's creeping me out."

"Are you afraid I'll fall? I thought you didn't care. Remember dead or alive?"

My cell phone was ringing in my bag.

"For crying out loud, answer it," Pickle said. "Don't worry about me, I'm only going to kill myself."

I did an exaggerated eye roll and answered the phone.

"Hey," Lula said. "Where are you? I been looking all over."

"I'm in the hotel at the end of the mall."

"I'm right outside of that hotel. What are you doing there? Do you have Pickle?"

"I don't exactly *have* Pickle. We're on the sixth floor, and he's thinking about jumping off the balcony."

I looked over the railing and saw Lula walk into the atrium. She looked up, and I waved at her.

"I see you," Lula said. "Tell Pickle he's gonna make a big mess if he jumps. This floor's marble, and his head's gonna crack open like a fresh egg, and there's gonna be brains and blood all over the place."

I disconnected and relayed the message to Pickle.

"I have a plan," he said. "I'm going to jump feet first. That way my head won't make such an impact when I land."

Pickle was getting noticed. People were dotted around the atrium, looking up at him. The elevator opened behind me and a man in a suit stepped out.

"What's going on here?" he wanted to know.

"Don't come near me!" Pickle yelled. "If you come near me, I'll jump."

"I'm the hotel manager," the man said. "Is there something I can do?"

"Do you have a giant net?" I asked him.

"Just go away," Pickle said. "I have big problems. I'm a pervert."

"You don't look like a pervert," the manager said.

"I whacked off in the multiplex," Pickle told him.

"Everybody whacks off in the multiplex," the manager said. "I like to go when there's one of those chick flicks playing, and I wear my wife's panties and I—"

"Jeez," Pickle said. "Too much information."

The manager disappeared behind the elevator doors and minutes later reappeared in the lobby. He stood in a small cluster of hotel employees, everyone with their heads back, their eyes glued to Pickle.

"You're making a scene," I said to Pickle.

"Yeah," Pickle said. "Pretty soon they're going to start yelling *'Jump.'* The human race is lacking. Have you noticed?"

"There are some good people," I told him.

"Oh yeah? Who's the best person you know? Of all the people you know personally, is there anyone who has a sense of right and wrong and lives by it?"

This was a sticky question because it would have to

be Ranger . . . but I suspected he occasionally killed people. Only *bad* people, of course, but still . . .

The crowd in the atrium was growing and now included some uniformed security guys and two Trenton cops. One of the cops was on his two-way, probably calling Morelli to tell him I was involved in yet another disaster. A cameraman and his assistant joined the crowd.

"We're on television," I told Pickle.

Pickle looked down, waved at the camera, and everyone cheered.

"This is getting too weird," I told Pickle. "I'm leaving."

"You can't leave. If you leave, I'll jump."

"I don't care, remember?"

"Of course you care. You'll be responsible for my death."

"Oh no. No, no, no." I wagged my finger at him. "That won't work with me. I grew up in the Burg. I was raised Catholic. I know guilt in and out. The first thirty years of my life were ruled by guilt. Not that guilt is an entirely bad thing. But you're not going to lay it on me. Whether you live or die is your choice. I have nothing to do with it. I'm not taking responsibility for the state of the pot roast anymore."

"Pot roast?"

"Every Friday I'm expected for dinner at my parents' house. Every Friday my mom makes pot roast. If I'm late, the pot roast cooks too long and gets dry, and it's all my fault."

"And?"

"And it's not my fault!"

"Of course it's your fault. You were late. They were nice enough to make a pot roast for you. Then they were nice enough to hold dinner for you even though it meant ruining the pot roast. Boy, you should learn some manners."

My cell phone rang again. It was my Grandma Mazur. She lives with my mom and dad. She moved in when Grandpa Mazur sailed off in a heaven-bound gravy boat.

"You're on television," she said. "I was trying to find Judge Judy, and you popped up. They said you were breaking news. Are you trying to rescue that guy on the railing, or are you trying to get him to jump?"

"In the beginning I was trying to rescue him," I said. "But I'm starting to change my mind."

"I gotta go now," Grandma said. "I gotta call Ruth Biablocki and tell her you're on television. She's always going on about her granddaughter and how she's got that good job at the bank. Well let's see her top this one. Her granddaughter don't get on television!"

"What are you so depressed about that you want to jump off this balcony?" I asked Pickle. "Jumping to your death is pretty severe."

"My life sucks! My wife left me and took everything, including my clothes and my dog. I got fired from my job and had to go to work in a shoe store. I have no money, so I had to move back home and live with my mother. And I got caught whacking off in a multiplex. Could it possibly get any worse?"

"You have your health."

"I think I'm getting a cold. I have a *huge oozing cold sore*!"

My phone rang again.

"Cupcake," Morelli said, "I don't like finding you in a hotel with another guy."

I looked down and saw Morelli standing next to Lula.

"He's a jumper," I told Morelli.

"Yeah," Morelli said. "I can see that. What's the story?"

"He got caught whacking off in the multiplex and doesn't want to go to jail."

"He won't get a lot of jail time for that," Morelli said.

"Maybe a couple weekends or community service. It's not a big deal. Everyone whacks off in the multiplex."

I relayed the message to Pickle.

"It's not just jail," Pickle said. "It's me. I'm a loser."

Morelli was still on the phone. "Now what?"

"He's a loser."

"You're on your own with that one," Morelli said. "Are you going to need help with this?"

"Maybe you need . . . vitamins," I said to Pickle.

Pickle looked at me. Hopeful. "Do you think that could be it?"

"Yeah. If you get off the railing we could go to the health food store and get some."

"You're just saying that to get me off the railing."

"True. When you get off the railing, the police will probably arrest you for being a nut. You'll have to go to the station and wait for Vinnie to get there to bond you out again."

"I can't afford to get bonded out again. I just walked off my job. I'm probably unemployed."

"Oh for the love of everything holy." I peeked at my watch. I didn't have time for this. I had other fish to fry. "How about this. We need someone to do filing at the bonds office. Maybe I can get Vinnie to hire you so you can work off the fee to get bonded out."

"Really? You'd do that for me?"

Morelli was still listening in. "Okay, so far we've promised him community service, vitamins, and a job. The only thing left that he could possibly want is gorilla sex. And if you promise that to him I'm not going to be happy."

I disconnected Morelli and put the phone back into my pocket.

"About the job," Pickle said. "Vinnie wouldn't mind that I'm a . . . you know, pervert?"

That was pretty funny. Vinnie minding that Pickle

whacked off at the multiplex. "It's probably the only thing you have going for you," I told Pickle.

"Okay," he said. "But you're going to have to help me get off this railing. I'm terrified to move."

I grabbed the back of his shirt and hauled him off the railing, and we both collapsed into a heap on the floor. The crowd reaction was mixed. Some cheers and some boos. We got to our feet, and I cuffed his hands behind his back and led him to the elevator.

Chapter TWO

Morelli was waiting for me when the doors opened at the atrium level. He stepped in with two uniforms, and we all rode one floor down to the parking garage where a cruiser was idling. I got Pickle into the back seat and promised to get him rebonded.

"And the vitamins," Pickle said. "Don't forget the vitamins."

"Sure."

The cruiser took off, and I turned to Morelli. He was standing, thumbs hooked into his jeans pockets, and he was smiling at me. Morelli is six feet tall and is all lean planes and angles and hard muscle. His complexion is Mediterranean. His hair is almost black and curls against his neck. His brown eyes are liquid chocolate when he's aroused.

"What?" I asked Morelli.

"Did you make any more promises after you hung up on me?"

"None you want to know about."

The smile widened. "Bob misses you. He hasn't seen you in a couple days."

Bob is Morelli's big orange dog. And this is Morelli's ploy when he wants me to do a sleepover. Not that he needs a ploy.

"I'll have to call you later this afternoon," I said. "I don't know how my day will go. I'm on a mission to clean up a bunch of FTAs for Vinnie."

He curled his fingers into my T-shirt, pulled me to him, and kissed me. There was a lot of tongue involved and some wandering hands. When he was done he held me at arm's length. "Be careful," he said.

"Too late," I told him.

He moved me five steps backward into the elevator, pushed the button, and sent me up to the atrium where Lula was waiting.

"I'm not even going to guess what went on in that parking garage," Lula said. "But you better wipe that goofy smile off your face, or people are gonna get the right idea."

I called Connie and told her about Pickle.

"Vinnie's out of town," she said. "I'll bond Pickle out. And before I forget, there was a woman in here asking for you. She said her name was Carmen."

Offhand, I couldn't think of anyone I knew named Carmen. "Did she say what she wanted?"

"She said it was personal. I'm guessing she was in her late twenties. Soft-spoken. Pretty. And crazy."

Great. "What kind of crazy are we talking about? Crazy stressed? Crazy dressed in clown shoes with a red rubber nose? Or crazy crazy?"

"Crazy stressed and crazy crazy. She was dressed all in black. Like Ranger. Black boots, black cargo pants, black T-shirt. And she was . . . intense. She said she would track you down. And then she asked about Ranger. I guess she's looking for him too."

"We got choices to make," Lula said when I put my phone away. "We could cruise for shoes, or we could embarrass ourselves some more by pretending to be bounty hunters."

"I think we're on a roll. I say we keep pretending to be bounty hunters."

"I want to see the woman who stabbed her husband in the ass," Lula said. "Let's do her next."

"She's in the Burg," I said to Lula, pulling the file on Mary Lee Truk. "I'll call my mom and see if she knows her."

The Burg is a small chunk of Trenton just outside the center of the city. It's a working-class neighborhood that can't keep a secret and takes care of its own. My parents live in the Burg. My best friend, Mary Lou Molnar, lives in the Burg. Morelli's family is in the Burg. Morelli and I have moved out . . . but we haven't moved far.

Grandma Mazur answered the phone. "Of course I know Mary Lee Truk," Grandma said. "I play bingo with her mother."

"Does Mary Lee get along with her husband?"

"Not since she stabbed him in the behind. I understand he got real cranky about that and packed up and left."

"Why did she stab him?"

"The story is that she asked him if he thought she was putting on weight, and he said *Yes,* and then she stabbed him. It was one of them spontaneous acts. Mary Lee's going through the change, and everyone knows you don't just up and tell a menopausal woman she's getting fat. I swear some men have no brains at all.

"And by the way, I forgot to tell you before, but some woman came to the house this afternoon, looking for you. I said I didn't know exactly where you were, and she said that was okay, that she'd find you with or without anyone's help. And she was dressed like that hottie you work with, Ranger."

Lula pulled the Firebird in to the curb, and we sat looking at the Truk house.

"I don't have a good feeling about this," Lula said.

"You were the one who wanted to do the butt stabber."

"That was before I knew the menopause story. What if she has a hot flash while we're there and goes looney tunes?"

"Just don't turn your back on her. And don't comment on her weight."

I got out of the car and walked to the door, and Lula followed. I was about to knock when the door was wrenched open, and Mary Lee glared out at me. She had short brown hair that looked like it had been styled with an electric mixer. She was fifty-two according to her bond papers. She was a couple inches shorter than me and a couple pounds heavier.

"What?" she asked.

"*Yow*!" Lula whispered to me.

I introduced myself and gave Mary Lee the routine about getting rebonded.

"I can't go with you," she wailed. "Look at my hair! I used to be so good with hair, but lately I can't do anything with this mess."

"I use conditioner on mine," Lula said. "Have you tried that?"

We both looked at Lula's hair. It was orangutan orange and the texture of boar bristles.

"How about a hat?" I said.

"A hat," Mary Lee sobbed. "My hair's so bad I need a hat!" Mary Lee's face got red, and she stripped her T-shirt off. "God, it's *hot* in here." She was in her bra, sweating, and fanning herself with her shirt.

Lula put her finger to the side of her head and made circles. The international sign for *bats in her belfry*.

"I saw that!" Mary Lee said, eyes narrowed. "You think I'm nuts. You think the big fatso is nuts!"

"Lady, you just took your shirt off," Lula said. "I used to do that but I made money on it."

Mary Lee looked at the shirt in her hand. "I don't remember taking it off."

Mary Lee's face wasn't red anymore, and she'd stopped sweating, so I took the shirt and tugged it over her head. "I can help you," I said. "I know just what you need." I rummaged through my shoulder bag, found my baseball cap, and clapped it onto her head and tucked most of her hair in. I did a fast walk through the house to make sure it was locked up and Mary Lee hadn't accidentally put the cat in the oven, and then Lula and I steered Mary Lee out of the house and into the car.

Five minutes later I had Mary Lee standing in front of the doughnut case at the bakery.

"Okay, take a deep breath and look over all the doughnuts," I told her. "Look at the strawberry doughnut with the rainbow sprinkles. Doesn't it make you happy?"

Mary Lee smiled at the doughnut. "Pretty."

"And the meringue that looks like a fluffy cloud. And the birthday cakes with the pink and yellow roses. And the chocolate cream pie."

"This is very relaxing," Mary Lee said.

I called Connie's cell phone. "Are you still at the courthouse?" I asked her. "I'm bringing Mary Lee Truk in and we're going to want to bond her out right away before she gets another hot flash."

"I hate to break into the moment," Marjorie Lando said. "But what'll it be?"

"A dozen assorted doughnuts to go," I told her.

Lula dropped me off in front of the bonds office. "That wasn't so bad," she said. "We helped two lost souls today. That's real good for my horizon expanding and positive karma stockpile. Usually we just piss people off, and that don't do me any good in the karma department. And it's only five o'clock. I got plenty of time to get to rehearsal. See you tomorrow."

"See you tomorrow," I said, and I waved Lula away and beeped my car open. I was driving a black and white Mini Cooper that I'd gotten from Honest Dan the Used Car Man. The interior space was a little cozy for carting bad guys off to jail, but the car had been the right price, and it was fun to drive. I slid behind the wheel and jumped when someone knocked on the driver's side window.

It was the woman dressed in black. She was young, maybe early twenties. And she was pretty in a normal kind of way. She had thick wavy brown hair that fell to her shoulders, blue eyes under long lashes, and full lips that looked like they could easily go pouty. She was maybe five feet five inches and had a nice shape with round breasts stretching the fabric of her black T-shirt.

I started the car and rolled the window down. "You wanted to speak to me?" I asked the woman.

The woman looked in the window. "You're Stephanie Plum?"

"Yes. And you would be . . ."

"My name is Carmen Manoso," she said. "I'm Ranger's wife."

My stomach went into a free fall. If I'd been hit in the head with a baseball bat, I wouldn't have been more stunned. I suppose I had to assume there were women in Ranger's life, but I'd never seen any women. There'd never been mention of any women. And there had never been evidence of any women. Much less a wife! Ranger was a very sexy guy, but he was also a lone wolf.

"I understand you're sleeping with my husband," the woman said.

"You're misinformed," I told her. Okay, once! But it was a while ago, and she'd put the accusation into present tense.

"You were living with him."

"I used his apartment as a safe house."

"I don't believe you," the woman said. "Where is he now? Is he in *your* apartment? I've been to his office, and he isn't there."

Keep calm, I told myself. This doesn't feel right. This woman could be *anyone*.

"I'm going to need some identification," I said to the woman.

She reached into a pocket on her black cargo pants and pulled out a slim credit card holder. It contained a Virginia driver's license issued to Carmen Manoso, plus two credit cards also issued to Carmen Manoso.

So this told me she was Carmen Manoso. It still didn't confirm that she was Ranger's wife.

"How long have you been married to Ranger?" I asked her.

"Almost six months. I knew he had an office here, and that he spent a lot of time here. I never had reason to think he was cheating. I trusted him. Until now."

"And you don't trust him now, why?"

"He moved out. Like a thief in the night. Cleaned out our bank account and stripped the office of all the files and computer equipment."

"When did this happen?"

"Last week. One minute he was in bed with me, telling me he was returning to Trenton in the morning. And then *poof!* Gone. His cell phone is no longer in service."

I punched Ranger's number into my cell phone and got his message service. "Call me," I said.

Carmen's eyes narrowed. "I knew you'd have a number for him. *Bitch!*" And she reached behind her and drew a gun.

I stomped on the gas and the Mini sprang off the curb and jumped forward. Carmen fired off two shots. One pinged off my rear fender.

Connie was right. Carmen Manoso was crazy. And maybe I was crazy too, because I was lost in a rush of insane emotions. Not the least of which was jealousy. Yikes, who would have thought *that* was hiding in the closet? Stephanie Plum, jealous of a woman claiming to be Ranger's wife. And the jealousy was mixed with anger and hurt feelings that this was kept from me. That Ranger had misrepresented himself. That this man I respected for his integrity and strength of character might be not at all what he'd seemed.

Okay, take a deep breath, I told myself. Don't go all hormonal. Get the facts straight. Have a mental doughnut.

I live in a no-frills, three-story apartment building that is for the most part inhabited by the newly wed and the nearly dead . . . except for me. I live on the second floor with my apartment windows looking out on the parking lot. Handy for those times when I need to keep watch over my car because some pissed-off woman might be inclined to take an axe to it. The building is in a convenient location, a couple miles from the bond office and, more important, just a couple miles from my mom's washer and dryer.

I rolled into the lot, parked, and got out to look at the damage. It wasn't bad, all things considered. A line slicing through the paint. A ding on point of impact. Considering that I once had a car smushed by a garbage truck, this hardly counted. I locked up and went into the building.

Mrs. Bestler was in the elevator. She was in her eighties, and her own personal elevator didn't quite go all the way to the top anymore. "Going up!" she sang out to me.

"Second floor," I said.

She pushed the button and smiled at me. "Second

floor, ladies' lingerie and better dresses. Watch your step, dear."

I thanked Mrs. Bestler for the ride and got out of the elevator. I walked the length of my hall and let myself into my apartment. One bedroom, one bath, kitchen, dining room, and living room. All beige, none of my choosing, redecorated by the building owner after an apartment fire. Beige walls, beige carpet, beige curtains. Total seventies orange and brown bathroom. My luck the fire didn't destroy the bathroom.

My hamster, Rex, lives in a glass cage on my beige kitchen counter. He poked his head out of his soup can when I came in. His whiskers twitched and his black button eyes were wide in expectation. I said *Hello* and dropped a couple Cheerios into his food dish. He rushed out, shoved the Cheerios into his mouth, and disappeared into his soup can. My kind of roommate.

I called Morelli and told him I'd be over in an hour. I took a shower, did the hair and makeup thing, put on some pretty undies, clean jeans, and a sexy little knit shirt, and checked my messages. No Ranger.

This was a dilemma. I didn't know what to do about Carmen. My instincts told me she wasn't what she said. My curiosity had me in a state. And my hormones still had me a teensy jealous. Probably I wouldn't be bothered so much if she wasn't so pretty. Truth is, she looked like a woman Ranger might find attractive, except for the crazy part. I couldn't see Ranger with an irrational woman. Ranger was organized. Ranger didn't act on impulse.

Anyway, here she was, and I seemed to be in the middle of something. Whether or not she was Ranger's wife wasn't my most pressing problem. The fact that Carmen felt comfortable shooting at me put her beyond the nuisance category and into the *yikes* category. I was supposed to call Tank if I needed help, but I wasn't ready to push that button just yet. If Tank thought I was in danger, he'd assign someone to follow me around whether I wanted it or not. My experience with Ranger's men is that this isn't desirable. They're big and hard to hide. And they're overly protective, since the fear is that Ranger might shoot them in the foot should they let anything bad happen to me.

I stuffed a change of clothes into my shoulder bag and locked my apartment up behind me. I headed out and did a fast check on my car before getting in. No spray-painted slogans suggesting I was a slut. Windows hadn't been broken by a sledgehammer. No ticking noises coming from the undercarriage. Looked to me like Carmen hadn't yet discovered my address.

I drove the short distance to Morelli's house and parked at the curb. Morelli lived in a pleasant neighborhood with narrow streets, small attached houses, and hard-working people. I spent enough time here that knocking wasn't a required formality. I let myself in and heard Bob galloping at me from the kitchen. He hurled himself against me, tail wagging, eyes bright. Bob was in theory a golden retriever, but his gene pool was questionable. He was big and orange and fluffy. He loved everybody, and he ate every*thing* . . . including table legs and upholstered chairs. I gave him a hug, he realized I didn't have any bakery bags, and he trotted away.

Morelli didn't gallop at me, but he didn't drag his feet either. He met me halfway to the kitchen, pressed me into the wall, plastered himself against me, and kissed me. Morelli was off-duty in jeans and a T-shirt and bare feet. And the only weapon Morelli was currently carrying was pressed into my stomach.

"Bob really missed you," he said, his mouth moving down my neck.

"Bob?"

"Yeah." He hooked a finger into my shirt and slid it off my shoulder so his mouth could kiss more of me. "Bob's been nuts without you."

"Sounds serious."

"Fucking pathetic."

His hands slid down to my waist, under my shirt, and in an instant the shirt was off.

"You aren't hungry, are you?" he asked.

"Not for what's in the kitchen."

I was dressed in one of Morelli's shirts and a pair of his sweatpants. I was beside Morelli, on his couch, and we were eating cold pizza and watching a ball game.

"I had an interesting experience today," I told him. "A woman introduced herself to me as Ranger's wife. And then she pulled a gun on me and got two rounds off at my car."

"Am I supposed to be surprised at this?"

There's a certain amount of professional respect between Morelli and Ranger. And from time to time they've worked together for the common good. Beyond that, Morelli thinks Ranger's a head case.

"Do you know anything about this woman?" I asked Morelli.

"No."

"Ranger left for Miami today. Do you know anything about that?"

"No."

"Do you know anything about anything?"

"I know a few things," Morelli said. "Tell me more about Ranger's wife."

"Her name is Carmen. I saw a Virginia driver's license issued to Carmen Manoso. And two credit cards. She's pretty. Sort of curly brown hair, blue eyes, about five-foot-five, Caucasian, nice shape. Fake boobs."

"How do you know the boobs are fake?"

"Actually, I'm just hoping they're fake. And she was dressed in black SWAT clothes."

"That's cute," Morelli said. "Mr. and Mrs. Ranger clothes."

"She said one minute they were in bed and then *poof*, he was gone. Cleaned out the bank account and emptied the office. And the cell number she has for him is out of service."

"And your cell number for him?"

"It's in service, but he's not answering."

"It doesn't work for me," Morelli said. "I can't see Ranger tying himself up in a marriage."

I happened to know that Ranger had been married for about twenty minutes when he was Special Forces. He has a ten-year-old daughter from that marriage, and the daughter lives in Miami with her mother and stepfather. So far as I know, he's been careful to avoid entanglements since. At least, that's what I believed, until a couple hours ago.

"Who is this woman if she's not his wife?" I asked.

"Wacked-out bimbo? Paid assassin? Demented relative?"

"Get serious."

"I *am* serious."

"Okay, different subject. Did you do the report on Melvin Pickle? Do you know his status?"

"Oswald did the report. Pickle shouldn't have any problem getting rebonded. Probably have to go through some kind of mental health screening." Morelli eyed the last piece of pizza. "Do you want it?" he asked.

"You can have it," I told him, "but it'll cost you."

"What's the price?"

"How about running Carmen Manoso through the system?"

"I'd need more than a piece of pizza for that," Morelli said. "I'd need a night of balls-to-the-wall sex."

"You're going to get that anyway," I told him.

Morelli was already out of the house when I dragged myself down the stairs and into the kitchen. I gave Bob a hug, scooped some coffee into the coffeemaker, added water, pushed the button, and listened to the magical gurgle of coffee brewing. Morelli had a loaf of raisin bread out on the counter. I considered toasting a slice, but it seemed like unnecessary work, so I ate a slice raw. I drank my coffee and read the paper Morelli had left behind.

"Gotta go to work," I said to Bob, pushing back from the table.

Bob didn't look like he cared a lot. Bob had found a patch of sun on the kitchen floor and was soaking it up.

I showered and got dressed in clean jeans and a little knit shirt. I swiped some mascara on my lashes and took off. I had two files pulled from the pack on the seat next to me. Leon James, the arsonist. And Lonnie Johnson. Both high bonds.

I drove the short distance to Hamilton and parked in front of the office. I got out of the Mini and looked across the street at the black SUV with Virginia plates and tinted windows. Carmen was on the job. I stuck my head into the office. Lula was on the couch reading a movie star magazine. Connie was at her desk.

"How long's the SUV been across the street?" I asked.

"It was there when I opened the office," Connie said.

"Anybody come in to say hello?"

"Nope."

I turned and walked across the street and rapped on the driver's side window of the SUV.

The window rolled down, and Carmen looked out at

me. "Looks to me like you spent the night with someone," she said. "Like maybe you spent the night with my husband."

"I spent the night with my boyfriend. Not that it's any of your business."

"I'm going to stick to you like nothing you've ever seen. I know you're going to lead me to the son of a bitch. And when I find him, I'm going to kill him. And then I'm going to kill you."

Carmen Manoso had said this with eyes narrowed and teeth clenched. And I realized that the jealousy I felt over her and Ranger was nothing compared to the jealousy she felt toward me. Like it or not, fact or fiction, I was the other woman.

"Maybe we should talk this over," I said. "There are some things that don't add up for me. Maybe I can help you. And I have a couple questions."

The gun appeared, pointed at a spot in the middle of my forehead. "I'm not answering any more questions," Carmen said.

I stepped to the rear of the SUV and got the plate. Then I hustled across the street and into the office.

"Well?" Connie asked.

"It's Carmen, the woman in black. She claims to be Ranger's wife. I've seen her driver's license. It reads Carmen Manoso. Her story is that he walked out on her last week, and she's looking for him."

"Holy crap," Lula said.

Connie started punching information into her computer. "Do you know anything else? Address?"

"Arlington. I didn't see her driver's license long enough to get more," I told her. "And I have the plate." I scribbled it on a piece of paper for her. "Supposedly Ranger had an office in the area, closed it without warning and disappeared."

This is the age of instant access. Connie had computer

programs that pulled everything from credit history to medical history to high school grades and movie preferences. Connie could find out if you were constipated in 1994.

"Here she is," Connie said. "Carmen Manoso. Twenty-two years old. Maiden name, Carmen Cruz. Married to Ricardo Carlos Manoso. Blah, blah, blah. I don't see anything especially interesting. She's originally from Lanham, Maryland, and then Springfield, Virginia. No children. No history of mental illness. No criminal history that I can see. Unimpressive work history. Mostly in retail sales. Waited tables at a bar in Springfield and most recently lists herself as self-employed, bounty hunter. Some financial information. The SUV is leased. Lives in a rental in Arlington. I can go deeper, but it'll take a day or two."

"What about Ranger? Can you run a check on him?"

"Connie and me try to run a check on him all the time," Lula said. "It's like he doesn't exist."

I looked at Connie. "Is that true?"

"I'm surprised his name showed up in Carmen's data base," Connie said. "He has a way of erasing himself."

I redialed Ranger's cell number and got his service again. "Hey, man of mystery," I said, "your wife is here, and she's looking for you with a gun in her hand."

"That would get my attention," Lula said.

"Only if you were near a cell tower," I told her. "And sometimes Ranger goes places where no cell tower has gone before. Let's saddle up. I want to see what Lonnie Johnson's house looks like today. See if anyone's shooting at him."

Lula's Firebird was parked in the small back lot, so we left through the back door and took her car. After a couple blocks I called Connie.

"Is Carmen still at the curb?"

"Yep. She didn't see your rear exit. Guess bounty

hunter skills aren't high on the list of things you learn when you're married to Ranger."

I hung up, and Lula cruised down Hamilton and hooked a right turn into Johnson's neighborhood. We were a block away when we saw the lone fire truck. It was parked in front of Johnson's house . . . or at least, what was left of it.

"Hunh," Lula said, creeping in for a closer look. "Hope he had insurance."

Johnson's house was a pile of blackened rubble.

I got out of the car and walked to the fire truck where two firemen were checking off a form on a clipboard.

"What happened?" I asked.

"The house burned down," one of them said.

They looked at each other and laughed. Fireman humor.

"Anyone hurt?"

"No. Everyone got out. Are you a friend?"

"I knew Lonnie Johnson. Do you know where he went?"

"No, but he went there fast. Left his girlfriend behind to sort through the mess. She said it was a kitchen fire, but there was no way."

How about this: maybe the *firebomb* landed in the kitchen.

I got back into the car and slouched in my seat.

"Look on the bright side," Lula said. "Nobody's shooting. And I don't see no rocket launcher."

Chapter THREE

"I think we'll file Lonnie Johnson in the lost cause file," I said to Lula. "If he has any sense at all, he's on a bus out of town."

"Good idea," Lula said. "Who we got next up?"

I'd planned to do the arsonist next, but he'd lost some appeal now that I had my nose clogged with barbecued house. I got the stack of files from the back seat and fingered through them.

Luis Queen had been picked up for solicitation. Not a high bond, but he'd be easy to find. I hauled Luis Queen in all the time. Unfortunately, it was too early for Queen. He wouldn't be on his corner turning tricks until mid-afternoon. Queen liked to sleep in.

Caroline Scarzolli held some potential. She was a low-bond shoplifter. First-time offender. Worked in a lingerie and gadget shop. I handed the file to Lula. "How about this one?"

"I like this one," Lula said. "Scarzolli will be at work now, and I've been wanting to take a look at this store. I gave up being a 'ho, but I still like to keep up on the technology."

Pleasure Treasures was on a side street in the middle of the city. The name on the front of the store was written in hot-pink neon light. The lingerie displayed in the window was exotic. Crotchless panties trimmed in faux fur, sequined thongs, nipple pasties, animal-print garter belts.

Lula parked in the small lot adjacent to the store, and we sauntered up to the front door. Actually, Lula was the only one sauntering. I was skulking, head down, hoping no one was looking.

An older woman walked by with her dog and our eyes met.

"I'm a bounty hunter, looking for someone," I said to her. "I'm not buying anything here. I've never even been here before."

The woman hurried on, and Lula shook her head at me.

"That is so sad," Lula said. "That shows low self-esteem. That shows you got no pride in your sexual side. You should've told that woman you were going in to get a vibrator and edible massage oils. This here's the twenty-first century. Just 'cause we're women don't mean we can't be sick as men."

"It's not the twenty-first century in the Burg. My mother would get an eye twitch if she heard I was shopping in the Pleasure Treasures."

"Yeah, but I bet your Grandma Mazur shops here all the time," Lula said, walking into the store, going into browse mode. "Look at all those dildos. A whole wall of dildos." Lula picked one off a shelf and pushed a button and it started to hum and rotate. "This here's a good one," she said. "It can sing and dance."

I had no frame of reference for dildos. "Yeah," I said, "it's . . . nice."

"It ain't nice!" Lula said, obviously impressed. "It's a nasty bugger."

"That's what I meant. Nice and nasty."

She handed me the dancing dildo. "Here, you hold it for me while I look around. I want to check out the DVD selection."

I followed Lula to the DVDs.

"They got a good selection," Lula said. "They got all the classics like *Debbie Does Dallas* and *Horny Little People*. And here's my personal favorite, *Big Boys*. Have you seen *Big Boys*?"

I shook my head no.

"You gotta see *Big Boys*. It'll change your life. I'm gonna buy *Big Boys* for you."

"That's okay, I don't—"

"It's a present from me." She handed me the DVD. "Hang on to it while I keep looking."

"We're supposed to be working," I said. "Remember how we came in here to apprehend Caroline Scarzolli?"

"Yeah, but that's her over there behind the counter, and she don't look like she's going anywhere. She looks just like her picture. I bet she's wearing a wig. Don't it look like a wig to you?"

Caroline was seventy-two years old, according to her bond sheet. She had skin like an alligator and bleached blond hair that was teased into a rat's nest. If it was a wig, she got swindled no matter what she paid. She was wearing orthopedic shoes, fishnet stockings, a tight spandex miniskirt, and a skimpy tank top that showed a lot of wrinkled cleavage. I was guessing she smoked three packs a day and slept naked in a tanning bed.

I glanced at my watch.

"Okay, I can see you're all antsy to make this bust. How about we check out, and then we give her the bad news?"

"Deal."

Lula took the dildo and the DVD to the register and handed Caroline her credit card.

"We're having a two-for-one sale on dildos," Caroline said. "Don't you want to pick out a second?"

"Hear that?" Lula said to me. "Two-for-one sale. Go get yourself a dildo."

"I don't actually need—"

"Two for one!" Lula said. "Pick one, for crying out loud. How many times in life do you get offered a free dildo?"

I took the first one I saw and brought it to Lula.

"That's a beauty," Caroline said. "You have good taste. It's our precision replica of the famous adult movie star Herbert Horsecock. It weighs five pounds and it's solid rubber. It's one of our few uncircumsized dildos. It even comes in a special-edition red velvet drawstring carrying sack."

Lula got her credit card back and took possession of the dildos. "Okay," she said to me. "Do your thing."

I gave Caroline my card and introduced myself and gave her the baloney about rebonding.

"Who's going to watch the store if I leave now?" she asked.

"Is there someone you can call to come in and babysit?"

"What, like my ninety-year-old mother?"

"You're not exactly doing a lot of business," I told her.

"Sweetie, I just sold over a hundred dollars' worth of shit."

"You sold it to Lula!"

"Yeah," Caroline said in her deep smoker's voice. "Life is good."

"It isn't *that* good," I told her. "You're going to have to come with me. Now."

"Okay," she said. "Just let me get something." And she dipped behind the counter.

"What are you getting?" I asked.

She reappeared with a sawed-off shotgun. "This big gun," she said. "That's what I'm getting. Take your dildos and march your ass out of my store."

Lula and I speed-walked out of the store and rammed ourselves into the Firebird.

"Look on the bright side," Lula said. "You got a free dildo. And you got a great movie. Happy birthday early."

"I don't need a dildo."

"Sure you do. You never know when it might come in handy. And this Herbert Horsecock dildo's got some heft to it. You could use it as a doorstop, or a paperweight, or you could decorate it with those little twinkle lights at Christmas."

"I need an apprehension. Vinnie isn't the only one worried about money. I need rent money." I shuffled through the files. "I want to do phone work on some of these. Make some calls to verify employment. See if anyone's at the home address. Let's go back to the office."

"Where am I supposed to park?" Lula wanted to know. "There's not supposed to be people parked in this lot back here. This is a private lot for the bonds office. We should call the cops on these people." She circled around the block and looked for a spot on the street. "I swear I've never seen so many cars. They must be having a party at the beauty parlor."

"Carmen hasn't moved from her spot," I said.

Lula glanced over as she crept down the street, looking for a parking space. "She's hunkered in. Ranger really pissed her off."

I was still having a hard time believing Carmen's story. I couldn't see Ranger married. And I couldn't see Ranger cleaning out the bank account. Ranger played a little loose with the law, but he had a very firm moral code. And from what I could see, he wasn't hurting for money.

I checked my phone to make sure it was on, and I hadn't missed a call.

"Still haven't heard from him?" Lula asked.

"No. He must be underground."

He'd only been gone for twenty-four hours. It was too early to be worried about his safety. But I was worried all the same. It was all too weird.

Lula parked two cars down from me, and we walked to the office. I watched the black SUV for a protruding gun barrel but saw none. When we got to the office we realized it was packed with people.

"What the heck?" Lula said, pushing through the mob to Connie.

Connie was at her desk, trying to talk to the people crowded directly in front of her.

"I ran an ad in the paper this morning for the bond enforcement agent job," she said to me. "And this is the response. And the phone hasn't stopped ringing. I had to turn it over to the answering service so I could try to clear this out."

"Looks like they emptied out the funny farm and everyone came here," Lula said. "Who *are* these people? They look like movie extras. They all look like that bounty hunter guy on television, only most of them have better hair. I tell you, they should take that TV bounty hunter guy to the beauty parlor."

Connie handed me a steno pad and pen. "You take the front of the room, and I'll take the back. Get names and phone numbers and some work information and tell them we'll be in touch. Put a star by anyone who has potential."

Forty-five minutes later, the last of the BEA wannabes walked out the door, and Connie hung out a CLOSED sign. Two people were left sitting on the couch. Joyce Barnhardt and Melvin Pickle.

Joyce was dressed in black leather, her eyes heavily

lined in black, her red hair teased and lacquered, her lips artificially inflated and painted red to match her hair. She had her arms crossed, and her legs crossed, and her foot jiggled impatiently in stiletto-heeled boots.

Joyce was a flesh-eating fungus. She'd been through more husbands than I could count, and each time she chewed them up and spit them out, she got richer. Three months of marriage to Joyce, and a man was willing to bankrupt himself to get free. When I was in first grade, Joyce threw my crayons in the toilet. When I was in second grade, she spit in my lunch. In third grade she told everybody I didn't wear underpants. In fourth grade she said I had three nipples. In high school she somehow took a picture of me in the girls' locker room and had it made into a flyer and distributed two hundred.

"I am *very* insulted by this whole piece of shit," Joyce said. "If you needed another bounty hunter, why didn't you call me? You *know* Vinnie brings me in when he needs help."

"First off," Connie said, "Vinnie doesn't bring you in when he needs help. He brings you in when he needs to fornicate with a barnyard animal. And second, I didn't call you because we all hate you."

"And?" Joyce said.

"And that's it," Connie said.

"So why didn't you call me?"

Melvin Pickle was sitting beside Joyce. He looked like he was trying to be invisible.

"Who's this little turd?" Joyce said, turning to Pickle.

"He's going to be doing some filing for us," Connie said.

"Why did he get a job, and I didn't get a job?" Joyce wanted to know. "What's so special about him?"

"I'm a pervert," Pickle said.

"And?" Joyce said. "*Hello-o-o.* What am I, chopped liver?"

"Why don't you let her work the LC file?" I said to Connie. "The one you keep in your bottom drawer."

"What's LC stand for?" Joyce asked.

"Large cash," I told her. Also, lost cause, but she probably didn't want to be bothered knowing that.

Connie pulled seven folders out of her bottom desk drawer and gave the top three to Joyce. "Here you go," she said to Joyce. "Good luck. Nice seeing you. Mazel tov."

Joyce took the folders and looked down at Pickle. "Love the herpes. Adds color to your face."

"Thank you," Pickle said, his hand to his mouth, covering the herpes. "Have a nice day."

Connie locked the door after her. "I swear she's the Antichrist. I always smell sulfur burning when she's in the office."

"Maybe it's the salve I put on my cold sore," Pickle said.

"I don't want to be mean about it," Lula said to Pickle, "but you might want to think about wearing a mask and rubber gloves when you do the filing."

"It's going away," Pickle said.

We all gave an involuntary shudder.

"I'll go through the list of freaks and line up some interviews," Connie said to me. "I'll schedule them for tomorrow morning. I'd like you to be here to help."

"Sure." I looked at my watch. One o'clock. Luis Queen would be on his corner. "New game plan," I said to Lula. "Let's go get Luis, and then I'll do my phone work from home."

Luis Queen is a slim, five-foot-four-inch Hispanic sweetie pie. He turns tricks for a living and doesn't discriminate between male and female. I've been told he'll do *anything,* and I prefer not to think about that too much.

He works the corner across from the train station. The police have pretty much cleaned that area out, except for Luis Queen. Luis refuses to leave. Which is why he got picked up for soliciting.

Luis was wearing a pristine white tank top today, the better to show the muscle definition in his arms and his freshly shaved chest. He was in tight jeans, trimmed out in a wide belt decorated with rhinestones. And he was strutting his stuff in his trademark black lizard-skin cowboy boots.

Lula pulled to the curb, and I rolled my window down to talk to him.

"Look who's here," Luis said, big smile. "My favorite bounty hunters. You girls need something from Luis? I got a few minutes for you. You need to get relaxed?"

"Tempting," I said, "but I had other plans for you. You missed your court date. You need to rebond. Get in the car, and we'll give you a ride."

"Oh man," Luis said. "You gonna ruin my business day. This is my housewife time. They come for a little tickle from Luis before the kiddies get out of school."

"Are you going to make me come out there and get you?"

"You think you could take me?" Luis said, still smiling. "Bring it on, momma. I do Pilates. I'm toned perfection."

"I've got two inches and ten pounds on you. And if I have Lula get out of the car, you'll be nothing but a grease spot on the pavement."

Luis did a frustrated arm flap and slid into the back seat. "I don't know why you bust my balls. I'm just out here making a living."

"You need a new corner."

"I like this corner. It got sunshine."

"It's also got cops."

"I know, but I can't move until I tell all my regulars."

"You need a mailing list," Lula said, heading for the courthouse. "You should get a Web site."

Luis opened the Pleasure Treasures bag on the back seat. "Looks like you ladies been shopping. Whoa, baby, that's a monster. I think I'm blushing."

"You can drop me at the office," I told Lula. "Then you can pick Connie up and take her to the courthouse with you and Luis, so she can get him released again."

Fifteen minutes later, I swapped seats with Connie.

"Don't forget your toys," Luis said, handing me the bag.

I took the bag, waved Luis and Connie and Lula away, and crossed the street to the SUV. The window slid down, and Carmen looked out at me.

I decided to try friendly. "How's it going?"

Carmen didn't say anything.

"Can I get you something? Lunch? Water?"

Nothing.

"I'd really like to ask you a few questions. I don't think—"

The gun came up.

"Okay then," I said. "Good talk."

I crossed the street, angled into the Mini, cranked it over, and eased into traffic. I drove two blocks on Hamilton and turned into the Burg at the hospital with Carmen close on my bumper.

I've had occasion to lose people, and I had a route that worked. I wound through the Burg, took Chambers to Liberty, and returned to the Burg. Between traffic and lights and the back alleys of the Burg I was always able to lose the faint of heart. And I lost Carmen. Probably she'd eventually go to my apartment building, but I thought *eventually* was better than *now*.

Chapter FOUR

I had the phone beside me while I worked at the dining room table. I was prioritizing the skips, making calls to check on addresses and employment histories, trying to determine who was where. And I was hoping for a call from Ranger. The call that finally came in was from my grandmother.

"Big news," she said. "The funeral parlor is having a viewing tonight. It's the first viewing with the new owners. Catherine Machenko is getting laid out. Dolly did her hair, and she gave me all the dirt. She said the new owners are from Jersey City. Never owned a funeral parlor before. Fresh out of mortuary school. Dolly said they were a nice young gay couple. Dave and Scooter. Dave is the mortician, and Scooter makes the cookies for the viewings. Isn't that something?"

Some communities have country clubs, some have senior centers, some have shopping malls and movie theaters. The Burg has two funeral parlors. Only Thursday night bingo occasionally draws a bigger crowd than a well-run viewing in the Burg.

"I tell you those homosexuals are all over the place," Grandma said. "And they get all the good jobs, too. They get to be cowboys and morticians. I never wanted to be a homosexual, but I *always* wanted to be a cowboy. What do you suppose it's like to be a homosexual? Do you think their privates look different?"

"*All* privates look different," I told her.

"I haven't seen too many. Mostly your grandfather's . . . and that wasn't a real pretty sight. I wouldn't mind seeing some others. I'd like to see some minority privates and maybe some blue ones. I was listening to one of them late-night radio shows and they were talking about blue balls. I thought that sounded colorful. I wouldn't mind seeing some blue balls."

My mother groaned in the background.

"Hold on, dear," Grandma Mazur said. "Your mother wants to talk to you."

"I'll do your laundry if you take your grandmother to the viewing," my mother said. "And I'll iron it if you make sure she doesn't get into trouble. If it's closed casket, I don't want her trying to get it open."

Grandma thinks if she made an effort to come out to a viewing, the least they can do is let her take a look at the dead guy. I guess I understand her point of view, but it makes for a scene when the lid is nailed down.

"That's asking a lot," I said to my mother. "I'll give her a ride, but I can't guarantee no trouble."

"Please," my mother said. "I'm begging you."

Carmen was in my lot when I exited the building. She was parked one space over from my Mini, and her windows were down to allow air into the car.

I waved when I walked past. "I'm going to pick up my grandmother," I said. "I'm taking her to a viewing on Hamilton. Then I'll take her home and probably stop in to see Morelli."

Carmen didn't say anything. She was wearing mirrored lenses, and she wasn't smiling. She followed me out of the lot, into the Burg, and she parked half a block down while I went in to get Grandma.

Grandma was at the door when I arrived. Her grey hair was tightly curled. Her face was powdered. Her nails were newly manicured and matched her red lipstick. She was wearing a navy dress and low-heeled patent leather pumps. She was ready to go.

"Isn't this exciting," Grandma said. "A new funeral director! Catherine is lucky to be his first. There'll be a real crowd there tonight."

My mother was in the foyer with my grandmother. "Try to behave yourself," she said to my grandmother. "Constantine had years of experience. He knew how to manage all the little disasters that happen when people get together. These two young men are brand new at this."

For as long as I can remember, Constantine Stiva owned the funeral parlor. He was a pillar of the community and the funeral director of choice for the Burg bereaved. As it turned out, he was also a little insane and had a homicidal past, and he's now spending his remaining years in maximum security at Rahway prison.

I've heard rumors that Con prefers prison life to seeing Grandma Mazur walk through his front door, but I'm not sure they're true.

My father was in the living room watching television. His eyes never left the screen, but he mumbled something that sounded like "poor unsuspecting bastard funeral director."

My father used to keep an old army-issue .45 in the house as protection against intruders. When Grandma Mazur moved in, my mother quietly got rid of the .45, fearing someday my father would lose patience and blow Grandma away. If it had been me, I would have also gotten rid of sharp knives. Personally, I think Grandma Mazur is a hoot. But then, I don't have to live with her.

"We'll be fine," I said to my mother. "Don't worry."

My mother made the sign of the cross and bit into her lower lip.

I drove the short distance to the funeral parlor and dropped Grandma in front of the building. "I'll find a parking place and meet you in there," I said.

Grandma tottered up the stairs to the big wide front porch, and I motored slowly down the street, followed by Carmen. I parked one block north, Carmen chugged past me, hooked a U-turn, and parked across the street.

I was in no rush to get back to the funeral parlor, so I called Ranger again. "Hi," I said to his answering service. "It's me. Things are looking up. Your wife is tailing me, but she hasn't shot at me yet today, so that's a good thing, right? And you need to answer your damn phone calls."

I cracked my knuckles and looked at my watch. I hated viewings. I hated the cloying smell of too many flowers. I hated the small talk I'd be forced to make. I hated the inevitable dead person. Maybe I could procrastinate with another phone call.

I called Morelli and told him I might be stopping around after the viewing. He said he'd take a nap in anticipation. That didn't take up nearly enough time so I called my best friend, Mary Lou.

"What?" she yelled into the phone. "I can't hear you. I'm putting the kids to bed."

Bedlam in the background.

"I'll call some other time," I said.

I disconnected Mary Lou and called my sister Valerie. "I'm feeding the baby," she said. "Is it important?"

"Just checking in," I said. "Nothing that can't wait."

Since I couldn't think of anyone else to call, I left the comfort of my Mini and trudged off to the funeral parlor.

I worked my way through the crush of people to slumber room number one where Catherine Machenko was laid to rest. Grandma was close to the casket, not wanting to miss any of the action. She was with Catherine Machenko's sisters and two young men dressed in black.

"This is the new funeral director," Grandma said to me. "Dave Nelson. And this is his partner, Scooter."

Dave looked like Paul Bunyan in a suit. He was huge. Dark hair, slightly receding. Head insignificant on his tree-trunk neck. Barrel-chested. Thighs bulging against his pants fabric.

"Dave used to be a wrestler," Grandma said.

No shit.

Scooter and Dave were yin and yang. Scooter was average height, slight build, blond hair nicely cut, pale blue eyes. Very Norwegian. Or maybe German. Definitely Nordic. I was guessing his suit was Armani and probably his tie cost more than my car.

They were wearing wedding bands. And when they looked at each other you knew they liked being together. I was a little jealous. Again. But in an entirely different way. I wondered if I ever looked like that when I was with Morelli.

Lucky for Dave and Scooter, the Burg wouldn't care about their sexual orientation as long as the cookies were good and they had some expertise at plugging the occasional bullet hole.

Both Dave and Scooter were beaming, proud of their first viewing, flushed with the success of the party. Very different from the calm, cool, solicitous demeanor always displayed by Constantine Stiva.

"I just heard they have one of those alerts out here in Trenton for a kidnapping," Grandma said to me. "A little girl was kidnapped in Florida, and they think she might be here in Trenton, because she was kidnapped by her father, and her father lives here. I bet you could find her."

"The little girl's name is Julie Martine," Scooter said. "It's all over the television. She's ten years old. And they think she's with her birth father, Carlos Manoso."

My heart stuttered in my chest, and for a moment there was no air around me. Ranger's legal name is Ricardo Carlos Manoso, but he never uses the Ricardo.

"What else did they say on television?" I asked him.

"That was mostly it. They showed a picture of the man from when he was in the army. Special Forces. And they showed a picture of the little girl."

I looked at my watch. "We can't stay much longer," I said to Grandma. "I promised Joe I'd come over tonight."

"That works perfectly for me," Grandma said. "I've seen everything, and there's a television show on in a half hour that I like to watch. It's a rerun of *The Crocodile Hunter.* That crocodile guy is a real cutie in those little shorts."

"Make sure you get a cookie before you leave," Scooter said. "I baked them myself. Chocolate chip and oatmeal raisin."

We hit the cookie table on the way out.

"Look at this," Grandma said, taking two cookies, "Scooter put them on doilies and everything. Such a nice young man. You can entrust your loved one to a funeral parlor that takes the time to use doilies."

I dropped Grandma off, and I went home to my apartment. I said hello to Rex, hung my bag and jacket on a hook in the hall, and went straight to my computer. I surfed a couple news sites and then went to the site for missing children. The little girl was pretty with an infectious smile. She had brown hair pulled into a ponytail and big brown eyes. She lived with her mom and stepdad in Miami. She was picked up on her way home from school and not seen since. She was with two girlfriends who said she got into a car with a man police believe to be her birth father. The description of the man that the girls gave to the police fit Ranger. And the photo shown was of Ranger.

I shut the computer down and called Morelli. "Have you gotten the missing child alert?" I asked him.

"Oswald just called me."

"Do you know anything I don't know?"

"Oswald got all his information from television."

"What do you think?"

"Ranger's not my favorite person. I think his wiring isn't code. And it wouldn't surprise me to hear he's kidnapped his daughter, but I'd be very surprised if he didn't have a good reason. Are you still planning on coming over?"

"I don't know. I'm really thrown by this. Carmen showing up, and now the little girl getting kidnapped."

"I have a cake," Morelli said. "Got it just for you."

"You don't!"

"Only one way to find out."

"Okay, I'll be there in ten minutes."

I hung up and called Tank.

"What's going on?" I asked him.

"Business as usual."

"What's going on with Ranger?"

"He's off-line."

"And?"

"Keep the faith."

I disconnected and made a mental note not to call Tank unless I was bleeding profusely and he was the only other person on earth.

Chapter FIVE

Morelli was slow to kill the alarm on his clock radio.

"You purposely let that ring so I'd wake up," I said to him.

"I didn't want you to miss anything."

"Such as . . . oh God, give me a break. What time is it? It's still dark out."

"There's this thing that happens when I wake up next to you," Morelli said. "It's very uncomfortable . . . in a good way."

"What about the cake you promised?"

"It's baking."

That was obvious.

"Can't you go back to sleep and pick this up in an hour or two?" I asked Morelli.

"I have to be at my desk in an hour or two. And my body doesn't work like that. Once the cake's in the oven, it keeps baking until it's done."

"I'm tired. Maybe this is one of those times when you can have your cake and eat it too. You know, all by yourself."

"Do you want to watch?"

"No! I want to sleep."

Morelli nibbled on my neck, and his hand snaked around to my breast. "Okay," he said with his voice all soft and old-whiskey smooth. "Go back to sleep. We'll do this some other time."

I blew out a sigh. "What kind of cake is it?" I asked. "Coffee cake? Birthday cake?"

We were lying spoon fashion, and I could feel Morelli laughing behind me.

"It's a cannoli," he said.

"Oh boy," Lula said when I swung into the office. "Only one thing puts *that* kind of smile on your face."

"I had cake for breakfast."

"Must have been damn good cake."

Melvin Pickle was working at filing. "I can't eat cake for breakfast," he said. "It's bad for my blood sugar level."

"She didn't mean *cake* cake," Lula said. "That was one of them double entendre things. Boy, you're awful slow on the pickup for a pervert."

"Did you hear about Ranger?" I asked Connie and Lula.

"It came up on my news service this morning," Connie said.

"What did the service say? Have they found him or his daughter?"

"No. It just said she was picked up after school by a man who met Ranger's description and not seen since. I tried paging him but he's not answering."

I glanced out the front window. "I see Carmen is back at the curb."

"This just gets weirder and weirder," Lula said. "This is like *Twilight Zone* shit."

Connie gave me a clipboard and then gave one to Lula. "I don't have time to think about it this morning. We have people coming in for the BEA job. I cut the group of applicants in half by eliminating everyone with a criminal record," she said. "The rest have been divided into three groups. I'm calling those groups Best, Okay, and God Help Us. Hopefully we'll find someone before we get to God Help Us. The Best group is coming in this morning. We're going to give everyone a fifteen-minute interview, so this shouldn't take all day. I know you're anxious to go out there and round up some bad guys."

"Yeah, I can't wait," Lula said. "I need to look like an idiot at least twice a day to keep myself humble."

My clipboard had seven bios on it. Connie had run simple background checks on today's group and gotten the basics. First up was George Panko. He was scheduled for a nine o'clock interview. At nine-fifteen we ripped his sheet off the clipboard.

"Guess he changed his mind," Lula said. "Probably decided to get a good job . . . like feeding lions or cleaning kennel cages."

Becky Willard strolled in at nine-twenty-five. "I figured you'd be running late," she said. "So I stopped for a latte, and the moron behind the counter took *so* long. And then he didn't put the right kind of milk in it. I asked for a skim milk latte, and I *know* he gave me regular milk. I mean, do I look stupid? So he had to make it over. And he took *so* long again." She looked around. "This office is *so* dreary. Would I have to spend much time here? And I get a company car, right? I mean, you don't expect me to use my own car to apprehend fugitives, do you?"

When Willard left, Connie ripped Willard's sheet off the clipboard. "Two down."

The nine-thirty interview was precisely on time. He was dressed in head-to-toe black leather and had a six-shooter strapped to his leg.

"That gun looks vintage," Lula said. "Is it real?"

"You bet your ass," he said. And he pulled the gun, twirled it around on his finger, and shot a hole in the front panel of Connie's desk. "Oops," he said. "Sorry about that. Slipsies."

Another sheet got ripped off the board. Four to go.

Anton Rudder was next in the hot seat. "I can do this job," he said. "I'll go out there and get those motherfuckers. They won't even know what hit them. I'll have their law-breakin' asses in the trunk of my car . . ."

"Actually, we almost never transport someone in the trunk," I said.

"Yeah, but that's because you're pussy," Anton said. "This whole office is pussy. I figure that's why I got the callback. You need a real man here."

"If we needed a real man, we wouldn't have called your runt ass," Lula said.

"No offense," Anton said. "I like pussy. I especially like fat black pussy. But it's not like pussy can do the same job a man can do. Everybody knows that. That's a scientific fact."

Lula was on her feet, rooting through her shoulder bag. "Excuse me? Did you just imply I was fat? Is that what I heard?"

"Probably you should leave before Lula finds her gun," I said to Anton.

Lula had her head in her bag. "It's in here somewhere."

Anton hustled out the door, and Connie ripped his sheet off her clipboard.

Three interviews left, and I was having a hard time concentrating. I was in a state over Ranger.

Martin Dorn arrived for his interview looking relatively normal with the exception of a mustache drawn onto his upper lip with a black Magic Marker.

"It's always been my lifelong dream to be a bounty hunter," Dorn said. "I watch all the television shows. And I went to bounty hunter school on the Internet. You could ask me anything about being a bounty hunter, and I bet I know the answer."

"That's promising," Connie said. "Do you know you have a Magic Marker mustache on your upper lip?"

"I tried to grow a real one, but I didn't have any luck at it," he said. "I'm good with a Magic Marker. I used one to draw a lightning bolt on my penis. Would you like to see it?"

Melvin Pickle was filing reports on the other side of the bank of cabinets. He popped his head up to take a look at Dorn, and Connie ripped Dorn's sheet off her clipboard.

The sixth applicant was a no-show.

The seventh was Brendan Yalenowski.

"I need to know my rights," Brendan said. "Am I allowed to shoot people? Suppose I shot someone while I was in the act of making an apprehension. Only suppose that person wasn't actually the guy I was looking for. Suppose it was someone who looked a little like the guy. And suppose he wasn't armed. And this is just theoretical, but suppose it turned out that I knew him and owed him money . . ."

Connie slouched in her seat when Brendan left. "Is it too early in the day to start drinking?"

"This was a big bust," Lula said. "Who'd think this would be so hard? It's not like we were gonna be picky. I mean, look what you got doing this job, a former 'ho and someone who used to sell cheap ladies' panties."

"I was a buyer," I said. "The job wasn't *that* bad."

"Yeah, but you got fired."

"Laid off. It wasn't my fault."

Vinnie's office door was closed. "Where's Vinnie?" I asked Connie. "I haven't seen him all week."

"He's in Biloxi. Bail bonds conference. And I hate to bring this up, but you need to bring in a couple of the high bonds. We need Lonnie Johnson and Leon James."

"I made some phone calls last night, and I couldn't get anything on Johnson. Someone a lot scarier than I am is after him, and he's on the run. I'll try Leon James today."

"I'll go with you," Lula said. "Only I gotta be careful because I just got my nails done, and I don't want to ruin them. This is my big night. I'm making my debut with the What tonight. We're gonna be at that bar on Third Street. The Hole."

"That's a pretty rough bar. I didn't know they had bands," I said to Lula.

"We're the first. They're trying something new. They said they wanted to expand their clientele."

"I hope Sally isn't going in drag to that bar."

"He's got a dress that's like mine only his is in red on account of he don't look good in gold. People be disappointed if Sally wasn't in drag. That's his thing. He's famous for his accessorizing."

Salvatore Sweet is a good friend in a constant state of reinvention. He's played lead guitar with a bunch of bands. The Funky Butts, the Pitts, Beggar Boys, and Howling Dogs. When I met him, he was playing in drag for the first time with the Lovelies, and that was where he hit the jackpot. Actually, it was just a local jackpot, but it was more success than he'd ever seen. When the band broke up, Sally continued to perform in drag. He's currently driving a school bus days and playing guitar nights. His bands are always a collection of misfits. Good musicians most of the time who, for one reason or another, don't fit in anywhere else. In a bizarre way, Lula would be a perfect addition.

"If he goes in drag to the Hole, he's going to be accessorizing in the hospital," Connie said.

"Something to think about," Lula said.

I glanced out the front window at the SUV. "Does

she ever get out?" I asked Connie. "Just to stretch? Walk around?"

"I haven't seen her out since that first time when she came into the office looking for you."

"I have a sick stomach over this Ranger thing," I told Connie. "I think we should get some background on Julie Martine's mother and stepfather. And maybe you could poke around in Arlington. I'd like to know more about Ranger's business there."

Ten minutes later, we were in Lula's car, on the way to Leon James's last known address, and I was on the phone with Morelli.

"I need some help," I told him. "I'd like to know the captures Ranger made through his Virginia office. And it would be helpful if I could get a photograph of the Virginia Ranger."

"The captures I should be able to get for you. The photo will only happen if he has a mug shot or a Virginia driver's license."

"Good enough. And remember, it's Friday, and we're expected for dinner at my parents' house."

"I'll be there," Morelli said.

Lula parked in front of a two-story brick row house in a neighborhood adjacent to the Burg. "Here it is," she said. "This is the address on the file."

Leon James had listed the house as his residence and had also used it to secure the bond. He was a penny-ante hitman, selling his services to anyone with a grudge. Usually evidence is scarce against him. And witnesses have been known to recant stories and occasionally to disappear. He was wanted for arson and attempted murder. He was a third-time offender, and this was going to be an ugly capture.

"How are we going to do this?" Lula wanted to know. "This isn't a nice guy. He kills people and burns down houses."

"I think we'll have to be tricky."

"Yeah, tricky. I like the sound of that."

"First thing, we need to get him out of his house and into someplace public. Then we need to distract him until we can get him cuffed."

"Okay," Lula said. "I'm with you."

"That's it. That's all I've got."

"That's not much," Lula said.

"Suppose one of us calls him and says she wants to hire him to do a job. And then she could set up a meeting."

"Good thinking. That's going to be you doing the calling, right? You're a way better liar than I am."

I cut my eyes to Lula. "You're an *excellent* liar."

"Maybe, but I gotta be saving myself for tonight. I can't afford to use my voice too much."

"That is so lame," I said to Lula.

"It's the best I could come up with."

I punched Leon's number into my cell phone. "I'd like to speak to Leon James," I said to the guy who answered.

"Speaking."

"I think I might need some help in solving a problem."

"Un-hunh."

"You were recommended."

"Oh yeah? Who recommended me?"

"Butchy."

"I don't know any Butchy."

"Well, he knows you. And he recommended you."

"What sort of problem we talking about?"

"I don't want to say on the phone."

"That sounds promising already," James said.

"I was hoping we could meet somewhere. I need to solve this problem fast."

"It'll cost you."

"I don't care. Just solve my friggin' problem, okay?"

* * *

I'd agreed to meet Leon James in a small park in the Burg. The park wasn't much more than a patch of grass half a block in size. It had a couple trees and a couple benches and that was it. Once in a while an old guy would sit on a bench and soak up sun. And once in a while a couple kids would sit on a bench and smoke some weed. And once in a while someone would walk his dog in the park.

Lula and I had driven to Morelli's house and commandeered Bob. The plan was that I'd meet Leon James at the bench, and while we were talking, Lula would mosey by with Bob. Then when James was distracted, one of us would zap him with a stun gun.

I dropped Lula and Bob off on a side street, turned a corner, and parked not far from the bench. I walked to the bench and sat down with my purse in my lap. After five minutes, a car pulled up behind Lula's Firebird, and James got out. He looked around, straightened his jacket, and walked toward me. It was eighty degrees out, and there was only one reason to be wearing a jacket.

James was five-foot-nine and stocky. The fact that he'd been caught numerous times for arson put him in the not-too-bright category. Arson is a respected profession among certain subcultures in Jersey, and the good ones don't get caught. The good ones channel lightning and mysterious acts of spontaneous combustion.

I fought stage fright as I watched James cut across the grass. My heart was racing, and I could feel panic sticking in my throat. Deep breath, I told myself. Be calm. Be cool.

"You looking for a problem solver?" James said, coming up to the bench.

"I might be."

He sat down. "What kind of problem you got?"

"A cheating husband."

"And?"

"I'm told it would be cheaper to pay you to take care of the bastard than it would be to divorce him and lose half of everything."

"Works for me."

James was turned toward me, and I could see Lula and Bob coming up behind him. Bob was straining at the leash, wanting to run, but with Lula at the other end it was like pulling a refrigerator.

"Are you interested, or what?"

"Sure. I'm a professional. I don't need to know *why*. I just need to know you'll pay."

"Good. Then it's settled. We just have to agree on a price."

"I don't negotiate price. My price is fixed. Ten big ones. Five now and five when the job is completed."

"Nobody told me that part," I said. "I don't have a lot of money on me."

"Then you have a problem."

"Do you take credit cards?"

"Lady, I'm not the Gap."

"How about a check?"

"How about cash," he said.

"Wait a minute, let me think. I just have to go to the bank. Can you wait while I go to the bank?"

"Sorry, no can do. I have a visibility problem."

Lula was about twenty feet away, and Bob was chugging like a freight train, pulling against his collar, trying to get to me.

James turned to see what was making all that noise behind him, I slipped the stun gun out of my bag, pushed the button, and the little *on* light didn't go on.

James turned back to me and saw the stun gun. "What the fuck?"

I looked at Lula in utter panic.

Lula let go of Bob's leash. Bob bounded over and took a flying leap for me, knocking me off the bench. James reached for his gun. And Lula roundhoused James on the side of the head with her purse. I still had the stun gun in my hand and suddenly the light blinked on. I shoved Bob out of the way, scrambled to grabbing distance of James, and caught him in the ankle with the prongs of the stun gun. James squeaked, slumped over, and slid to the ground.

I flopped over and lay spread-eagle on my back, hand to my heart for a moment. I was breathing hard, and I was leaking nervous fear, sweating in places I didn't think had sweat glands.

"What the heck was that?" Lula wanted to know. "You had a expression on your face like you just had a irritable bowel experience."

I looked at the stun gun. The light was off again. "Low battery," I said.

"Don't you hate when that happens?"

"What have you got in your purse? It sounded like you hit him with a frying pan."

"I got my gun in there. And I got a couple rolls of quarters for meters. And I got a Maglite. And a stun gun. And cuffs." She pulled the cuffs out and handed them to me. "I guess you should cuff him, except it seems like a shame to ruin Bob's fun."

Bob was jumping around on James, trying to get him to play. He'd snuffle James, and then he'd jump up and land on James with all four feet and do a growly thing, and then he'd jump around some more.

"Gonna be hard to explain all those muddy Bob-sized footprints on him," Lula said. "Gonna be even harder to explain all the dog slobber on his crotch."

I dragged Bob off, and I cuffed James behind his back and stood. "Do you have any shackles?"

"I got shackles in the trunk," Lula said. "You baby-sit, and I'll go get them."

James moaned and sucked in some air and squinted up at me. "Fuck. What happened?"

"Bond enforcement," I said. "Lula hit you with her purse."

He sat up and looked at his slacks.

"What's all over my pants? Why are my pants wet?"

"Lula fell in love," I told him. I thought that would put him in a better mood than telling him it was Bob slime.

Chapter SIX

"Are we hot, or what?" Lula said. "We captured Leon James."

We'd done a drive-through at Cluck-in-a-Bucket to celebrate our success, and then we'd processed James, picked up our body receipt, and now we were back in the office.

Connie was smiling. "The morning was a downer, but the rest of the day was good. That was a big bond. And it turns out our Melvin Pickle is a filing demon."

Bob was sitting on my foot, pressing his body against my leg. He'd gone for a walk, eaten two pieces of chicken, slurped up a bowl of water, and now he was ready to nap.

"I'm taking Bob home," I told Connie. "If any information comes in on Ranger, give me a call on my cell."

"Yeah, and I'm going home too," Lula said. "I gotta get ready for tonight."

"We have another batch of job applicants coming in tomorrow," Connie said. "Starting at nine o'clock."

I loaded Bob into the back seat of the Mini and rolled the window down so he could stick his head out. The car was wall-to-wall dog, but Bob looked happy on the cushy leather.

I turned the engine over and moved into the stream

of traffic with my eyes on Carmen, expecting her to follow. When I stopped for the light at the corner, the SUV was still at the curb, no sign of life. Carmen had probably fallen asleep at the wheel. Or maybe she'd gone for a walk. Or maybe she was in a second car, using the SUV as a decoy. I wound through the Burg watching my rearview mirror for a tail. No tail appeared, so I drove to Morelli's.

I deposited Bob in the house, locked up, and got back into the Mini. I motored the short distance to my apartment, parked, and rode the elevator with Mrs. Bestler.

"How was your day, dear?" she asked, pressing the button for the second floor.

"Very good. And yours?"

"My day was excellent. I visited the chiropodist this morning. That's always exciting." The doors opened, and Mrs. Bestler sang out, "Second floor, ladies' lounge."

Here's the thing about my apartment: no matter how chaotic my day has been, my apartment is usually calm and silent. There was a time when my answering machine would be filled with messages when I came home, but my answering machine broke and was never replaced, so now everyone calls my cell. Rex is happy about this, since no one disturbs him while he's sleeping. I don't cook, so the kitchen is never messy. My furnishings are sparse, since the clutter went up in flames with the fire. And the bathroom doesn't count. The bathroom is always a wreck.

I filled Rex's food dish with hamster crunchies, a peanut, a green bean, and a piece of pretzel. I gave him fresh water. I said "Hello."

Rex backed out of his soup can, stuffed the green bean and pretzel into his cheek, and rushed back into his can.

It was four o'clock, and I had to be at my parents' house at six. I turned my computer on and surfed the net for news of Ranger. I went to the site for missing children, and I visited some of the news sites. No information beyond what was initially released.

Vinnie belongs to PBUS. Professional Bail Agents of the United States. PBUS shares information and loosely links agencies nationwide. A couple months ago, a Virginia agency needed help locating a guy who'd skipped out of their area and was believed to be in Trenton. I found the guy and held him until the agency could get someone to Trenton to take possession. I had a business card from John Nash, the agent who collected the FTA, and I thought he might be willing to do me a favor.

I e-mailed Nash and asked if he knew anything about Ranger. Bail bonds is a small world. Agents know when new competition pops up in their neighborhood.

I ran through my spam box and deleted sixty-four ads for penis enhancement, seventeen ads for animal porn sites, and two ads for cheap credit.

Beautification was next on my list. I jumped into the shower, did what I could to improve on nature by way of makeup and hair gel, got dressed in my best jeans and sexy little shirt, and took off for my parents' house.

Morelli arrived a beat after I did.

"Everyone to the table," my mother said. "Stephanie, you get the mashed potatoes from the kitchen."

Dinner in my parents' house happens precisely at six o'clock. Five minutes late, and it could all be ruined. Burned pot roast, cold potatoes, overcooked green beans. A disaster of biblical proportions.

My father was first to sit. He had his fork in hand and his attention focused on the kitchen door, waiting for my mother to emerge with the pot roast. Grandma Mazur set the beans on the table and took her place across from Morelli and me. My mother followed with the meat, and we all dug in.

If a man attended enough pot roast dinners in the

presence of a single woman and her family, it was a marriage in the eyes of the Burg, if not God. And Morelli was dangerously close to marriage by pot roast. There's a part of me that likes the comfortable intimacy between Morelli and me at the table. I like the way his knee snuggles against mine. And I like the way he accepts my family. And I like the way he looks with a glass of red wine in his hand, relaxed and confident, his dark eyes not missing anything. In fact, there isn't a lot *not* to like about Morelli. So the hesitancy I have to commit is confusing. I suppose it has something to do with the fact that I'm horribly attracted to Ranger. Not that I would ever commit to Ranger. Ranger is an accident waiting to happen. Still, the heat is there.

"I was talking to Merle Greber today," Grandma Mazur said. "She lives two houses down from Mary Lee Truk, and she said Mary Lee's feeling much better. I guess she's got the hot flashes under control. And the stitches came out on her husband's behind from where she stabbed him, and word is he's thinking about dropping the charges against her and moving back home. Merle said, only problem now is it looks like Mary Lee's putting on weight."

The unfortunate result of acquiring happiness at the bakery.

"Anyone hear anything about that little girl who was kidnapped?" Grandma asked.

"She's still missing," I said.

"People are saying Ranger took her. I hope for her sake that's true, because he wouldn't hurt her. It's still a terrible thing."

We all lapsed into silence after that. Not that silence was abnormal at my parents' table. We tended not to multitask body functions. When we sat down to eat, we got to it.

* * *

"Oh man, you're kidding," Morelli said. "You want me to do what?"

It was eight-thirty, and we were walking Bob around Morelli's neighborhood, so Bob could do one last tinkle.

"I want you to go to the Hole with me. Lula's singing there tonight, and I feel like I should be supportive. And I thought it wouldn't hurt to have an armed cop in the room."

"Lula can't sing. I've heard her sing. She's tone-deaf."

"Yeah, but she looks good in her dress." As long as she doesn't bend over. "And she's singing with Sally Sweet and his band. None of them can sing. They just play loud enough to drown themselves out."

"I had plans for tonight," Morelli said.

"Would those be the same plans you had for last night?"

"The basic plan is the same, but I have a few variations I thought I'd throw in."

"Look on the positive side. You could try to get me liquored up at the Hole, and I might come up with some of my own variations. I'm an animal when I'm liquored up."

Morelli smiled at me. "Good point."

"Did you have any luck getting information for me on Ranger?"

"No photo. He doesn't have a Virginia driver's license. And no captures on record. Sorry."

"That's okay. I suspected there wouldn't be anything, but I thought it was worth a try."

"What about the woman? Have you talked to her?" Morelli asked.

"Carmen? I can hear her release the safety on her Glock when I get within two feet of her."

"Do you want me to roust her?"

"No. At least this way I know where to find her. And

as long as there's distance between us, I don't think she's dangerous. She's not exactly a sharpshooter."

We took Bob back to the house, locked up, and headed off in Morelli's SUV. Morelli used to have a truck, but he traded it in so Bob could ride with him and be more comfy in bad weather.

The Hole was on Third, in an area top-loaded with bars, pawnshops, and adult video stores. Sandwiched between the bottom-feeder businesses were bedraggled drugstores, convenience stores, rooming houses, and fast-food franchises.

Morelli drove around three blocks, looking for a parking space, finding none. He turned into the alley behind the Hole and found a space reserved for employees.

"It's good to be a cop," I said to him.

"Sometimes."

We entered through the back door, skirted around the kitchen, walked past the restrooms, and stepped into a large room packed with people. The stagnant air was saturated with kitchen grease and smelled like beer and booze and weed. There was a small stage at one end. The stage was set with amps and standup mics. A mahogany bar stretched the length of one wall, and everywhere else there were round tables crammed with chairs. There was at least one person sitting in every chair. The noise level was set at *roar.* Most of the women were in tube tops and shorts. The men wore jeans and muscle shirts, chains and tattoos. I was still in my jeans and little T-shirt. Morelli was wearing a gun on his ankle and at his back, both covered by clothes.

Morelli snagged a waitress by the strap on her tank top, gave her a twenty, and ordered two Coronas.

"You're disturbingly good at this," I said to him.

"I had a wild youth."

That was an understatement. Morelli had been a

womanizer and a bar brawler of the first magnitude. I slipped my hand into his, and we smiled at each other, and it was one of those moments of understanding that happens between people with a long history together.

I chugged down a cold Corona and stood close to Morelli. The lights blinked, and the What appeared onstage. There was a guy on drums, a guy on keyboard, and a guy on bass. They set up and rapped out a fanfare. No one on the floor paid any attention. And then Lula and Sally came out and everyone turned and gaped.

Lula was wearing the gold dress and spike-heeled shoes, and Sally was wearing his guitar, dangly red sparkly earrings, four-inch red sequined heels with two-inch platform soles, and a red-sequined thong. He'd forgone his usual platinum Marilyn Monroe wig and was au naturel in his shoulder-length, kinky curled black hair. His big, gangly, hairy body ambled up to the mic, and he gave a loud strum on the guitar that brought the house down.

"I usually wear a dress," Sally said. "But people told me it might not go over here, so I wore this thong instead. What do you think?"

Everyone whistled and hooted. Morelli had his arm around me and a grin on his face. I was smiling too, but I was afraid the good mood of the audience wasn't going to last. It looked to me like this was a crowd with a short attention span.

Sally Sweet has been punk, funk, rock, country western, and everything in between. This band looked to me like a seventies cover band, since the first song was "Love Machine."

Lula had a handheld mic and was doing a routine somewhere between Tina Turner and a Baptist revival meeting. It wasn't bad, but every time she raised her arms the skimpy gold dress would hike up, and she'd have to tug it back down over her ass. Halfway through the song Lula lost her place and gave up on the lyrics and started singing, "Love machine, la la la la love machine." Not that it mattered. The entire audience was mesmerized by the fleeting glimpses of Lula's size XXX-Large leopard thong.

When the song ended someone yelled out that he wanted to hear "Love Shack."

"No way," came back from the other side of the room. "'Disco Inferno.'"

"'Disco Inferno' is gay," the first guy yelled. "Only pussies like 'Disco Inferno.'"

"Pussy this," the Disco Inferno guy said. And he threw a beer bottle at the Love Shack guy.

"You better stop that," Lula said to the Disco guy. "That's rude behavior."

An onion ring came sailing out of the audience, hit Lula in the head, and dropped onto her chest.

"Now I'm getting mad," Lula said. "Who did that? I got a big grease spot on my dress now. You're getting my dry cleaning bill."

"Hey," someone yelled to Lula, "show us the rest of those big tits. I want to see your tits."

"How about you want to see my foot up your ass," Lula said.

A show-us-your-tits chant went up and a bunch of the women flashed headlights.

The drunk next to me grabbed my shirt and attempted to pull it over my head. "Show me *your* tits," he said.

And that was the last thing he said because Morelli shoved his fist into the guy's face.

It pretty much went downhill after that. Beer bottles were flying, and the room looked like a WWE cage match with a frenzied mob smashing furniture, scratching and clawing and punching each other out.

Sally went off the stage with a war whoop, wading

into the mess, whacking guys with his guitar, and Lula crawled under a table. Morelli wrapped an arm around my middle, lifted me two inches off the floor, and fought his way toward the hall leading to the restrooms and rear door, laying waste to anyone in his way. He got me outside, and he went back in for Lula. He shoved Lula out the rear door just as the police arrived, front and rear.

Eddie Gazarra was in one of the squad cars angled behind Morelli's SUV. He was a good friend, and he was married to my cousin, Shirley-the-Whiner. He was with three other cops, and they all had big smiles when they saw Morelli and Lula and me.

"What's going on?" Gazarra wanted to know, working hard not to totally crack up.

"I got hit with an onion ring," Lula said.

"Anything else?" he asked Morelli.

"Nope, that's about it," Morelli said, hands loose at his sides, knuckles scraped and bleeding, bruise flowering on his right cheekbone. "Be nice if you'd move your car, so we could get out of here. And when you go inside, you might look for a guy in a red thong. He's with us."

Morelli was slouched on the couch, holding an ice pack to his bruised cheek, taking in the last minutes of a West Coast ball game.

"It could have been worse," I said.

"It could have been a *lot* worse. We could have had to listen to another set of songs."

"We'd probably be sitting in jail right now if you weren't a cop."

"My being a cop had nothing to do with it. Gazarra would never arrest you. I went along for the ride on this one."

"You don't talk much about being a cop anymore."

Morelli tossed the ice pack to the floor. "I'm working homicide. There's not much I'd want to talk about. I'm up to my armpits in gang-related killings. The only decent part is usually they kill each other." He clicked the game off. "This game is boring. I bet we can find more interesting things to look at if we go upstairs."

The first applicant was already in the office when I arrived. He was wearing chaps, and he had a sawed-off strapped to his back.

"We don't actually dress like bounty hunters in this office," Connie was explaining to him. "We find it's . . . too obvious."

"Yeah, and chaps makes your ass look big," Lula said. "You go around looking like that and the fashion police gonna come after you."

"I always dress like this," the guy said. "I ride a Hog."

"What about the sawed-off?" Connie asked.

"What about it?"

Two more applicants came and went after the guy with the chaps. I cracked my knuckles through both of them, wanting to move on. I had three FTAs targeted for today, plus Caroline Scarzolli was still at large. And Lonnie Johnson was out there, somewhere. And the truth was, I didn't want to find any of these people. I wanted to find Ranger.

When the last applicant walked out the door, Connie wrenched her bottom drawer open, unscrewed a bottle of Jack Daniel's, and chugged some down.

"Okay," she said. "I feel better now."

"I like this job interviewing shit," Lula said. "It's a real boost to my self-esteem. Even with my damaged early years, I'm looking good up against these freaks."

"Where's Pickle?" I asked Connie.

"He's working Monday through Friday. Since we

usually only work half-day on Saturday anyway, I gave him weekends off."

I looked out the front window at the black SUV. It was starting to feel eerie. No one ever saw Carmen. Just the tinted black windows.

"The SUV is still out there," I said. "When was the last time anyone saw that SUV move?"

"It was here when I arrived this morning, and I guess it was here when I left last night," Connie said.

I took a slurp of booze from Connie's bottle. "I need to take a look at the car."

I crossed the street, and I knocked on the driver's side window but nothing happened. I looked in through the windshield. Nobody home. Blood everywhere. I turned and slid down the car until I reached pavement. I sat there with my head between my knees until the nausea was under control and the noise subsided in my head. I got to my knees, waited a moment for the fog to clear, and then got to my feet. I walked to the rear of the SUV where the smell of decomposing flesh was strong. I put my face to the glass and squinted through the tinted window. A tarp had been pulled across the cargo area.

I took my cell phone out and called Morelli. "You might want to get over here," I said. "I think I have a body for you."

Chapter SEVEN

Connie and Lula and I waited across the street in front of the bonds office while the police did their thing. I was so terrified at what would be found that my fingers were numb, and I could feel tears welling behind my eyes. I suspected Carmen was in the back of the SUV, but it could as easily be Ranger or his little girl, Julie.

Morelli stood to the side watching while a uniform opened the back hatch and slid the tarp aside. Morelli's eyes flicked to the body in the cargo area and then to me. *Carmen,* he mouthed to me.

I wasn't sure what I felt. A mixture of emotion. Horror for Carmen and relief that it wasn't Ranger or the child.

"Did we get information back on Julie's mother and stepfather?" I asked Connie. "Anything on the Virginia business?"

"I saw reports come in, but I didn't read them."

We went into the office, and Connie pulled up the reports. Rachel Martine had no work history. High school graduate. Lived her whole life in Miami. Nothing derogatory in her credit file. Her banking history showed a steady money stream from Ranger. No criminal history. She married Ronald Martine eight years ago. They bought a house shortly after they were married, and they were still at that same address. Ronald

Martine was seven years older than his wife. Also a high school graduate. No college, but he had gone to school to repair air-conditioning systems and had been working at his trade for eighteen years. Both seemed to be very stable. There were two other Martine children, a seven-year-old girl and a four-year-old boy. They attended the local Catholic church. You couldn't get much cleaner than Rachel and Ronald Martine.

RangeManoso showed up on the Virginia business report. Described as bail enforcement and fugitive apprehension. The business had leased office space in Arlington. The proprietor was Rxyzzlo Xnelos Zzuvemo. In six months of operation it had incurred a long list of delinquent bills.

"I love the way he's coded his name every time it pops up in a data base," Lula said. "It's genius."

"This doesn't sound right," Connie said. "Ranger runs a tight business. He pays his bills on time."

"I saw a TV show on identity theft," Lula said. "Maybe someone's posing as Ranger."

I'd actually been thinking the same thing for some time. And the fact that Ranger's name is always in code probably helped to hide the theft.

I dialed Tank. I'd sworn I'd never again dial Tank, but I couldn't help myself. I didn't know what else to do.

"They just found Carmen Manoso dead in her SUV in front of the bonds office," I told him. "If Ranger's looking for his body double, there's a good chance he's here in Trenton."

"Ten four." And Tank hung up.

"So you don't think Ranger offed Carmen?" Lula asked.

"Ranger wouldn't have left her in front of the bonds office for us to find. Ranger would have made her disappear, never to be found again. Ranger likes to keep things tidy."

Morelli stuck his head in the office and crooked his finger at me. "Can I see you outside?"

I left the bonds office, and we stood by the side of the building.

"Her driver's license identifies her as Carmen Manoso," Morelli said. "She seems to be the woman you described to me. I didn't think you'd want to see for yourself. She's been dead a while. It's not good. A single bullet in the head."

"Could it have been self-inflicted?"

"No. Her gun was unfired on the driver's side floor."

"I have a theory."

"Oh boy."

I gave Morelli a copy of the Virginia business report. "I think some nut is posing as Ranger."

"Identity theft."

"Yeah, only maybe it's not that simple. Maybe this guy is wacked-out. He got married as Ranger. That's carrying identity theft a little far."

"You still haven't heard from Ranger?"

"No. I've talked to Tank a couple times, but that's like talking to a wall."

"What about the kid? Any more theories?"

"I think one of the Rangers took her."

"And?"

"And I think it's the wrong one. The little girl's parents look solid. And Ranger's been regularly sending child support. I don't think he'd take the girl without telling her mom. A while ago, Ranger mentioned that he had a daughter, but I got the impression it wasn't common knowledge. So either it's someone who was at one time very close to Ranger, or else it's someone close to the little girl or her family."

"And I want to know this because . . ."

"Because you want to close Carmen's case, and it's possible she was shot by the Un-Ranger."

"Something I've learned with police work," Morelli said. "It's good to have theories, but don't lock yourself into them. In the end, it's facts that count, not theories. Carmen could have been killed by some random maniac. And Ranger could easily be leading his own double life. No one knows what's in Ranger's head. There are too many times a crime doesn't get solved because the investigator followed an obvious but wrong lead and ignored looking for anything else until it was too late and all other leads were cold."

"Point taken," I said.

"Well?" Lula asked when I returned to the office.

"A single bullet to the head," I told her. "Not self-inflicted."

"Right in front of the office," Lula said. "Gives me the creeps."

"I'm feeling stressed," Connie said. "This has been a really shitty morning."

"I bet I got something that'll cheer you up," Lula said. "This here specialty shop I know about was open this morning, and I stopped on my way to the office. I got another singing gig tonight, and I needed a new outfit. Everybody wait here, and I'll try it on."

Five minutes later, Lula swung out of the bathroom and paraded around the bonds office in a one-piece jumpsuit-type thing made out of glaring white vinyl. The bottom was short-shorts that sort of got lost in Lula's ass, and the top was strapless, squishing her boobs up so they bulged out everywhere. The outfit was accessorized with four-inch-spike-heeled white vinyl boots that came to just below her knee.

"Now when someone hits me with a onion ring and it leaves a grease spot I can just wipe it off with Lysol," Lula said.

"Smart," I said to Lula. "Are you sure you want to do this?"

"Fuckin' A. I'm expanding my horizons, remember? This could be a whole new career for me. Not that I don't like bounty huntering, but I feel this is a time when I should be open to new opportunities. Anyways, the What's got a job lined up at the Golden Times Senior Center in Mercerville tonight."

Connie and I were speechless. Lula was going to perform in a white vinyl Band-Aid in front of a bunch of impaired senior citizens.

"I know what you're probably thinking," Lula said. "You're thinking I probably don't have to worry about them throwing onion rings . . . but you never know. Some of those old people are real feisty."

"That's not what I was thinking," Connie said. "I was thinking you're going to give them all a heart attack if you wear that getup."

Lula looked down at herself. "You think it's too much?"

"I think it's not enough," Connie said.

"What's Sally wearing?" I asked Lula.

"I got him a matching thong." Lula glanced down at her watch. "I gotta go. We got a rehearsal this afternoon, and then we're playing at six o'clock on account of the old folks don't stay up real late."

"Life just gets weirder and weirder," Connie said, taking in the full rear view of Lula running off to the bathroom to change.

I grabbed my shoulder bag and headed for the door. "See you Monday."

"Don't be late," Connie said. "We have the last group of mutants to interview Monday morning."

Goody. Goody.

Morelli was still standing across the street, hands on hips, keeping watch over the crime scene. The medical examiner had arrived, along with the meat wagon. A tech truck was angled into the curb, the back doors open. A squad car was double-parked, strobe flashing. A uniform was keeping traffic moving.

I didn't often see Morelli at work, and I was struck by a few things that I already knew but didn't always think about. He was movie-star handsome in a rugged, lean, and muscled way. He was good at his job. He carried more responsibility than I could manage. And his job was really crappy. Every day he slogged through death and misery, seeing the worst side of society. I suppose once in a while good people walked through his life, but I didn't think it was the norm.

I slid behind the wheel of the Mini and motored off. In a few minutes I was back at my condo. I went straight to my computer and brought my e-mail up. Five more ads for penis enhancement, three ads for big-busted women, two ads for cheap mortgage money, and an answer from Nash in Virginia.

The e-mail from Nash read:

KNOW THE GUY YOU'RE LOOKING FOR. ONE OF THOSE IDIOTS DRESSING IN BLACK, TEARING POSTERS OFF THE POST OFFICE WALL. HAD A ONE-ROOM OFFICE IN A STRIP MALL BUT IT'S CLOSED UP. I CHECKED FOR YOU. DON'T KNOW ANY MORE THAN THAT. MET HIM ONCE WHILE I WAS ON A STAKEOUT AND HE WANDERED ONTO MY TURF. I TOLD HIM HE WAS POACHING AND HE LEFT.

So I was more and more convinced there was a guy out there pretending to be Ranger. What I didn't have was a name for the guy. Or a face. He obviously resembled Ranger in build and coloring and had to be close in age. He was able to get a fake ID. Not a hard thing to do. Every sixteen-year-old kid has a fake ID.

Ranger was probably riding the wind, looking for the guy. And any well-adjusted person would walk away and let Ranger do his thing. Unfortunately, I wasn't that well adjusted. I possess an abnormal amount of curiosity, undoubtedly a Grandma Mazur gene. And dwarfing the curiosity was concern. I was worried. Really worried. Not to mention I had all these hormonal Ranger feelings that I hadn't a clue how to control.

I'd exhausted all my search possibilities, but I knew where there was more information. Ranger's computer. I'd worked for Ranger for a brief amount of time, running searches in the RangeMan office. I knew the programs available, and I knew how they worked. Connie had good programs, but Ranger had better. And I suspected Ranger had a way of recognizing his own name.

I had a key to Ranger's apartment, but I couldn't get into it without Tank knowing. Ranger resided on the seventh floor of his office building. The building was secure, from the sidewalk in front to the rooftop. Every inch, with the exception of the interior of the apartments, was monitored.

I could go to Tank and tell him I was using Ranger's apartment, but the thought practically made me break out in hives. Tank was intimidating. I had no real relationship with Tank. And I was pretty sure he thought I was a pain in the ass.

Well, what the hell, half the people in New Jersey probably thought I was a pain in the ass. A girl can't let something like that stand in her way, can she? Besides, this was all Ranger's fault for not returning my calls.

I made myself a peanut butter and olive sandwich, washed it down with a diet soda, beefed up my courage by adding another layer of mascara to my lashes, and set out for RangeMan headquarters.

Ranger's building was on a quiet side street in city center. It was an unremarkable building. Neatly maintained. Only identified by a small plaque by the front door and the security cameras at the entrance to the underground garage. I pulled the Mini up to the garage entrance and flashed my key pass. The gate opened and I whipped the Mini into one of Ranger's four parking places. Ranger drove a Porsche Turbo, a Porsche Cayenne, and a big-ass truck. All three were parked. I waved at the security camera facing me and stepped into the elevator. I used my key to get to the seventh floor and stepped out into the small foyer.

I dialed Tank on my cell phone.

"Tank here."

"Are you in the control center?" I asked him.

"Yeah."

"Then you know I'm upstairs in the foyer. I thought I'd call and make sure Ranger wasn't inside and naked."

Silence. Tank didn't know what to say to this.

"I'm taking your silence as an affirmative that it's okay to go in," I said to Tank.

"Let me know if you need anything," Tank said.

I unlocked Ranger's lair, opened the door, and stepped over the threshold. I closed and locked the door and took a moment to let the cool calm wash over me. Ranger's apartment was tastefully decorated by a professional and perfectly kept by a housekeeper. It was masculine and sophisticated and slightly Zen. Everything had a place, and I'd spent some time as Ranger's guest so I knew the routine. Keys went in a dish on the sideboard in the front entrance hall. Also on the sideboard were fresh flowers in a small glass vase. Probably the flowers were never once noticed by Ranger. Mail was stacked in a silver tray.

I leafed through the mail, checking the postmarks. It looked like Ranger hadn't been in his apartment since I saw him in the bakery. I called "Hello," just in case. No one answered.

I walked past the kitchen, dining area, and small living room and went to Ranger's office just off the bedroom. I sat at his desk and turned his computer on. This felt invasive but I didn't know what else to do. I couldn't just sit on my hands while Ranger was suspected of kidnapping and possibly murder.

I stood and stretched and looked at my watch. It was almost seven o'clock, and I still hadn't found what I was looking for. I couldn't track the Un-Ranger because I couldn't decode Ranger's name. And Carmen and RangeManoso always came to a dead end. I went to the kitchen and looked through the cupboards and fridge. Not a lot I was interested in. Ranger didn't exactly keep a ton of food on hand. There'd be sandwiches downstairs in the control center kitchen, but I didn't want to go there. I finally settled on a beer and some cheese and crackers.

I went back to the computer and looked around Ranger's office. No photographs. No personal doodads. Only articles selected by the housekeeper or the decorator. This was a place where Ranger slept and worked. This was the Batcave. This wasn't his home. I knew Ranger had other properties. And one of those properties was home. I hadn't a clue where it was located or what it looked like.

I slouched back in the leather desk chair and closed my eyes. Let's go at this from a different direction, I thought. Straight computer searches weren't working. Pretend Ranger's an FTA. What do I know? He was going to Miami. Why? Not on normal BEA business. He would have told me. And Tank wouldn't be this uncommunicative. Ranger had said it was "bad business."

So just to choose a direction, let's assume the Un-Ranger popped up on the radar screen. Ranger would have shut him down . . . professionally and personally. Possibly permanently. Since it doesn't look like that happened, the next assumption would be that the

Un-Ranger moved on before Ranger got to him in Virginia. And maybe he moved to Miami. And that would be his undoing, because there was a RangeMan office in Miami. And Ranger's computer guru was at that office. His name was Silvio, and I was betting he knew how to decode Ranger's name.

So let's assume the Un-Ranger tried to set up shop in Miami and Silvio found out. And Ranger took off for Miami to take care of the Un-Ranger. But before Ranger got to the Un-Ranger, the little girl was kidnapped. And now Ranger was looking for both of them.

Lots of assumptions. Still no facts. Still no name. No Un-Ranger face. I went into Ranger's mail program. The in-box was empty. "Sent items" was empty. Nothing in "Deleted items." Ranger kept things clean. I went to his hard drive and started opening files. This took some time because Ranger numbered his files but didn't name them. File XB112 contained two JPGs. I opened the JPGs and there was the Un-Ranger. Both photos had clearly been taken without the man's knowledge. He was walking toward a car. The shots were full frontal and head turned slightly.

The man was dressed in black. He was a little less muscular than Ranger. Maybe a little wider in the hip. His hair was colored and styled like Ranger's. Sideburns cut at an angle. His skin tone was close. Maybe a half-shade lighter than Ranger's. Facial features were startlingly similar. It was easy to see how a description of this man would fit Ranger. The foliage in the background was tropical. Florida plates on the cars in the photo.

I printed both JPGs and then e-mailed them to myself. Then I permanently erased the e-mail from "Sent items."

My cell phone rang and was so startling in the silent apartment, it had me out of my seat.

"I'm still at work," Morelli said. "This is going to be a late night."

"That's okay," I said. "I'm at work, too. Maybe I'll see you tomorrow."

I didn't have a name, but I had a picture. And I knew Ranger was on top of it all. I shut his computer down, shut the lights off, and locked up behind myself. I rode the elevator to the garage, waved good-bye at the security camera, and drove away.

I stopped at Pino's on the way home and picked up a pizza and a six-pack. Then I rode past the bonds office out of morbid curiosity. Not much to see, thank heaven. The car had been removed.

I carted the pizza and beer upstairs, opened my door, and realized the lights were on in my apartment. I experienced a nanosecond of terror until I saw Ranger sitting in my living room.

"*Jeez!*" I said. "You scared the crap out of me. I thought you were in Florida."

Ranger unfolded himself and closed the space between us. "I just got back."

He took the pizza box and the beer and carried them to the kitchen. We each took a beer and a slice of pizza and ate standing at the counter.

"Did you water my plants?" Ranger wanted to know.

"Ella waters your plants."

He went to my shoulder bag, rummaged around in it, and pulled out the two pieces of paper with the Un-Ranger pictures.

"I'm impressed. Where did you find them?" he asked.

"In a file in your hard drive. I couldn't get anything else because I couldn't decode your name. If I'd been really desperate, I would have called Silvio."

"Tank wasn't helpful?"

"Tank's entire vocabulary consists of seven words.

Ten, tops. You could have returned a phone call and saved me a lot of trouble," I said.

"People can listen in on phone calls."

Ranger took an unheard-of third piece of pizza.

"Wow," I said. "You must be hungry."

His eyes were dark when he looked at me. "Babe, you don't want to go there."

My heart skipped a beat. "Probably not," I said. I picked the Un-Ranger picture off the counter. "Do you know who this is?"

"No name. Just this photo. It was taken two days before the kidnapping. We thought it was simple identity theft and didn't have him under twenty-four-hour surveillance. Big mistake, because he checked out of his motel in the middle of the night and the next day he kidnapped Julie. We've been two steps behind him ever since."

"Everyone thinks *you* kidnapped Julie."

"Not everyone. Rachel and Ron know I didn't take her. I have a good relationship with them. And the lead agency man knows. We made a decision to go this route and hope the kidnapper feels comfortable enough to get sloppy. The downside is my picture's been all over the media and now my movement is limited. So I could use some help."

"Why don't you just go blond?"

"I've been blond. When I go blond I look like I should be singing with the Village People."

I burst out laughing. The visual was so perfect.

"You have a sense of humor," I said to him. "Who would have thought?"

"There are lots of things you don't know about me."

"Just about everything." I gave Rex a piece of pizza crust. "Your cars were all parked at RangeMan."

"I can't drive them. Every poser cowboy bounty

hunter in the country is looking for me, along with a lot of law enforcement. I've got a green Explorer parked on the street."

"And a new wardrobe."

Ranger was total Abercrombie in jeans, olive-drab T-shirt, and a loose-fitting button-down shirt, worn untucked.

"You aren't going to give me grief over this, are you?" he asked.

I smiled at him. "You look cute."

"*Cute,*" Ranger repeated. "That just dropped my testosterone level."

The Pleasure Treasures bag was sitting forgotten on my counter. "Looks like I'm not the only one who's been shopping," Ranger said, reaching for the bag.

"*No!* Don't touch that."

Too late. He had it in his hands.

"This is embarrassing," I said. "Give me the bag."

Ranger held the bag out of my reach. "Want to wrestle me for it?"

At another time this exchange might have felt flirty. Tonight there was an edge to Ranger. Anger simmering just below the surface. And I thought it wouldn't take too much provocation for him to rearrange someone's face. Not mine, of course. He liked my face. Still, he was a little scary.

I narrowed my eyes at him. "Just give me the damn bag."

"I let you snoop in my computer," Ranger said. "The least you can do is let me see in this bag."

"I don't think so."

"Not much you can do about it, babe."

"I'll be mad at you."

"You can't be mad at me," Ranger said. "I'm cute. I might even be adorable."

"Try *jerk* on for size."

"Sticks and stones." He looked in the bag and gave a single soft bark of laughter. "Nice," he said, taking the dildo out, setting it on the counter, balls down, shaft up, like a giant pink rubber mushroom.

I'm not one of those women who blushes easily, but I could feel my ears burning.

"Having problems with Morelli?" Ranger asked, the edge gone. Anger replaced by something much softer . . . amusement, exhaustion, affection.

"The woman working in the Pleasure Treasures store went FTA, and Lula and I went in to make an apprehension, and Lula got this dancing dildo, but they were having a two-for-one sale, and somehow I ended up with this. It's the Herbert Horsecock model."

"It's impressive."

"It's frightening," I told him.

He took the DVD out of the bag. "*Big Boys,*" he said. "I'm seeing a theme here."

"Lula said it would change my life."

Ranger put the dildo and the DVD back in the bag. "Does your life need changing?"

"I don't know. I thought so a while ago, but it feels comfortable now . . . except for a commitment dilemma."

He pulled me to him and kissed me in a way that more than made up for the benign kiss in the bakery. "Let me know when you figure it out," he said.

I realized that sometime during the kiss I'd inserted my leg between his and had plastered myself to him in all the strategic places. I inched away and smoothed out the wrinkles I'd made when I gripped his shirt.

"Is there something I should be doing tonight to find Julie?" I asked him.

"Not tonight, but I have some legwork for you to do tomorrow if you have time."

"Of course I have time. Are you managing this okay?"

"It's not the first time I've had to find someone important to me. You learn to keep moving forward. And you go deep into denial."

"Are you scared?"

"Yeah," Ranger said. "I'm scared for Julie."

"Do you have a place to stay?"

"I have a safe house in North Trenton. I'll pick you up tomorrow morning at eight." He reached out to kiss me again, but I jumped away. Another kiss like the last one and he wouldn't leave. . . . I'd make sure of it.

"Still think I'm cute?" Ranger asked with the almost nonexistent smile curving the corners of his mouth. And he left.

Chapter EIGHT

I opened an eye and squinted at my bedside clock. Six-thirty. In the morning! My alarm wasn't set to go off for another hour, but something had dragged me awake. I opened the other eye and did some deep breathing, sucking in the smell of coffee brewing. I rolled out of bed and shuffled into the dining room.

Ranger was at the table, using my laptop.

"Unh," I said.

"Coffee's in the kitchen."

"What are you doing here?"

"No computer in the safe house, and I thought this was easier than getting Tank to try to get a laptop to me. I had some things I wanted to run down."

"I don't have very good programs."

"I don't need programs. Silvio is sending me information from Miami."

"How long have you been here?"

"About an hour." He stood and stretched and headed for the kitchen. He got two mugs out of the cabinet, filled them with coffee, added milk, and gave one to me.

I was wearing short cotton pajama bottoms and a knit tank top, and I could see Ranger was enjoying the tank top.

"I'm feeling self-conscious," I said to him.

"That's not what I'm feeling."

No kidding! "Go back to work," I told him. "I'm going to take my coffee into the shower. I'll be ready to go in a half hour."

Ranger had parked on a side street a block away from my building. He left through the front door and walked to his car. I left through the back door, got into the Mini, and drove around three blocks until I was sure I wasn't being followed. I parked behind Ranger, beeped the Mini locked, and slipped into the green Explorer.

"Now what?" I asked.

Ranger pulled into traffic and went north on Hamilton. "I want you to canvass a neighborhood for me."

Ranger isn't an especially talkative guy. He doesn't do small talk, and he doesn't usually initiate conversation, but he'll talk about the job if he feels there's a genuine interest. In this case, I definitely had interest.

"I'd really like to know the history on this," I said to him. "I've only got bits and pieces."

"Two weeks ago someone started using a credit card issued to RangeManoso Enterprises with my name on it. Silvio found it during a routine scan. Silvio traced down RangeManoso, and to the best of our knowledge this guy appeared in Arlington six months ago and set up shop. I was about to go to Arlington and shut him down when we discovered he'd moved on. And then all of a sudden he started using the card in Miami. We assumed he was there reestablishing himself, but in retrospect, I think he was there to get Julie."

"So you went to Miami to find this guy and before you got to him he took Julie."

"Yes. And until you called Tank and told him someone smoked Carmen we had no reason to think he was in Jersey. We thought either he hunkered down somewhere in Florida or else he was in a car moving around.

We didn't think he'd be able to get Julie through security and onto a plane. And the FBI was combing passenger lists for Julie Martine and Carlos Manoso and not finding anything."

"If he stole your identity, I guess he could steal others."

"Two others turned up when Silvio ran through the RangeManoso credit history. He paid some early bills with cards issued to Steve Scullen and Dale Small. Silvio had been watching passenger lists for both those identities, but nothing there either."

"No leads in Miami from the crime scene?"

"Miami went cold. Julie got picked up in a stolen car. It was found abandoned two blocks from the pickup point. The police issued a bulletin, and they're doing the follow-up on calls coming in."

"It was my impression that not many people knew you had a daughter."

"You and Tank and relatives."

"And Julie's mother and stepfather."

"Rachel and Ron are working with the people in Miami, trying to trace down anyone who might have known about me. They didn't hide the fact that Ron was Julie's stepfather, but they didn't tell a lot of people the details. Julie knew. My name is on her birth certificate, but Ron adopted her, and she's always thought of herself as Julie Martine."

"Is that painful?"

"It might be painful if she wasn't happy, but Rachel and Ron are good parents. Rachel is a nice Catholic girl I took advantage of one night on leave when I was in the military. She got pregnant, and I married her and gave the baby my name and financial support. We divorced after the baby was born. I'm involved only as much as Rachel wants me to be."

"She didn't want you to stick around and be a permanent husband?"

"That was never an option either of us would have considered."

We were on Route 1, driving north. It was early Sunday morning and traffic was light. I was in my usual uniform of jeans and T-shirt. Ranger was in homeboy clothes.

"From the way you're dressed, I'd guess we were canvassing the ghetto today," I said to Ranger.

"You'd guess right."

His jeans were loose-fit but not falling off his ass. "Think you can pull it off in those jeans?"

"They'll have to do. You can't chase someone down if your pants are around your ankles."

True enough. I'd actually chased guys who'd literally run out of their pants.

"And I'm a little old for the homey look. I was shooting for Latino Gap," Ranger said. "I don't plan to get out of the car, but just in case, I wanted to blend."

Ranger took the turnpike and got off at the Newark exit. When they nicknamed New Jersey the Garden State, they weren't talking about Newark. The neighborhoods we drove through were bleak by anyone's standards. If I'd been with anyone other than Ranger, I'd have turned tail and gotten back on the turnpike.

"This is a scary neighborhood," I said, taking in the graffiti, the occasional condemned building, the sullen faces of the kids hanging on street corners.

"I grew up here," Ranger said. "It hasn't changed much in twenty years."

"Were you one of those guys on the corner?"

Ranger cut his eyes to a group of teens. "Eventually. When I was a kid, I was little and I didn't fit, so I got beat up a lot. My skin color was too light for the blacks and too dark for the Cubans. And I had straight brown hair that made me look like a girl."

"How awful."

Ranger shrugged. "I found out I could survive a beating. And I learned to be quick, and to watch my back, and to fight dirty."

"All good skills," I said.

"For street thugs and bounty hunters."

"I thought you lived in Miami for a while."

"When I was fourteen I got arrested for stealing a car and spent some time in juvie. When I got out, my parents sent me to Miami to live with my grandmother. I went to high school in Miami. I moved back to Jersey to take a shot at college, and then I came back when I got out of the army."

Ranger found a place at the curb in front of a deli. "My parents live on the next block," Ranger said. "This neighborhood we're in right now really isn't so bad. It's actually the Cuban equivalent to the Burg. Problem is, you have to go through the bad neighborhood to get anywhere, including the school."

Ranger clipped a little gizmo onto my jeans waistband. "Panic button. If you have a problem, just push it, and I'll come to you. I want you to take the photo you got off my computer and see if someone knows this guy. He has to have some association with me."

"All the signs are in Spanish. Will I be able to talk to anyone?"

"Everyone speaks English. Except for my Grandma Rosa, and we're going to try hard not to run into her."

I left Ranger sitting in the SUV and took the picture into the deli. It was a little mom-and-pop business. A butcher in the back behind a glass case filled with sausages and pork roasts and chicken parts. Shelves filled with sacks of rice, spices, cereals, canned goods. Baskets of vegetables. More shelves with breads and packaged cakes and cookies.

A middle-aged woman was at the register. I waited

for her to check out a customer before introducing myself.

"I'm looking for this man," I said, showing her the photo. "Do you know him?"

"Yes, I know him," the woman behind the counter said. "This is Carlos Manoso."

"No," I said to her. "I know Carlos, and this isn't him."

I showed the picture to the butcher and to a woman waiting to have a pork roast boned and rolled. They both thought it was Carlos Manoso, the man the police were looking for. They said they'd seen his photo on television.

It was close to noon when I returned to the green Explorer. My nose was sunburned, and I had sweat running in a river down my breastbone.

"Nothing," I said to Ranger. "Everyone thinks it's you."

Ranger looked at the picture. "I need to get back to the gym."

"It's not the body. It's the clothes and the face. He's spent some time studying you. He's got the clothes down. And he's had his hair cut like yours. Hard to tell from this picture if the skin tone is the same or if he's tanned himself to mimic your coloring."

"This is the third day, and I still haven't got anything," Ranger said. "We worked Miami really hard. Mostly talking to relatives and neighbors, going with the idea that he knew me, that he was close enough to someone in my circle to know about Julie."

"Is this the first you've started looking in Jersey?"

"We went to relatives and friends right away. This is the first neighborhood search. And this is the only neighborhood where he'd pick up information on Julie. It would have to come from one of my relatives. No one in Trenton knew."

"Okay, so we seem to be at a dead end on the Ranger

connection. Let's go in another direction. He married Carmen Cruz from Springfield, Virginia, and he set up an office in Arlington. Maybe that's where he originates. Not in Arlington but close enough to feel comfortable with the area. Maybe we should talk to Carmen's parents."

Ranger put the SUV in gear and called Tank. "Run Carmen Cruz in Springfield, Virginia, and get Stephanie and me on a train out of Newark going to northern Virginia. I'll be traveling as Marc Pardo."

"Stolen identity?" I asked him.

"No. It's all mine."

"Wouldn't it be faster to fly?"

"I can't take a gun on a plane."

Ranger left the green SUV in the train station parking lot. Good luck with that one. One of his guys was supposed to pick it up, but I was giving it a half hour tops before it was on the way to a chop shop.

I was sitting next to Ranger, I had a box of food in front of me from the café car, and the rocking of the train was hypnotic and soothing and exciting all at the same time. We were rolling through the country's backyards, seeing America with its pants down.

Ranger was on the phone with Tank, taking down information on Carmen Cruz and arranging for a rental car.

"About the cell phone," I said, when Ranger disconnected. "Why is it okay to talk to Tank when you couldn't call me?"

"Tank has a secure phone."

"Like it's scrambled?"

"No. They're just phones under different names. It's a way to make sure no one's listening. If someone's trying to get a line on me, they're not going to tap Larry Baker's phone."

"Spending time with you is always a learning experience."

"There are other things I could teach you," Ranger said.

It was four o'clock by the time we picked up the rental car and rolled out of Union Station. Ranger had the GPS gadget set to take us to the Cruz house in Springfield, and it was talking us through downtown Washington.

"Turn left in twenty feet," the mechanical voice told us. "Move to the left lane. Take a right at the bottom of the off-ramp. Merge into traffic."

"This thing's giving me an eye twitch," Ranger said. "Can you get the sound off?"

I started pressing buttons and the screen went blank.

"How's that?" I asked.

"Babe, you shut the system down."

"Yes, but the sound is off."

"Reprogram it."

"No need to get testy," I told him.

"I don't know where I'm going."

"I have a map. You just get on I-95 south and take the Springfield exit."

"And then what?"

"Then you'll have to pull over and reprogram the GPS."

Ranger cut his eyes to me and there was the tiniest of smiles on his mouth. I was amusing him.

"You're a very strange man," I told him.

"Yeah," he said. "That's what I hear."

I had my cell phone clipped to my waist, and I could feel it buzzing. I looked at the screen. Morelli.

"Howdy," I said.

"Can I buy you dinner and a movie and a room at Hotel Morelli?"

"Sounds good but I'm working."

"After work."

"After work will be late," I said.

"How late?"

"Monday or Tuesday."

"Where are you?" Morelli wanted to know.

"I can't tell you that," I said.

"Goddamn it, you're with Ranger, aren't you? I should have known. He's up to his armpits in murder and kidnapping, and he's going to drag you into it with him."

Ranger reached over, grabbed my phone, and shut it down.

"Hey!" I said. "That was Morelli."

"If you stay on too long, it can be traced down. I'm sure he understands."

"Yeah, he understands. If he knew where we were, you'd be seeing his Kojak light in your rearview mirror."

"Then I'm glad he doesn't know where we are because I wouldn't want to have to square off with Morelli. It wouldn't end well for either of us."

We moved onto I-95 south, and I tightened my seat belt. Driving out of D.C. into northern Virginia is like NASCAR on a flat straight track, racing bumper-to-bumper six wide, twenty miles deep. And attached to that is another identical race going six wide in the opposite direction. Two-story-high sound barriers rise out of the breakdown lanes and form a cement canyon filled with wall-to-wall noise and insanity. We hurtled forward to the appropriate exit, catapulted ourselves down the chute, and peeled off toward Springfield.

Ranger pulled onto the shoulder and reprogrammed the GPS system.

"Lucky for you, you look good in a T-shirt," Ranger said.

"Lucky for you I don't have a gun on me."

Ranger turned to me. His voice was low and even, but there was a whisper of incredulous disbelief. “You’re not carrying a gun?”

“Didn’t seem necessary for us *both* to have one.”

Chapter NINE

It was a little after five o'clock when we drove past the Cruz house. We were in a development of middle-income homes, mostly little ranches sitting on small plots of land. Every third house was the same. From the maturity of trees and shrubs, I'd have guessed the houses were maybe ten years old.

The Cruz house was pale yellow with white trim and a teal-green front door. The landscaping was economy grade but neat. There were several cars in the driveway and two at the curb. I imagined friends and relatives were sharing the Cruzes' grief over their daughter.

Ranger drove two blocks over and parked. We were in front of a small public access to a bike path that wound through a narrow greenbelt behind the houses.

"I'm going to wait here," he said. "You take the car and go do your thing."

"Are you sure you want to give me the car after making sexist remarks about my mechanical skills? I might not come back for you."

"I'd find you," Ranger said. He took my hand, kissed the palm, and got out of the car.

I exchanged seats, put the car in gear, and drove back to the Cruzes'. I parked at the curb and blew out a sigh. I was going to feel like a real shit for intruding at a time like this. I set off for the house, and just as I got to the porch two young women came out to have a cigarette. They lit up, took a deep drag, and sat down on the step to enjoy the rest in comfort.

I extended my hand. "Stephanie Plum," I said. "Were you friends with Carmen?"

They both nodded.

"I'm Sasha," one said.

"Lorraine."

"I'm part of the task force investigating the crime," I told them. "Would you mind if I asked some questions?"

Lorraine looked down at my jeans.

"You're going to have to excuse my dress," I said. "I was called in on my day off, and I didn't get a chance to change."

"What do you want to know?"

"Do you know her husband?"

"Carmen talked about him in the beginning. Ranger, Ranger, Ranger. I mean, how lame is that? Who calls himself Ranger?"

"Did she ever mention his real name?"

"Carlos."

"Would you recognize him if you saw a picture?"

"No. None of us actually saw him. And then all of a sudden she was married and living in Arlington and she sort of fell off the earth."

"Is he from this area?"

"I don't know where he's originally from," Lorraine said. "He was working as a security guard at Potomac Mills Mall when she met him. He told her it was only a temporary job until his business took off."

"What business was that?"

"He was a bounty hunter. Carmen thought that was real cool. From what I hear, she cashed in an insurance policy so they could buy computers and shit." A tear ran down Lorraine's cheek, and she wiped her nose with the back of her hand. "The people on television are saying the bastard shot her."

"Thanks," I said. "This has been helpful."

I got directions to the mall, drove back to the bike path, and picked Ranger up.

"When Carmen met this guy, he was working as a security guard at Potomac Mills. It's a mall off I-95 a couple miles south of here," I told Ranger.

Ranger punched Potomac Mills into the GPS. "Okay, sweetheart," he said to the GPS. "Talk to me."

If you entered Potomac Mills at one end and stared down the length of the mall, you would be sure it ended in Kansas. We were standing in front of a mall map getting the lay of the land, looking for the security office and not finding it.

"The mall closes at seven," Ranger said. "We've got a little over an hour to get someone to ID our man. I'm going to have Tank see if he can do something by phone. Meanwhile, you try to find security people to talk to. I'll be fifty paces behind you."

I looked down the mall and saw two uniformed guards standing back on their heels watching the shoppers. Man and woman. In their twenties. The woman looked like she'd gained some weight since they'd issued her uniform. Her partner was tall and gangly. Bad complexion. I was guessing they ate a lot of meals at the food court.

I came up to them with a smile. Friendly. Needing assistance.

"Excuse me," I said. "I'm looking for a guy who used to work as a security guard here. I can't remember his name but he was medium build, dark brown hair, kind of nice-looking. Caucasian, I think, but with dark skin. Probably hasn't been here for maybe six months."

"Doesn't ring a bell," the woman said. "Did he work weekends? We only work weekends."

"I'm not sure."

"You should talk to Dan," she said. "He's been here forever. He knows everyone. He's sort of heavyset and balding, and he's probably down toward the other end. He might be around Linens-N-Things, unless he got a call."

I wasn't sure where Linens-N-Things was located, but with the way this mall was looking it could be a couple miles. I took off at a fast walk, trying not to be distracted by the stores. I made it past Banana Republic and the Gap but instinctively stopped in front of Victoria's Secret.

I felt Ranger at my back, his hand warm on my waist. "If you buy something, you have to model it," he said.

I got a rush at the thought, panic followed . . . and then guilt. "Just looking," I said.

"I hate to ruin this moment, but there's a guard at three o'clock."

"Is he overweight and balding?"

"Hard to tell if he's balding from here, but he's overweight. He's standing by the kiosk, four or five stores down."

"I see him."

I read his name tag as I approached him. Dan Whitten. "Excuse me," I said. "I'm looking for a guy who used to be a security guard here. I can't remember his name. Medium build. Caucasian but sort of dark skin. Dark brown hair."

"That's a pretty broad description. What do you want with him?"

"I met him in a bar a couple days ago, and he walked away with my iPod. We were comparing MP3 players, and he got a phone call and had to leave. I didn't realize until too late that he'd walked off with my iPod and left me with his piece of junk. Anyway, all I remembered was that he said he used to work here. And he said now he was working as a bounty hunter."

"Edward Scrog. You should kiss that iPod good-bye. The guy is a nutcase. He got fired for harassment."

"You mean sexual harassment?"

"*All* kinds of harassment. Some guys go power-goofy when they get a badge and a uniform. This guy thinks he's Wyatt Earp or something. Walked around with his hand on his flashlight like it was a gun." He broke into a smile. "Scrog used to pat women down. He'd claim they looked suspicious. That was ultimately his undoing. Tried to do a pat-down on a fed. She pulled a move on him and had him on the floor with her foot on his neck. Then she filed charges."

"I don't suppose you know where I can find him?"

"No. It wasn't like we were friends."

"Well, thanks," I said. "This has been helpful."

"Let me give you some advice you didn't ask for. Stay away from Scrog. He's got a screw loose. When they fired him, they walked him to his locker, made him clean it out and leave the premises. I was there to make sure he left, and I saw what was in the locker. He had it filled with guns and ammo. And he had pictures pasted on the door like a kid does with baseball stars and then later on with girls with big hooters. Only this guy had pictures of SWAT guys taking people down. It's like he's seen too many cop movies. When he first came on the job, he was applying to all the local police academies, only no one would give him a call back.

"After he was here a couple months he started talking about the bounty hunter thing. Watched all the shows on television. Apparently he was hooked on some bounty hunter in Jersey who was supposed to be a real hotshot, and he said he was studying him. Used to take off weekends so he could 'observe' this guy. So maybe he's in Jersey now. Good for Virginia, that's my opinion.

"You look like a nice girl," he said. "Take my advice and buy yourself a new iPod."

I walked back to Ranger and gave him the whole story. "I imagine the hotshot Jersey bounty hunter would be you," I said to Ranger.

Ranger called Tank and gave him the name. "Run an address history for me," Ranger said. "I want to know what's open."

We found the food court and sat at a table while we ate pizza and waited for Tank to call back. The call came in at five minutes to seven. Ranger took two addresses down and disconnected.

"We have Scrog's parents' house in Fairfax and an apartment in Dale City."

"Did you ever search his office or the apartment he shared with Carmen?"

"We went through the office in Arlington on the first pass. He didn't leave anything. Same with the apartment. He didn't leave on an impulse. He'd removed everything that could identify him. There were some clothes hanging in the closet and some things in the dresser. Everything else belonged to Carmen."

Scrog's Dale City apartment building was a two-story cinderblock bunker with a parking lot and a close-up view of the interstate. Scrog was on the second floor. Unit 209. Ten units to a floor. Stained carpet. Strong burrito aroma coming out of 206.

Ranger knocked on the door of 209. No answer. He tried the knob. Locked. "I don't suppose you have anything helpful in your bag?" he asked me.

"Like a set of burglary tools? No."

Ranger put his foot to the door, kicked it open, and

stepped inside. I followed behind him and tried to get the door to stay closed.

"Don't worry about it," Ranger said, flipping the light on. "We won't be in here long. There's not a lot to see."

It was a one-bath studio apartment with a small kitchenette along one wall. The blinds were drawn on the single window. There was a sofa bed open and unmade, a small table with two wooden ladder-back chairs, a two-drawer metal file cabinet, and two laundry baskets holding a computer and accessories.

"This guy travels light," Ranger said.

"Maybe he has stuff stored with his parents."

Ranger opened a closet and a bunch of guns fell out. He stepped over the guns and squatted in front of the file cabinet and opened the top drawer.

"He has a file labeled 'Captures' but it's empty. He also has a file labeled 'Wanted,' and it's filled with pictures he's ripped off federal bulletin boards."

Ranger pulled the bottom drawer open, removed a scrapbook, and handed it over to me. "I have a bad feeling about this scrapbook. Scan it while I look through the cupboards."

"Your bad feeling is justified," I said, flipping pages. "This is an homage to Ranger. It looks to me like he was following you around. There are pictures in here of your office building and your cars. There are pictures of you. Pictures of you with me. Pictures of . . . omigod."

It was a picture of Carmen naked. The handwriting on the bottom read: OUR WEDDING NIGHT. PRACTICING FOR THE REAL THING. And it was followed by a snapshot of me. And for the first time I saw the resemblance between Carmen and me. Not that we'd pass for twins, more that we were similar in coloring and build.

Ranger looked over my shoulder. "This guy is sick."

"Do you think he married Carmen because she looks a little like me?"

"Yes. I think he's trying to move into my life."

"He left her behind and killed her."

"Guess he's done practicing," Ranger said.

The next page had a picture of Ranger in front of the Martines' house, talking to Ron. The caption read: RANGER MAKES A MYSTERIOUS VISIT AND I KNOW HIS SECRET. This was followed by pictures of Julie.

Ranger went dead still. He stared at the pictures of his daughter and his face showed no emotion, but he wasn't breathing. It was as if the oxygen had been sucked out of the room. His hands were loose at his sides and his eyes were focused on the pictures. He was looking at a little girl with silky brown hair, intelligent brown eyes, and flawless light brown skin . . . the image of her father. I slipped my hand in his and waited for him to pull himself together.

"She'll be okay," I said. "He's playing a role. He's going to act like he's her dad."

Ranger nodded. "I'd like to think that was true. Let's pack up. I'm going to take the computer and the scrapbook. I don't see anything else of value to us."

We carted Scrog's stuff downstairs and out to the car and put it in the trunk. The sun had set, and the parking lot was dark. Traffic noise carried over the apartment building.

"Now what?" I said to Ranger. "Do you want to talk to his parents?"

"No. I have what I need. Let's go home."

We took I-95 north to the beltway, driving in silence, Ranger in his zone. We were following taillights in the dark, gliding through the night like disembodied spirits. We were between time and place, encapsulated in steel and fiberglass. All this much more poetic than the reality of the moment, which was that my ass was falling asleep. I'd like to say I was in a zone like Ranger, but the truth was, I'd never in my life achieved a zone. In fact, I couldn't even imagine a zone, and didn't really know what one was. If I had to describe my condition, I'd have to say I was freaked.

I fell asleep somewhere in Maryland and didn't wake up until we were on Broad Street. I stretched and looked at Ranger. His hand was loose on the wheel. His breathing was even. At first glance, he seemed relaxed. If you looked more closely, the tension around his eyes and the corners of his mouth was visible. I wondered what was really inside him. And at what cost he kept it hidden.

He parked in my lot and got out of the car. "I'm going to see you upstairs," he said.

"Not necessary."

He beeped the car locked and moved me toward the building. "It is necessary. There's some psycho running around wanting to add you to his Ranger memorabilia."

"You're right," I said. "Thanks. I'm happy to be escorted."

We got upstairs without incident, Ranger opened the door to my apartment and flicked the lights on. Rex was quietly running on his wheel.

"The attack hamster is on the job," Ranger said.

I dropped a peanut into Rex's cage and turned back to Ranger. He looked tired under the kitchen light. He had dark smudges under his eyes and his mouth was tight, fighting sleep. "You look exhausted," I said to him.

"Long day."

"You have another half-hour drive to get to your safe house. Would you like to stay here tonight?"

"Yes."

"This isn't a sexual invitation," I said.

"I know. The couch will be fine."

Chapter TEN

I woke up slowly. I opened my eyes and saw there was a bar of light shining through the crack between my bedroom curtains. It was morning. And I was in my own bed, feeling incredibly comfy. I looked down and realized there was a man's arm thrown across my chest, the hand lightly curled around my breast.

Ranger.

I moved my head ever so slightly on the pillow and looked over at him. He was still asleep. He had a decent beard growth going and his hair had fallen across his forehead. I was pretty sure he wasn't in my bed when I fell asleep. I looked under the covers. I was wearing my knit tank top and short pajama bottoms. Ranger was wearing briefs. Could be worse, I thought.

"Hey," I said.

He wrapped his arms around me and cuddled me into him, his eyes still closed.

"Ranger!"

"Mmm."

"What are you doing in my bed?"

"So far I'm not doing anything, but that could change."

"You said you were going to sleep on the couch."

"I lied."

This was bad because he felt *way* too good. I looked beyond him to the clock. Nine o'clock. "I have to go to work," I said. "I'm already late."

He drew me in a little closer and stroked his thumb across my breast. "Are you *sure* you want to go to work now?"

I got a rush that was so strong it might have been an orgasm, and I think I might have moaned a little. Mentally, I was working hard to be faithful to Morelli, but the physical part of me wasn't cooperating.

Ranger kissed my shoulder, and the phone rang. Ordinarily, at a time like this you'd rip the phone line out of the wall. But these were scary days, and we both went still at the sound.

"Let me get it," I said, reaching across Ranger.

There was a lot of noise at the other end, and then Melvin's voice came on. "Thank God, you answered," he yelled into the phone. "I'm all alone here, and this mob's getting ugly. And Joyce Barnhardt is here, and she's frightening me!"

"Where're Connie and Lula?"

"I don't know where Lula is. Connie had to go bond someone out."

I heard a gun go off in the background, Melvin shrieked and the line went dead. I pushed away from Ranger, and I rolled out of bed. "I have to go. Melvin's alone at the bonds office, and he's got problems."

I grabbed some clothes and ran into the bathroom.

"Who's Melvin?" Ranger said to my back.

I slid to a stop in front of the bonds office and jumped out of the Mini. The plate glass window was filled with lettering advertising bail bonds. Beyond the lettering I could see that the small front office was filled with people dressed like television bounty hunters. I pushed through the door and shouted for Melvin.

"Here," he yelled back. "Under the desk."

I plowed through the crowd and looked under the desk at Melvin. "Why are all these people here? I thought they were scheduled throughout the morning."

"Something got messed up, and they were all told to come in at nine."

"What was the gunshot I heard?"

"Two guys were playing quick draw and one of them accidentally shot the phone."

I glanced over at the phone. Shot dead.

I reached into the petty cash drawer and took out a wad of money. "Hey!" I said. "Listen up."

No one listened, so I climbed onto the desk and tried again. "*Hey!*" I yelled. "Everyone shut the fuck up and listen to me."

This got their attention.

"I'm very sorry but the appointments got screwed up," I told them. "I'm going to reschedule you, and I'm going to give everyone five dollars to go have breakfast while you wait for your appointment time. So I want everyone to line up single file."

Pandemonium. Everyone wanted to be first. Someone got knocked to the ground, and someone got punched in the face. And there was a lot of cussing and shouting and eye gouging and biting.

I got Connie's gun out of her desk drawer and fired a round into the ceiling. A chunk of plaster fell onto the desktop and plaster dust sifted onto my hair and shoulders.

"If you don't get in line nicely, I'm going to shoot you," I said.

This got them to sullenly line up with just a minimum amount of pushing and shoving. I gave out fifteen-minute appointments to eleven people. They each got five dollars. All but one left.

"You can come out from under the desk now," I told

Melvin. "What happened to Joyce? I thought Joyce was here."

"She left. She said she'd be back later this morning. She was real mad. Something about getting sent on a wild goose chase."

I dragged a folding chair over to the desk and told the first bounty hunter impersonator to sit down. The folding chair was old and scarred and said STIVA FUNERAL HOME on the back. I sat in Connie's chair and called Lula on my cell.

"Where the heck are you?" I asked Lula.

"I had to go shopping. We were a big hit at the old people's home, and we got a new gig out of it. And I need a new outfit."

"You're supposed to be here helping with the interviews."

"I figured you didn't need me. They're all losers, anyway."

I looked at the guy in the folding chair. He was dressed in black leather pants and a black leather vest that showed a lot of chest hair. A roll of fat oozed out from under the vest and spilled over his belt buckle. He'd accessorized with black leather wristbands that were studded with the metal things you see on Rottweiler collars. And he was wearing a blond mullet wig.

"You're right," I said to Lula. "Happy shopping."

"So," I said to the guy in front of me, "what makes you qualified to be a bond enforcement agent?"

"I watch all the television shows, and I know I could do this. I don't take shit from anyone, and I got a gun."

"That would be the one that's strapped to your leg?"

"Yeah. And I'm not afraid to use it. I don't take crap from blacks, spics, chinks, Polacks, or commies. I swear, I'll kill all the motherfuckers if I have to."

"Good to know," I said. "You can go get breakfast now."

Connie rolled in while I was interviewing idiot number 5. "How's it going?" she asked. "Sorry I'm late. I had to bond someone out. Is that a bullet in my phone?"

"We had some problems in the beginning, but it's all straightened out now," I told her. "So far I've seen two psychos, one gay hut, a guy who got a boner talking about guns, and this gentleman here who seems to be wearing black leather chaps, cowboy boots, and nothing else."

Connie looked down at the guy in the chair. "Nice boots," she said to him.

When he left, we sprayed the chair with Lysol and invited the next candidate to sit.

"I'm here on a mission from God," he said. "I'm here to save your immortal souls."

"I thought you were here for the bond enforcement position," Connie said.

"God loves sinners and what better place to find them?"

"He's got a point," I said to Connie.

Connie ripped his application off her clipboard.

Lula bustled in as the last guy was leaving. "I can't believe how hard it is to find clothes when you're a rock star. It's not like us singers can wear just any old thing. And now Sally and me are getting famous for dressing together, and so I gotta find something that'll match up with a thong for him. I tell you, it's not easy."

"Why can't you wear the white outfit again?" I asked her.

"It turns out all that shiny white isn't good for the old folks. They got macular shit and cataracts, and they were getting seizures from the light reflection off my ass." Lula pulled a wad of pink feathers out of her shopping bag. "I finally found this here flamingo feather dress. Only thing is, I couldn't find a flamingo feather thong, so I got a boa, and I figure we can sew some of it on a jock strap or something."

"That's a lot of flamingo feathers," Connie said. "They aren't real, are they?"

"It says here they're genuine farm-raised dyed fowl. You want me to try it on?"

"No!" Connie and I said in unison.

Lula looked a little put off, so I told her it was just that we were starving, and maybe she'd show us after lunch.

"I'm hungry, too," Lula said. "I'm feeling like spaghetti and meatballs."

"I could go for some spaghetti," Connie said. "I'll get Pino's to deliver."

"I want a meatball sub," I told her.

"And a side of potato salad," Lula said. "And a piece of their chocolate cake. Now that I'm doing all this entertaining I gotta keep my strength up."

"Melvin?" Connie yelled out. "We're ordering from Pino's. Do you want something?"

"No," Melvin said from behind the first bank of file cabinets. "I brought my lunch. I have to save my money in case I go to jail. I hear if you can't afford to buy cigarettes for everyone, you have to be someone's bitch."

"Is that why you didn't show up for your trial?" Lula asked. "On account of you didn't want to be someone's bitch?"

"Yeah. I know I'm a pervert and all, but I'm not that *kind* of a pervert. I'm sort of a specialist. I'm like a do-it-yourself pervert."

"I hear you," Lula said. "I've shopped in that aisle."

Connie put the order in and shoved a stack of files to the middle of her desk. "We have to pick one of these . . . for lack of a better word, *people*."

"These *people* are gonna lower the quality of our

work," Lula said. "And God knows it's already pretty low."

"How are we doing?" I asked Connie. "Are we catching up enough to do without a third person?"

"The problem is, you catch up but then we get a couple new FTAs, and we're behind the curve again. I'm going to divide these files between us and everyone has to pick the best person in their stack. Then we'll choose one of those three people."

We were still reading through the files when the Pino's guy arrived. We set the files aside, spread the food out on Connie's desk, and pulled up more of the funeral home folding chairs. I had my sub in my hand when Joyce Barnhardt stormed in and threw a file on the table, splattering Lula's spaghetti sauce.

"What the fuck's the matter with you?" Lula said. "You got a problem?"

"Yeah, I got a problem, fatso. I don't like getting sent off on a goddamn wild goose chase with those LC files. I bet you all thought it was funny. See if Joyce can find Willie Reese, right?"

"What's wrong with finding Willie Reese?" Connie asked. "Those were legitimate files I gave you."

"He's friggin' dead. He's been friggin' dead for almost a year. What do you want me to do, dig him up and cart him in here?"

"No," Connie said. "I want you to bring me a copy of his death certificate, so we can close the case and get our money back."

"Oh," Joyce said. "I didn't know I could do that."

"I don't like being called a fatso," Lula said. "I think you should apologize."

"If the shoe fits," Joyce said. "Or in your case, if nothing but a *tent* fits . . ."

"I'm not that fat," Lula said. "I'm just a big woman. I'm Rubenesque. You wouldn't know that because you're ignorant. I know all about it because I took an art course at the community college last semester."

"I know fat," Joyce said. "And you're fat."

I didn't like Joyce frightening Melvin Pickle. And I didn't like Joyce calling Lula fat. And I *really hated* that Joyce was able to find stupid dead Willie Reese when I hadn't been able to find him.

"Hey Joyce," I said.

Joyce turned to look at me, and I threw one of my meatballs at her. It hit her square in the forehead and left a big splotch of marinara sauce.

"Bitch," Joyce said, narrowing her eyes at me.

I narrowed my eyes back. "Slut."

"Skank."

"Hag."

Joyce grabbed Lula's spaghetti and dumped it on my head. "I am *not* a hag," she said.

"That was my lunch!" Lula said to Joyce. And she dumped Connie's chocolate milkshake down Joyce's cleavage.

Joyce pulled a gun on Lula, and Lula pulled a gun on Joyce, and they stood there pointing guns at each other.

"I'm going to fucking kill you," Joyce said.

"Yeah, maybe, but I got a better gun than you," Lula said.

"Your gun's a piece of shit compared to my gun," Joyce said.

"I got a big whup-ass gun," Lula said.

"Puleeze," Joyce said. "I've got dildos bigger than that gun."

"Oh yeah? Well I bet Stephanie could out-dildo you any day of the week. She's got a Herbert Horsecock."

"Are you shitting me?"

"No, honest to God. Tell her, Stephanie. You got a genuine Herbert Horsecock, right?"

"It was a two-for-one sale," I said.

Melvin had managed to crawl under Connie's desk while all this was going on. I looked down and saw him reach out and tag Joyce in the leg with a stun gun. Joyce gave a squeak, went limp, and crumpled to the floor.

"I hope it was okay that I did that," Melvin said. "I was afraid she was going to shoot someone. I've never used one of these before. Will she be all right?"

"You did good," Lula said. "And don't worry about Joyce. We zap her all the time. When she opens her eyes, we'll tell her she slipped in the marinara sauce and knocked herself out hitting her head on the desk."

I had noodles in my hair and noodles hanging off my ears and noodles sliding down my face.

"You're a magnet for mess," Lula said to me. "I've never seen anything like it."

I picked some noodles off my shirt and dropped them on Joyce. "I have to go home to change. I'll be back later to go through my stack of losers."

It was hard to go out through the bonds office front door and not look across the street. Even if I didn't look, if I kept my head down and my eyes diverted, I felt the eerie sadness that always lingers on a murder scene.

I drove back to my apartment, checking periodically for a tail, but so far as I could see, no one was following. I parked and trudged up to my apartment. I opened the door and ran into Ranger in my kitchen.

He looked me over and gave his head an almost imperceptible shake. "Babe."

"Food fight with Joyce Barnhardt." I noticed Ranger had changed clothes and was looking comfy in washed-out jeans and a T-shirt. "I'm surprised to still find you here," I said to him.

"Tank had to put a threatened witness in the safe

house, so I'm going to need to stay here. We've got federal surveillance on the office."

"I thought you were working with them."

"I'm working with one man, and he's not sharing that information with anyone."

"Morelli isn't going to understand this arrangement."

"You can't tell Morelli I'm here. He's a cop. He's supposed to arrest me if he finds me."

Ranger opened the refrigerator and took out a plastic-wrapped sandwich.

"Where'd that come from?" I asked him.

"Hal brought me some food and clothes and equipment."

"Equipment?"

He unwrapped his sandwich and ate it standing. "In the dining room."

I looked in at the dining room and had to do deep breathing to keep from screaming. There were two computers, a printer and fax machine, four cell phones with chargers, two cases that I knew contained guns, four boxes of ammo, a large Maglite and a small Maglite, the scrapbook, a stack of folders that I knew were case files, and three sets of car keys.

"Two computers?" I asked.

"One's mine, and the other we took from the apartment in Virginia."

"Anything interesting on it?"

"His surfing history is what you'd expect. Fascination with martial arts, guns, law enforcement, some porn. He has one basic search program. No information stored that would be of any use. He's done some blogging. Talking about wanting to be a cop. Then wanting to be a bounty hunter. Then he starts mixing fantasy and reality. He talks about working with a superstar bounty hunter. How he's learning a lot but has no respect for his mentor. There's a brief mention of a manhunt where he tracks his quarry to Florida. And the blog stops at that point."

"I imagine you were the quarry he was stalking."

"Yes. His scrapbook is filled with photographs from that visit. That's how he knew about Julie. He followed me, did his homework, and put the facts together."

"You never suspected you were being stalked?"

"No. I try to always be vigilant, but I didn't pick this guy up. It was a complicated surveillance, too. He had to follow me when I left the office, and then follow me into the terminal, learn my destination, and then buy a ticket in time to get on the plane."

"Do you think he had an accomplice?"

"There's no mention of anyone else."

"What about Carmen?"

"He'd already assumed his Ranger identity when he met Carmen. He only uses her name once and then she becomes Stephanie. And that's the main reason I'm staying here. I'm sure he's going to come after you. I want to be there when he does."

"You'll use me to get to Julie."

"Are you okay with that?"

"Of course."

Ranger picked a spaghetti noodle out of my hair. "I'd like to think I was protecting you at the same time."

"You mean I won't be a sacrificial virgin?"

"Too late for that, babe."

My cell phone rang, and I looked at the screen. Morelli.

"How's it going?" I asked him.

"The ME is releasing Carmen's body today. We didn't get anything off the car. Doubtful if we'll get any DNA off Carmen. There wasn't a struggle. She was shot at close range through the open driver's side window.

If you're reading the papers you'll see this is getting a lot of press. Daughter of Trenton bounty hunter is kidnapped and wife murdered."

"Do you have any theories? Suspects?"

"I'm working on some angles. And I'm under a lot of pressure from above to bring Ranger in."

"Understood."

"Where are you?"

"I'm at home. There was an incident at the bonds office, and I ended up wearing my lunch. So I came home to change."

"You aren't harboring a fugitive, are you?"

"Who, me?"

Morelli gave a disgusted sigh and hung up.

"Sounds like that went well," Ranger said.

"Yeah. If I get caught with you I'll go to jail for a thousand years."

Ranger gave me a smile that didn't quite make it to his eyes. "I could make it worthwhile."

"I'll hold that thought. Right now I need to take a shower and get the noodles out of my hair."

I went into my bedroom, closed the door, and stripped out of the spaghetti clothes. I hopped into the bathroom and stopped short when I looked at the sink. Ranger's razor and shaving gel, Ranger's toothbrush. I went back to the bedroom and looked in my closet. Ranger's clothes. Ranger had moved in. I locked myself in the bathroom and did some more deep breathing.

Chapter ELEVEN

Ranger was slouched back in his chair, long legs stretched out under the dining room table, his attention on the computer screen.

"How's the search going?" I asked him.

"It's going in slow motion. It feels like two lifetimes have gone by since he took Julie."

"Anything new?"

"Pictures and background on Scrog. His mother is Puerto Rican. He comes by his skin and hair naturally. Nothing that has a big orange arrow on it saying 'Look Here.' A profiler would find him interesting. Some of his makeup is classic and some is off the map.

"He's an only child. Early school reports are that he's smart, but he doesn't apply himself. He's a dreamer. Shy. Doesn't participate in class activities. Middle school, he does a nosedive. Failing grades. One of twelve boys questioned about molestation by a local priest. He receives counseling and the diagnosis is that he has low self-esteem and has difficulty separating fact from fiction, leading to a poor sense of consequence for his actions. High school, he's tracked with underachievers, doing some remedial work. At home he's spending hours playing computer games. His mother thinks he's a genius. His counselor thinks he might be borderline psychopath. His work history is erratic. He can't keep a job. He resents authority. Most of his jobs are sales. Music stores, movie theaters. Had a good run managing a comic book store with a gaming room. Took some computer courses at a community college but nothing came of it."

"Were you able to find his connection to you?"

"Do you remember Zak Campbell? He was caught in a drug bust two years ago. He skipped and while he was in the wind they tied him to a double homicide. I tracked him to Virginia, and Tank and I made the apprehension in a music and video store. Scrog was working in the store at the time. I don't remember him, and I didn't have any contact with him that I remember. It was a quiet bust. We went in with mall security waiting at the store entrance. I approached Campbell, introduced myself, cuffed him, and walked him out."

"No guns drawn?"

"No. Not necessary."

"I guess you made an impression."

"Apparently. That was the only connection I could find."

I went into the kitchen and investigated the refrigerator. It was filled with Ranger food. Sandwiches, fruit, low-fat cream cheese, yogurt, and assorted snack vegetables all cut and washed. I selected a baby carrot and dropped it into Rex's cage. I looked at the phone on the counter by the cage and saw that I now had a working answering machine.

"I don't want an answering machine," I yelled at Ranger.

"When this is over you can throw it away."

I took a turkey sandwich and brought it to the table to eat.

"I thought you had spaghetti for lunch," Ranger said.

"I wore it. I didn't get to eat any. The entire country's

looking for Scrog. Hard to believe he hasn't been caught."

"He's enjoying the game," Ranger said. "Probably has Julie stashed somewhere and goes out in disguise. He'll be careful at first, but the longer the game goes on the more chances he'll take."

"Is there something I can do?"

"You can go about your business, so he has a chance to make a move on you." He took a cell phone from the table. "If you need to call me, use this phone. My number's programmed in. And make sure you're always wearing the panic button. It's tied into the RangeMan network. I can track you if you're wearing the button. If you catch someone following you, don't try to lose him."

I looked at the car keys on the table.

"I'll be in a blue Honda Civic, a silver BMW sedan, or a silver Toyota Corolla," Ranger said. "And Tank will be in a green Ford Explorer."

"I'll be in a black and white Mini Cooper," I said. And my knees will be knocking.

I drove to the bonds office and parked at the curb where I could easily be seen. Stephanie Plum, psycho bait. Lula and Connie and Melvin were huddled around Connie's desk, debating the files in front of them.

"These people all creep me out," Lula said. "I don't want to work with none of them."

"I liked the blond woman with the eagle tattooed on her big huge breast," Melvin said.

We all turned to look at him, and he blushed bright red.

"Pickle, if you want to be a pervert you gotta stop blushing like that," Lula said. "You're gonna give perverts a bad name."

The door opened and a woman walked in. "I heard

you're looking for someone to do bond enforcement," she said.

We looked her over. No black leather, no tattoos that were visible, no gun strapped to her leg, no obvious missing teeth. Already she was ahead of everyone else. She was about my height and weight. Maybe a little chunkier. She had short brown hair cut into a bob. Not a lot of makeup. Some lip gloss. She was wearing a three-button collared knit shirt and tan slacks. She was perfectly pleasant-looking and amazingly forgettable.

She extended her hand. "Meri Maisonet."

"Maisonet," Lula said. "Isn't that a puppet?"

"That's marionette," Connie said.

"I haven't got a lot of experience," Meri said, "but I'm a fast learner. My dad was a cop in Chicago, so I grew up around law enforcement types."

Connie gave her one of the forms we'd printed out, asking for name and vital statistics . . . like human being, yes or no. When she left, Connie punched her name into the computer.

"She looked sort of normal," Lula said. "What's with that?"

The information started flooding in.

"Everything checks out," Connie said. "Never been convicted of a crime, good credit. High school graduate. Waited tables for two years. The rest of her work history is on the line at a small brewery in Illinois. Relocated here two months ago, following her boyfriend. Twenty-eight years old."

"You could start her in the office doing telephone work and computer searches," I said. "Then after she gets a feel for the job we can take her on some road trips."

"Okay," Connie said. "If everyone's agreed, I'll call her and see if she can start tomorrow."

"I'm getting restless," Lula said. "I feel like I need to go out and apprehend a scumbag."

"Lonnie Johnson's still open, but I don't know where to begin with him," I said.

"I'm chuffed over Caroline Scarzolli," Lula said. "We should have nabbed her. How does it look to get run over by a freaky old lady like that?"

"If we go back to the store she'll shoot us."

"Not if we buy something."

"No! I'm not buying any more dildos."

"Don't have to be a dildo. They got lots of good stuff in that store. I might need a pair of panties."

"Okay, fine," I said. "I'll wait in the car, and you can go in and buy panties."

"I'm not just going for the panties," Lula said. "It's my cover. This here's serious shit. I'm gonna make an apprehension."

I grabbed my shoulder bag and palmed my keys. "I'll drive."

I drove eyes forward, and I avoided checking the rearview mirror. If Ranger was following me to Pleasure Treasures, I preferred not to know. I parked on the street, two doors down from the store.

"I'm not going in," I said. "If she shoots you, you're going to have to drag your ass out the door, because I'm not going in to pick you up."

"Hunh," Lula said. "I thought we were partners. How's that for a partner to act? I'd go in there for *you.* I'd walk on fire for you. I'd bitch-slap the devil for you. You wouldn't catch me sitting in no car if my partner goes into the danger zone. If it was you in there getting shot for upholding the law of this great land, I'd be there right behind you."

"Oh for crissake," I said, wrenching the door open. "Just shut up. I'll go with you."

Caroline looked up and narrowed her eyes when we walked in.

"We're just shopping today," Lula said. "I was real happy with my dildo, and I thought I'd come back and browse."

"We've got a one-day special sale on electronics," Caroline said. "In case you're interested."

"I might be interested," Lula said. "I had a Madam Orgasmo, but I burned out the motor."

I made an unsuccessful attempt to choke back a snort of nervous laughter. I turned my back on Lula and made a show of being engrossed in a display of erotic oils. There was Lickit and Luvitt Chocolate Love Cream. Kama Sutra Slick, rub it and it gets hot, blow on it and it gets hotter. Spank Me Peppermint Cooling Cream. Pleasure Jelly to minimize friction and avoid irritation, enriched with vitamin E and completely edible.

Here's the thing about all this stuff . . . some of it I thought looked like fun. And truth was, I wouldn't have minded if Joe brought some of it home. I just felt like an idiot buying it for myself.

"She's got some good electronics," Lula said to me. "You want to come take a look?"

"No, that's okay," I said. "I'm trying to decide on these oils."

"I think you should come take a look," Lula said. "I might need you to, you know, help me out here."

"Those oils are all overpriced," Caroline said. "You're better off buying one of these vibrating miracle makers and they throw the oil in for free. It's a lot better bargain."

"Gee, I really don't need a miracle maker though," I said. "I got a house full of them already."

"Well, I need a miracle right now," Lula said to me.

"You got any miracle makers in your bag? Do you see what I'm saying?"

"Sorry," I told her. "I left my miracle maker at home. It's in my cookie jar."

"What's going on?" Caroline said. "You two aren't thinking about trying anything funny, are you?"

Lula reached in her bag to get her gun, but Caroline was faster. Caroline hauled the shotgun out from under the counter and pointed it at Lula's head.

"You better be reaching in that bag to get your credit card," Caroline said.

"That's just what I'm doing," Lula said. "You sure are an untrusting person."

"I'm thinking you both want to buy one of these Lady Workhorse cordless personal massagers. And I'm even going to throw in extra oil," Caroline said.

I glared at Lula and forked over my credit card.

"It's not so bad," Lula said when we were in the Mini. "It's not like you got something useless. You'll get years of satisfaction out of this machine. Just don't go for thirds on account of apparently that's what freezes up the motor."

I dropped Lula back at the office and sat at the curb for a while. I wanted Scrog to find me. I wanted to make contact and be done with it. I wanted the nightmare to be over for Julie and Ranger and everyone involved. After a couple minutes, I called Ranger.

"Is anyone tailing me?"

"Not that I can tell."

"Where are you?"

"Across the street, half a block south."

"Now what?"

"Now we go home and order take-out."

Fifteen minutes later, I opened the door to my apartment and Ranger followed me in.

"This is frustrating," I said.

"He's out there, waiting for the right time to make his move. Probably he's enjoying the foreplay. We need to be patient. The police are scrambling, looking for him to be recognized. We're working from a different direction. We're playing the game with him."

I tossed my purse and the Pleasure Treasures bag onto the kitchen counter and rooted through the drawer where I kept all the take-out menus.

"What do you feel like?" I asked Ranger. "Chinese, Italian, pizza, fried chicken?"

Ranger shuffled through the menus. "Chinese. I'll have brown rice, steamed vegetables, and lemon chicken."

And this is the problem with Ranger. I could spend a lot of time in bed with him, but he'd drive me nuts in the kitchen. I called the order in, adding Kung Pao chicken, fried rice, fried dumplings, and a piece of their Great Wall of Chocolate cake.

"When was the last time you talked to Morelli?" Ranger wanted to know.

"When I came home to change clothes."

"You should check in with him. See if anything new is going on. Let him know you're working tonight."

I slouched against the counter. "I hate lying to Morelli."

"You're not lying," Ranger said. "You're omitting some information. And if it makes you feel better, I'll make sure you work tonight."

I did an eye roll and dialed Morelli.

"What?" Morelli said.

"I was just checking in."

"Sorry, I'm still at work. Some big bad gangsta just took about fifty rounds in front of the B&B Car Wash and set a new world record for leaking out body fluids. They're not going to have to embalm this guy."

"Anything new on Julie Martine or Carmen?"

"Nothing. We're waiting on DNA from Carmen. I'd

like to spend some time talking to you, but I have to go. I'll be doing paperwork on this until tomorrow morning. Miss you. Be careful." And Morelli disconnected.

"Some guy got ventilated in front of the B&B Car Wash," I told Ranger. "Morelli's working it."

"Morelli's a good man with a sucky job," Ranger said.

We were still in the kitchen and Ranger glanced over at the Pleasure Treasures bag. "You must really like that store. You keep going back."

"I don't want to talk about it."

He looked in the bag and smiled. "Lady Workhorse?" Ranger read the hype on the box. "Hours of pleasure guaranteed."

"You're going to torture me with this, aren't you?" I said.

Ranger took the gadget out of the box. "I think we should take it for a test drive." He turned it on, and it hummed in his hand. "Feels good," he said. "Gentle action."

"You're an expert?"

"No," he said, shutting it off, setting it on the counter. "I'm not really a gadget man." He took the bottle of oil out of the bag. "This holds more interest for me. Let's see what this does." He opened the bottle, poured a drop into the palm of my hand and rubbed it with his fingertip. "What do you think?"

"It's warm!"

"It says on the bottle it tastes like cherries."

He touched his tongue to my oiled palm, and I felt myself go damp, and I worried my knees might buckle.

"W-w-well?" I asked.

"Cherries."

The doorbell rang, and I sucked in some air.

"Are you expecting anyone?" Ranger asked.

"The food."

"This fast?"

"They're just around the corner on Hamilton."

Ranger capped the oil and got the door. And we carted the food into the living room to eat in front of the television.

"Scrog has been in Jersey for five days," I said. "He has to be staying somewhere. He has to be buying food. Why aren't we turning anything up? Where's he getting his money from?"

"You don't need money if you have a credit card. And he knows how to scam credit cards."

I speared a dumpling. "I'm not good at waiting."

"I've noticed."

Chapter TWELVE

I woke up wrapped in Ranger's arms, our legs entwined, my face snuggled into his neck. He smelled nice, and he felt even better . . . warm and friendly. I enjoyed it for a moment before reality took hold.

"This is a little déjà vu," I said to him. "Didn't you start the night out on the couch?"

"No. I was on the computer when you went to bed. You were already asleep by the time I was done."

"So you climbed in next to me? I thought when you moved in you'd be sleeping on the couch."

"You thought wrong."

"You can't sleep in my bed. It just isn't done. I have a boyfriend. He's a nice guy, but he's not good with sharing."

"Babe, we're sharing a bed, not a sexual experience. I can control myself if you can."

"Oh great."

Ranger's face creased into a smile. "You can't control yourself?"

I bit into my lower lip.

"Stephanie," he said. "You shouldn't tell me things like that. I'll take advantage."

I blew out a sigh and rolled away from him. "No you won't. You're Ranger. You're the guy who protects me."

"Yes, but not from myself!"

I kicked the covers off and slid out of bed. I needed to find Edward Scrog. I needed to find him *now*! I couldn't manage another morning of waking up next to Ranger.

I took a shower and called Morelli.

"What's going on?" I said.

"I don't know," Morelli said, sounding half asleep. "Give me a hint?"

"With Carmen. With Julie Martine. Why hasn't someone found Julie Martine yet? What the heck are you guys doing? I don't understand what's taking so long."

"What time is it?" Morelli wanted to know. I heard some fumbling and then swearing. "It's seven-fucking-thirty," Morelli said. "It was after two when I got to bed."

"Did I wake you?"

"Mmm."

"Sorry. You always get up so early."

"Not today. Talk to you later." And he hung up.

I stomped out of the bedroom and into the kitchen where Ranger was making coffee. "I'm going out," I said.

"Where are you going?"

"I'm going out for muffins."

"Give me five minutes to get my shoes on."

"I don't have five minutes," I said. "I have things to do. I've got the panic button. I'll be fine. I'll bring a muffin back for you. What do you want, zucchini, no fat, no sugar, extra bran?"

I turned to go and Ranger scooped me up and carried me into the bedroom and tossed me onto the bed. "Five minutes," he said, lacing his shoes.

I lay there spread-eagle, waiting for him. "Very macho," I said.

He grabbed my hand and yanked me to my feet. "Sometimes you try my patience."

"You don't like it? You can leave."

He slammed me into the wall and kissed me. "I didn't say I didn't like it."

"Okay, good to get that straightened out," I said. "Are we going to get muffins, or what?"

He walked to the lot with me, stuffed me into the passenger seat of the Mini, and got behind the wheel.

"I thought you were supposed to be secretly following me. I thought I was supposed to be luring Scrog into action."

"This morning we're both luring him into action. Where do you want to go for muffins?"

"Tasty Pastry. And then Italian Bakery. And then Prizolli's. And then Cluck-in-a-Bucket for a breakfast muffin. And then the convenience store on Hamilton for a paper."

"Trying to get yourself kidnapped?"

"Do you have a better idea?"

Ranger drove out of the lot and headed for Hamilton. "Nice to know you're going proactive."

By the time we got to the convenience store we had the Mini filled with muffin bags. "Get coffee and a couple papers," Ranger said. "We'll have a picnic."

Ten minutes later, we were on a bench in front of a used-book store on Hamilton, next to the bonds office. The only way we'd have higher visibility would be to stand in the middle of the road.

"Anybody following us?" I asked Ranger.

"Three cars. Tank in the green SUV, a grey Taurus, and a minivan."

"Aren't you afraid you'll get arrested?"

"I'm more afraid I'll get shot by some good Samaritan citizen who saw my picture on *America's Most Wanted*." He took a coffee and called Tank. "Do you have a fix on the Taurus and minivan?"

I chose a carrot cake muffin and waited through a

couple beats of silence while Ranger took in the information.

"Amateur bounty hunters," Ranger finally said to me. "Disable them," he said to Tank. "I don't want Stephanie dragging that clutter around with her." He disconnected, and we sat there for a half hour eating our muffins, drinking our coffee, and reading the paper. We were ready to leave for greener pastures when Morelli drove by, came to a screeching halt, and pulled to the curb. He got out of his SUV and walked over to us.

"You want to explain this to me?"

I told him about Edward Scrog and the scrapbook and the computer blogs.

"So you're sitting here trying to provoke him into making a move?"

"Yep."

"This is a dangerous, stupid idea. He shot his wife and there's no reason to think he won't shoot you."

"Yeah," I said. "But I don't think he'll shoot me right away."

"That makes me feel a lot better," Morelli said. "I'll tell that to my acid reflux."

"I'll be fine. I swear!" I told him.

Morelli made a disgusted hand gesture. "I didn't see this," Morelli said. "But I want to be kept apprised of the evidence you gather. And if you overstep boundaries with Stephanie and move in on me," he said, turning to Ranger, "I'll find you, and it won't be good."

Morelli took a blueberry muffin out of a bag, jogged back to his car, and took off.

Ranger smiled at me. "Just so you know, that's not going to stop me from trying to move in on him."

"You and Morelli have an entirely different agenda. Morelli wants to marry me, and you want to . . ."

I stopped because I wasn't sure what word I wanted

to insert. Not that any word was necessary. We both knew what Ranger wanted.

"Babe," Ranger said. "What I want to do to you is no secret. And I want to do it bad. But I can think with two body parts simultaneously, and I'm not going to do anything stupid."

"That includes marriage?"

"Marriage, pregnancy, and anything nonconsensual." He ran a finger under the strap on my tank top. "I *will* make a move with partial consent."

Ranger collected the bags and empty coffee cups and newspapers. He let himself into the bonds office, shut down the alarm, and dumped the trash into Connie's wastebasket. He reset the alarm, exited the office, and locked the door.

"I need to go back to your apartment," he said. "I have work to do this morning. Tank will stay with you, and I'll join him later in the day in a separate car. Try to move around and be visible. Remember to always wear your panic button."

Ranger pulled me to him and kissed me before we got into the Mini.

"Just in case Scrog is watching, I don't want to miss an opportunity to piss him off," Ranger said.

Connie, Lula, and Melvin Pickle were in the office when I returned.

"Meri Maisonet is scheduled to start this morning," Connie said. "I'm going to have her run some of the simple search programs. If you have phone work or background checks, just put your file in the queue."

I dropped Charles Chin, Lonnie Johnson, and Dooby Biagi onto the Maisonet "to-do" stack, writing a brief note for each. For Chin and Biagi I asked for work and residence histories, followed by phone verification of the most current. For Johnson, I simply said "Find him."

Johnson's file was already thick with information. I didn't expect Maisonet to find him, but sometimes a new set of eyes saw things previously missed.

I paged through the remaining files and looked for jobs that didn't require the help of a partner. Edward Scrog would be more likely to approach me if I was alone.

I put Bernard Brown at the top of the list. He was low bond and low risk. His danger quotient was close to zero. Bernard had gotten drunk off his ass at Marilyn Gorley's wedding and in a display of ill-timed homage had set fire to a floor-to-ceiling drapery while holding his lighter aloft during a John Lennon song. The result was approximately $80,000 in damages to the banquet room of Littuchy's Restaurante. Probably no criminal charges would have been pressed, but Bernard had panicked and punched out the maitre d' when the man had attempted to extinguish Bernard's flaming hair with a bottle of beer.

Bernard was a self-employed accountant working out of his house. Should be an easy catch.

"I'm going to help Bernard Brown get reregistered for court," I said to Lula. "It's not a two-man job. Maybe you want to stay here and help Meri get started. Tell her about being a BEA."

"Sure, I could do that. I got a lot of things I could tell her."

I avoided looking at Connie and whisked myself out of the office before I got stuck with Lula. I was on the sidewalk when I got a call from Morelli.

"I thought you should know we just towed an abandoned rental. It was rented at Newark Airport on Thursday around eight P.M. The name on the rental agreement was Carmen Manoso. That's why it bounced back to me. Not sure how it slipped through the FBI search. Maybe no one thought to look for something registered to Carmen. Anyway, I've got the car impounded and we're going through it. It looks like blood on the back seat. No way of knowing whose blood it is right now."

"Is it a lot of blood?"

"Doesn't look like someone died there if that's what you're asking. The bad news is there was also a scrunchie on the floor of the back seat. You know, one of those things the kids use to tie up a ponytail. We photographed it and e-mailed it to Rachel Martine, and it's tentatively been identified as belonging to Julie Martine."

"Where did you find the car?"

"It was by the train station."

I called Ranger and gave him the news. Then I got into the Mini and drove along Hamilton. I was following Ranger's advice. Keep moving forward. Try not to think about the blood in the car.

Bernard Brown lived in a neighborhood that was adjacent to the Burg, just past Saint Francis Hospital. I drove down his street, checking off house numbers, parking when I reached his duplex.

Brown was forty-three years old and divorced. His house was neat but showing wear. A small sign next to Bernard's front door read BERNARD BROWN, CPA.

I rang his bell and waited, resisting the urge to burst into tears or frantically look around for stalkers.

Bernard answered the door in his pajamas and a knit cap. "Yes?"

I gave him my card and introduced myself.

"I'll be a laughingstock if I go into court," he said. "I know people. I do taxes for half the cops. I'll have to take my hat off, and I'll never live it down."

My eyes went to the knit cap. Eighty degrees out, and he was wearing a knit cap. I looked at the mug shot on his bond agreement. Yow! Torched hair.

"Anything go up in flames besides your hair?" I asked him.

"The entire north side of the banquet room. Luckily no one was hurt. Except for the maitre d'. I broke his nose when he threw beer on me. That was before I knew my hair was on fire."

"It's probably not so bad," I said. "Take your hat off. Maybe we can fix it."

He took his hat off, and I tried not to grimace. He had patches of angry red scalp and tufts of singed hair. And it was all greasy with salve.

"Have you been to a doctor?"

"Yeah," he said. "He gave me the salve to put on."

"You should shave your head. Shaved heads are sexy these days."

He rolled his eyes up like he was trying to see the top of his head. "I guess so, but I don't think I can do it myself."

"Get dressed and we'll go to a hair salon before I take you to court."

"Okay, but not the one on Hamilton. She's a big busybody. And not the one on Chambers Street. My ex-wife goes there. And I don't want to go to the mall. Everyone looks at you. And it's all women in there. I'd feel funny. Maybe you could find someplace where men get shaved."

"What's this?" Bernie asked. "Why are we here?"

"This is the only place I could think of where men regularly get shaved."

"This is a funeral parlor."

"Yeah, have you ever seen anyone laid out with a two-day-old beard? No. Everyone's perfectly groomed when they get put in the box. And it's very private. And I just met these guys. They're new here. And they seem nice. And they make their own cookies."

"It's creepy."

"Don't be such a whiner. This is what I came up with. Take it or leave it."

Bernie got out of the Mini and followed me into the funeral home. I walked through the lobby and saw that the office door was open. I could see Dave Nelson at his desk. He was wearing a crisp white dress shirt and navy slacks. He looked up and smiled when I got close.

"We have a problem," I told him.

"Oh dear. I'm so sorry."

"Not that kind of problem. Bernie here has had a hair disaster and needs someone to shave his head. I know you guys shave men all the time, so I thought maybe you could help us out."

Bernie took his hat off, and Dave yelled for his partner. "Scooter is here somewhere," Dave said. "He's wonderful with makeup and hair. He's wonderful at it. He used to work at the Estée Lauder counter at Saks."

"Estée Lauder," Bernie said. "I don't know. That's women's stuff."

Scooter came up behind us. "Estée Lauder has a wonderful line just for men. A dab of their eye serum each night would take years off your face," he said to Bernie. He extended his hand. "I'm Scooter. I was in the kitchen making cookies for tonight's viewing. I chose snickerdoodles for Mrs. Kessman and big-chunk chocolate chip for Mr. Stanko. I wanted something masculine for Mr. Stanko. He was a truck driver. That's such a guy job, don't you think?"

Bernie shook Scooter's hand, and there was bolt-and-run all over Bernie's face, so I clapped a bracelet on him and attached the other half to my wrist.

"Just a formality," I said to Bernie. "Don't give it another thought."

"Oh dear," Scooter said. "Is he a criminal?"

"No," I told Scooter. "He's having a bad hair month, and I thought he looked like he was getting cold feet. We were wondering if you could shave his head."

"Of course I can shave his head," Scooter said. "He'll

look wonderful. And I have some moisturizer which will be much better than that dreadful grease he's using now. Follow me back to my workroom."

We crossed the lobby and trailed after Scooter into the new addition to the rambling funeral home. "We'll use treatment room number two," Scooter said. "Number one is occupied."

Bernie and I peeked into the room. Tilt-top stainless steel grooved table. Slight odor of formaldehyde. Carts filled with instruments best not seen in the light of day.

"This is an embalming room!" Bernie said.

"Isn't it wonderful?" Scooter said. "State-of-the-art. And it has excellent light. Sit on the little stool by the table, and I'll get my razor. I've gotten used to working on people who are horizontal, so this will be a fun experience."

"Oh fuck," Bernie whispered. "Get me out of here!"

"Chill," I told him. "He's going to shave your head, not drain your body fluids. It's not a big deal. And when he's done, I bet he'll give you a cookie."

"I guess congratulations are in order," I said to Scooter when he got into position behind Bernie. "Sounds like you've got a full house. Mrs. Kessman and Mr. Stanko. And a third body in prep."

"The third body is just a holdover. It's poor Carmen Manoso. They autopsied her and released her, but we can't ship the body until Thursday. I had some free time, so I was trying to get her prettied up a little. Not much you can do to someone who's had their brain surgically removed, not to mention has a big bullet hole in the head, but I did what I could to soften it for her parents in case they open the casket."

Carmen Manoso! And she was hanging out with nothing to do until Thursday.

"She needs a viewing," I said to Scooter.

"Excuse me?"

"She's famous. The Burg loves a murder. You won't be able to shoehorn all the mourners in. You'll have to give out tickets like at the bakery."

"I don't know. I'd have to check with her parents."

"She doesn't belong to her parents. She belongs to her husband."

"The murderer?"

"He's still her husband. And I bet he'd want her to have a viewing."

"Interesting," Scooter said. "I'd have to bake *a lot* of cookies."

I called Ranger on the special cell phone. "You're not going to believe this. . . . I'm at the funeral home on Hamilton, and they've got Carmen here."

"Should I ask what you're doing at the funeral home?"

"No. It's not important. The important thing is, Carmen is here and isn't getting shipped off to Virginia until Thursday. And I thought since you're her husband you might want to hold a viewing so her friends and relatives who might be in the area could see her one last time."

"Gruesome but clever," Ranger said. "Let me talk to whoever is in charge."

I passed the phone over to Scooter.

"Is this Mr. Manoso?" Scooter asked. "The husband of the deceased?"

Chapter THIRTEEN

"Run this by me again," Lula said. "You took Bernie Brown to the funeral home to get his head shaved?"

"Yes. And it worked out great. And I checked him in at the courthouse after he got shaved, and he's already bonded out again."

"And while you were at the funeral home, you ran into Carmen Manoso?"

"Yep. She was passed on to the funeral home for transport back to Virginia. Only they can't do it until Thursday."

"And while you were there, Ranger called in and arranged for her to have a viewing?"

"He *is* her husband of record. And as such, he has a right to a viewing."

"I don't suppose you got to talk to him?"

"Mostly he talked to Scooter. Financial arrangements and everything."

Connie had been the one to rebond Bernie. She'd gotten back to the office minutes before me and was in the process of repairing a chipped nail. "I don't usually go to viewings, but I'm going to that one," she said, adding a fresh coat of fire engine red to her index finger.

Meri Maisonet was on the couch with a stack of files, making notes, not saying anything, but not missing much either. I wasn't sure how I felt about her. She seemed likeable enough, but something was off. Usually people are a little nervous on a new job. They try too hard. Or they try to become background. Meri Maisonet didn't show any of that. She was dressed in running shoes, jeans, and another of the three-button knit shirts. No big hair lacquered with hair spray. Only lip gloss. Not exactly a Jersey girl, but then, she hadn't been in Jersey for very long.

"How's it going?" I said to her.

"I have the information you asked me to get on Charles Chin and Dooby Biagi. I haven't had a chance to make the phone calls. I was going to do that now. I haven't done anything on Lonnie Johnson yet. Sorry."

"It's okay. Lonnie Johnson is probably in Peru. I've run into a brick wall on him. I thought it wouldn't hurt to have someone new take a look. Don't spend a lot of time and energy on him, but maybe you can make a feeler phone call once in a while to one of the contacts."

"I read about Ranger and Carmen in the paper," she said. "And the little girl . . . Julie Martine. How terrible. What a tragedy."

"Yeah," Lula said. "It's pretty freaky. Is there any information on the viewing yet?" she asked me. "I don't want to miss that one."

"Tomorrow at six."

"Darn. I got a gig tomorrow at seven. I'm wearing my new feather outfit, and Sally and me got a new song rehearsed. I'll have to get there when the doors open, so I can fit it all in."

"Isn't seven early for a band to play?"

"It's another old people's home. They get medicated at eight, and it's lights out at nine," Lula said.

"It's a little creepy that her husband murdered her, and now he's arranging a viewing," Meri said. "Is he here in Trenton?"

"I don't know," I said to Meri. "He made the arrangements over the phone."

"I never heard for sure that anyone said he murdered her," Lula said.

"The paper said he was wanted for *suspicion,*" Meri said. "Do you know him? Does he work for this office?"

"Yeah, we all know him," Lula said. "He's a good guy, too. If he does something bad, it's because he has a good reason."

"Hard to believe there's a good reason for murdering your wife," Meri said.

"Maybe she was a spy," Lula said. "She could have been a secret agent or a terrorist."

"Or an alien from Mars," Connie said.

"Hunh," Lula said. "You're making fun of me, but I was serious. Who's to know if she was a double agent or something?"

"She wasn't a double agent," I said. "She was a woman on the edge."

"She shot at Stephanie," Lula told Meri. "Put a ding in her car."

"Why did she do that?" Meri asked.

"Frustrated because she couldn't find her husband," I said. "I approached her at the wrong time."

"Now what are we going to do?" Lula wanted to know. "You got someone on target for this afternoon?"

"I have some errands I have to run, and then tonight I'm going after Caroline Scarzolli."

"I'm surprised to hear you say that," Lula said. "You must have some room left on your credit card."

"I have no room left on my credit card, and I'm fed up with this woman. She's going down."

"And how are you planning on doing this?"

"I'm going to wait outside and ambush her when she closes up shop."

"You gotta be careful," Lula said. "She's seventy-two. You could break something that can't be fixed. Hard to find spare parts for something that old."

A more likely scenario was that she'd beat the crap out of me.

"Are you riding with me for Scarzolli?"

"Hell yeah," Lula said. "I'm not missing you duke it out with a seventy-two-year-old porn peddler."

"The store closes at eight o'clock. I'll meet you at the corner of Elm and Twelfth Street at seven-thirty."

I left the bonds office and sat in the Mini for a couple minutes. I looked around and adjusted the rearview mirror. Didn't see anyone, but that didn't mean much. I edged out into traffic and drove toward the center of the city. I turned onto Ryder and then Haywood Street. Two blocks later, I was in front of Ranger's office building. I nosed the Mini up to the garage gates, remoted them open, and slid into the garage interior. I sat there for ten minutes with my motor off.

I didn't have business here. I was simply riding around, trying to attract attention. The plan was to cruise every location Scrog might be watching and try to get him to follow me. I left the RangeMan garage and drove toward the train station. I turned onto Montgomery and got a call from Tank.

"You've picked up two more bandits," Tank said. "One of them is an idiot. And the other is a federal idiot. We're going to get rid of them for you. Don't look back."

I didn't know exactly what that meant, but I didn't look back. I drove past the train station. I drove up and down Hamilton. I stopped at Cluck-in-a-Bucket for a soda. I drove past the bonds office. I drove through the Burg, and I stopped at my parents' house.

"Did you hear?" Grandma Mazur said. "There's gonna be a viewing for that poor Carmen Manoso. Not often you get to see someone's been autopsied."

"I'm sure it'll be closed casket," I said to Grandma.

"That would be a shame," Grandma said. "Of course, sometimes those lids just spring open."

We were in the kitchen, and I saw my mother flick a quick look to the cabinet by the sink where she kept her emergency liquor stash.

"I might have to get a new dress for tomorrow night," Grandma said. "It's gonna be a big hoo-ha there. I hear they're thinking about giving out numbered wristbands if you want to get up by the casket. And there's a rumor that Ranger will show up. I bet the place will be crawling with hot FBI guys."

I found myself wishfully staring at the liquor cabinet with my mother. Tomorrow night was going to be hideous. If there was any justice in this world, Edward Scrog would be caught and Julie Martine would be found unharmed before tomorrow night's viewing.

"I'm going with Lorraine Shlein," Grandma said to me. "You're welcome to come with us, if you want."

"Gee, thanks, but I'm going to pass," I told her. "I might just pop in for a minute or two on my own."

My mother latched on to my arm. "You will get there on time, and you will watch your grandmother every second, do you hear me? You will not allow her to pry that casket lid open. You will not take her to a nudie bar after the viewing, no matter how much she begs. And you will not allow her to spike the punch bowl."

"Why me?"

"You're responsible for this. It's one of your crime schemes. I can feel it in my bones. Myra Sklar said she saw you going into the funeral home today."

"Coincidence," I said.

I looked up and down the street when I left my parents' house. No suspicious cars in sight. I got into the Mini, drove to the cross street, and my phone rang. "You just picked up a hitchhiker," Ranger said. "He's in a silver

Honda Civic half a block behind you. He's wearing a black ball cap, and from this distance he's looking good. We're running the plate on the car. Take him home with you."

I drove out of the Burg and turned right onto Hamilton. It was close to five, and Hamilton was clogged with cars and impatient Jersey drivers. I watched my rearview mirror and saw the Civic make the turn. He was four cars back. I went through a green light and the Civic got a red.

Ranger was still open on the phone. "Don't worry about it," he said. "I've got a visual on him. I don't want him to suspect he's been spotted. Go home and park and go up to your apartment. We'll take it from here."

An hour later Ranger let himself into my apartment and threw his keys on the kitchen counter. "We lost him. He turned around before he got to your apartment and drove to the government complex. Then he went into a parking garage and didn't come out. Dumped the car and left on foot and somehow we missed him."

"Do you think he saw you?"

"Don't know."

"You think it was Scrog?"

"Yes. The car was stolen. From what we could see he fit the description." Ranger stood with his hands flat on the counter and his head down. "I can't believe I lost him. I didn't want to get too close to him in the parking garage. I wanted him to lead us to Julie."

"You'll have another chance," I said. "He's not going away until he completes his family." I opened the refrigerator door. "And look at this. Here's a piece of good news. While we were gone the food fairy arrived and filled the refrigerator."

Ranger grabbed a beer and a roast beef sandwich.

"It's too bad this guy is crazy," Ranger said. "He's

not stupid. And he has good instincts. If he was even the slightest bit sane, I'd hire him."

Ranger took his beer and sandwich into the living room and turned the television on. He slouched on the couch and surfed until he found local news. His picture came up and then Carmen's. The anchor read a short clip about the viewing and the fact that there was still an alert for the missing child.

Ranger sunk lower into the couch. "They said I was armed and dangerous."

"Yeah," I said. "They got that right."

Ranger crooked an arm around my neck and kissed me at my hairline.

"I talked to Rachel this afternoon," he said. "She's falling apart. She had to be sedated after they showed her the hair scrunchie. I know this isn't my fault, but I feel responsible. I wish I could do more."

"It looks to me like you have every resource available to you working to find Julie. I don't know what more anyone could do."

"I feel guilty sitting here."

"Make the most of it. In a half hour you'll be following me around again. I'm determined to get Caroline Scarzolli. I'm going to jump her when she closes the store tonight."

"I think you should go shopping first. I like when you bring all that kinky stuff home."

I walked out the back door alone, but I knew Ranger was watching. He'd gotten a ten-minute head start on me and was waiting to follow me to Elm and Twelfth where I'd hook up with Lula. Tank was there too. And God knows who else. Bad enough I was going to look like a moron running down Caroline Scarzolli . . . now I was going to do it in front of Ranger and his men.

I didn't get any warning phone calls, so I assumed the only people following me were good guys. I saw Lula's red Firebird parked on Elm. I pulled up behind her and got out of the Mini. I had cuffs tucked into the waistband on my jeans, and a stun gun and pepper spray stuffed into my two back pockets.

"Looks like you're loaded for bear," Lula said.

"I just want to get this over and done."

"I hope you know this is probably gonna ruin it for me to go shopping here. And I was starting to like this store."

"Are you ready?"

"Sure I'm ready," Lula said. And she hauled a Glock out of her handbag.

"Caroline Scarzolli is a first-time shoplifter," I said. "You can't shoot her."

"Every time we see her she pulls a gun on us."

"I don't care. You can't shoot her. That's the rule."

"Boy, who died and made you boss?"

"I've always been the boss."

"Hunh," Lula said. "I was just gonna scare her anyway."

"From what I've seen so far, it's going to take more than you and me and that gun to scare her. This time we're going to try *surprising* her."

We walked to where we could look into the store from the opposite side of the street. We were partially hidden behind a panel van, and we could see Scarzolli moving around, doing nothing. At five of eight she started to go through the closing ritual, and Lula and I crossed the street and hid in the narrow alley separating the store from the neighboring business.

The front lights went out, and we heard the door open and close and the deadbolt get thrown. I peeked around the corner and saw that Scarzolli was walking in the wrong direction. She was walking *away* from us. I popped out from the alley and tiptoed after her, closing the gap. She sensed I was there, turned and uttered an oath, and took off at a fast shuffle. I was almost within arm's reach of her when Tank stepped out of a shadow, blocking her way.

"Excuse me, ma'am," Tank said.

Scarzolli backed up a step and kicked Tank in the nuts. Hard to believe anyone that old could get her leg up that high, but Scarzolli scored a direct hit. Tank turned white and went down to his knees, hands at his crotch. Ranger was behind him, doubled over laughing.

I tackled Scarzolli and wrestled her to the ground. "Someone friggin' cuff her!" I yelled.

"I'm trying," Lula said. "You gotta hold her still. She's like a octopus, waving her arms and legs around."

I had at least ten pounds on Scarzolli, and I used my weight to pin her. I saw Ranger's denim-clad legs straddle us both, saw his hands reach over and attach a cuff to Scarzolli's one wrist, and then the other. He was still smiling wide when he lifted me off Scarzolli and got me up on my feet.

"I can always count on you to brighten my day," Ranger said.

"You just liked seeing Tank get kicked in the nuts."

"Yeah," Ranger said on a whisper of laughter. "That was worth the ticket."

Tank was up, trying to walk it off.

"Hope you didn't permanently damage anything," Lula said to him. "I always had an attraction to you."

"Most women don't like me," Tank said. "On account of I'm too big."

"I'm not most women," Lula said. "I could handle a big man. I *like* them big. The bigger, the better, is what I say."

Scarzolli was still on the ground. She was making angry cat sounds, and she kicked out with her feet when anyone came near her.

"It's just a crappy first-time shoplifting charge," I said to her. "Get a grip."

Ranger got her under the armpits, dragged her to the green SUV, and eased her into the back seat.

"Take her to the station," he said to Tank. "Bring her around to the back door. Stephanie will follow you in."

"I'll leave my car here and go with you," Lula said to Tank. "The crazy old lady might get out of control, and you might need some help. And after we drop her off, we could go get a burger or something."

"I'm supposed to watch Stephanie," Tank said.

"Don't worry about it," Ranger said. "I'll take care of Stephanie."

Chapter FOURTEEN

It was a little after ten when I finally walked into my apartment. No sign of Ranger, so I called Morelli while I waited.

"Long time no see," Morelli said.

"Miss me?"

"No. Joyce Barnhardt is here with her trained dogs."

"You're not going to get me going on that one. You hate Joyce Barnhardt."

"Yeah, but Bob might like the dog part," Morelli said.

"I just took down the old lady who runs the porn shop on Twelfth. Tank tried to help me, and she kicked him in the nuts."

"I'm sorry I missed it. I'm not being sarcastic either. I'm *really* sorry I missed it. I assume you've got a full contingent of Ranger's Merry Men watching your back."

"Yep. Mostly I pick up vigilantes, but we think Scrog followed me for a while this afternoon."

"Ranger called it in to me, and we determined the car was stolen. I reached the parking garage shortly after Ranger. Scrog slipped through my fingers, too."

"Will you be at Carmen's viewing tomorrow?"

"Yeah. We've called in the National Guard to help with crowd control."

"You haven't!"

"No, but we probably should. I was getting ready to go to bed," Morelli said. "I don't suppose you want to join me?"

"That would be nice, but I have to stay here and hope there's an attempt made to kidnap me."

"Other men have girlfriends with safe normal jobs," Morelli said. "Like swallowing swords and getting shot out of a cannon." And he hung up.

Ranger walked in and caught me with my head in the refrigerator.

"The food fairy left sandwiches, salad, fresh fruit, bagels and cream cheese and lox from Nova Scotia. But no dessert," I told Ranger.

"I don't eat dessert."

"Yes, but it's *my* refrigerator."

Ranger removed the gun he'd been wearing and placed it on the kitchen counter beside his car keys. "I'll pass the word to Ella."

I nuked a bag of microwave popcorn and dumped it into a bowl. "I talked to Morelli. He said you brought him in to help tail Scrog this afternoon. That was very classy."

"Yeah, I'm a classy guy." Ranger scooped up a handful of popcorn. "A little girl's life is at stake. That doesn't leave much room for ego and turf wars."

I brought the popcorn into the living room and turned the television on. "Has anyone talked to Scrog's parents?"

"They're being watched, but no contact has been made. The feds are running that show, and they're playing it very quiet. My understanding is that Scrog was estranged from his parents. He wanted to be a cop, and they wanted him to go into a monastery."

"Any news from the underground that he's trying to buy drugs or guns?"

"No. Nothing."

"Sightings?"

"Constantly. They go to the hotline. So far they aren't seeing a pattern. There was a rash of sightings in South Beach yesterday, but it turned out to be Ricky Martin."

I was working my way through my 472 worthless cable stations, and Ranger's cell phone rang. He answered and in a moment was on his feet, yanking me to mine.

"One of my men just got shot," Ranger said.

He had his hand wrapped around my wrist, moving me through the apartment. He grabbed his keys and his gun off the kitchen counter without breaking stride. He was out the door and down the hall, his legs longer than mine, forcing me to run to keep up.

It's pretty much a straight shot down Hamilton to Saint Francis Hospital from my apartment building. If there's no traffic and you hit the lights right, it can be done in less than ten minutes. We were in the silver BMW with Ranger behind the wheel, his cell phone on drive mode.

Hal was on the line, fielding calls through Ranger's central dispatch. "Manuel and Zero responded to a break-in at the bonds office," Hal said. "Manuel approached the office and was shot three times, through the plate glass window. The perp left through the back door. Do you want me to patch you through to Zero? He just arrived at the hospital with Manuel."

"No," Ranger said. "I'll take it from here."

We were a block from the bonds office and traffic was stopped in front of us. Police strobes pulsed beyond the traffic. Ranger turned off Hamilton and wove his way through side streets. Five minutes later, Ranger turned onto the street leading to the emergency entrance at the hospital.

"I can't go in," he said. "I'm going to drop you off, and then I'm going to loop around and park on Mifflin. Send Zero out to see me. Remind him to check that he isn't followed. You're wearing the panic button, and you have a secure phone. Call me when you know something about Manuel."

I hopped out of the BMW and hurried to the emergency room entrance. I saw Ranger wait until I was inside, and then he took off. Zero was sitting in the waiting room. Easy to find him in his RangeMan uniform.

"How's Manuel?" I asked.

"He's in the back. He was hit three times, but he was wearing a vest, so the two he took in the chest just knocked him back. The third got him in the arm. He's waiting for a doctor. It's a zoo in here tonight."

Zero was right about the zoo. The waiting room was packed with the walking wounded and their relatives. I sent Zero out to talk to Ranger, and I looked around to see who was on duty. Growing up in the Burg meant you almost always knew someone working emergency. Not that it mattered. There was always so much traffic in the ER, if you knew the drill you could just walk through to the treatment area.

I got two cups of coffee from the machine and walked past the ER desk.

"Excuse me," the woman on duty said.

"Just taking coffee to my husband," I told her. "I'll be right out."

I went bed to bed, peeking around curtains, until I found Manuel. He was on his back, hooked up to an IV. His shirt was off and his bicep was wrapped in a bloody towel. Gail Mangianni was with him. I went to high school with Gail. Her sister is married to my cousin Marty. Gail is an ER nurse and almost always works a night shift.

"Hey girlfriend," Gail said. "What's up?"

"Came to see my husband Manuel Whatshisname."

"Lucky for you we allow wives back here," Gail said. "Otherwise you'd have to leave."

"How's he doing?"

"He's going to be flying in a couple minutes. I just gave him a shot."

"I need to talk to him before he takes off," I said.

"You better talk fast. He's starting to drool."

"Do you know who shot you?" I asked Manuel.

"It was weird. I looked into the glass and this guy looked back out at me, and it was like looking at Ranger. I sort of freaked, you know, like I was confused. And then he raised his gun and the whole time I swear he never blinked, he just kept staring into my eyes while he was shooting me."

I felt the skin crawl along the nape of my neck. Edward Scrog had executed his wife and gunned down Ranger's man in cold blood. He'd looked Manuel in the eye and shot him without hesitation. And now, I imagined, Edward Scrog was returning to his hiding place and his ten-year-old hostage. Julie Martine was locked away somewhere, waiting for the monster to return. The horror of it all pressed against the backs of my eyes and clogged my throat. I was gripping the metal bed rail, and I looked down and saw that my knuckles were white. I made an effort to relax and focused on Manuel.

"You could see in the dark office?"

"I had a flashlight on him. I was right up to the glass, trying to see in."

"What happens next?" I asked Gail.

"I'm waiting on a doctor. Probably we'll take him into the OR to remove the bullet, but I don't think it's major surgery. He's going to have some bruising on his chest from where the bullets impacted the vest. I imagine we'll monitor him and keep him overnight."

"Can I see him when he comes out of surgery?"

"Sure," Gail said. "You're his wife." She looked over at his chart. "You're Mrs. Manuel Ramos."

I returned to the waiting room and called Connie. Since Vinnie was still out of town, Connie would get called in to check out the office.

I heard the connection open and there was a lot of background noise and police band squawk.

"*Hello,*" Connie yelled over the noise.

"I imagine you're at the office."

"Yeah, and you would be where?"

"At the hospital checking on the guy who got shot."

"How is he?"

"He'll be okay. What are you finding at the office?"

"Guns and ammo missing. That's about it. He left the petty cash. Probably didn't have time to look. It was locked away. Didn't want a George Foreman grill."

"The police having any luck finding him?"

"No. He was long gone by the time they got here. My understanding is that he set off the alarm when he entered, and RangeMan responded fast because they already had men in the area. I guess he shot the one guy and then took off out the back door."

"Is Morelli there?"

"No. We got a bunch of uniforms and two suits. A guy from out of state named Rhodenbarr. I don't know any of them. They tell me a lot of the men are at an awards banquet for Joe Juniak who was just appointed Emperor of the Universe."

"Do you need help?"

"No. I'm fine. And Meri is here. She was on her way to pick up a pizza and she saw all the cop cars so she stopped."

I called Ranger next and told him everything I knew. "I'm going to wait until Manuel is out of surgery," I said.

"Stay inside the hospital. Call me when you're ready to leave."

"Is Tank back on the job?"

"Yeah. And he's smiling but completely wasted. I saw him run a half marathon once and look better than this."

"He's had a tough day. First he got his clock cleaned by an old lady, and then he had to buy Lula a burger."

"Must have been some burger."

I thought Ranger sounded a little wistful.

I was in my knit tank top and cotton boxers. My teeth were brushed, and my face was washed and moisturized. I was exhausted. I wanted to go to sleep. Problem was . . . there was a man in my bed. And I didn't exactly know what to do with him. I knew what I *wanted* to do with him. And I knew what I *should* do with him. Unfortunately, what I *wanted* to do and what I *should* do were two very different things. Even without Morelli I'd have a dilemma deciding on a path of action with Ranger. I blew out a sigh. Stephanie, Stephanie, Stephanie, I said to myself. That's a big fib. You know exactly what you'd do about Ranger if Morelli wasn't in the picture. You'd ride him like Zorro.

Ranger was watching me. "Are you coming to bed?"

"I'm thinking about it," I told him.

"Come closer, and I'll help you decide."

"Omigod," I said on a sudden flash of sleep-deprived insight. "You're the big bad wolf."

"There are some similarities."

I grabbed my pillow and took the extra blanket draped over the chair. "I'm too tired to wrestle with this tonight. Since you can't sleep on the couch, I'll sleep on the couch."

I stomped off to the living room with my pillow and blanket, flipped the lights off, and flopped onto the couch. Turns out the couch is too short. No matter, just curl up a little, I told myself. Turns out the couch is too narrow. And the cushions were sliding around. And there was a ridge of something sticking up into my back. I threw the pillow and blanket onto the floor and tried sleeping on the floor. Too hard. Too flat.

I stomped back into the bedroom, climbed over Ranger, and slid under the covers.

"The princess returns," Ranger said.

"Don't start."

I rolled around in the dark, trying to get comfortable.

"Now what?" Ranger said.

"I left my pillow in the living room."

Ranger reached out and gathered me into him. "You can share mine. Just don't climb on top of me like you did last night or those cute little pajamas you're wearing will be on the floor when you wake up."

"I didn't climb on top of you!"

"Babe, you were all over me."

"You wish. And your hand is on my ass."

"My hand on your ass is the least of your worries."

I woke up completely entangled with Ranger.

"Uh-oh," I said. "Sorry! I seem to be on top of you."

Ranger kissed my neck and slid the strap to my tank top off my shoulder. And then his hand was under my little knit top, his fingers skimming across my breast. He kissed me, and our tongues touched, and his mouth moved lower and lower . . . and lower! And this is the thing I knew about Ranger from the one time we'd been together. *Ranger made love.* And Ranger liked to kiss. Ranger kissed *everything. A lot.*

Ranger froze in mid kiss.

"What?" I asked.

"Someone's at your door. I just heard the lock tumble."

"How could you possibly hear the lock tumble? You had your head under the covers!"

He moved off me, slipped out of bed, and started for the door.

"Holy cow!" I said. "You can't go to the door like that!"

"My gun's in the kitchen."

"Yes, but your underwear's on the floor in my bedroom!" And that wasn't the biggest problem.

The front door to my apartment opened, and the chain caught with a snap. There was a moment's silence, and then Morelli's voice sounding impatient.

"Steph?"

There've been times in my life when I couldn't get a decent date. Long dry spells with no boyfriend, no sex, no relationship prospects. And now I had *two* men. Life was a bitch. I scrounged under the covers for my pajamas, rammed myself into them, and jumped out of bed. I padded barefoot to my front door and peeked at Morelli over the chain.

"Hi," I said.

"Are you going to let me in?"

"Sure."

I slid the chain back and opened the door for him.

"I'm not staying," he said. "I'm just dropping off." And he tossed a duffle bag into the foyer.

"What's this?" I asked.

"I'm moving in."

Oh boy.

Morelli looked at the pillow and blanket in the living room. "Who's sleeping on the floor?"

"Ranger's here."

"Going to be tight in the bathroom in the morning," Morelli said. And he kissed me and left.

I made coffee and ate a Pop-Tart while Ranger showered. Then I went across the hall and swiped

Mr. Wolesky's newspaper. I was standing in the kitchen, reading about the shooting, when Ranger strolled in. He was dressed in jeans and a T-shirt, his hair still damp.

"That was close," he said, helping himself to coffee.

"Yeah, you almost opened the door to Morelli."

"I wasn't talking about Morelli. I was talking about us."

"That too," I said.

Ranger sliced a bagel and looked for the toaster.

"It's broken," I told him.

He turned the broiler on and slid the bagel into the oven.

"That's surprisingly domestic for the man of mystery," I said to him.

He looked at me over the rim of his coffee mug. "I like things hot."

Chapter FIFTEEN

The sidewalk in front of the bonds office was wet from being scrubbed down and hosed off in an attempt to remove the bloodstains, and two guys were working to repair the front window. I parked the Mini in front of the used bookstore, carefully stepped around the men and the glass, and walked through the open front door.

It was after nine, and I was the last to arrive for work. Connie was at her desk. Meri was at a card table with a phone and a laptop, Melvin Pickle was a filing demon, and Lula was on the couch reading *Star* magazine.

"How's Ranger's man?" Connie wanted to know.

"He's okay. I stayed at the hospital until he was out of recovery. They wanted him to spend the night, but he refused. Lucky for him he was wearing a vest."

"He told the police it looked like Ranger shooting him," Meri said.

"Yes, but when I talked to him in the hospital he said that was a first impression. He said it freaked him out, and he didn't respond because of it. His second impression was that it wasn't Ranger. It was someone who was dressed in black and resembled Ranger."

"How could he be sure it wasn't Ranger?" Meri asked. "I mean, he was getting shot!"

"He said he was right up to the window, shining his flashlight on the guy. He said the guy looked him in the eyes and raised the gun and shot him without blinking."

"Gives me the heebie jeebies," Lula said. "That's so cold. And I bet he's the one who's got the little girl. How terrible is that? That child must be terrified."

"I don't know," Meri said. "I'm having a hard time with this. Everything always points back to this Ranger person. How can you be so sure it's not actually him? I mean, he could have gone nutso. From what I hear, he was dark anyway, like Batman. Silent. Tortured soul. Always dressed in black."

"The all-black clothes just make things easy," I said. "He doesn't have to mix and match. He doesn't have any decisions in the morning. His housekeeper doesn't have to worry about colors running."

Meri's eyes got wide. "Do you know him *that* well?"

"Um, no," I said. "I was sort of putting myself in his place." Okay, so that was liar, liar pants on fire, but there was something about Meri that had me on guard. Hard to say what it was, but she still felt off to me. Something about her manner, the way she looked, the way she asked questions, the way she showed up and was too good to be believed . . . too perfect for the job.

"Your problem is you don't know him," Lula said to Meri. "If you knew him you'd understand. He's dark in a good way. And besides, anybody *that hot* can't be all bad."

"What's happening with Dooby Biagi and Charles Chin?" I asked Meri.

She handed the files over to me. "They're both business as usual. I made some phone calls and neither seems to have skipped town."

"Ready to ride?" I asked Lula.

"Yeah, I gotta talk to you anyway."

We took my Mini, and Lula waited until we were away from the curb before she spoke.

"I got three things," she said. "First is, there's something bothering me about Meri. I don't know what it is. Second thing, where the heck did Ranger and Tank come from last night? Tank doesn't talk. He wouldn't say nothing. And third is, Tank don't need to talk because he was right about being big. It's like wrestling some prehistoric monster. Like having a go at King Kong. And he's big all over the place, if you know what I mean. I tell you I'm in love. I don't need to go visiting that Pleasure Treasures on account of I found my own pleasure treasure and his name is Tank. Probably he has some other name, but I don't know what it is. He wouldn't tell me that either."

"Maybe it's just that Meri is new."

"Melvin is new, and I don't feel like that about him. And it isn't that I don't like Meri. She's real likeable. I just don't feel comfortable somehow."

I had Dooby Biagi's file on top. Dooby worked the counter at one of the fast-food places and got caught with his hand in the cash register. He said he was making change, but the day manager found more than change in Dooby's pocket. Dooby had a couple hundred plus a pipe and a dime bag of crack.

Dooby lived in a row house in the Burg. According to Meri's research, Dooby rented with three other guys. And needless to say, Dooby was unemployed.

I idled in front of Dooby's house, and Lula and I stared out at it, neither of us moving.

"I don't feel like doing this," I finally said.

"Me either," Lula said. "I'm wore out with this job. I'm tired of dragging these people off to jail. Nobody's ever happy. I feel like the Grinch."

"Somebody's got to do it," I said, trying to convince myself of my worth.

"I know that," Lula said. "This here's for the good of society. It's not like the police have time to find these people. I just think I need a mental health day."

I looked in my rearview mirror for Ranger.

Lula looked too. "He's back there, isn't he? He's following you around, right? That's how come they were at the Pleasure Treasures."

"We're hoping the Ranger impostor will come after me. And then when he nabs me he'll lead us to Julie."

"That's a pretty good plan," Lula said. "Unless the Ranger impostor decides to kill you instead."

I slumped a little lower in my seat.

"It's gonna be a hot one today," Lula said. "You know what I'd like to do? I'd like to go to Point Pleasant and play the claw machine in the arcade and get one of them orange and vanilla swirly frozen custard ice creams."

I put the Mini into gear, hooked a U-turn, and drove back to the office. "We need to take your car," I said. "Is it parked in back?"

"Yep. It's in the lot. The glass truck was parked in my usual spot on the street."

"Just changing cars," I said to Connie, as we breezed through the office.

I selected a gun from the cabinet, took a box of rounds, and left the panic button in the gun cabinet. I dropped the gun and the ammo in my bag, and Lula and I went out the back door.

"I know this is the wrong thing to do," I said to Lula, "but I need a break from all the sad scary things. And I need to get away from Ranger for a couple hours."

"I don't see nobody back here," Lula said. "I think we tricked them."

Ranger called when we were on the bridge, crossing the Manasquan Inlet. "Where are you?" he asked.

"I'm taking a day off."

"You removed the panic button."

"Yes, but I took a gun. And it's even loaded. And I have extra bullets. And Lula is with me."

Silence.

"Hello?" I said. "Are you mad?"

"Mad doesn't come close. Are you going to tell me where you are?"

"Not when you're in this kind of mood."

More silence.

"Are you trying to control yourself?" I asked. Easy to be brave when Ranger was in Trenton, and I was in Point Pleasant.

"Don't push me," Ranger said.

"You can just keep going and going and going," I told him. "I'm not that strong. I'm running low on happy. And I hardly have any brave left at all. We were careful not to be followed. We're armed. We're sober. I'll be home this afternoon. I'll call you when I get to Trenton." I disconnected and broke into a nervous sweat. "That was Ranger."

"No shit."

"It gets worse," I told her. "He's been staying in my apartment, and this morning Morelli moved in."

"Let me get this straight. You got Ranger and Morelli living with you. At the same time."

"Looks that way."

Lula pulled into the lot at the pavilion. "Girl, you got a problem. You can't put two alpha dogs in the same kennel. They'll kill each other. It's not like those two are ordinary men. They got enough testosterone between them that if testosterone was electricity they could light up New York City for the month of August."

"I don't want to talk about it. I want to get some ice cream and sit in the sun and listen to the ocean."

* * *

Ranger was brooding in the parking lot in front of my condo when I pulled in. He was in a RangeMan SUV, which meant it was new, it was immaculate, it had the big engine, it was black with black tinted windows, and it had the big-bucks chrome wheel covers.

He got out of the SUV and silently escorted me to my apartment.

"Is Morelli here?" I asked him.

"No. Not yet, but it's almost five, so I imagine he'll be rolling in soon." He unlocked the apartment door, stepped in first, and looked around before he motioned me in. "Your nose is sunburned," he said. "They don't sell sunscreen at Point Pleasant?"

"Are you sure I was at Point Pleasant?"

"I knew it was either the mall or Point Pleasant, and there were no background mall sounds when you talked to me."

"You followed me down there?"

"No. I sent Hal and Roy."

"I didn't see them."

"That's my point. Hal doesn't blend in. It's like being followed by a stegosaurus. So if you didn't see Hal, you sure as hell weren't going to pick out Edward Scrog." He tossed his keys on the kitchen counter. "If you have an issue with me, I expect you to tell me about it, not run away."

"You don't listen."

"I always listen," Ranger said. "I don't always *agree.* I have a problem right now that I can't seem to solve by myself. I need you to help me find my daughter. And there's an even bigger problem involved. I feel a financial and moral obligation to my daughter. I send child support, I send birthday and Christmas presents, I visit when I'm invited. But I've kept myself emotionally distanced. I'm *not* emotionally distanced from *you.* I couldn't live with myself if something happened to you because I was using you to find someone . . . even if that someone was my daughter. So I have to make every effort to keep you safe."

"You're a little smothering."

"Deal with it." He looked over at Morelli's duffle bag still sitting in the foyer. "This should be interesting."

"You're not going to do something stupid and macho, are you?"

"I try hard not to do things that are stupid. I'm willing to make an exception in this case. I'm not leaving. And if you sleep with him while I'm here, I'll have to kill him."

If anyone else had said that I'd burst out laughing, but there was a slight chance Ranger was serious.

I took a shower and spent a few minutes on makeup and used the roller brush on my hair. Then I spent a few more minutes on makeup. I wiggled into a little black dress and stepped into black heels. I sashayed out of the bedroom and found Morelli and Ranger in the kitchen, eating.

Ranger was eating a chopped salad with grilled chicken. Morelli was eating a meatball sub. I checked out the refrigerator and discovered Ella had dropped off a cheesecake . . . so that's what *I* ate. No one said anything.

I finished off the cheesecake and glanced at my watch. Six o'clock. "Gotta go," I said. "Don't want to be late for the viewing."

Ranger had the panic button in his hand, and he was looking my dress over. If we'd been alone, he would have slipped it into my cleavage, but Morelli was watching with his hand on his gun.

"Oh, for God's sake," I said. "Just give me the stupid thing." I took the panic button and stuck it into my Super Sexy Miracle Bra.

"GPS," Ranger said to Morelli.

"Probably I can find her breast without it," Morelli said. "But it's good to know there's a navigational system on board if I need it."

I saw Ranger's mouth twitch, and I was pretty sure it was a smile. I wasn't sure what the smile meant. First guess would be he was thinking he had no problem finding my breast without GPS either.

I grabbed my handbag and swung my ass out of the kitchen, out of the apartment, and down the hall. I was thinking I might get into the Mini and drive to California. Start over. New job. New boyfriend. No forwarding address. I checked my rearview mirror. Ranger in the silver BMW. Morelli in his green SUV. Two RangeMan goons in a black SUV, too far back to see their identity. I was leading a friggin' parade. And the parade would follow me to California.

"Stephanie," I said, "you're in deep shit."

The little lot attached to the funeral home was packed by the time I got there. I drove up and down the streets, but the curbside parking was taken for blocks. I double-parked and got out of the car. The shiny black RangeMan SUV rolled up to me, the window slid down, and Hal looked out from the passenger seat.

"RangeMan valet parking?" I asked.

Hal got out, rammed himself into the Mini, and I thought I saw the tires flatten a little. Both cars drove off. One mark on the tally for Ranger. *Employees available for valet parking.* On the Morelli side was *hates salad.*

I fought my way through the crush of people on the funeral home porch and wormed my way through the crowd in the lobby. I felt a hand at my back and heard Morelli's voice in my ear.

"Go do your thing, and I'll keep you in sight," Morelli said. "Ranger has some men in here who are also watching you. Probably there are a couple feds as well."

I got into the viewing room, but there was a wall of people in front of me. I looked left and saw a head rising above all else. It was Sally Sweet, close to seven feet tall in his heels. I inched closer and saw he was wearing shocking pink platform pumps with a five-inch stiletto heel and a raincoat. Lula was beside him, also in pink heels and a raincoat. I looked at the ground and saw they were molting pink feathers.

"This here's a mess," Lula yelled when she saw me. "I can't go forward, and I can't go back."

Grandma elbowed her way over to us. "I lost my sense of direction. Which way's the casket? I can't see a darned thing."

Sally picked Grandma up and held her over his head.

"Okay," Grandma yelled to Sally. "I got a fix on it. You can set me down now." And Grandma took off, burrowing through the bodies.

Chapter SIXTEEN

I tried following, but Grandma was instantly swallowed up by the mob of mourners.

"Can you see her?" I asked Sally.

"I can't exactly see her, but I can see people moving to get out of her way. She's almost all the way up front. She should pop out any minute now. Yep, there she is. She's right in front of the casket. Looks like the funeral director standing firm to one side, and everyone else is milling around, jockeying for position. And there's Granny, holding her ground. I can only see the tops of heads," Sally said. "Hold on, something's happening. People are scrambling. The funeral director's waving his arms and bobbing around."

I heard someone shouting to stand back. Then some hysterical screaming. And a loud crash. Someone yelled out, "*Get her!*"

"What's going on?" I asked Sally.

"It looks like a riot. Someone just got knocked into a big floral arrangement, and it all went over. And I think the funeral director's thrown himself on top of the casket. Looks like there's someone under him. I can see two feet sticking out. It's someone in patent leather pumps. Omigod, I think it's your granny."

"I bet she tried to get the lid up," Lula said. "You know how she hates when she can't see nothing."

My mother was going to kill me.

"Everybody looks real angry," Sally said. "We should probably try to rescue Granny."

"Coming through," Lula said, head down, plowing her way to the front. "'Scuse me, move your bony little ass, outta my way, make way for mama."

Sally and I rode in her wake, stumbling up to the casket, coming nose to nose with Dave Nelson.

Nelson grabbed me by the front of my shirt. "You have to help me. These people are insane. Your grandmother is insane. She started it all. Somehow she got the lid up. And now *everyone* wants to see!"

"Is there a problem with that?" I asked.

"Carmen Manoso has been autopsied! She makes Frankenstein look *good.* She's had her brain taken out and weighed and put back in!"

"Oh yeah," I said. "I forgot."

"I drove here from Perth Amboy," some lady said. "I'm not leaving until I get to see the body."

"Yeah," everyone said. "We want to see."

"They're going to take my mortuary apart, brick by brick," Dave whispered. "These people are all ghouls."

"They just want to be entertained," I told them. "I bet you ran out of cookies."

I stood on a chair and yelled at the crowd. "Everybody quiet down. We can't open the casket, but we've got some exciting entertainment. Two members of the What band have agreed to do a special performance."

"We can't do that," Lula said. "We don't have any music. And besides, we're professionals. We don't do this shit for nothing."

"All kinds of people have come to see Carmen," I told Lula. "I wouldn't be surprised if a bunch of television crews were here. And I think I saw Al Roker when I walked in."

"Al Roker! I love Al Roker. Do you think he's married?"

"I thought you were in love with Tank."

"Yeah, but Al is so cute. And I hear he has his own barbecue sauce. You gotta love a man's got his own barbecue sauce. Boy, it'd be real hard to have to choose between Al and Tank."

"There's a stage behind the casket," I said. "And there's even a microphone on that pulpit thing. This could be your big break."

Okay, so I didn't really see Al Roker and this was probably a rotten thing to do, but I couldn't figure anything else out. And who knows, maybe there were television people in the viewing room. From where I was standing, it looked like half the state was here.

Lula and Sally took the stage and stood there in their pink high heels and raincoats and the whole room went silent. They took their raincoats off and the room went nuts. Lula looked like a big round pink puffball in her genuine domestic farm-raised fowl feather dress. Sally looked like nothing anyone had ever seen before. He was wearing the heels and the flamingo feather thong. The thong sack looked like dyed dead bird. And the rest of Sally made a strong case for full body waxing.

"Hey all you fuckin' mourners," Sally yelled. "Are you fuckin' ready for this?"

Everyone cheered and clapped and hooted. Jersey's always fuckin' ready for anything. Especially if it's hairy and in a thong.

Lula and Sally started singing and waving their arms and dancing around and the mourners all backed up a couple feet. Feathers were flying, and Lula was sweating, and the room was starting to smell like wet water fowl. By the time Lula and Sally got through the second song the room had emptied out some.

"Thanks," I said to Lula. "That did the trick. Everybody's happy now. I think you can stop singing."

"Yeah," Lula said, climbing off the stage. "We were pretty good. Too bad, I didn't see Al Roker out there. But I think I saw Meri. Guess she didn't want to be left out."

"I always wanted to be in a rock-and-roll band," Grandma said. "I could do all those dancing moves too. I'm old, but I still got legs. I can't play any instruments though."

"Can you sing?" Sally asked.

"Sure. I'm a good singer," Grandma said.

"I've been thinking now that we're playing all these geezer gigs we could use an older demographic in the band. You'd have to get some outfits, and we practice once a week."

"I could do all that," Grandma said.

"Sometimes we're not done until ten o'clock when we do assisted living," Sally said. "Those cats get to stay up later. Can you stay up that late?"

"Sure," Grandma said. "Sometimes I even watch the ten o'clock news."

"We could dress her up like us," Lula said to Sally. "And I'll teach her my moves."

"Do you wear these feather outfits all the time?" Grandma asked. "They look real pretty, but they don't seem practical. Sally's doodle sack lost all its feathers. Not that it don't look good bald like that, but it must be a lot of work putting those feathers back all the time."

"Yeah, the feathers didn't totally work out," Lula said. "I got feathers up my ass. I gotta go shopping again."

"Looks like the crowd's thinned out," Grandma said. "I'm going to see if there's any cookies left in the kitchen."

"Sorry about the casket getting opened," I said to Dave. "I was supposed to keep an eye on Grandma, but she got away from me in the crowd."

"It worked out okay," Dave said. "But it was scary there for a while. I was doing the best I could to protect your grandmother and the deceased, but I couldn't have held them off much longer. Good thing you arrived with the band."

"We gotta get going," Lula said, looking at her watch. "The old folks don't like when you're late. They get real cranky."

Lula and Sally had driven a lot of people out of the viewing room, but there was still a huge bottleneck in the lobby. I pushed my way into the gridlock and inched forward. I looked over my shoulder and spotted Morelli. He was keeping watch over me with people five or six deep between us.

"Look *here,*" someone said directly behind me.

I followed the voice and experienced the same flash of confusion Ranger's security man had described. For a nanosecond I thought I was looking at Ranger. And then all the hairs raised on my arm and the back of my neck, and I realized I was looking at Edward Scrog.

"I only have a moment," he said. "I know you're waiting for me to come get you, but there are too many people watching us here. You have to be patient. We'll be together soon enough, and then we'll never be parted again. We'll go to the angels together."

"Where's Julie?"

"Julie is at home, waiting for you. I told her I was going to bring her a mommy soon. And then we'll be a family, and I can finish my work."

"She's okay?"

"I love you," Scrog said.

I grabbed hold of his sleeve and opened my mouth

to yell for Morelli. I heard something sizzle, and everything went black.

Even before I opened my eyes I knew what had happened. I felt the familiar tingle and then the feeling getting restored to my fingertips. The noise in my head went from a buzz to a hum and then disappeared, replaced by voices.

Morelli's face swam into focus. He looked worried. "Are you okay?" he asked. "I was watching you, and all of a sudden you collapsed."

"I think I was stun-gunned by Scrog. Did you see him?"

"I saw you say something to the guy behind you. I couldn't see his face, and from the back he didn't resemble Ranger. The skin tone might have been the same, but the hair, and the build, and the clothes were all different. You had Tank two people away to the side of you, and he didn't spot Scrog either."

Morelli helped me to my feet and wrapped a supporting arm around my waist. People had been cleared away from me. A paramedic had just arrived and was standing to the side.

"Thanks," I said to the paramedic. "I'm okay."

"We had men at every exit," Morelli said. "The instant you went down we sealed the building. We're letting people out one by one. Do you remember anything about him? What he was wearing?"

"I didn't notice, but I don't think he was in black. For a split second I thought it was Ranger. I think it's the face shape and coloring and haircut from the front. He's shorter than Ranger. His eyes and mouth are different when you see him up close."

"I'm turning you over to Tank," Morelli said. "He'll see that you get home. I'm going to stay here until they empty and search the building. It shouldn't take long. They're moving people out fast. Seventy percent of the people here are women."

Tank was sitting in my living room, looking uncomfortable. Ranger had given him orders not to leave me alone, and I was worried if I had to use the bathroom he might follow me in. I had a ball game on the television, but Tank kept nervously looking around at me, as if I'd suddenly vanish into thin air. I'd made him stop at a convenience store on the way home, and I'd gotten a week's worth of comfort food. Tastykakes, Cheez Doodles, candy bars, Suzy Q's, barbecued chips. I'd just started working my way through the bag when Morelli and Bob came in, followed by Ranger.

Some sort of silent communication happened between Ranger and Tank, and Tank got up and left without saying a word.

Ranger threw his keys on the kitchen counter. Removed his gun and left it alongside his keys. Morelli did the same. At first glance this looked like they were safe at home, relaxed and unarmed, but I knew they both carried ankle guns. And Ranger always had a knife.

No one said anything. They were both wearing cop faces. Wary, emotionally inaccessible. Not hard to tell they were both in a vile mood.

"How did the search go?" I asked.

"We didn't get him. It looks like he went out a back window," Morelli said.

I repeated the conversation I'd had with Scrog. No one said anything else. Morelli put a bowl of water on the floor for Bob, got a beer out of the refrigerator, and slouched in front of the television with it. Ranger went to the computer. I stayed in the kitchen and shoved Butterscotch Krimpets into my face.

I couldn't imagine what was going to happen next. I had one bed and one couch. The numbers didn't add up. Even if the sleeping arrangements were resolved, I couldn't live with both of them under my roof.

"This is uncomfortable," I said. "I'm going to bed. And I'm locking my door."

Both men looked over at me. We all knew a locked door was meaningless. Morelli and Ranger went where they wanted to go. I blew out a sigh and closed the bedroom door behind me.

I got a tote bag out of the closet, stuffed clothes and cosmetics into it, quietly opened my bedroom window, and climbed out onto the fire escape. I tossed the tote bag and my shoulder bag to the ground, lowered the ladder, and jumped the remaining couple feet. I turned and bumped into Morelli and Ranger, standing hands on hips, not amused.

"How did you know?" I asked.

"Tank called," Ranger said. "He's watching the lot."

"I'm divorcing both of you," I said. "I'm moving in with my parents. You can stay here," I said to Ranger. "Remember to give Rex fresh water and food in the morning." I turned to Morelli. "You and Bob should go home. You'll be more comfortable there."

Silence.

I gathered my tote bag and shoulder bag up from the ground.

"One of us should stop her," Ranger said to Morelli, his eyes fixed on me.

"Not going to be me," Morelli said. "Have you ever tried to stop her from doing something she wanted to do?"

"Haven't had much success at it," Ranger said.

Morelli rocked back on his heels. "One thing I've learned about Stephanie over the years, she's not good at taking orders."

"Has authority issues," Ranger said.

"And if you piss her off, she'll get even. She ran over me with her father's Buick once and broke my leg."

That got a small smile out of Ranger.

"Nice to see you boys bonding," I said.

I hiked the tote up onto my shoulder and left them still standing hands on hips. I crossed the lot to the Mini and got in. I cranked the engine over and drove out of the lot. I looked in my rearview mirror. Tank was following. Fine by me. I was actually very scared. I was scared for me, and I was scared for little Julie.

It was a little after nine when I got to my parents' house. I parked in the driveway and looked around for Tank. I didn't see him, but I knew he was there. He'd probably work shifts with Hal or Ranger doing surveillance on me. My mother and grandmother were at the door waiting for me. How they always knew I was in the neighborhood was a mystery. Some female homing device that announced the approach of a daughter.

"I'm letting a friend use my apartment," I told them. "I was wondering if I could stay here for a couple days."

"Of course you can stay here," my mother said. "But what about Joseph? I thought you two were . . . you know, almost married."

I dropped the tote bag in the little hall foyer. "He has a full case load and is really busy. He's spending a lot of hours on the Manoso murder and kidnapping."

"The phone's been ringing off the hook," my mother said. "Everyone calling about the viewing. They said you fainted."

"They had way too many people in the funeral home. It was hot, and it smelled like funeral flowers, and I hadn't eaten any dinner. I'm fine now. And Joe was there to catch me."

The buzzwords in that explanation were *hadn't*

eaten dinner. Those were the words that without fail got my mother up and running every time.

"No dinner!" my mother said. "No wonder you fainted in that crush. Come into the kitchen, and I'll make you a nice roast beef sandwich."

My mother pulled a bunch of dishes out of the refrigerator and put them on the small kitchen table. Cole slaw, potato salad, three-bean salad, macaroni. She hauled out a chunk of roast beef, bread, mustard, olives, pickled beets, lettuce, sliced tomatoes, sliced provolone.

"This is great," I said, filling my plate.

"Good," my mother said, "and after you've had something to eat, you can tell me how your grandmother managed to get the lid open on the casket."

Chapter SEVENTEEN

Morelli and my parents live in houses that are almost identical, but Morelli's house feels larger. Morelli's house has less furniture, fewer people, and one more bathroom. My parents' house is filled with overstuffed couches and chairs and end tables and candy dishes, vases, fruit bowls, china doo-dads, stacks of magazines, afghans, area rugs, and kid things for my sister Valerie's three girls. My parents' house smells like pot roast and lemon furniture polish and fresh-baked chocolate chip cookies. Morelli's house rarely has a smell, except when it rains . . . then it smells like wet Bob.

There are three tiny bedrooms and the bathroom on the second floor of my parents' house. At the crack of dawn my mother gets up and is the first in the bathroom. She's quiet and efficient, taking a shower, putting on her face, neatening up after herself. After my mother it's a battle between my grandmother and my father. They rush at the bathroom and the first one there elbows in and slams and locks the door. Whoever is left on the outside starts yelling.

"For crissake, what are you doing in there?" my father will yell. "You've been in there for *days*. I need to take a crap. I need to go to work. It's not like I sit around watching television all day."

"Blow it out your you-know-what," my grandmother will fire back.

So it's not like I ever have to worry about oversleeping at my parents' house. Toilets are flushing, people are yelling and stomping around. And morning kitchen smells work their way upstairs. Coffee brewing, sweet rolls in the oven, bacon frying.

My room hasn't changed much since I moved out. My sister and her kids took the room over while she was regrouping after her divorce, but they're in their own house now, and the room has reestablished itself. Same floral quilted bedspread, same white ruffled curtains, same pictures on the walls, same chenille bathrobe hanging in the closet, same small chest of drawers that I left behind when I went off on my own. I sleep like a rock in the room. It feels safe . . . even when it isn't.

By the time I got down to the kitchen my father had already left. He's retired from the post office and drives a cab part time. He has a few regulars that need rides in the morning, to work or the train station, but mostly he picks his cronies up and takes them to the lodge to play cards. And then he stays and plays cards too.

My grandmother was in the kitchen, hooked up to my mother's iPod. "Before you break my heart . . . think it *oh oh ver,*" she sang, eyes closed, bony arms in the air, shuffling around in her white tennies.

"She tells me she's got a *gig,*" my mother said. "Just exactly what's going on?"

"Sally has a new band, and they have a bunch of jobs playing for seniors. He thought Grandma was an appropriate addition."

"Sweet Jesus!" And my mother made the sign of the cross.

I poured out some coffee and added milk. "It might not be so bad. They get done early because everyone in the audience gets medicated and falls asleep. And no one can sing, so Grandma will fit right in."

My mother watched Grandma gyrating and flailing her arms. "She looks ridiculous!"

I got a cinnamon roll and took it to the table with my coffee. "Maybe she just needs a costume."

Grandma paused while there was a song change on the iPod, and then she started skipping and strutting around the kitchen. "I can't get no satisfaction!" she yelled. "*No, no, no!*"

"Actually, she looks a lot like Jagger," my mother said.

Ranger's cell phone rang, and I opened the connection. "Yeah?"

"Your friend Scrog called early this morning. I have him on the machine. I want you to come over and listen to this."

"I knew it was a mistake to get an answering machine."

"The mistake was to leave last night. If you'd been here this morning you could have talked to him."

"Omigod, what the heck would I say?"

"You could keep him on long enough for a trace," Ranger said.

"My line is bugged?"

"Of course it's bugged."

I looked at my watch. It was almost nine. "Is it okay if I stop at the office first?"

"As long as you're here by noon. I want you to change your recording."

"I have to go to work," I said to my mother.

"It's Thursday," my mother said. "And I know you usually come for dinner on Friday, but Valerie and the girls and Albert are coming tomorrow. Would you and Joseph rather come for dinner tonight?"

"Probably. I'll have to ask him."

* * *

I walked into the bonds office and noticed that for the first time in almost two weeks the inner sanctum door was cracked open. I threw my shoulder bag on the couch and gave Connie raised eyebrows.

"He's back," she said.

I heard rustling in the inner office, the sort of sound rats make running through leaves, and Vinnie opened the door wide and stuck his head out.

"Hah," Vinnie said to me. "Decided to show up for work?"

"You got a problem?" I asked him.

"I'm drowning in FTAs. What the hell do you do all day?"

Vinnie is a cousin on my father's side of the family, and it's not a comfortable thought that he swam out of the Plum gene pool. He's slim and boneless with slicked-back hair and pointy-toed shoes and Mediterranean coloring. The thought of him married and reproducing sends chills through me. Still, in spite of his shortcomings as a human being, or maybe *because* of them, Vinnie is a pretty good bail bondsman. Vinnie is an excellent judge of sleaze.

"You're writing too much bond," I told him.

"I need the money. Lucille wants a new house. She says the one we have now is too small. She wants one with a home theater. What the fuck is that, anyway?"

Meri was watching from her card table. "Maybe I could start going out with Stephanie and Lula," she said. "I wouldn't be any help in the beginning but maybe eventually I could pick up some of the easier skips."

"Maybe eventually," Lula said.

"Not eventually," Vinnie said. "Now! Get out there *now*. I'm hemorrhaging money, for crissake. Lucille's gonna kill me."

Connie, Lula, and I knew who would kill him, and it

wouldn't be Lucille. It would be Lucille's father, Harry the Hammer. Harry didn't like when Lucille was disappointed.

"How did the nursing home go last night?" I asked Lula.

"We had to quit early. The feathers gave two people an asthma attack. I'm going out on my lunchtime to get us new outfits. We have a big job coming up Sunday night at the Brothers of the Loyal Sons, and we're calling an emergency practice so Grandma can learn the moves. We're doing a dress rehearsal and everything."

A floral delivery van double-parked in front of the office and a guy got out and carted a vase of flowers into the office. "Is there a Stephanie Plum here?"

"Uh-oh," Lula said. "Morelli must have done something wrong."

I took the vase and put it on Connie's desk and read the card. TILL DEATH DO US PART. NOT LONG NOW.

"What the heck?" Lula said.

"One of my many secret admirers," I said. "Probably some serial killer who just broke out of prison."

"Yeah," Lula said. "I bet that's it. Those serial killers are known for being romantic."

"Did we get any new skips in?" I asked Connie.

"None this morning. The one high-end bond we still have out is Lonnie Johnson. I'd really like it if you could get a line on him."

The front door banged open, and Joyce Barnhardt stalked in. She was still in black leather, wearing the stiletto-heeled black leather boots and the skin-tight, low-slung black leather pants and black leather bustier with her boobs squishing out the top. Her red hair was teased, her long artificial nails were polished and sharpened, her glossy red lips looked about to explode.

"I've got it! I've got the death certificate," she said.

She let the paper float down onto Connie's desk and she turned her attention to Meri. "Who's this?"

"New BEA," Connie said.

"You look like a cop," Joyce said to Meri. "Did you used to be a cop?"

"No," Meri said. "But my father was a cop."

Joyce turned back to Connie. "I want my money. This is as good as a body receipt, right?"

Connie wrote Joyce a check, and Joyce tucked the check into the pocket on her black leather pants.

"Aren't those pants hot?" Meri asked Joyce.

"Gotta look the part," Joyce said. "And nothing says bounty hunter like black leather. Toodles, ladies, I've got a date with a bad guy."

"Maybe that's my problem," Lula said when Joyce left the office. "I don't look like a bounty hunter. But hell, I'd sweat like a pig in those pants."

"I have things to do," I told everyone. "I just wanted to check in. I'll be back in an hour or so, and then we should go after Charles Chin."

Lula walked me to my car. "It was the Ranger nut who sent you those flowers, wasn't it?" she asked.

"Yes. And he left a message on my phone this morning."

"And what about the funeral home? We left out the back door, but Meri said she was there, and you fainted, and then they locked all the doors and let people out one at a time. They were checking for the Ranger nut, weren't they?"

"He got behind me in the lobby somehow. We had a short conversation, and then he stun-gunned me."

"You saw him?"

"Yes. It's strange. For a second, when you first see this guy, you think Ranger. But then when you actually look at him, you know it's not Ranger. And apparently he doesn't look like Ranger from the back or the side. Morelli and Tank weren't that far from me and they didn't pick him out."

"You be careful," Lula said. "You sure you want to go off on your own? I could ride with you."

"Thanks, but I've got RangeMan surveillance. I'll be okay."

Lula went back into the office; I locked myself into the Mini and called Morelli on my own cell phone.

"How's it going?" I asked him.

"Bob misses you."

"I bet. What's on your dance card for today?"

"I'm doing a follow-up on a gang slaying. Between the feds and RangeMan and the maverick bounty hunters, there are so many people working the Carmen Manoso murder I get lost in the crowd."

"The maverick bounty hunters are a problem. They're clutter."

"Rangerman is working to get rid of them," Morelli said, "but they're like lemmings. You push a bunch off a cliff, and there are twice as many behind them."

"I got a call from an old boyfriend this morning. I wasn't home when he called, so he left a message on the machine. And then he sent flowers to the office."

"You're not going out with him, are you?"

"I don't have any plans at the moment. If I change my mind, you'll be the first to know."

"Appreciate that," Morelli said.

"Everyone at the office thought the flowers were from you. Figured you'd done something bad."

"What about you? Did you think they were from me?"

"No. You don't send makeup flowers. You send makeup pizza and beer."

Ranger was at the dining room table, watching the computer screen. "Last night Tank noticed there were security cameras in the funeral home. Common practice to lower insurance rates. The cameras aren't monitored, they're just there to record in case a negligence claim is filed. We thought there was a chance Scrog got caught on video, so we got the cards out of the cameras last night and have been going over them."

"Does Dave know you have these cards?"

"Dave looked tired. We didn't want to disturb Dave."

"I'm surprised you didn't have to wrestle the FBI for camera access."

"They have to follow procedure. And they don't have the specialists I have."

"Cat burglars?"

"The best in the business, not behind bars. We copied the cards, and the originals are already back in the cameras. We want the FBI to have access to this." Ranger pulled a frame up and started the video rolling. "Here's our man. He comes in from the side and moves directly behind you the instant you enter the lobby. Tank is on the wrong side to see him. Morelli is behind two women who are partially blocking his view. And when Morelli can see Scrog, this is what he gets . . ." Ranger did a stop frame and isolated the man behind me. "Scrog is shorter and slimmer and is partially bald at the crown. The skin tone looks similar, but the overall appearance is very different. And he's not in black. Hard to tell from the camera angle exactly what he's wearing, but he's not dressed in SWAT clothes."

Ranger wasn't in black either. Ranger was in jeans and a washed-out, loose-fitting grey sleeveless Big Dog T-shirt. He looked comfortable in the clothes and relaxed in my apartment. His hair was growing out, curling around his ears and falling across his forehead. It was a younger, softer look for him, and it was disconcerting. I didn't know this Ranger.

"Who are you?" I asked him.

"I'm always the same person," he said. "Don't judge me by my clothes."

He hit play on the video, and I watched Scrog approach me. Scrog and I had a brief conversation, I grabbed his sleeve and opened my mouth, and in the next instant I went down and Scrog moved off and was lost in the swell of people.

"This is helpful," I said. "We know what he looks like from the back."

Ranger paused the video and pushed his chair back. "Come into the kitchen, and I'll play the message back for you."

"It was great seeing you last night," Scrog said. "I probably shouldn't have taken a chance like that, but I couldn't help myself. I wanted to get close to you. I know the police are looking for me. They don't understand why I had to rescue Julie from those people. That's okay. I'm used to being misunderstood and underestimated. Soon I'll be able to rescue you, and then we'll all be together forever. Sorry I had to stun you last night, but you were getting too excited. You would have given us away."

I instinctively moved closer to Ranger. "Listening to him makes my stomach cramp."

"So far he's textbook. Cautious at first and becoming increasingly bold . . . and careless. I want you to record a new greeting giving callers your cell phone. I don't want you to miss another opportunity to talk to him."

"He sent flowers to the office. The card read, 'Till death do us part. Not long now.'"

"We saw the delivery and already checked it out. He phoned it in and paid for it with a stolen credit card. You have to give this guy credit. He's got skills."

I recorded a greeting on the answering machine and gave my cell number.

"I should get back to work," I told Ranger. "Vinnie

is in the office today, and he's on a mission to clean up the FTAs."

"Keep in touch. And make sure you're always wearing the panic button," Ranger said. "And make sure it's hidden. If you get to talk to Scrog, I want you to push him. Tell him you like when he dresses in black bounty hunter clothes. Tell him they're sexy. Ask him if he's working, hunting anyone down. Let's try to get him out of his hiding place so he might get recognized. And ask about Julie. Tell him you're anxious to see Julie. Try to get to talk to her. Tell him you think he's lying to you, that he doesn't really have her. Now that he's made contact with you, things should move faster."

"Okey dokey," I said.

Ranger hung my bag on my shoulder and looked at me. "Are you okay with all this?"

"Actually, I feel like throwing up a lot."

"It's the doughnuts."

"It's my life."

Chapter EIGHTEEN

Lula wasn't looking happy. "Meri got a line on Lonnie Johnson," she said. "Personally, I'd rather stick a fork in my eye than go after Lonnie Johnson. I have a real bad feeling about Lonnie Johnson."

I took the file from Meri. "What have you got?"

"You told me to check on him once in a while so I ran his credit and got a hit. He applied for a car loan two days ago and gave an address."

I looked at the credit report and sucked in some air. Stark Street. Just about the worst possible address. Stark Street made Johnson's last address look like high rent.

"Were you able to do any phone verification?" I asked Meri.

"No landline given. He gave a cell, but I didn't know if you wanted me to call it. I checked the by-street address and there was no phone listed."

"Probably a rooming house at that end of Stark," Lula said. "Either that or a cardboard box on the sidewalk."

"What kind of car did he get?" I asked Meri.

"I don't know."

"Find out. And then get the temporary plate number."

"Boy, you're smart," Lula said to me. "I would never have thought to look for the car."

Mostly I was a big chicken. I was on the same page as Lula. I didn't want to go after Lonnie Johnson. He was a scary guy, and I wasn't exactly at the top of my game. I was too distracted by Edward Scrog. It was now the eighth day for Julie Martine. Eight days that she was away from her mom. Eight days that she was held captive by a psychotic killer.

I noticed Lula looking at her phone. "Expecting a call?" I asked her.

"Yeah, a certain big guy works all the time. I've been getting a lot of phone calls, but I'm not getting any action."

"You've been getting phone calls? With the big guy actually saying something on the other end?"

"Well I gotta do most of the talking, but I can hear him breathing."

"Big guy?" Connie said. "What's that about?"

"Lula's having a thing with Tank," I told her.

"Get the hell out," Connie said. "Shut up."

"It's only the beginning stages," Lula said. "But I think this could be it. I tell you, he's a hunk of burning love. He's a sex bomb. He's a big ol' honey bear."

"Who's Tank?" Meri wanted to know.

"He's Ranger's top guy," Lula said. "He watches Ranger's back, and he takes over when Ranger's away."

"So I guess he's in charge now?" Meri asked.

"Yeah, sort of," Lula said.

A black Corvette with red, orange, and green flame detailing screeched to a stop in front of the office and angled into the curb in front of Lula's Firebird.

"Here comes Vampira again," Lula said. "Wouldn't you think once a day was enough? What did we do to deserve this?"

"Connie hired her," I said.

We all glared at Connie.

"I gave her three impossible files. I didn't think we'd

ever see her again. I thought I was getting *rid* of her. And anyway, you were the one who suggested giving her the impossibles!" Connie said to me, glaring back. "I'm not taking the fall for this all by myself."

Joyce Barnhardt shoved through the front door and stood in the middle of the floor looking like something fresh out of an S&M movie. She'd improved on the black leather outfit by adding a black leather utility belt that carried a can of Mace, a stun gun, a Glock, and cuffs. Only the whip was missing.

"These two files you gave me are impossible," she said, tossing them onto Connie's desk.

"And?" Connie said.

"There are no leads. Everything hits a wall. These assholes aren't even dead. I want something else."

"Everything else is assigned," Connie said.

"Then reassign someone." Joyce looked at the Lonnie Johnson file open on Connie's desk. "I want this one. I saw this guy on the wall in the post office. This is worth something. Armed robbery. I could get my teeth into this one."

"Yeah, but you're supposed to bring them in to get rebooked, not gnaw on them," Lula said.

"Shut up, fatso."

Lula was out of her seat, and Connie and I jumped between her and Joyce.

"Take it," Connie said to Joyce. "Just get out of here!"

Joyce snatched the file and swished out of the office.

"Never mind finding the make of the car and the license number," I said to Meri.

"Boy, too bad," Lula said. "I was looking forward to going after Lonnie Johnson."

"Me too," I said. "I'm real disappointed."

Lula's phone rang. She looked at the readout, pumped her fist in the air, did a victory dance, and bustled outside to have some privacy.

"Is she really going out with Tank?" Connie wanted to know.

"Looks that way," I said.

"How did that happen?"

"I think it was fate." And Caroline Scarzolli.

"I guess we're left with Charles Chin," Meri said.

I looked at Chin's file. White-collar crime. He'd embezzled close to $15,000 while working at one of the local banks. He had a house in a nice neighborhood in North Trenton. And he hadn't shown up for his court appearance.

"He answered the phone sounding *very* drunk," Meri said.

"When did you call?"

"About an hour ago."

I grabbed my bag and stuffed the file in it. "Let's roll."

Meri looked hopeful. "Me too?"

"Yes. We shouldn't have a problem with this. We'll let Lula do her shopping."

I took the Mini and didn't bother to check for a tail. Best not to know, I thought. Meri, on the other hand, kept checking her mirror.

"Don't look," I told her.

"But what if we're followed?"

I didn't want to explain the whole process to her so I conceded. "You're right," I said. "Let me know if we're followed."

"I thought we were being followed when we first left the office but then the car disappeared."

Imagine that.

I turned onto Cherry Street and Meri read off the house numbers.

"It's on the right," she said. "The grey house with the white shutters."

I parked in front of the house and tucked my cuffs

into the back of my jeans and slipped a small canister of pepper spray into my jeans pocket.

"Just stand behind me and smile like you're friendly and let me do the talking," I told Meri.

We walked to the small front porch and rang the bell and waited. No answer. I rang again, and I heard something crash into the door. I stepped away from the door and looked in the front window. There was a man lying on the floor in front of the door.

"Try the door and see if it opens," I told Meri.

Meri turned the knob and pushed. "Nope. Locked."

I walked around to the back of the house and tried the back door. Also locked. I returned to the front and started looking for a key. Not under the mat. Not in a fake rock alongside the step. Not in the flowerpot.

"Everyone leaves a key somewhere," I said to Meri.

I felt on top of the doorjamb. Bingo. The key. The door opened a crack but wouldn't go any further. The body was in the way. I forced the door to open enough for me to get my foot in, and then I shoved the body with my foot.

We squeezed in, carefully stepping over the body. We compared the body to the picture on the bond agreement. Charles Chin, all right.

"Is he dead?" Meri wanted to know.

I bent to take a closer look. He was breathing, and he smelled like he just crawled out of a bottle.

"Drunk," I said, clapping the cuffs on him. "I love apprehending unconscious people."

We each got under an armpit and dragged Charles Chin out of his house and stuffed him into the back seat of my car. I went back to lock up and my phone rang.

"He isn't dead, is he?" Ranger asked.

"No. Drunk. Where are you?"

"I'm almost a block away. Tank was supposed to be

keeping his eye on you, but he had a nooner, so I'm filling in. Who's riding with you?"

"Meri Maisonet. She's the new BEA. No experience, but she seems okay."

I disconnected, locked up, and went back to the car.

"Now what?" Meri asked.

"Now we take him to the police station and get him checked in. If he was sober, I'd call Vinnie or Connie and try to get him rebooked while court was in session. Since he's out like a light, he's going to have to sleep it off in a cell."

It was mid-afternoon by the time we returned to the bonds office. Lula was out shopping. Melvin had gone through all the filing and was making new tabs for the file cabinets. Connie was surfing eBay. Vinnie's door was closed.

I gave Connie my body receipt. "Anything new I should know about?"

"Nope. Nothing new. All the bad guys have gone to the shore for the weekend."

"I'm heading out then. See you tomorrow."

I slid behind the wheel and called Morelli.

"What's happening?" I asked.

"Murder, mayhem. The usual stuff."

"Are you up for dinner with my parents?"

"Yeah, I'm afraid if I don't fill that seat you'll bring in the second team."

"Very funny. See you there at six."

Ranger followed me into my apartment. "My radar is humming so loud it's giving me a headache. This guy is watching you. I know he's there. And I can't get a fix on him." He removed his gun and put it on the counter next to his keys. "What do you know about Meri Maisonet?"

"Almost nothing. New to the area. Didn't show up for the interview in black leather, and didn't say she wanted to kill people, so we hired her."

"She has *cop* written all over her."

"She said her father was a cop. Connie ran her, and she seemed to check out."

Ranger punched her into his computer. "Let's see what we get."

Twenty minutes into the computer search, my phone rang. I answered on speaker phone so Ranger could hear. There was a pause, and then Scrog's voice.

"I followed you around today. I saw you make the capture. Not bad, but I could teach you some things," Scrog said.

"Like what?"

"I could teach you to shoot. I know a lot about guns. I could teach you about everything. And I don't like that you look so unprofessional. You don't look like a bounty hunter. If we're going to work together, you have to dress better. You should look like that other bounty hunter who came to the office. The one with the red hair."

"Joyce Barnhardt?"

"I don't know. The one in the black leather. She looked great. You need to dress like that from now on if you want to hook up with me."

I glanced at Ranger and caught him almost smiling.

"Maybe," I said to Scrog.

"No! You'll do as I say. We're a team. You have to do as I say."

"Okay, I'll dress like that if you will. Is that a deal?"

"Yeah. Okay. It's a deal."

"So, what are you doing these days? Have you made any captures lately?"

"I captured my daughter."

"That wasn't a capture. She probably wanted to go with you."

"Yeah, but it was tricky. I had to get her on a plane and everything."

I could hear his voice ratchet up a notch. He wanted to brag about his kidnapping success. "How did you do that?"

"You're going to love this. I drugged her, and then I wrapped her leg in one of those inflatable casts and put her in a wheelchair. Everyone thought she was drugged because she was in all this pain and flying to Jersey for special medical help. Pretty good, huh?"

"Is she there now?"

"Yeah."

"Can I talk to her?"

"I don't think that's a good idea. You have to wait until you see her."

"When do I get to see her?"

"I don't know. I have to figure a way to get you here. You're always being followed. It's starting to get on my nerves."

"I don't believe you. I bet she isn't there."

His voice ratcheted up again. "Of course she's here. Where the hell do you think she'd be?"

"I don't know. I thought maybe she ran away."

"Okay, you can talk to her, but make it quick." There was some fumbling noise, and I heard Scrog prod Julie. "Talk," he said off stage.

"Hello," I said. "Julie? Are you there?"

"Who's this?" she asked whisper-soft.

"It's Stephanie. Are you okay?"

She took a moment, and I was unable to breathe, waiting for her answer.

"Yes," she said. Her little girl voice wobbled. "Do you know my father?"

"Yes," I said. "We're friends. I work with your father."

She absorbed that for a beat. "Well, I hope you come visit before we move on again."

There was a yelp and the line went dead.

I looked over at Ranger. His face was devoid of expression, and his breathing was slow and measured. Ranger was in lockdown mode.

I didn't have a lockdown mode. Tears swarmed behind my eyes, and a large, painful undefined emotion clogged my throat. I blinked the tears away and blew out some air. "Jeez," I said.

Ranger cut his eyes to me and gave me a moment to get myself together. "You have a goal," he finally said quietly. "The goal is to rescue Julie. You have to focus on the goal. If you give yourself up to unproductive emotion, you can't focus on the goal. Let's think this through. Scrog wouldn't risk taking Julie in the car when he was following you around. So he saw you go into this building and then he returned to his hiding place. That means he's no more than twenty minutes away. And Julie said they were moving around. That might mean they're in a camper or a motor home."

"Can you run stolen property checks?" I asked Ranger.

"Yes, but the police have faster access."

I called Morelli on his cell. "Can you run a stolen property check for me? I want you to see if any campers or motor homes have been reported stolen in the last two weeks. All of New Jersey and eastern Pennsylvania."

I hung up and my phone rang again.

"I had to hang up," Scrog said. "If you stay on too long, they can trace you."

"How do you know all these things?" I asked him.

"I know everything. I'm the best bounty hunter in the world. Anyway, everybody knows about tracing.

They always talk about it on television and in the movies. I called back because I have a plan. The feds are watching you, so you have to act natural. I want you to dress like a bounty hunter so they think you're going to work all the time. And then I'm going to show you how to lose them. I want you to be in your car driving around at midnight tonight. I'll call you on your cell phone."

"Can't we do this earlier? I don't stay up that late."

"Midnight. It's so the people following you will be tired. Jesus, take a nap or something. What's your cell phone number?"

I gave him the number and he hung up.

"He's created an odd world for himself," I said to Ranger.

"If the stakes weren't so high, I'd probably think some of this was funny." Ranger returned to the computer. "You need to get some bounty hunter clothes."

"I don't know where to go to get bounty hunter clothes." I looked at my watch. "And I haven't got a lot of time. I'm supposed to be at my parents' house at six. Maybe I could wear your clothes."

"You're welcome to wear my clothes any time of the day or night, but I don't think that's what Scrog had in mind. I'll send Ella out shopping. She knows your size."

"Are you getting anything on Meri?"

"Not at first look, but I think her history feels constructed. It's too perfect. I'm going to give this to Silvio."

Chapter NINETEEN

"I made lasagna today," my mother said. "Your father wanted Italian. It's in the oven staying warm. And there's extra gravy on the stove. Maybe you can help your grandmother with the bread and salad."

"I already got the bread and the salad," Grandma said. "And I got some antipasto going. We got salami and olives and anchovies and cheese."

It was five minutes before six o'clock, and my mother was counting down. "Grated cheese? Butter? Olive oil?"

I pulled the butter and cheese out of the refrigerator and got the olive oil out of the cabinet. I set them all on the table. The red wine was already uncorked. A bottle at each end.

The front door opened, and Morelli and Bob walked in, and *bang* we were off and running for the dining room. My father was first to sit. My grandmother skidded in right behind him.

"We don't want dinner to run over," my grandmother said. "Sally's coming here at seven and we're going to rehearse."

My father was concentrating on the dish of lasagna, tuning my grandmother out. He mumbled something, and we all leaned forward to hear.

"Say again?" I said to him.

"*Gravy.*"

My mother sent the red sauce down to him, and he poured it over everything and dug in, never raising his head. At first glance the best you might say for my parents' marriage is that my mother never stabbed my father in the ass with the carving knife. If you look closer, you see they've found a lifestyle designed for the long haul. My father makes a huge effort to ignore my grandmother. My mother has a few rituals that make my father feel like he counts. And there's an underlying affection that's expressed mostly through tolerance.

Morelli filled his plate and passed on the wine.

"Working tonight?" I asked him.

"I don't think these are days when I'd want to risk impaired judgment."

I admired his work ethic, but I had no intention of following it. I *really needed* a glass of wine.

"Did you find any stolen property?" I asked him.

He pulled a file card out of his shirt pocket. "I got two hits. I have the details here for you. And the license numbers. You might not want to put too much stock in the license. If you have a smart thief, he'll swap out the plate. Should we be working harder to find these vehicles?"

"Yes, but you should be careful when approaching. I'll explain it all later."

I called Ranger and gave him the camper descriptions. I disconnected, and Morelli watched me clip the phone onto my jeans. I now had two cell phones and the panic button clamped on to my waistband.

"New phone?" he asked.

"Goes directly to the Batcave."

Morelli reached across me for the bottle of wine. "Maybe just one glass."

* * *

Grandma jumped when the doorbell rang. "That's my band!" she said, running for the door.

My father had a plate of Italian cookies in front of him and a cup of coffee. "Band?"

"You don't want to know," I told him. "Eat your cookies. Enjoy your coffee."

Sally and his crew trooped in, carrying instruments and amps.

"Man, this is so cool that we can rehearse here," Sally said. "We've been kicked out of every place else."

Lula was the last in. She was carrying a bunch of bags, and she was wearing a blond wig.

"Wait until you see what I got," she said. "It's the bomb. This is the best outfit yet. And it hasn't got any feathers."

Sally started setting up in the living room, plugging the amps in, unpacking his guitar. The other three guys were working, hauling in a drum set, keyboard, bass.

"What the heck?" my father said. "What's going on?"

"I thought Sally was coming over for dessert," my mother said. "Who are these people?"

"The *band,*" my grandmother said. "Nobody listens to me."

"Of course no one listens to you, you old bat," my father said. "I'd have to blow my brains out if I listened to you. How am I going to watch television? There's a ball game tonight. The Yankees are playing. Get these people out of my living room. Someone call the police."

We all looked at Morelli.

"Do something," my father said to Morelli.

Morelli slid his arm across the back of my chair and whispered into my ear. "Help."

"Wait a minute," my grandmother yelled. "I live here too. And this here's an important moment in my life. And you know how old I am . . . I might not have many more moments left."

Clearly that statement represented the pot of gold at the end of the rainbow for my father.

"We gotta go upstairs and get dressed," Lula said to Grandma. "And I got a wig for you too."

"Maybe you should go to the lodge," I said to my father. "I thought Thursday was pinochle night."

"It's always pinochle night at the lodge. I wanted to see the ball game tonight."

"Don't they have a television at the lodge?"

"Yeah, they got one in the bar." He looked at his coffee and cookies. "I'm not done eating."

"A bag!" I said to my mother. "For God's sake, put his cookies in a bag."

"I have to get changed," Sally said, going upstairs. "I'll only be a minute."

"*Hurry!*" I shouted to my mother. "What's holding up that bag?"

The bass player started tuning, adjusting the volume on the amp. The first sound that came out was *Wanggggggg!*

"Holy crap," my father said. "What in the beejeezus was *that*?"

"Bass," Morelli said, eyeing a cookie on my father's plate.

"I see you looking at my cookies," my father said to Morelli. "Don't even think about it. Go get your own cookies."

I poured myself another glass of wine.

"Okay," Lula shouted from the top of the stairs, "don't anybody look. Everybody close their eyes until we get into position."

"I'm not closing my eyes," my father said. "The Italian Stallion here will eat my cookies."

The drummer beat out a couple heart-thumping bars, the bass and keyboard came on at a deafening level, and the dining room chandelier jiggled and swayed on its chain. Plates danced across the dining room table.

A half-eaten cookie fell out of my father's mouth. And Bob tipped his head back and howled.

My mother ran in from the kitchen with the bag, but it was too late. Lula and Grandma and Sally were onstage in front of us. Grandma and Lula were wearing black leather hot pants and ice-cream-cone bras. Grandma looked like a soup chicken dressed up like Madonna. She was all slack skin and knobby knees and slightly bowed legs. Her blond wig was slightly askew, and her ice-cream-cone bra hung low, not from the weight of her breasts but from breast location. Gravity hadn't been kind to Grandma. Lula's body spilled out of her outfit. The hot pants were reduced to black leather camel-toes in front and what looked like a leather thong in the rear. And the ice-cream-cone bra precariously perched at the end of Lula's basketball breasts. They were in big platform heels and they had spiked leather dog collars around their necks. Sally was in a dog collar, black leather thong with a silver zipper inexplicably running the length of his package, and over-the-knee swashbuckling black leather high-heeled boots with huge platform soles.

My mother made the sign of the cross and staggered into a dining room chair. Morelli had his teeth sunk hard into his bottom lip to keep from laughing out loud. My father's face was stroke red. And Bob ran upstairs.

Lula and Grandma went into their dance routine and Morelli broke out in a sweat from the effort of maintaining composure. Grandma wobbled into an amp, snagged her heel on the cord, and fell over into the drum set, taking the bass player down with her. She was on her back, under cymbals and the bass player, with only her platform shoes showing. She looked like the Wicked Witch of the East when Dorothy's house fell on her. We all jumped up and rushed to help Grandma, except for my father, who stayed like stone in his seat, his face still red.

We got Grandma up on her feet and fixed her wig and adjusted her breasts.

"I'm okay," Grandma said. "I just caught my heel on the wire and unplugged the thingy."

Grandma bent to plug the amp back in and farted in the black leather hot pants.

"Oops," Grandma said. "Someone step on a duck?" She farted again. "Broccoli in the salad," she said. "Boy, I feel a lot better now."

I looked over at Morelli and saw that he had a cookie in his hand. "Is that my father's cookie? You're in big trouble."

"He's beyond noticing," Morelli said. "I've seen that look on people passing by horrific car crashes. Trust me, he's lost count of the cookies."

"Maybe you should turn the amp back a little," I said to Sally. "I think I heard glasses breaking in the kitchen."

My mother had her fingers curled tight into the front of my T-shirt. "You have to stop her," she said. "I'm begging you."

"Me? Why me?"

"She'll listen to you."

"If this works out I think I'll try to get a gig with the Stones," Grandma said. "I'd fit right in with them. They could use a chick in the band. I wouldn't mind going on one of them tours. And I can do that walk like Jagger. Look at me walk."

We all watched Grandma strut around like Jagger.

"She's surprisingly good," Morelli said.

My mother's eyes cut to the kitchen door, and I knew she was thinking about the booze in the cabinet by the sink.

"What do you think of this outfit?" Lula asked me. "Do you think it's too small? They didn't have my size."

"It looks painful," I told her.

"Yeah, I think I'm starting to get a hemorrhoid."

"Maybe tomorrow we can go out together and look for new costumes," I said. "It would be fun to go shopping together."

"That's a deal," Lula said. "We could have lunch and everything."

"You name it," my mother said to me. "What do you want? Pineapple upside-down cake? Chocolate cream pie? I'll make any dessert you want if you can guarantee me that your grandmother won't wear that leather outfit."

Chapter TWENTY

A low cloud cover had rolled in, obscuring moon and stars. Morelli and I walked Bob in the dark, down sidewalks I knew inch by inch from my childhood. I'd roller-skated on them, drawn chalk pictures on them, biked on them, walked to school on them, spied on boys and skinned my knees on these sidewalks. I knew the people who lived here. I knew their dogs, their secrets, their tragedies, failures, successes, and bedtimes. It was just a little past nine, and dogs were being let out for the last tinkle of the night. Televisions flickered through front windows. Air conditioners hummed.

Morelli and I were holding hands, following after Bob, who happily plodded around blocks, sniffing bushes. I'd filled Morelli in on the phone call and my midnight appointment with Scrog. Now Morelli and I were walking Bob, and I was feeling a little like a heart patient waiting to undergo surgery. Nervous. Looking forward to the end. Hoping it ends well. Anxious to get started.

I looked up from the sidewalk and realized we'd walked for an hour and come full circle. We were in front of my parents' house, still holding hands, still silent.

"Now what?" Morelli said.

"I'm going back to the apartment. Scrog wants me

dressed like a bounty hunter, and Ella went shopping for clothes for me."

"Anything I can do to help you?"

"It's Ranger's daughter. I think this is his show, and he has his whole organization behind him. And probably the FBI is involved. Ranger seems to be communicating with them at some level."

"We're all communicating with them," Morelli said.

"Just do your cop thing. Whatever it is you're supposed to do. And then do your boyfriend thing and make sure there's cold beer in your refrigerator. When this is all over, I'm going to need a few."

"When this is over and I get you back into my house, you're not going to have time for beer. I'm going to get you naked and make sure all the scary, bad thoughts are pushed out of your mind. Be careful tonight. Put the panic button someplace where it can't easily be found. I'll be around if you need me."

"I don't believe I'm in this outfit," I said to Ranger. "I feel like an idiot."

Ranger slid a black nylon-web gun belt through the loops on his jeans. "You're dressed like a real honest-to-gosh bounty hunter, babe."

I was wearing black biker boots, black leather pants that fit like skin, and a black leather vest that had a layer of Kevlar sewn into it. The pants were cut low and a swath of skin showed between pants and vest.

"Ella was optimistic about my weight," I said. "A size up would have been better."

"Not from where I'm standing," Ranger said, buckling his gun onto the belt. "But you might want to remember to sit with your back to the wall."

I felt the back of the pants. Yikes. I needed another inch of leather. "This is embarrassing," I said.

Ranger clipped *his* cell phone with earbud on one

side of my pants. "Once you start driving, you're going to have a lot more on your mind than these pants. Let's hope this works and everyone comes out healthy." He clipped *my* cell phone with earbud to the other side. "My phone is voice activated, and you can leave it on at all times. Where's the panic button?"

"Hidden."

"I'm afraid to ask."

"Good, because I don't want to say it out loud."

"If this wasn't so deadly serious and we had more time, I'd find out for myself. Go out ahead of me. Everyone's in place. I'll leave through the side door."

I took the stairs, crossed the lot, and angled into the Mini. I had a route planned out. I was going to keep it simple and drive up and down Hamilton until I got the call. Once I was in the car and out of the lot, I settled down. I had Ranger in my ear. He wasn't saying anything, but I knew he was there. Not a lot of cars on Hamilton. That made it difficult to follow and stay hidden. Ranger could do it because he had multiple cars on the job. Scrog would find it much more challenging.

I drove for fifteen minutes and was making my second pass on the bonds office when my phone rang and adrenaline shot into my system.

"I like the outfit," Scrog said. "Much better. Now as soon as you lose the people following you, we can be together. Don't worry about them. I have it figured out. Just keep following my instructions. The first thing you have to do is go to the municipal building parking lot at the corner of Main and Fifteenth Street. You're to go to the middle of the lot and wait." And the line went dead.

"I'm going to the municipal building lot at the corner of Main and Fifteenth," I told Ranger.

"That lot will be empty at this time of the night with the exception of a few maintenance workers. Take your time getting there. I'm sending someone to check it out."

Ten minutes later I was approaching the lot and Ranger came back on the phone. "There's a lone car sitting in the middle of the lot. A blue Honda Civic. We didn't want to get close to it, but it looks okay from a distance. No one in it. Probably he wants you to swap out cars."

I drove into the lot and stopped a short distance from the car Ranger had described. My phone rang.

"Good," Scrog said. "Now get out of your car and stand with your hands in the air and turn around.

"Why?"

"Just do it!"

I took Ranger's earbud out of my ear, tucked it into my pants, and got out of the Mini and stood with my hands in the air.

"What have you got clipped on to your pants?" Scrog wanted to know.

I was in the middle of an acre of blacktop, washed in the eerie glow from overhead security lights. And somewhere beyond the light Scrog sat watching me. He could see the two phones, so he was using a scope. Probably binoculars, but it could as easily be a rifle scope.

"That's my phone," I told him.

"There are two of them."

"I have a backup."

"I want you to take both phones and leave them on the ground. Then I want you to get into the Honda. The keys are in the ignition and there are instructions on the passenger seat. Follow the instructions."

I unclipped the two phones and set them on the blacktop. I got into the Honda, cranked the car over, and read the instructions. Scrog wanted me to go to the parking garage three blocks down on Main. I was to park the car on the second level, take the stairs to the street, and walk east on Dennis Street, toward the center of the city. When I got to the condo building at 375 Dennis, I was to enter through the front door and go to the elevator.

Okay, I no longer had a phone, but I had my little tracker gizmo. And probably forty people were following me. And the FBI probably had a helicopter flying around with infrared equipment keeping watch on my every move. I stuck my head out the window and looked up at the sky. No helicopter. Cheap-ass FBI.

I followed the instructions and parked on the second level of the garage. I got out of the Honda and my heartbeat picked up. It was late, and dark, and the garage was deserted. I was lucky if I didn't get mugged before I made contact with Scrog.

I took the stairs to street level and went east on Dennis. I walked a block and a half and found myself in front of the condo building. I stood there for a couple minutes, trying to give Ranger time to get into position, trying to get my feet to move forward. My feet didn't want to go into the building. For that matter, none of my other parts wanted to go into the building either. It was five stories of mid-range housing. Probably constructed in the fifties and renovated a couple years ago when it switched from apartments to condos. I was able to look through the double glass doors to the small foyer. Dimly lit. Unattended. Elevator to the right. A bank of mailboxes to the left. No Scrog.

It was in the seventies, but I'd started to sweat at my hairline. A little girl's life is at stake, I told myself. You can do this. It's important. Be brave. And if you can't be brave . . . fake it.

I took a deep breath and entered the foyer. Very quiet. No one there. I saw a piece of paper taped to the wall by the elevator. RIDE THE ELEVATOR TO THE GARAGE.

Damn. I didn't want to go to the garage. Garages were creepy at night. Anything could happen in a garage. I cracked my knuckles, got into the elevator, and pushed the button. I felt the elevator move, and I got another shot of adrenaline. I had so much adrenaline going through me I felt like my hair was on fire and I could hear a pin drop a mile away.

The doors opened, I stepped out, and a woman moved into view from behind a van. She walked toward me, and I realized it was Scrog. No wonder it was so hard to spot him. He constantly stole new cars, and he went out in drag.

I watched him come closer, and I thought he made a pretty decent woman. If I was looking at him in a car, I wouldn't guess he was a guy. It was the walk that gave him away.

"Surprised?" he asked.

I nodded. And oddly relieved. Men in dresses don't inspire terror.

"It's all about packaging," Scrog said. "Now it's time to change yours. You're going to have to get undressed."

"No way."

"There's no one here. Just you and me." He had a tote bag over his shoulder and a gun in his hand. He tossed the tote at me. "I have new clothes for you."

"What about dressing like a bounty hunter?"

"This is in case something goes wrong and someone sees you. Everyone will be looking for the bounty hunter in black leather. And not that I don't trust you, but I have to make sure you're not wearing a wire. So take your clothes off. All of them."

"You're going to have to shoot me to get these clothes off, because the only way they're coming off is if I'm dead."

Scrog thought about it. "You have to at least let me

pat you down. Turn around and put your hands on this car."

"Just don't get too friendly," I said, turning around.

Scrog moved behind me. "You're going to have to get over this modesty. We're together now."

There was a familiar sizzle, and it was lights out.

It took me a while to get smart, but I finally put it together. I was in the trunk of a car. Been there, done that. It was pitch black. I had no idea of time. The car was moving, turning corners. My hands were handcuffed behind my back. I was pretty sure I'd been stun-gunned again. I hoped I wasn't naked. I felt around with my hands and was relieved to feel clothes. Unfortunately they weren't the clothes I remembered wearing. Scrog had undressed me while I was unconscious. How icky is that?

The car stopped. The engine cut out. A car door slammed shut. And then the trunk opened, and I saw Scrog again. Still in drag in the brown wig.

"Feeling better?" he asked.

"No, I'm not feeling better. I'm feeling pissed off that you keep stun-gunning me."

"That's the reward for bad behavior. You have to learn to obey me."

He hauled me out of the trunk, and I saw that we were in a wooded area. I could hear cars in the distance, but I couldn't see lights. The road was dirt. A motor home was parked in front of us. It wasn't one of the motor homes reported stolen. It was old and partially rusted out around the rear wheels.

"Home sweet home," Scrog said.

"Where are we?"

"We're home. That's all you need to know. Get in."

I was wearing a white T-shirt and lightweight grey sweatpants. "Where are my clothes?"

"In the tote bag. Except for the little gadget you had

cleverly hidden in your . . . pants area. I thought it best to leave that behind."

I felt myself go cold and my heart stop dead in my chest for a moment. I was so cold I was chattering inside, and I thought, *This is fear.* Debilitating. Gut-clenching. Cold fear. Ranger had no way to find me.

I climbed rickety steps and wrenched the door open. It was dark inside. No electricity. I toed my way into the sweltering-hot room and stopped when I ran into something that felt like a table.

"Don't move," Scrog said. "I have a battery-powered light."

Stay calm, I told myself. At least this rattrap doesn't smell like death. Just keep thinking. Don't panic.

He switched on what looked like a small electric lantern. The light was dim, and I thought this was a good thing. Best not to look too closely at the motor home. It seemed to be composed of two rooms. I was in the living room, dining room, kitchen area. Upholstery was filthy and torn. The floor had been patched with odd pieces of linoleum. Water stains ran down walls. The Formica tabletop and kitchen countertop were riddled with cigarette burns and knife scars. A lumpy soiled pillow and threadbare blanket had been left on the bench seat behind the table.

"I figure once we get the business up and running we can get something nice, but for now this will have to do," Scrog said. There was a closed door at the end of the kitchen area. It had to lead to a small bedroom and maybe bathroom of sorts. I was hoping Julie was okay behind the door.

"Where's Julie?" I asked him. "I'm anxious to see her."

"She's in the bedroom. You can go on in. The door isn't locked."

I called ahead. "Julie? It's Stephanie. I'm coming in."

No one answered, so I pushed the door open and peered inside. Too dark to see anything.

"Do you have another lantern?" I asked Scrog.

"No," he said. "You can have this one. I have eyes like a cat. I don't need light."

He moved past me into the room and set the lantern on a small bedside built-in. Julie was huddled on the bed. Her brown hair was snarled and her eyes were huge. Her face was filthy and there were days-old tear tracks on her cheeks. I'd read a description of her when she was kidnapped, and it looked to me like she was wearing the same clothes. Maybe that was a good thing. At least he hadn't undressed her. Her feet were bare, and she was chained to the bed with an ankle shackle.

She looked at me, and then she looked at Scrog. She didn't say anything.

"It's late," Scrog said. "You girls must be tired. You need to go to sleep. Tomorrow will be a big day. Special things doing tomorrow." He reached under the bed and pulled out another length of chain with a shackle attached. "I'll just clamp this onto your ankle," he said to me, "and then I can unlock the handcuffs."

He reached for my ankle, and I kicked him in the head as hard as I could. I booted him back about three feet. He landed on his ass, and I went after him, catching him in the side with another kick. He managed to scoot away from me; he reached behind him, his hand moved toward me, and I got another jolt from the stun gun.

Chapter TWENTY-ONE

When I came around I was on my back on the grungy floor in the bedroom. My shoes and socks had been removed, and the ankle shackle was locked in place. I waited for the noise to go away in my head and for everything to stop tingling before I tried to stand.

Julie was sitting up in bed, watching me. "Good one," she said.

That knocked me over. *Good one.* Julie Martine had grit. Maybe more than me at this point. I did a head roll and shrugged off the muscle cramps that come with taking a bunch of volts and crashing to the floor.

"It was lame," I told her. "Your father would have finished him off."

"Do you mean Ranger? I don't know him real well."

"He's very special."

Julie lowered her voice. "He's going to kill him. That's what he meant by tomorrow being a big day. Chuck says he can't be whole until Ranger is dead."

"Who's Chuck?"

"That man. He wants me to call him Dad, but I won't do it. I call him Chuck. I don't think he even cares about you and me so much. I think it's Ranger he really wants."

I wasn't completely surprised. It had crossed my

mind that eventually Scrog would feel the need to eliminate Ranger.

"Chuck's crazy, isn't he?" Julie asked. "He told me he's killed people. Like he was bragging about it. Has he really killed people?"

"I think he might have."

"That's so horrible," Julie said.

"Has he treated you okay?"

"Yeah. I mean, I'm chained in here like an animal but he hasn't, you know, done anything to me. And my chain can reach to the bathroom."

The sound of snoring carried from the other room. Murder and kidnapping obviously didn't weigh on Scrog's conscience. No tossing and turning trying to sleep. No late-night pacing.

So now what? Now you suck it up and look for a way out, I told myself. You do what Ranger told you to do. Focus on the goal. Push unproductive emotion away.

I got down on my hands and knees and looked to see how the chains were fastened. "Thc bed is bolted to the floor and the chains are padlocked around the steel frame," I told Julie.

"I know. I looked. I couldn't find a way to get free."

I took the lantern and prowled the bedroom, looking for something that might be helpful, not finding anything.

"Tomorrow I'll look again when there's daylight," I said to Julie.

"There's no daylight," she said. "He's blacked out all the windows. Half the time I don't know if it's night or day."

"Rise and shine, ladies," Scrog said, throwing a couple bags onto the bed. "Breakfast is here."

I looked in one of the bags. Twinkies, Ring Dings,

Hostess pies, tiny bags of salted nuts, little boxes of raisins, candy bars. More of the same in the second bag.

"He robs convenience stores," Julie said, selecting a box of raisins.

"It's an easy hit if you get there when they're opening up," Scrog said. "Problem is, they never have a lot of money. I need more money."

"Where's the coffee?" I asked him.

"There's no coffee."

"I can't get through the morning without coffee," I told him. "Do you have any idea how nuts I'm going to be without caffeine? *I need coffee in the morning!*"

Julie made a big pretense of opening a package of peanuts, but I could see she was enjoying my show.

"Jeez, don't go all PMS on me," Scrog said. "How was I supposed to know?"

I narrowed my eyes at him. "Are you going to get me coffee?"

"No. I haven't got the time. I'm in the middle of something here. Boy, you think you're doing something nice for people and all you get is yelled at. I didn't have to rob that store, you know. I did it for you and the kid."

He went back to the living area, leaving the bedroom door open. I heard him raise a shade, and some light filtered in to the bedroom.

"What are you doing out there?" I asked him.

"I'm building a bomb."

Julie and I looked at each other, mouths open wide.

"What kind of bomb?" I asked Scrog.

"What do you mean? It's a bomb, for crissake. I got it off the Internet."

"You have a computer here?"

"No. I went to the library. They have computers you can use."

"So, what are you going to do with the bomb?"

"Shut up. I can't concentrate with you yammering.

I'm almost done. I just have to connect a couple things. Eat a goddamn doughnut or something."

"I already ate a doughnut and now I'm thirsty."

"There's water in the bathroom. And anyway, we're going out, and you can get something to drink then."

"Where are we going?"

"We're going to get money. I need more money."

Scrog came into the bedroom carrying a packet that was about four inches by four inches and maybe an inch thick and entirely wrapped in duct tape. "I'm gonna toss this onto the bed real gentle, along with the tape, and you're gonna strap it onto yourself," he said.

"Is that the bomb?"

"Yeah. It's supposed to be pretty stable," he said. "It's not supposed to go off unless I push the button."

"Not *supposed* to?"

"Hey, cut me some slack. This is my first bomb."

"I'm not strapping a bomb to myself," I said.

"Well great, then how about I shoot the kid in the foot?"

"You wouldn't do that. You wouldn't shoot your kid."

"I would if I had to. I'd shoot her in the foot, so she wouldn't die, and maybe she'd walk with a limp, but she'd get over it. It's in everyone's best interest. I need more money, and I don't trust you to just go out with me yet."

"Why do you need all this money?" I asked him.

"I got a plan. I figure now that we're together we'll escape to Australia. No one will find us there. And we can all be bounty hunters. All we have to do is lay low for a while and everybody will forget about us. Like, while we're laying low we can drive to California. Then we get on a plane and next thing, we're in Australia."

"Yeah, that's a good plan," I said. "What about passports?"

"Passports?"

"You can't move between countries without a passport."

"Are you sure? Even Australia?"

"Duh-uh," Julie whispered.

"Shit. I didn't think about passports. Okay, we'll just change the plan a little. We'll go to Mexico. Hell, we could go to Mexico in a little boat. Just sneak in after dark. Or we could probably just walk across in Texas. It would be cheaper, too. I wouldn't have to risk robbing a bank. I could keep robbing these little stores. I've already got a couple hundred saved up."

"I know how we can get some money," I told him. "There's a high-risk bond that I just got a line on. If we could capture him, my BEA fee would be around five thousand dollars. But there's a catch. If I get the money for you, you have to let us go."

Not for a single minute did I think Scrog would let us go. What I thought was that he'd use me to get the money and in the process feed his ego and fulfill his bounty hunter fantasy. I figured if he had his way, he'd come back to this piece-of-shit motor home, lure Ranger here, and then kill us all.

I was just hoping to buy some time and get us out in the open where we might be seen. Ranger was in tracking mode, sniffing the bushes like Bob on a rampage. And if I was lucky enough to make the capture, I'd have a chance to pass information on. I'd have to walk my FTA into the police station.

"Who is this guy?" Scrog wanted to know.

"Lonnie Johnson. Wanted for armed robbery. He didn't show for his court appearance. Lula and I went after him but he disappeared from the face of the earth. Then yesterday he popped back into the area. I have a new address for him."

"And he'd be worth five thousand dollars?"

"Yep."

"Maybe I should just ransom you for the money."

"Ransoming takes time. All that back-and-forth negotiating. And then the FBI gets involved. And you have to give directions for making the money drop. Anyway, I thought you wanted to be a bounty hunter."

"Is this address a sure thing?"

"I don't know. We couldn't do a phone verification. He tried to get a line of credit, and he gave an address."

"Tell me how this is gonna get us the money again."

"We make the capture. I turn him over to the police. Connie gives me the money I've earned."

"I'm a little fuzzy on the part where we turn him over to the police. You don't think I'm going to let you walk into the police station, do you?"

"That's usually the way it works."

"Boy, you must think I'm stupid. You'll go in there and blab everything."

"Okay, I have another idea. Lonnie Johnson shot a guy who was servicing an automatic teller, and Johnson walked away with $32,000 and change. I'm betting he's still got most of it. Suppose we rob Lonnie Johnson?"

"You mean we like, take him down and force him to tell us where the money is?"

"Yeah."

I knew in my heart that Lonnie Johnson pissed away every cent he stole. The fact that he was trying to get a loan to buy a car would seem to support my theory. No point bothering Scrog with this line of reasoning.

"Okay, I guess I don't see any harm in trying," Scrog said. "You're going to have to strap the bomb on though, and I swear if you do anything stupid I'll blow you to bits."

I got the bomb strapped on, and I looked over at him. "Unlock the ankle bracelet. If we go out now, we might catch him at home."

Scrog stepped back. He had the little detonator in

one hand, and he threw the key onto the bed with the other. I unlocked the shackle and skated the key back to him across the linoleum floor.

"Now you have to get dressed in your bounty hunter clothes," he said. "If I'm going to do this, I'm going to do it right. We need to look like a couple badasses."

"Sure," I said, "but you have to get dressed up too."

"Don't worry about me. I'll be dressed."

I went into the little bathroom and wriggled into the black leather pants. I took the T-shirt off and put the vest on and stepped out. "What about the bomb?" I said. "You can see I have a bomb strapped to my stomach."

Julie was on the bed behind me. "That's not all you can see," she said, giggling.

Scrog had changed into black leather pants and a black T-shirt and was wearing a black leather Sam Brown belt armed with cuffs and stun gun and Glock. It was better than the ladies' dress, but he sure as hell was no Ranger. Ranger would crack a smile at the thought of someone impersonating him in leather pants.

"Put the T-shirt on over the vest," Scrog said. "It's the best we can do right now."

I dropped the T-shirt over my head and walked ahead of Scrog, out of the motor home. I stood blinking in the bright sunlight, waiting for my eyes to adjust, trying not to get hysterical over the fact that I had a bomb strapped to my stomach.

"Jeez," Scrog said. "Now that you're out in the sun you look like the Bride of Frankenstein. Can't you do something with your hair?"

"Maybe if you'd stop running electricity through me, my hair would look better! Ever think of that? And what do you think, hair just happens? I need a roller brush. I need gel and hair spray and a hair dryer. Next time you rob something, make it a hair salon."

"Cripes, just trying to be helpful. I figured you cared about your appearance."

"If I cared about my appearance I wouldn't be wearing these butt-crack pants," I snapped back at him.

"Yeah, they're kind of small," he said. "Maybe you should lay off the doughnuts."

I thought this was a good chance to get hysterical and try to rattle Scrog.

"You have a lot of nerve," I said, all emotional. "All you brought me to eat for breakfast was cake and candy. If I'm so fat, why didn't you bring me some fruit? You didn't even bring me coffee. All I wanted was coffee. Was that so much to ask?"

And to my surprise I'd actually popped out a couple tears and gotten my nose to run a little.

"I'm sorry!" Scrog said. "Hold it down, will you? I'll get you some coffee. I swear to God, this isn't turning out like I thought." Scrog opened the trunk of the car. "Get in, and we'll go get coffee."

"I'm not getting into the trunk! I've got a bomb strapped to me," I said, hiccupping back sobs that were only half fake. "What if I roll around? And anyway, it's demeaning. How would you feel if I made *you* ride in the trunk?"

I couldn't believe I was actually saying this. *Demeaning.* How was I thinking of this crap?

"It's so you can't see where we are. It's for your own good."

I wiped my nose with the back of my hand. "It's not for my own good if I blow myself up."

"Oh man, you have to stop crying. You got mascara running all down your face."

"It's all your fault. You started it. You said I was fat."

"I didn't say you were fat. You're putting words in

my mouth. Hell, get in the car. I'm starting to think it would be a relief to go to jail."

"This is a nice car," I said, buckling myself in. "Is it new?"

"Yeah, I picked it up this morning when I went out for breakfast."

"You should steal a Lexus next time. I hear they're really comfy."

"I'll keep that in mind."

"We're coming out of the woods now, so I want you to close your eyes and put your head down so you can't see."

"Oh, for crying out loud."

"Just do it. I'm ready to blow you up just to shut you up."

I thought I'd pushed him about as far as I could, so I bent in my seat and put my head between my knees. The car swerved off the dirt road and skidded to a stop in a patch of grass.

"What the heck was that?" I yelled.

"Shoot, I'm sorry," Scrog said. "But you haven't got much leather back there when you bend over like that."

I pulled the T-shirt down. "If you were a gentleman, you wouldn't look."

"Wasn't my fault. I was just about blinded by all that white ass."

I felt my eyes bug out of my head. "Excuse me? All that white ass?"

"That didn't come out good," Scrog said. "I didn't mean it exactly that way. You're not gonna start crying again, are you?"

"Just drive. Just get the heck back on the road."

"Actually, after looking at your uh, backside, I wouldn't mind taking some time here to get better acquainted, if you know what I mean."

"Let me get this straight. You have me wired to explode and now you want to get friendly?"

"Well, yeah."

"I am so sorry to tell you that as long as I am a walking bomb I am not engaging in friendly activities. If you want to get friendly, you're going to have to take this bomb off me."

"I can't do that. Last time I wasn't careful with you, you kicked me in the head."

I wasn't sure what to say to that. First chance I got I was going to *shoot* him in the head, but I didn't want to spook him. I folded my arms across my chest and tried to look petulant. I'd never looked petulant before but it seemed like it fit the role I was playing.

"Is that *no*?" he asked.

I did an exaggerated pout. "I've said my last word on the subject."

Scrog blew out a sigh and backed the car out of the grass and onto the dirt road. "Where are we going?"

"Stark Street."

Chapter TWENTY-TWO

We were on East State Street, driving toward the center of the city, and we were looking for a Dunkin' Donuts drive-through.

"We passed a bunch of shit," Scrog said. "I don't see why it's gotta be Dunkin' Donuts."

"They make the best coffee. Everybody knows that."

"They just put a lot of cream in it," Scrog said. "All it does is clog your arteries up. And I don't ever remember seeing a Dunkin' Donuts here anyway."

"Maybe if you go to Greenwood."

"I hate to keep thinking ill of you, but I'm starting to wonder if you're making us drive around so someone sees us."

"That's silly. You drive around all the time, and you're never spotted."

"Yeah, but I'm mostly dressed up like a woman when I'm driving around. I have three different wigs, too."

"Well, I'm sure there's a drive-through on Greenwood."

"Okay, but that's the last street we're gonna try. After Greenwood we gotta go after Lonnie Johnson."

* * *

"This is it," I said to Scrog. "It's the building on the right with the door missing and the boarded-up windows on the ground floor."

"It looks deserted."

"Lots of these buildings look like this. Some are even condemned, but people still live in them. If you look at the windows on the second and third floors, you can see signs that the units are being used. A sheet tacked up for privacy. A couple empty beer bottles on the window sill."

Friday morning was a quiet time on Stark Street. Everyone was sleeping off something . . . drink, drugs, desperation. In another hour the bars would open, and the hookers would start to stake out corners. Traffic would pick up and security cages would get rolled back on local groceries, adult videos, pawnshops, hash shops, and liquor stores. And little by little the bedraggled, angry, lost souls of Stark Street would roll out of their sweat-soaked beds and make their way to cement stoops and street-side folding chairs and discarded sofas to enjoy the first smoke of this steamy summer day.

There was a new black Cadillac Escalade with temporary plates parked in the alley next to Johnson's building. So there was a slim chance Johnson was inside.

I had no idea how this would play out. I was with a man who floated in and out of varying degrees of insanity. He wanted to take over Ranger's life, but there was a corner of his brain that always knew it was a sham. He didn't mind shooting people, but I doubted he was much of a match for Lonnie Johnson. Scrog was nuts. Lonnie Johnson was *bad.* My real concern was that Johnson would unload a clip into Scrog, and Scrog would fall on the detonator, and I'd be dust.

I suspected Scrog hadn't any idea what to do next, but I didn't think he'd want me running the show, so I sat back and let him wing it. He circled the block and parked in front of Johnson's building. He sat there for a minute, and I swear I could see him calling up his Ranger personality.

"Let's do it," he finally said, and I had to look closely because the change was striking. He wasn't Ranger, but he wasn't Edward Scrog either. "Do you know which unit this guy is in?"

"No," I said. "He just gave the address."

We got out of the car and entered the building. It was dark and musty. No bulb in the overhead foyer light. The stairwell smelled like urine and fast-food burgers. Paint peeling off the wall. A dead roach, feet up, on the third step.

"You go first," Scrog said. "I want to keep an eye on you. Sniff this guy out."

It wasn't a big building. Three floors. Two units on each floor. No one in the two ground-floor apartments. The doors were missing. It looked like they were using 1B to dump garbage. A stained mattress and a bunch of fast-food wrappers on the floor in 1A. A rat as big as a beaver rustled through the wrappers.

I hurried up the stairs. Doors were closed to 2A and 2B. I listened at the doors. Spanish coming out of 2A. I didn't have Lonnie Johnson pegged as bilingual. Nothing in 2B. I knocked, and no one answered. I was losing patience. I put my boot to the door, and the door crashed open. I was totally impressed with myself. I'd never kicked a door open before.

"Nice," Scrog said. "Now go in and look around."

Someone was living there, but it was hard to tell who it was. Junkyard furniture. Mattresses on the floor. Empty beer bottles filling the sink. Didn't feel like Lonnie Johnson.

I went to floor three and did the same routine, listening at doors. A woman answered my knock on 3A. She was hollow-eyed and rail-thin. I looked beyond her to a man on a mattress. He was equally wasted. No Lonnie there. She didn't know who was across the hall. No one answered 3B, so I crashed that door open, too. The apartment was empty but neat. This felt more like Johnson. A pair of men's sneakers had been placed on the floor beside a small stack of clothes.

"If I had $32,000, I wouldn't be living in this dump," Scrog said.

"I'm not the only one after him. Someone shot up his house and then burned it down. That was when he disappeared. Something brought him back, but this is probably just a short visit before he moves on."

We went back down the stairs and out of the building. A man was walking our way, carrying a brown grocery bag. I looked him in the eye and I knew. "Lonnie Johnson?" I asked.

"Yeah?"

"We'd like to talk to you, if you wouldn't mind stepping inside."

Johnson was big. Late thirties and about 250 pounds. Lots of those pounds were fried dough and beer, but there was some muscle, too. His eyes were small and close-set and radiated mean.

"Fuck off," Johnson said.

I took two steps back and left Scrog standing face-to-face with Godzilla.

"We have a business proposition," Scrog said.

"What kinda proposition? You look like that stupid bounty hunter on television."

Scrog glanced over at me and smiled as if to say, *See? Now we look like bounty hunters!*

"We need to go upstairs to talk about it," Scrog said. "I don't want to talk about it here on the street."

I heard the staccato tap of heels on the sidewalk behind me. I turned and saw Joyce Barnhardt striding toward us.

"What the hell's going on?" she wanted to know. "This guy belongs to me. I was here first. I've had this building under surveillance since yesterday. You think I'm sitting in this shit-hole neighborhood for my health? Back off."

"I need to talk to him," Scrog said.

Joyce planted her hands on her hips and got into Scrog's face.

"And you would be, who?"

"None of your business. You can have him when I'm done."

"Yeah, right," Joyce said. "That makes me feel all warm and fucking fuzzy. Like I'm going to hand this guy over to Ms. Plumber Butt and Mini Ranger. I don't think so. Go find your own meal ticket." And she gave Scrog a hard shot to the chest, knocking him on his ass.

Scrog and Barnhardt both pulled guns. Scrog squeezed off two rounds. The first went wide of Joyce and blew out a tire on Scrog's stolen car. The second stovepiped and jammed the gun. Joyce's first shot caught Scrog in the foot, ripping off a chunk of boot. Scrog yelped and rolled. And Lonnie Johnson bolted, shoving into Joyce, sending her gun flying out of her hand, skittering halfway down the block.

Meanwhile I was furiously working at the tape that was holding the bomb to me. It was heavy-duty electrician's tape, and it was wrapped around and around my torso. Scrog had the detonator stuffed into his utility belt. I kept one eye on Scrog's hand to make sure it wasn't going for the detonator, and I clawed at the tape. Scrog had momentarily forgotten about me, more focused on Joyce and Lonnie Johnson. I had a length of the tape ripped free. One piece to go. Scrog looked over at me and went for his stun gun and not the detonator. I gave a frantic yank on the tape and the bomb broke loose and went sailing into the street.

Lonnie Johnson peeled out of the alley in his Escalade. He whipped the wheel around, put his foot to the floor, and laid down a quarter inch of rubber before he took off down Stark. His back tire ran over the bomb and there was a fireball explosion. The Escalade jumped up a couple feet and came down on its side, the undercarriage smoking.

I was now face to face with Scrog. He had the stun gun. I had a lot of rage.

"Bring it on," I said to him. "Come get me."

Scrog cut his eyes to his car. Flat tire, and the Escalade was blocking his exit. The only way he was going to get me to go with him was to stun me and drag me. And if that wasn't bad enough, his foot was bleeding where he'd been shot.

He turned to leave, and I grabbed him by the back of his shirt and took him down to the sidewalk, cracking his head on the cement. I punched him in the face and then the son of a bitch did it again.

I was struggling to get to my feet, my brain still fried, and I realized the hands helping me stand belonged to Morelli. After a moment his face came into focus. His eyes were red-rimmed and shadowed from fatigue. His shirt was soaked in sweat.

"Jeez," I said. "You look like crap."

"This is nothing. You should see Ranger. We worked through the night looking for you."

"I got zapped again."

"I heard. I was a couple blocks away, following a lead, when the call came in on the explosion and shooting. Joyce called it in. She wanted to make sure she got credit for her capture. She had Johnson cuffed to his steering wheel when we got here."

"How is he?"

"Let's just say it wasn't necessary to cuff him. And if he ever gets out of jail, he'll remember to wear a seat belt."

"You have to get to Julie before Scrog. I know where she is. He's got her in a rusted-out motor home at the end of a dirt road. The road goes off Ledger. It looks like nothing is down there. You go past an abandoned house with a tar paper roof and then it's the next left."

Morelli called it in.

"He can't have that much of a head start," I said. "Joyce shot him in the foot. And he didn't have a car. He had to steal one."

"He got a car right away. He flagged a guy down and yanked him from behind the wheel and drove off. We got a description of the car, and it's already gone out. The driver didn't say anything about Scrog's foot. He said Scrog was bleeding from the nose."

"I punched him."

"And would you know how the Escalade happened to explode?"

"I had a bomb strapped to me, and when Scrog and Joyce were arguing I managed to work the bomb loose, and when it ripped free it flew into the street, and Johnson accidentally ran over it."

"You had a bomb strapped to you," Morelli said, sounding a little dazed.

"Scrog made it. It was only supposed to go off when he pushed the detonator, but obviously getting run over by an SUV could do it too."

"You had a bomb strapped to you," Morelli repeated.

"Yeah. It was really scary at first, but terror is a strange thing. It's such a strong emotion it can't sustain itself. After a while a numbness sets in, and the terror starts to feel normal. And that's a good thing because it allows you to function."

Morelli hugged me against him. "I need a new girlfriend. I need someone who doesn't wear bombs."

"You're squeezing me too tight," I said. "I can't breathe."

"I can't let go."

"Look at me. I'm okay."

"*I'm not!* I thought . . . I don't know what I thought, but I'm not sure I ever got to the numb-and-functioning stage. I've been at the terror level ever since you dropped off the radar screen." He blew out a sigh. "And where the hell did you get these pants? Half your ass is hanging out."

We slowed when we reached the entrance to the dirt road and maneuvered around the cop cars that had been first on the scene. We'd already heard the motor home was deserted, but I wanted to see with my own eyes. A uniform was ringing the area with crime scene tape. One of the first cars in was a black RangeMan SUV. No reason for Ranger to remain hidden. Everyone knew about Scrog.

Morelli and I ducked under the tape and went to the motor home. The door was open. There were blood splotches on the steps leading in. I went inside and raised the shades and pulled taped cardboard off windows. The shackles were still chained to the bed, but Julie was gone. Scrog had cleared out in a hurry. He'd left the wigs and the few pieces of clothing he possessed behind. It looked to me like he grabbed Julie and took off. Even at that, I was surprised he hadn't run into the police.

Ranger was standing hands on hips, waiting for me

when I came out of the motor home. Morelli was right. Ranger didn't look good. Our eyes met and a very, very small smile played at the corners of his mouth.

"I'm okay," I said to Ranger. "And Julie was okay when I left her this morning."

Morelli was behind me. "Find anything?" he asked Ranger.

"Scrog had a back door. The green Dodge that's parked here is the car he took on Stark Street. It looks to me like he went through the woods with Julie. If you follow the trail he left, you come to another dirt road. He probably had a car stashed there. There are fresh tire treads on the road. Tank is walking the road. I'm going to drive out and meet him."

Meri Maisonet and a guy in a dress shirt and suit pants walked toward us. I crooked an eyebrow at Ranger.

"Feds," Ranger said.

I looked at Morelli. "Did you know?"

"Yeah. I knew."

"And you didn't tell me."

"Nope," Morelli said.

I gave him a raised eyebrow that shouted *angry girlfriend.*

"Keep me in the loop," Ranger said. And he jogged to his car.

"What are you doing now?" I asked Morelli.

"This ties to my homicide. I'm going to stay here and get the crime lab started. I'll get a uniform to take you home . . . wherever that is."

"I'm going to my parents' house. My mother owes me a cake."

Chapter
TWENTY-THREE

"Where were you?" Grandma asked me. "You look like you've been on an all-night bender."

"I was working. I'm going upstairs to take a shower and change my clothes."

Here's one of the great things about going home. Whatever clothes happen to be left in my mother's care magically get cleaned and pressed. I don't leave a lot of clothes there, but whatever's in the closet is ready to go. Nothing stays left in a heap on the floor.

I stood in the shower until I ran out of hot water. I brushed my teeth three times. I fluffed my hair dry and pulled it back into a ponytail. I got dressed in jeans and a T-shirt and went downstairs in search of food.

I settled on a chunk of leftover lasagna. I took it to the table and forked into it cold. It seemed like a lot of effort to nuke it. I could see my mother trying hard not to interfere, but I knew she really wanted to heat the stupid lasagna. I dragged myself out of my chair and slid the lasagna into the microwave. My mother looked enormously relieved. Her daughter wasn't a total loser. She heated her lasagna like a civilized person. I took the warm lasagna back to the table and dug in.

My mother gave me a padded envelope. "Before I

forget, this just came for you. A young man dressed in black delivered it while you were in the shower."

"One of them RangeMan hunks," Grandma said.

I looked in the envelope and found the two cell phones I left in the parking lot, plus the keys to my Mini. I went to the living room and peered out to the street. The Mini was parked at the curb. I went back to the kitchen and finished the lasagna.

"Are you going shopping for a new band outfit today?" I asked Grandma.

"I gave up on the band," Grandma said. "I threw my back out with all that wiggling around. I had to sleep on the heating pad all night. I don't know how those rock-and-roll people do it. Some of those people are as old as me."

"Nobody's as old as you," my father yelled from the living room. "You're older than dirt."

"Yeah, but I'm pretty good for being so old," Grandma said. "I'm thinking I might be better with getting a gig as one of them piano bar singers. I could wear one of them slinky dresses with the slit up the side."

When I was done with the lasagna, I plodded upstairs to my bedroom, flopped onto the bed, and crawled under the covers. I was exhausted. I needed a couple hours of sleep before rejoining the hunt for Julie. Probably there were better-equipped people than me out there, but I'd make whatever contribution I could.

Grandma hovered over me. "Are you awake?" she asked.

"I am now."

"We're eating. I figured you'd want to know."

"I'll be down right away."

I sat on the edge of the bed and called Morelli. "Anything?"

"No. This guy is good at disappearing."

"I think part of his success is that he thinks ahead

and then he moves fast. He was already on the plane heading north before the word went out in Miami. He was out of the parking garage with me in the trunk of his car before anyone realized the panic button was left behind. And he had a car ready and waiting to make an exit from the motor home. And I'm betting he knew exactly where he wanted to go."

"Most people at this stage would just keep driving. Put as much distance as possible between point A and point B."

"He talked about going to Mexico to start a new life, but I don't think he can do that until he gets his fantasy together. I think he has to get rid of Ranger first."

"I can identify with that one," Morelli said.

I disconnected Morelli and called Ranger.

"Are you okay?" I asked him.

"I'm managing."

"Any luck?"

"It's like the earth swallowed this guy."

"He needs to eliminate you before he can move on."

"Many have tried. None have succeeded. Tell me about Julie."

"She was a little bedraggled-looking, but she seemed healthy. She's a lot like you. Brave and resilient. She said she hadn't been molested. I think women might be something Scrog needs to acquire to play his role, but I don't think he's a sexual deviant. He's constructed this weird world for himself. It's like he moves in and out of a game. And he kills people who get in his way. I think Julie will be safe with him. At least for a while."

"Do you have any idea where he might be hiding?"

"I don't think he'll go far. He gets food and spare change by robbing convenience stores. He goes out early in the morning and brings back a couple bags of candy bars and snack cakes. You might be able to do something with that. And he's going to be stalking you. Aside from that, I just don't know."

"What's your plan?"

"I don't have much of a plan. I'm at my parents' house right now, but I think I'll go back to my apartment tonight. Morelli's in his own house, and you don't need to camp out anymore. That leaves Rex all by himself."

"Are you evicting me?"

"Yes."

"We have unfinished business," Ranger said.

"We *always* have unfinished business. Just out of morbid curiosity, how would you define your role in my life?"

"I'm dessert," he said.

"Something that gives me pleasure, but isn't especially good for me?"

"Something that could never be the base of your food pyramid."

See, here's where I was in trouble. Dessert *was* the base of my food pyramid!

I was holding a bag of leftovers from my mom, and a bag of clean clothes, plus the shoulder bag I'd left in the Mini when I changed cars in the parking lot. I juggled the bags, fumbled with the key, and let myself into my dark, quiet apartment. I maneuvered into the kitchen and dumped everything on the counter.

Rex was on his wheel, running, running, running. I tapped on the case and said *hello.* It was good to be home. Good to be alone. Ranger had just very nicely uncomplicated my life. Don't count on me to be meat and potatoes, babe. Decent of him to be honest. Not that I didn't already know it. Still, it helped to have it articulated. I blew out a sigh. Who was I kidding? It didn't help at all. Any more than the attempt to come back to my apartment and normalize my life helped to erase Julie from my thoughts. Julie Martine was a dull ache in my chest. The ache was constant, and all the more painful since I had no clue how to help in her search. At least when I was bait I had some purpose. I was sidelined now, left with nothing to do but wait. I couldn't imagine what it must be like for her mom. Truly terrible.

I pulled a package of sliced turkey out of the left-over bag. Some rolls fresh from the bakery. A wedge of chocolate cake. And then . . . *sizzle*. Again. *Shit!*

I didn't have a lot of furniture. A table and four chairs in the dining room. A couch and a comfy chair in the living room. A televison on a low chest. A coffee table in front of the couch. When I came around I was in the living room, facing in such a way that I could see people entering from the little entrance foyer. I was sitting on a dining room chair, held to it by electrician's tape, my hands painfully cuffed behind the chair.

Julie was slumped in the single comfy chair. Her face was ghost-white and slack. Her eyes were drugged slits, barely open, unseeing. Her hands lay loose in her lap.

"What did you do to her?" I asked Scrog.

"She's okay. Just knocked out. I had to leave the motor home in a hurry. I didn't have time to make another bomb. Easier to zap her and give her a shot."

"How did you get in here?"

"I used a pick I bought on the Internet."

Scrog looked terrible. He had blood all over him from when I'd punched him in the nose. His eyes were black and swollen. His lip was cut. His foot was still in his shoe, and the shoe was wrapped around and around with the electrician's tape. He was sitting in the living room with me, in another of my dining room chairs, pulled to the side, out of view from the front door. He had a gun in his hand.

“I feel sick,” I whispered, head down. I was dripping drool and snot and my stomach was in a nauseous free fall. I was scared and horrified, and I'd been stun-gunned one too many times.

“Are you gonna throw up?”

“Yeah.”

He limped to the bathroom and came back with the wastebasket just in time for me to fill it with my mother's roast turkey and chocolate cake.

“That's disgusting,” he said.

“Maybe if you'd stop stun-gunning me . . .”

He limped back to the bathroom, and I heard him flush the toilet. He limped back and eased himself into his chair.

“You look like you could use some of the joy juice you gave Julie,” I said to him.

“I took some Advil.”

“Are you still going to Mexico?”

“Yeah. Maybe I'll work my way south and go to Guatemala. I think I heard they need bounty hunters there.”

If I didn't hate him so much, I might feel sorry for him. Poor stupid crazy moron.

“Why are you here?” I asked him. “Why don't you just steal a car and start driving?”

“I can't. It won't work unless I get rid of him.” He rubbed his temple with his fingertips. “Headache,” he said. “I think I might have a concussion from when I hit my head on the sidewalk. That was really bad of you. You're such a bitch. I was going to take you with me, but now I think I'll get rid of you too. I even know how I'll do it. I'll execute you. I'll put the barrel of the gun to your head and *bang*. A bullet in the brain.”

“You don't need to get rid of anyone,” I said. “It'll just slow you down. You should leave now before someone finds you.”

"I can't. Don't you understand? He's ruining it. I hate him. He's stolen my destiny. He has *my* identity."

Oh boy. "Why Ranger?" I asked.

"I was supposed to be him. The minute I saw him I knew. I was working in this dorky record store, and one day he came in with his partner and arrested some slimebag. It was like a movie. He was all dressed in black like a SWAT guy, and he just walked up to this creep and cuffed him. He was wearing a gun, but he didn't draw. He just cuffed him and marched him out. Man, it was so cool. And the more I thought about it, the more I realized something went wrong. I was supposed to be *him.* I even look like him. So I asked the guard at the door who he was, and I started finding out about him. That he was a bounty hunter and all. I figured I had to find a way to get what was mine, you know, like my identity, my destiny. Before that I was going to be a cop. I was all set. I was working part time at another mall doing security, waiting for my cop job to start. So it was lucky it all happened when it did, because I might have been a cop, and that would have been all wrong."

"Couldn't Edward Scrog be a bounty hunter?"

"I guess, but it wouldn't be right. It got mixed up somehow. I just knew I was supposed to take over. I always knew I'd have to kill him. I always knew it was just a matter of time," Scrog said. "I had to get my ducks in a row first." He squinched his eyes together. "This headache is bad. I can hardly think."

"Maybe you should lay down. Sleep it off."

"I can't. I have to be ready. He's going to come here. I can feel it. He's living here with you. All his stuff's here. I just have to kill him, and then I can get some sleep." Scrog had his head down, between his knees. "As soon as I kill him it'll all get better."

I glanced over at Julie and realized her color was

improved. She was still slack-faced and slumped in the chair, but she was watching Scrog through slitty eyes. The drug was wearing off, I thought.

It had to be maybe nine-thirty. It was true that Ranger had his computer here, but that wasn't reason enough for him to return. I'd told him he was evicted. I wasn't sure what would happen as the evening wore on and Ranger didn't show. I worried Scrog would become more erratic, more desperate.

"Ranger isn't living here anymore," I said. "He was just staying here because the police were looking for him, and he couldn't go home. Now that the police aren't looking for him he'll go back to RangeMan."

"I don't believe you. His clothes are here. His computer is here. He was staying here so I couldn't get to you." His hands were at his head again, and he was rocking with the pain. "I hate him. I hate him. And he isn't Ranger. Stop calling him that. *I'm* Ranger."

I looked over at Julie, and her eyes tracked to me. Her lids were still lowered, but her eyes were clear and focused. Julie was faking the drug.

"My hands hurt," I said to Scrog. "You have me all taped up to this chair. Why do I have to be handcuffed, too? If you'd just take the cuffs off, I'll be good. I swear."

"You broke my nose! You're a maniac. Those cuffs aren't coming off until you're cold and dead."

"It was an accident," I said. "I was—"

"Shut up!" he said, pointing the gun at me. "If you don't shut up I'll kill you now. The only reason you're alive is so you can see him die, but I'll kill you now if it's the only way to shut you up."

We all sat in silence for what seemed like a long time. Julie was slumped in her fake drug-induced slumber. I squirmed in my seat, hoping to little by little stretch out the tape. Scrog stayed vigilant in his chair, breathing heavy, cradling his gun in his lap, never letting go of the gun.

The only sound in the apartment was the occasional squeak of Rex's wheel. And then we all heard the lock tumble on my front door.

Scrog was out of his chair, moving forward toward the foyer. He flattened himself to the living room wall and took the safety off the gun. "If you say anything," he whispered to me, "I'll shoot the girl."

His face was flushed, and his eyes were feverish and crazy, and I absolutely believed him.

I saw Julie's hand clench and then release. She was fighting to stay slack in the chair.

I had my heart in my throat. I thought chances were better that Morelli would walk through the door than Ranger. Someone was going to get shot, and I was powerless to stop it.

Chapter TWENTY-FOUR

The door opened and closed. There was a moment of silence and then the soft sound of unhurried footsteps. My heart was pounding in my chest, and I didn't know what to wish. . . . Scrog was going to shoot whoever walked into the living room. He had the gun raised and ready, two-handing it for accuracy. One of the men in my life was about to be eliminated. I was sacrificing him for a little girl. A sob escaped from somewhere deep in my throat, disturbing the silence. Scrog didn't hear the sob. Scrog was concentrating on the slight rustle of clothes and scuff of shoes on carpet.

And then Ranger appeared in the living room. He was back to his SWAT uniform of black cargo pants and long-sleeved black collared shirt, rolled to the elbow. Our eyes met and there was no shock of surprise in Ranger's eyes. He had hands raised. He'd walked in knowing Scrog was here. He turned his head and looked directly at Scrog. And Scrog shot him.

I didn't know how many rounds went into Ranger. It was a blur of sound and movement. The force of the gunshot knocked him back. He crumpled to the floor and Scrog moved over him. Scrog looked at him for a moment, gun poised. "Execution time," Scrog said.

"No!" Julie shrieked, catapulting herself out of the

chair. She flew into Scrog, clawing at him, eyes wild. They went to the carpet with Julie scratching and kicking and screaming. The gun fell out of Scrog's hand. They both lunged for it. There was a shot. Scrog scrambled away from Julie. She had the gun. She aimed and fired. A bloodstain flowered on Scrog's shirt. She was about to shoot again, and the room filled with people. Trenton cops, federal agents, paramedics. Morelli.

Morelli had me up and walking around. I couldn't remember getting the cuffs removed or the tape cut away. I clung to Morelli, and I couldn't breathe. They brought oxygen to me, but I still couldn't breathe. From the corner of my eye I could see them working over Ranger. Hooking him to an IV, shouting orders, running with equipment. And I just couldn't breathe. I was crying and choking and there wasn't enough air in the room.

Morelli scooped me up and carried me outside to the hall, away from the insanity in the apartment. He was talking to me, but I couldn't hear what he was saying. He moved me flat to the wall, and they came through with Ranger. They had the elevator doors open and waiting. They rolled him past me. His eyes were closed. Oxygen mask over his mouth and nose. Shirt cut away. Blood everywhere.

Julie was running beside the stretcher, her hand clenched onto the strap holding Ranger secure. Someone tried to stop her, and she slapped him away.

"This is my father," she said. "I'm going with him."

Morelli turned to me with a small rueful smile. "The apple didn't fall far from the tree with that one."

I nodded.

"Do you want to follow them to the hospital?" Morelli asked.

I nodded again.

Morelli took me down the stairs and through the

lobby. Ranger was already on his way out of the lot when we walked through the doors. A black Range-Man SUV followed the EMS truck.

Morelli buckled me in and ran around to the driver's side. "He might be okay," Morelli said. "They'll know more when they get him into X-ray. He was wearing a vest. From what I could see he took four in the chest. One of them penetrated. Maybe not entirely. Even if it hadn't, at that close range they'd knock him out. He took two more. One in the shoulder and one sliced into his neck. It was the neck wound that produced all the blood. Sunny Raspich was working EMT, and he said he thought it looked worse than it actually was. He said it looked like a clean slice that didn't hit anything vital."

Morelli had his Kojak light on the SUV roof, but he didn't speed to the hospital. He drove sane and steady, and he kept an eye on me.

By the time we got to Hamilton I was breathing almost normally. "I'm okay," I said to Morelli. "I just had a slightly overdue panic attack back there."

"I've seen you in the middle of a lot of disasters. I've never seen you in that bad shape."

"I didn't know who was walking into my living room, but I knew it had to be you or Ranger. Scrog was hiding with his gun in his hand, and he said he'd shoot Julie if I said anything. It was like I had to choose who lived and who died. And I didn't know what to do. And then when Ranger was shot . . ."

Morelli pulled to the side and put his arm around me because tears were running down my face, dripping off my chin and soaking into my shirt.

"It wasn't your fault that Ranger got shot," Morelli said. "There were no good choices for you to make. It would all have played out the same. Except you probably saved Julie from getting shot. Ranger went in as a target. He had Tank still doing surveillance on you. When you went back to your apartment, Ranger swept the area and discovered the car Scrog had used. How he picked that car out is a miracle. It was parked two blocks away, looking like any other car in the dark. I think he's psychic sometimes. Scrog left some trace bloodstains on the seat. I would never have found them."

"I was stupid. I thought Scrog didn't want to have any more to do with me. I should have thought he'd go to my apartment and wait for Ranger."

"Sometimes it's the obvious that we miss. I remember you saying the reason Scrog succeeds is that he thinks ahead and moves fast. And that's exactly what he did. He went directly from the motor home, to the car he had hidden, to your apartment."

I had myself back under control, so Morelli put the car in gear and pulled into traffic.

"Ranger called me and said he found the car, and he thought Scrog was camped out in your apartment with you and Julie. We pulled a task force together and decided on a plan. Ranger knew Scrog wanted him, so he thought the safest way to go was to give himself up. He went in hoping he could talk to Scrog. And he knew there was a good possibility he'd get shot. He had the vest on. We had the EMT parked around the corner. Maybe Ranger was a mess inside, but he didn't show anything. He was eerily calm. I think if it was me I might have at least had to make a trip to the bathroom."

"Something became very clear to me when I was waiting to see who was going to walk into my apartment," I said to Morelli.

He looked over at me.

"I love you," I told him.

"Yeah," Morelli said. "I know. But it's nice to hear you say it. I love you, too."

What wasn't said was that I also loved Ranger, but one thing at a time, right?

Morelli parked in a small lot reserved for emergency vehicles, and we went into the ER together. The waiting room was filled with guys in black RangeMan uniforms.

"Blood donors," Morelli said.

And it was horrible, but true.

Tank was standing with an arm around Julie.

"How is he?" I asked Tank.

"Don't know. We're waiting to hear. They took him right into the OR. He was awake when he came in, so maybe that's a good sign."

"Have you called your mom?" I asked Julie.

"Yes. I just got off the phone with her. She was really happy that I was okay. Her and my dad are going to fly up here to get me. She said she wasn't putting me on a plane alone. And she told Tank he wasn't to let me out of his sight." Julie grinned. "She's a little overprotective."

I pulled Morelli to a quiet corner. "Did she kill Scrog?"

"He wasn't dead when they hauled him out. I hate to bring this up, but you don't smell great."

"I threw up."

"That would do it."

Melvin Pickle was in a state. He was sitting rigid on the faux leather couch in the bond office with his hands tightly clenched in his lap. His hair was newly cut and combed. His shoes were polished. His badly fitting clothes were clean and pressed. It was Monday, and he was scheduled for court. He was armed with a verification of employment from Connie and a letter of apology to the theater.

I was on hand to drive Melvin to court and make

sure he got through the ordeal without jumping off a bridge. I was dressed in my court outfit of black heels, a little black suit, and a white knit tank top. Melvin was first up, and with any luck we'd all be done by noon.

"Joyce got the money for capturing Lonnie Johnson, didn't she?" I asked Connie.

"It just about killed me to have to give it to her," Connie said.

Lula was on the couch next to Pickle. "She should have at least split it with you. You were the one who blew Johnson up. She would have never got him if it wasn't for you."

"And we're keeping her on?" I asked, already knowing the hideous answer.

"Damn right, we're keeping her on," Vinnie yelled from his office. "She brought in two big bonds. Count them. *Two!*"

"Life is so unfair," I said to Connie.

"I'm really nervous," Pickle said. "I don't want to go to jail."

"You won't go to jail," Lula said. "And even if you do, it won't be for real long. I mean, how much time can a little chicken-shit pervert like you get? And then when you get out, we're gonna go look for an apartment for you, so you don't have to live with your mother. Now that you got a job here, you can move out."

"We have to go," I said to Pickle. "We don't want to be late."

Connie handed me two folders. "New FTAs," she said. "Nothing exciting. A wife beater and grand theft auto."

I shoved the files into my shoulder bag. Maybe I'd look at them tomorrow. Maybe never. Maybe I needed a new job. Problem was, I'd gone that route recently, and it hadn't turned out great. But maybe I'd just lacked direction. Maybe if I had a plan this time . . . like opening a business. That could be exciting, right?

"You got that look," Lula said to me. "Like you're gonna start driving and not stop until you get to Hawaii."

I eased the Mini to the curb in front of the bonds office, and I was smiling along with Pickle.

"Ten days of community service," Pickle said for the hundredth time. "And I can do it on weekends. And probably it'll be fun. Maybe I can work at an old people's home or an animal shelter. I can't wait to tell Lula and Connie."

I was genuinely happy for Melvin Pickle. It turns out he's a nice guy. And I mean, who doesn't occasionally whack off in the multiplex? I've never tried it personally, but who am I to judge?

I dropped Pickle at the door, and I drove two blocks to Giorvichinni's Market and got some cut flowers. It was almost noon. Ranger was scheduled to leave the hospital this morning, so he should be home by now, back in his apartment at RangeMan. Morelli had taken Scrog's computer and scrapbook as evidence. I had Ranger's computer and various office machines in my trunk and back seat.

I let myself into the underground RangeMan garage and parked in one of Ranger's private spaces. I left the office equipment in the car, took the flowers and a bakery box, and stepped into the elevator. I waved at the security camera and used my passkey to get to Ranger's private floor. I keyed his apartment door open and stuck my head in and called to him.

"In my office," he said.

He was at his desk, dressed in grey sweatpants and a sleeveless grey sweatshirt. A large square bandage was taped to his neck, and his right shoulder was wrapped in heavy gauze and held tight to his body in a canvas sling. I could see his chest was wrapped in tape where the bullet had penetrated the Kevlar vest and splintered a rib.

"I'd get up," he said, "but the rib is a killer when I move."

"No need to get up," I told him. I moved some papers out of the way, sat my ass on his desk so that I was facing him, and gave him the flowers and the gift box. "I brought get-well presents."

He looked into the box. "Birthday cake?"

"I thought your food pyramid might need some cheering up."

"It says 'Happy Birthday Stanley.'"

"It also isn't your birthday, but I don't see why that should stop us from eating cake. Have you had lunch?"

"No. Ella brought a tray, but I wasn't hungry."

"Are you hungry now?"

He looked down at my bare legs and little skirt. "I'm getting there."

I slid off his desk and went to the kitchen. I prowled around and found some sandwiches and brought them in on the tray along with some forks. I set the tray on his desk and pulled a chair over for myself.

"Things are going to be pretty dull around here with only one Ranger," I said.

Ranger forked an icing rose off the cake and fed it to me. "One Ranger is all you'll ever need."

LEAN MEAN THIRTEEN

Hugs and thank-yous to my fabulous editor—
SuperJen Enderlin

Thanks to Sara Parker
for suggesting the title for this book

ONE

For the last five minutes, I'd been parked outside my cousin Vinnie's bail bonds office in my crapola car, debating whether to continue on with my day, or return to my apartment and crawl back into bed. My name is Stephanie Plum, and Sensible Stephanie wanted to go back to bed. Loco Stephanie was thinking she should get on with it.

I was about to do something I knew I shouldn't do. The signs were all there in front of me. Sick stomach. Feeling of impending disaster. Knowledge that it was illegal. And yet, I was going to forge ahead with the plan. Not that this was especially unusual. Truth is, I've been dealing with impending doom for as long as I can remember. Heck, when I was six years old I sprinkled sugar on my head, convinced myself it was pixie dust, wished myself invisible, and walked into the boys' bathroom at school. I mean, you don't know the water's over your head until you jump in, right?

The door to the bonds office opened, and Lula stuck her head out. "Are you gonna sit there all day, or what?" she yelled at me.

Lula is a black woman with a Rubenesque body and a Vegas wardrobe that's four sizes too small. She is a former 'ho, currently working as a file clerk for the office and a wheelman for me . . . when the mood strikes. Today, she was wearing big fake-fur Sasquatch boots, and her ass was packed into poison-green spandex pants. Her pink sweatshirt had *Love Goddess* spelled out in sequins across her boobs.

My wardrobe runs a lot more casual than Lula's. I was wearing jeans and a long-sleeved knit shirt from the Gap. My feet were stuffed into knock-off Ugg boots, and I was bundled into a big quilted jacket. I have naturally curly brown hair that looks okay when I wear it shoulder length. When it's short, the best you can say is that it has energy. I'd swiped on some extra mascara today, hoping to boost my bravado. I had a favor to perform that I suspected was going to come back to haunt me. I grabbed my bag, wrenched the driver's side door open, and angled myself out of the car.

It was the end of February, and there was gloom as far as the eye could see. It was almost ten A.M., but the streetlights were on, and visibility in the swirling snow was about six inches. A truck chugged past, throwing slush halfway up my leg, soaking my jeans, bringing out my trash mouth. Winter wonderland Jersey-style.

Connie Rosolli looked around her computer at me when I walked into the office. Connie is Vinnie's office manager and his first line of defense against the stream of pissed-off bondees, bookies, hookers, various bill collectors, and stiffed smut peddlers hoping to reach Vinnie's inner sanctum. Connie was a couple years older than me, a couple pounds heavier, a couple inches shorter, a couple cups bigger, and had hair a couple inches higher than mine. Connie was pretty in a kick-ass, central Jersey, third-generation Italian kind of way.

"I have three new skips," Connie said. "One of them is Simon Diggery again."

Skips are people who fail to show for a court appearance after Vinnie has bonded them out of jail.

Vinnie loses money when bondees fail to appear, so that's where I come in. I work for Vinnie as a fugitive apprehension agent, better known as bounty hunter, and my job is to find the skips and drag them back into the system.

"Don't look to me to help you out with Simon Diggery," Lula said, plunking herself down on the brown Naugahyde couch, picking up her copy of *Star* magazine. "Been there, done that. Not doing it again. No way."

"He's an easy catch," I said. "We know exactly where to find him."

"There's no 'we' gonna happen. You're on your own. I'm not freezing my sweet Jesus, sitting in some bone orchard in the dead of night, waiting for Simon Diggery to show up."

Diggery was, among other things, a professional grave robber, relieving the recently deceased of rings, watches, and the occasional Brooks Brothers suit if it was Diggery's size. Last time Diggery was in violation of his bond, Lula and I caught him hacksawing a cocktail ring off Miriam Lukach. We chased him all over the cemetery before I tackled him in front of the crematorium.

I took the three new files from Connie and shoved them into my shoulder bag. "I'm off."

"Where you going?" Lula wanted to know. "It's almost lunchtime. I don't suppose you're gonna be passing by some place I could get a meatball sub. I could use a meatball sub on a nasty day like this."

"I'm going downtown," I told her. "I need to talk to Dickie."

"Say what?" Lula was up on her feet. "Did I hear you right? Is this the Dickie that called the police on you last time you were in his office? Is this the Dickie you told to go fuck hisself? Is this the Dickie you were married to for fifteen minutes in another life?"

"Yep. That's the Dickie."

Lula grabbed her coat and scarf from the chair. "I'll ride with you. I gotta see this. Hell, I don't even care about the meatball sub anymore."

"Okay, but we're not making a scene," I said to Lula. "I need to talk to Dickie about a legal issue. This is going to be non-confrontational."

"I know that. Non-confrontational. Like two civilized people."

"Hold on. I'm going too," Connie said, getting her purse from her bottom desk drawer. "I don't want to miss this. I'll close the office for a couple hours for this one."

"I'm not making a scene," I told her.

"Sure, but I'm packin' just in case it gets ugly," Connie said.

"Me too," Lula said. "It isn't diamonds that's a girl's best friend. It's a .9mm Glock."

Connie and Lula looked at me.

"What are *you* carrying?" Connie asked.

"A brand-new can of hairspray and this lip gloss I've got on."

"It's a pretty good lip gloss," Lula said, "but it wouldn't hurt to have a piece as a backup."

Connie stuffed herself into her coat. "I can't imagine what legal problem you'd want to discuss with Dickie, but it must be a bitch to get you out in this weather."

"It's sort of personal," I said, relying on the one really decent bounty hunter skill I possessed . . . the ability to fib. "It dates back to when we were married. It has to do with . . . taxes."

We all went head-down into the cold. Connie locked the office door, and we got into Lula's red Firebird. Lula cranked the engine over, hip-hop blasted out of the CD player, and Lula motored off.

"Is Dickie still downtown?" Lula wanted to know.

"Yes, but he's in a new office. 3240 Brian Place. His firm is Petiak, Smullen, Gorvich, and Orr."

Lula cruised down Hamilton and turned onto North Broad. The wind had cut back, and it was no longer snowing, but there was still a thick cloud cover overhead. At best, the weather could now be described as grim. I was silently rehearsing my fake speech about how I needed information for an audit. And I was making promises to myself as performance incentive. I was seeing macaroni and cheese in my near future. Butterscotch Tastykakes. Onion rings. Snickers bars. Okay, so this had all the makings of a cluster fuck, but there was a Dairy Queen Oreo CheeseQuake Blizzard waiting for me somewhere.

Lula took a left at Brian and found a parking place half a block from Dickie's office building.

"I'm gonna smack you on the head if you don't stop cracking your knuckles," Lula said to me. "You gotta chill. You need some tax information, and he's gotta give it to you." Lula cut her eyes to me. "That's all there is to it, right?"

"Pretty much."

"Uh oh," Lula said. "There's more, isn't there?"

We all got out of the Firebird and stood huddled against the cold.

"Actually, I have to plant a couple bugs on him for Ranger," I told Lula. There it was, out in the open, swinging in the breeze . . . the favor from hell.

Carlos Manoso goes by the street name Ranger. He's my friend, my bounty hunter mentor, and in this case . . . my partner in crime. He's Cuban American with dark skin and dark eyes and dark brown hair recently cut short. He's half a head taller than I am, and two months older. I've seen him naked, and when I say *every* part of him is perfect you can take it to the bank. He was Special Forces, and while he's no longer military, he's still got the skills and the muscle. He owns a security company named RangeMan now. Plus, he does the high-bond skips for Vinnie. He's a hot guy, and there are strong feelings between us, but I try to keep some distance. Ranger plays by his own set of rules, and I don't have a complete copy.

"I knew it!" Lula said. "I knew this would be good."

"You need something better than taxes," Connie said. "You're going to need a diversion if you want to plant bugs."

"Yeah," Lula said. "You need us to go along with you. You need some hustle and bustle."

"How about if we say we want to start a business together," Connie said. "And we need advice on permits and partnership agreements."

"What kind of business we got?" Lula asked. "I gotta know what I'm getting into with you."

"It's not a real business," Connie said. "We're just pretending."

"I still gotta know," Lula said. "I'm not putting my good name on just any old thing."

"For crissake," Connie said, flapping her arms and stamping her feet to keep warm. "It could be anything. We could cater parties."

"Yeah, that's believable," Lula said. "On account of we're all such gourmet cooks. The only time I turn my oven on is to heat up my apartment. And Stephanie probably don't even know where her oven is."

"Okay, how about a dry cleaner, or chauffeured limos, or dog walking—or we could buy a shrimp boat?" Connie offered.

"I like the limo idea," Lula said. "We could buy a Lincoln and dress up in bad-ass uniforms. Something with some bling."

"It's okay with me," Connie said.

I nodded and pulled my scarf up over my nose. "Me too. Let's go inside. I'm freezing."

"Wait," Lula said. "We need a name. You can't have a limo company without a name."

"Lucky Limos," Connie said.

"The hell," Lula said. "I'm not joining up with a limo company's got a lame name like that."

"Then *you* name it," Connie said to Lula. "I don't give a fig what the friggin' company is called. My feet are numb."

"It should be something that reflects on us," Lula said. "Like The Bitches Limos."

"That's a stupid name. No one's going to hire a limo from a company with a name like that," Connie said.

"I know some people," Lula said.

"Lovely Limos, Lonely Limos, Loser Limos, Lumpy Limos, Looney Limos, La De Da Limos, Limos for Liars, Lampshade Limos, Landfill Limos, Leaky Limos, Lemon Limos, Long Limos, Large Limos, Lazy Limos, Loosey Goosey Limos," I said.

Connie looked at me and grimaced.

"Maybe it should be called Lula's Limos," I said.

"Yeah, that got a ring to it," Lula said.

"Then it's a deal. Lula's Limos."

"Deal," Connie said. "Get out of my way, so I can get inside and defrost."

We all pushed through the front door to Dickie's building and stood in the foyer, sopping up the sudden blast of heat. The foyer opened to a reception area, and I was relieved to see an unfamiliar face behind the desk. If anyone had recognized me from my last visit, they would have immediately called for security.

"Let me do the talking," I said to Lula.

"Sure," Lula said. "I'll be quiet as a mouse. I'll zip my lip."

I approached the desk and made an attempt at demure. "We'd like to see Mr. Orr," I told the woman.

"Do you have an appointment?"

"No," I said. "I'm terribly sorry to drop in like this, but we're starting a new business, and we need some legal advice. We were down the street looking at real estate and thought we'd take a chance that Mr. Orr might have a moment for us."

"Of course," the woman said. "Let me see if he's available. The name?"

"Capital City Limos."

"Hunh," Lula said behind me.

The woman buzzed Dickie and relayed our information. She got off the phone and smiled. "He has a few minutes between appointments. You can take the elevator to your left. Second floor."

We all moved into the elevator, and I pushed the button for the second floor.

"What was that?" Lula wanted to know. "Capital City Limos?"

"It just popped out, but it sounds classy, right?"

"Not as classy as Lula's Limos," Lula said. "I'd call Lula's Limos any day of the week over Capital City Limos. Capital City Limos sounds like it got a stick up its ass, but you'd be in for a good time in Lula's Limos."

The door opened, and we spilled out of the elevator into another reception room with another new face at the desk.

"Mr. Orr is expecting you," the woman said. "His office is at the end of the corridor."

I led the parade in a sedate march to Dickie's office. I got to his open door and rapped lightly. I peeked in and smiled. Friendly. Non-threatening.

Dickie looked up and gasped.

He'd put on a few pounds since the last time I saw him. His brown hair was thinning at the top, and he was wearing glasses. He was dressed in a white shirt, red and blue striped tie, and dark blue suit. I'd thought he was handsome when I married him, and he was still a nice-looking guy, in a corporate sort of way. But he felt soft compared to Joe Morelli and Ranger, the two men who were currently in my life. Dickie lacked the heat and raw male energy that surrounded Morelli and Ranger. And of course, I now knew Dickie was an asshole.

"No need for alarm," I said calmly. "I'm here as a client. I needed a lawyer, and I thought of you."

"Lucky me," Dickie said.

I felt my eyes involuntarily narrow and did some mental deep breathing.

"Lula and Connie and I are thinking about starting a limo service," I said to Dickie.

"You bet your ass," Lula said. "Lula's Limos."

"And?" Dickie said.

"We don't know anything about starting a business," I said. "Do we need some sort of partnership agreement? Do we need a business license? Should we incorporate?"

Dickie slid a piece of paper across his desk. "Here are the law firm rates for services."

"Wow," I said, looking at the rates. "This is a lot of money. I don't know if we can afford you."

"Again, lucky me."

I felt my blood pressure edge up a notch. I planted my hands on my hips and glared down at him. "Am I to assume you would rather not have us as clients?"

"Let me think about that for a nanosecond," Dickie said. "Yes! Last time you were in my office you tried to kill me."

"That's an exaggeration. Maim you, yes. Kill you, probably not."

"Let me give you some free advice," Dickie said.

"Keep your day jobs. The three of you in business will be a disaster, and if you last long enough to go into menopause as business partners, you'll turn into cannibals."

"Did I just get insulted?" Lula asked.

Okay, so he's a jerk, I said to myself. That doesn't change the mission. You have to keep your eye on the prize. You need to be cordial and find a way to plant the bugs. Hard to do when Dickie was in his chair behind the desk, and I was standing in front of it.

"You're probably right," I said to Dickie. I looked around and moved to the mahogany shelves that lined one wall. Law books interspersed with personal flotsam. Photographs, awards, a couple carved-wood ducks, some art glass. "You have a wonderful office," I told him. I went from photograph to photograph. A picture of Dickie with his brother. A picture of Dickie with his parents. A picture of Dickie with his grandparents. A picture of Dickie graduating from college. A picture of Dickie on some ski slope. No pictures of Dickie's ex-wife.

I'd inched my way along his wall, and I was now slightly behind him. I cleverly turned to admire the handsome desk set . . . and that was when I saw it. A picture of Dickie and Joyce Barnhardt. Dickie had his arm around Joyce, and they were laughing. And I knew it was recent because Dickie's forehead was unusually high in the photograph.

I sucked in some air and told myself to stay calm, but I could feel pressure building in my fingertips, and I worried my scalp might be on fire.

"Uh oh," Lula said, watching me.

"Is that J-J-Joyce?" I asked Dickie.

"Yeah," Dickie said. "We've reconnected. I had a thing with her a bunch of years ago, and I guess I never got over the attraction."

"I know exactly how many years ago. I caught you porking that pig on *my* dining room table fifteen minutes before I filed for divorce, you scum-sucking, dog-fucking lump of goose shit."

Joyce Barnhardt had been a fat, buck-toothed, sneaky little kid who spread rumors, picked at emotional wounds, spit on my dessert at lunchtime, and made my school years a nightmare. By the time she was twenty, the fat had all gone to the right places. She dyed her hair red, had her breasts enlarged and her lips plumped, and she set out on her chosen career of home wrecker and gold digger. Looking back on it all, I had to admit Joyce had done me a favor by being the catalyst to get me out of my marriage to Dickie. That didn't alter the fact that Joyce will never be my favorite person, though.

"That's right," Dickie said. "Now I remember. I thought I could finish up before you got home, but you came home early."

And next thing, Dickie was on the floor, my hands around his neck. He was yelling as best he could, considering I was choking him, and Lula and Connie were in the mix. By the time Lula and Connie wrestled me off him, the room was filled with clerical staff.

Dickie dragged himself up and looked at me wild-eyed. "You're all witnesses," he said to the roomful of people. "She tried to kill me. She's insane. She should be locked up in a looney bin. Call the police. Call animal control. Call my lawyer. I want a restraining order."

"You deserve Joyce," I said to Dickie. "What you *don't* deserve is this desk clock. It was a wedding present from my Aunt Tootsie." And I took the clock, turned on my heel, tipped my nose up ever so slightly, and flounced out of his office, Connie and Lula right behind me.

Dickie scrambled after us. "Give me that clock! That's *my* clock!"

Lula whipped out her Glock and pointed it at Dickie's nose. "Were you paying attention? Her Aunt Tootsie gave her that clock. Now get your little runt ass back in your office and close the door before I put a big hole in your head."

We took the stairs for fear the elevator might be too slow, barreled out the front door, and speed-walked down the block before the police could show up and haul me off to the clink. I saw the shiny black SUV parked across the street. Tinted windows. Motor running. I paused and gave the car a thumbs-up, and the lights flashed at me. Ranger was listening to the bugs I'd just left in Dickie's pockets.

We rammed ourselves into Lula's Firebird, and Lula rocketed the car away from the curb.

"I swear, I thought you were gonna burst into flames when you saw that picture of Dickhead and Joyce," Lula said. "It was like you had those glowing demon eyes you see in horror movies. I thought your head was gonna rotate."

"Yeah, but then a calm came over me," I said. "And I saw I had a chance to plant the bugs in Dickie's pockets."

"The calm must have come while you were squeezing his neck and banging his head against the floor," Connie said.

I blew out a sigh. "Yep. That was about the time."

We had food spread all over Connie's desk. Meatball subs in wax paper wrappers, a big tub of coleslaw, potato chips, pickles, and diet sodas.

"This was a good idea," I said to Lula. "I was starved."

"Guess going apeshit makes you hungry," Lula said. "What's up next?"

"I thought I'd do some phone work on Simon Diggery. Maybe I can get a lead on him that'll take me someplace other than a graveyard."

Diggery was a wiry little guy in his early fifties. His brown hair was shot with gray and tied back in a ponytail. His skin looked like old leather. And he had arms like Popeye from years of hauling dirt. Most often, he worked alone, but on occasion he could be seen walking the streets at two in the morning with his brother Melvin, shovels on their shoulders like Army rifles.

"You're not going to get anywhere with phone calls," Lula said. "Those Diggerys are wily."

I pulled a previous file on Diggery and copied phone numbers and places of employment. In the past, Diggery had delivered pizzas, bagged groceries, pumped gas, and cleaned kennel cages.

"It's a place to start," I said to Lula. "Better than knocking on their doors."

The Diggerys all lived together in a raggedy doublewide in Bordentown. Simon, Melvin, Melvin's wife, Melvin's six kids, Melvin's pet python, and Uncle Bill Diggery. If you knocked on the door to the doublewide, you'd only find the python. The Diggerys were like feral cats. They scattered into the woods behind their home the minute a car stopped in the driveway.

When the weather was especially bad and the ground was frozen, grave robbing was slow work and Simon would sometimes take odd jobs. I was hoping to catch him at one of those jobs. Since the jobs were random, the only way to learn of them was to trick a family member or neighbor into giving Simon up.

"What's the charge this time?" Lula asked.

I paged through the file. "Drunk and disorderly, destruction of private property, attempted assault."

Everyone knew Diggery was Trenton's premier grave robber, but his arrests were seldom associated with desecration of the dead. He was most often arrested for disorderly conduct and assault. When Simon Diggery got drunk, he swung a mean shovel.

I gathered my information together and stuffed it into my bag along with the clock. "I'm working at home for the rest of the day."

"I feel like working at home until July," Lula said. "I'm fed up with this weather."

I'd just gotten into my car when my mom called on my cell.

"Where are you?" she wanted to know. "Are you at the bail bonds office?"

"I was just leaving."

"I was wondering if you would stop at Giovichinni's for me on your way home. Your father is out in the taxi all day, and my car won't start. I think I need a new battery. I want a half-pound of liverwurst, a half-pound of ham, a half-pound of olive loaf, and a half-pound of turkey. Then you can get me some Swiss cheese and some good rye. And a rump roast. And get an Entenmann's. Your grandmother likes the raspberry coffee cake."

"Sure," I said. "I'm on my way."

The bail bonds office sits with its back to downtown Trenton and its front to a small ethnic neighborhood known as the Burg. I was born and raised in the Burg, and while I now live outside Burg limits, I'm still tethered to it by family and history. Once a Burgerbit, always a Burgerbit. Giovichinni's is a small family-owned deli a short distance down on Hamilton, and it's the Burg deli of choice. It's also a hotbed of gossip, and I was certain news of my rampage was circulating through every corner of the Burg, including Giovichinni's.

I was currently driving a burgundy Crown Vic that used to be a cop car. I'd needed a car fast, and this was the only car I could afford at Crazy Iggy's Used Car

Emporium. I promised myself the Vic was temporary, put it in gear, and motored to Giovichinni's.

I hurried through the store, head down, all business, hoping no one would mention Dickie. I walked away from the butcher unscathed, rushed past Mrs. Landau and Mrs. Ruiz without saying hello, and I stood in line at the checkout behind Mrs. Martinelli. Thank goodness, she didn't speak English. I looked past Mrs. Martinelli and knew my luck had run out. Lucy Giovichinni was at the register.

"I hear you trashed your ex's office this morning," Lucy said, checking my groceries. "Is it true you threatened to kill him?"

"No! I was there with Lula and Connie. We had some legal issues we wanted to run by him. Honestly, I don't know how these rumors get started."

And this was only the beginning. I could see it coming. This was going to turn into a disaster of biblical proportions.

I carried my bags to the Vic, loaded them into the trunk along with Aunt Tootsie's desk clock, and got behind the wheel. By the time I reached my parents' house, sleet was slanting onto the windshield. I parked in the driveway and dragged the bags to the front door, where my Grandma Mazur was waiting.

Grandma Mazur came to live with my parents when my Grandpa Mazur bypassed the FDA and took his trans-fat needs to a higher authority.

"Did you get the coffee cake?" Grandma asked.

"Yep. I got the coffee cake." I slid past her and carried everything to the kitchen, where my mother was ironing.

"How long has she been ironing?" I asked Grandma.

"She's been at it for about twenty minutes. Ever since the call came in about you sending Dickie to the hospital and then eluding the police."

My mother ironed when she was stressed. Sometimes she ironed the same shirt for hours.

"I didn't send Dickie to the hospital. And there were no police involved." At least none that I ran across. "Lula and Connie and I went to Dickie for some legal advice and somehow these rumors got started."

My mother stopped ironing and set the iron on end. "I never hear rumors about Miriam Zowicki's daughter, or Esther Marchese's daughter, or Elaine Rosenbach's daughter. Why are there always rumors about *my* daughter?"

I cut myself a slice of coffee cake, wolfed it down, and crammed my hands into my jeans pockets to keep from eating the whole cake.

Grandma was stowing the food in the fridge. "Stephanie and me are just colorful people, so we get talked about a lot. Look at all the crazy things they say about me. I swear, people will say anything."

My mother and I exchanged glances because almost everything crazy that was said about Grandma Mazur was true. If a mortuary viewing was closed casket, she pried the lid open to take a peek. She sneaked out to Chippendales performances when the road show hit town. She drove like a maniac until she finally lost her license. And she punched Morelli's Grandma Bella in the nose last year when Bella threatened to put the curse on me.

"Would you like a sandwich?" my mother asked. "Can you stay for dinner?"

"Nope. Gotta go. I have phone work to do."

Joe Morelli is my off-again, on-again boyfriend. Patience has never been his strong suit, but he's settled into a waiting game while we both struggle with commitment issues. He's six feet of hard muscle and Italian libido. His hair is currently longer than he would prefer, more out of laziness than fashion choice. He's a plainclothes Trenton cop who tolerates my job and my association with Ranger, but would prefer I go a safer route . . . like working as a human cannonball. Morelli owns a little fixer-upper house not far from my parents, but he sleeps over when all the planets are lined up correctly. For almost two weeks now, the planets have been misaligned, but it looked like today was about to improve because Morelli's SUV was parked in the lot next to my apartment building.

I pulled up next to Morelli's car and cut the Vic's engine. I looked up at my windows and saw that lights were on. I live on the second floor of a no-frills three-story brick building on the edge of Trenton. My unit overlooks the parking lot, and that's fine by me. I can amuse myself watching the seniors smash into each other trying to park.

I grabbed my shoulder bag with my failure to appear files, and hurried into the building. I took the elevator, swung my ass down the second-floor hall, opened the door to my apartment, and stood looking at Morelli. He'd left his boots in my small foyer, and he was at the stove, stirring a pot of spaghetti sauce. He was head-to-toe gorgeous male in thick gray socks and a faded Blue Claws T-shirt that hung loose over his jeans. He had a large spoon in one hand and a glass of red wine in the other. His big, goofy, orange dog, Bob, was at his feet. Morelli smiled and put the spoon and the glass down when he saw me.

"You're home early," he said. "I thought I'd surprise you with dinner. This feels like a spaghetti night."

Who would have thought Joe Morelli, the scourge of the Burg, the bad boy every girl wanted and every mother feared, would grow up and get domesticated?

I went to his side and looked into the pot. "Smells wonderful. Do I see hot sausages in there?"

"Yep. From Giovichinni's. And fresh basil and green peppers and oregano. Only a little garlic since I have big plans for tonight."

My hamster, Rex, lives in an aquarium on the kitchen counter. Rex likes to snooze in his soup can during the day, but Morelli had fed Rex some green pepper, and he was out of his can, busy stuffing the pepper pieces into his cheeks.

I tapped on the side of the cage by way of saying hello, and sipped some of Morelli's wine.

"You look good with a spoon in your hand," I said to Morelli.

"I'm gender secure. I can cook. Especially if it's man food. I draw the line at folding laundry." He draped an arm across my shoulders, and nuzzled my neck. "You feel cold, and I'm feeling very warm. I could share some of my heat with you."

"What about the sauce?"

"Needs to simmer for a couple more hours. I don't have that problem. I've been simmering for days."

TWO

I rolled out of bed a little after eight A.M. and went to the window. Not snowing or sleeting, but not great weather either. Gray skies, and it looked cold. Morelli was gone. He'd caught a double homicide at ten last night and never returned. Bob had stayed with me, and Bob was now pacing between my bedroom and the front door.

I pulled on some sweats, stuffed my feet into my boots, grabbed my coat, and hooked Bob up to his leash.

"Okay, big guy," I said to Bob. "Let's make tracks."

We walked around a couple blocks until Bob was empty, and then we went back to my apartment for breakfast. I made coffee, and while the coffee brewed, Bob and I ate the cold spaghetti.

I dropped a couple noodles into Rex's food dish, and gave him fresh water. There was some upheaval in the wood chips in front of the soup can, Rex's nose poked through and did some twitching, and Rex emerged. He scurried to his food dish, packed the noodles into his cheeks, and scurried back to his soup can. This is pretty much the extent of my relationship with Rex. Still, he was a heartbeat in the apartment, and I loved him.

I carried my coffee into the bathroom and took a long, hot shower. I blasted my hair with the hair dryer and swiped some mascara on my lashes. I got dressed in a sweater and jeans and boots, and took the phone and my paperwork into the dining room. I was working my way through Diggery's neighbors and a second cup of coffee when I heard the lock tumble on my front door.

Morelli strolled into the kitchen and poured himself a cup of coffee. "I have news."

"Good news or bad news?"

"Hard to tell," Morelli said. "I guess it depends on your point of view. Dickie Orr is missing."

"And?"

"Forced entry on his front door. Blood on the floor. Two bullets extracted from his living room wall. Skid marks on the wood floor in the foyer as if something had been dragged across it."

"Get out!"

"Police responded when his neighbors called saying they heard shots. Chip Burlew and Barrelhead Baker were the first on the scene. They got there a few minutes before midnight. Front door open. No Dickie. And it gets better. Marty Gobel caught the case, and when he talked to Dickie's office first thing this morning, everyone fingered you."

"Why would they do that?"

"Possibly because you went gonzo on him yesterday?"

"Oh yeah. I forgot."

"What was that about?"

"Lula and Connie and I wanted to get some legal advice, and I sort of lost it when I saw a picture of Dickie and Joyce Barnhardt. He had it on his desk."

"I thought you were over Dickie."

"Turns out there was some hostility left."

And now Dickie might be dead, and I wasn't sure *what* I felt. It seemed mean-spirited to be happy, but I wasn't experiencing a lot of remorse. The best I could manage on short notice was that there would be a hole in my life where Dickie used to reside. But then, maybe not. Maybe there wasn't even much of a hole.

Morelli sipped his coffee. He was wearing a gray sweatshirt under a navy jacket, and his black hair curled over his ears and fell across his forehead. I had a flashback of him in bed when his hair was damp against the nape of his neck, and his eyes were dilated black and focused on me.

"Good thing I have an alibi," I said.

"And that would be what?"

"You were here."

"I left at ten to take the murders in the Berringer Building."

Uh oh. "Do you think I killed Dickie?" I asked Morelli.

"No. You were naked and satisfied when I left. I can't see you leaving that mellow state and going off to Dickie's house."

"Let me analyze this a little," I said to Morelli. "Your expertise in bed is my alibi."

"Pretty much."

"Do you think that will hold up in a court of law?"

"No, but it'll look good for me in the tabloids."

"And if it wasn't for all that good sex and spaghetti, you'd think I was capable of killing Dickie?"

"Cupcake, I think you're capable of most anything."

Morelli was grinning, and I knew he was playing with me, but there was some truth in what he was saying as well.

"I have limits," I told him.

He slipped an arm around my waist and kissed my neck. "Fortunately, not too many."

Okay, so probably I should tell Morelli about Ranger and the bugging, but things were going so well I hated to put a fly in the ointment. If I tell Morelli about the bugging, he'll do his Italian thing, yelling at me and waving his arms and forbidding me to work with Ranger. Then, since I'm of Hungarian descent on my mother's side, I'll have to do my Hungarian thing and glare at him, hands on hips, and tell him I'll work with whoever I damn well want. Then he'll stomp out of my apartment, and I won't see him for a week, during which time we'll both be upset.

"Are you staying for a while?" I asked Morelli.

"No. I need to talk to someone in Hamilton Township about the Berringer murders. I was passing by and thought you'd want to know about Dickie." Morelli looked over my shoulder at the open file. "Diggery again? What's he done this time?"

"Got drunk and trashed a bar on Ninth Street with his shovel. Smashed about two thousand dollars' worth of booze and glassware, and chased the bartender down the street."

"You aren't spending the night in the cemetery, are you?"

"Wasn't planning on it. The ground is frozen. Diggery will wait until someone new is planted and the digging is easier. I checked the obits. No one was buried yesterday, and there aren't any funerals today. Is there a specific reason you're interested, or are you just making conversation?"

"I was thinking about the leftover spaghetti."

"Bob and I ate it for breakfast."

"In that case, I'll bring dinner," Morelli said. "Do you have a preference? Chinese? Pizza? Fried chicken?"

"Surprise me."

Morelli set his cup on the dining room table and kissed the top of my head. "Gotta go. I'll take Bob with me."

And Morelli and Bob were gone.

I dialed Lula. "I'm not having any luck getting information out of Diggery's relatives. I'm going to take a ride over there and look around for myself. Do you want to ride along?"

"Hell no. Last time we were in his shit-hole trailer, you opened a closet door and a twenty-foot snake fell out."

"You can stay in the car. That way, if the snake gets me, and you don't see me after an hour's gone by, you can call to have someone haul my cold dead body out of the house."

"As long as I don't have to get out of the car."

"I'll pick you up in a half hour."

I gathered my files together, turned my computer off, and called Ranger.

"Yo," Ranger said.

"Yo yourself. Dickie's disappeared."

"That's what I hear."

"I have a few questions."

"It wouldn't be smart to answer those questions on the phone," Ranger said.

"I'm going out with Lula this morning to look for Diggery, but maybe we can get together this afternoon."

"Keep your eyes open for the snake."

And Ranger disconnected.

I bundled myself up in my big quilted coat, scarf, and gloves, took the elevator to the lobby, and pushed out into the cold. I walked to the burgundy Crown Vic and gave it a kick to the driver's side door with my boot.

"I hate you," I said to the car.

I got in, cranked the engine over, and drove to the office.

Lula came out when I drove up. She wrenched the passenger side door open and looked in at me. "What the heck is this?"

"A Crown Vic."

"I know it's a Crown Vic. Everybody knows a Crown Vic. What are you doing driving one? Three days ago, you were driving an Escape."

"A tree fell on it. It was totaled."

"Must have been a big tree."

"Are you going to get in?"

"I'm weighing the consequences. People see me in this, they think I'm arrested . . . again. It's gonna be damaging to my good reputation. Even without that, it'll be humiliating. Hard enough being hot without overcoming a humiliating automotive experience. I got a image to think about."

"We could use your car."

"Yeah, but suppose by some miracle you catch Diggery? I'm not putting his moldy ass in my Firebird."

"Well, I'm not driving to Bordentown in this POS all by myself. I'll buy you lunch if you'll get in the car."

Lula slid onto the passenger seat and buckled up. "I got a craving for a Cluck Burger Deluxe today. And a large fries. And maybe one of them Clucky Apple Pies."

I had sixteen dollars and fifty-seven cents in my purse, and it had to last me until I brought in a skip and got a new infusion of money. Two-fifty for a Cluck Burger Deluxe. A dollar-fifty for fries. Another dollar for the pie. Then she'd need a drink. And I'd get a bargain-meal cheeseburger for ninety-nine cents. That would give me ten dollars left for an emergency. Good thing Morelli was bringing dinner.

I took Hamilton to Broad and headed south. I thought I was hearing a strange grinding sound coming from under the hood, so I turned the radio up.

"You're not gonna guess what Connie picked up on the police band this morning," Lula said. "Dickie's missing, and it don't look good. There was blood and bullets all over the place. Hope you got a alibi."

"I was with Morelli." Earlier in the evening.

"Don't come much better than that," Lula said.

"Did you hear if they have any suspects?"

"You mean besides you?"

"Yeah."

"Nope. You're it, so far as I could tell." Lula cut her eyes to me. "I don't suppose it was you."

"No."

"Okay, so it wasn't you directly, but it might have had something to do with the bugs you put on him."

"You didn't just say that. And you're never going to say that again," I said to Lula. "In fact, yesterday you didn't see or hear *anything* about bugs."

"I must have hallucinated it."

"Exactly."

"My lips are sealed."

I turned off South Broad and took Route 206 to Groveville Road. I crossed the railroad tracks and started looking for the road that led to Diggery's house.

"This don't look familiar," Lula said.

"That's because we were here in the summer last time."

"I think it's 'cause we're in the wrong place. You should have MapQuested this," Lula said. "I always MapQuest."

"We're not in the wrong place. We just missed a road."

"Do you know the name of the road?"

"No."

"See, you needed to MapQuest."

A rusted-out pickup blew past us. It had a gun rack across the back window, a Grateful Dead sticker on the bumper, and a rebel flag flying from the antenna. It looked to me like it belonged in Diggery's neighborhood, so I hung a U-turn and kept it in sight, leaving Groveville Road for a winding two-lane road strewn with potholes.

"This looks more like it," Lula said, watching the countryside fly by. "I remember some of these pathetic excuses for a house."

We passed a shanty constructed of tar paper and particleboard, eased around a bend in the road, and Diggery's trailer was to the left, set back about fifty feet. I continued driving until I was out of sight of the trailer. I turned around, cruised past Diggery's again, and parked just beyond the bend. If Diggery saw me parking in front of his house, he'd be halfway to Newark by the time I got out of my car.

"I don't think anybody's home," Lula said. "I didn't see any cars in the yard."

"I'm going to snoop around anyway. Are you coming?"

"I suppose, but if I see that snake, I'm outta there. I *hate* snakes. I don't care if that snake wraps itself around your neck, I'm telling you right now, I'm not staying to help."

Diggery lived on a sad patch of parched and frozen hardscrabble. His double-wide trailer had rust stains running from top to bottom, with cankerous rot eating at the trailer floor. The piece of junk was set a foot off the ground on cinderblocks and was held together with duct tape. Grave robbing obviously didn't pay all that well. There were hardwoods behind the trailer. No leaves at this time of year, just barren, naked stalks of trees. It was late morning, but there was little light filtering through the thick gray cloud cover.

"There's a back door on the other side," I said to Lula. "You take the back door, and I'll take the front door."

"The hell I will," Lula said. "First off, I don't want no Diggery opening that door and knocking me on my ass trying to get to the woods. And second . . . well, that's all there is. There's no second. I'm going in behind you, so I can be first out if the snake's there."

There was no answer when I knocked on the door, but then, I hadn't expected an answer. The little Diggerys were in school. The big Diggerys were probably picking through Dumpsters, looking for lunch. I pushed the door open and cautiously looked inside. I flipped a switch by the door and a forty-watt bulb blinked on in what might pass for the living room. I stepped in and listened for rustling, slithering sounds.

Lula stuck her head in and sniffed the air. "I smell snake," she said.

I didn't know what a snake smelled like, but I suspected it was a lot like a Diggery.

"Snoop around and see if you can find something that tells us where Simon is working," I said to Lula. "A pay stub, a matchbook, a map with a big orange X on it."

"We should have brought rubber gloves," Lula said. "I bet this place is covered with snake spit."

"The snake stuff is getting old," I said to her. "Could you back off from the snake stuff?"

"Just trying to be vigilant. If you don't want me reminding you to be careful, hey, okay by me. You're on your own."

Lula opened a closet door and a mop fell out at her.

"Snake!" Lula screamed. "Snake, snake, snake!" And she ran out of the trailer.

I looked out at Lula. "It was a mop."

"Are you sure? It looked like a snake to me."

"It was a mop."

"I think I wet my pants."

"Too much information," I said to her.

Lula crept back into the trailer and looked at the mop lying on the floor. "Scared the bejeezus out of me," she said.

We made our way through the living area and the kitchen. We looked through a tiny bedroom that was stacked with bunks. We opened the door to the master bedroom and there it was . . . the snake. It was curled on the bed, and it was looking at us with lazy snake eyes. It had a lump in its throat that was about the size of the family dog, or maybe a small Diggery.

I was paralyzed with fear and horror and gob-stopping fascination. My feet wouldn't move, and I could barely breathe.

"We're disturbing him," Lula whispered. "We should leave now and let him finish his breakfast."

The snake swallowed and the lump moved six inches farther down its throat.

"Oh crap," Lula whispered.

And next thing I knew, I was in my car.

"How did I get in the car?" I asked Lula.

"You let out a shriek and ran out of the trailer and all the way here. I bet I got footprints on my back where you ran over me."

I slouched in my seat and concentrated on getting my heart to stop racing. "That wasn't a snake. Snakes aren't that big, are they?"

"It was the snake from hell. It was a motherfucking mutant reptile." Lula shook her finger at me. "I told you we didn't want to go in there. You wouldn't listen."

I was still shaky enough that I had to two-hand the key to get it in the ignition. "Took me by surprise," I said.

"Yeah, me too," Lula said. "Do I get my lunch now?"

I dropped Lula at the office and looked at my watch. It was a little after one. I had more skips sitting in my bag, waiting to get found, but I was having a hard time working up enthusiasm for the whole bounty hunter thing. I decided procrastination was the way to go, so I called Morelli.

"Is there anything new on Dickie?" I asked him.

"No. As far as I know, he's still missing. Where are you?"

"I'm in my car in front of the office, and I'm trying to calm myself."

I could hear Morelli smile over the phone line. "How's the snake?"

"Big."

"Did you catch a Diggery?"

"No. Didn't even come close."

I disconnected Morelli and called Ranger.

"Can we talk?" I asked him.

"Your place or mine?"

"Yours."

"I'm parked behind you."

I looked in my rearview mirror and locked eyes with him. He was in the Porsche Cayenne.

"Sometimes you freak me out," I said to Ranger.

"Babe."

I got out of my garbage-scow Crown Vic and into Ranger's shiny, immaculate SUV.

"You involved me in a murder," I said to Ranger.

"And you have no alibi," Ranger said.

"Is there anything you don't know?"

"I don't know what happened to Dickie."

"So I guess that means you didn't snatch him?"

"I don't leave bloodstains," Ranger said.

Ranger was dressed in his usual black. Black Vibram-soled boots, black jeans, black shirt, black wool pea coat, and his black Navy SEAL ball cap. Ranger was a shadow. A mystery man. A man who had no time or desire to mix and match colors.

"Those bugs I planted on Dickie . . . what was that about?" I asked him.

"You don't want to know."

"Yes, I do."

"You *don't*."

I stared him down. "I *do*."

Ranger did what for him was a sigh. The barest whisper of expelled breath. I was being a pain in the keester.

"I'm looking for a guy named Ziggy Zabar. His brother, Zip, works for me and came to me for help when Ziggy disappeared last week. Ziggy's a CPA with a firm downtown. They prepare the tax reports for Petiak, Smullen, Gorvich, and Orr. Every Monday, the partners hold a meeting off-site, and Ziggy had the meeting on his calendar. He was seen getting into his car to go to the meeting, and then he disappeared. The four partners swear Zabar never showed up, but I don't believe it. There's something not right about the firm. Dickie has legitimate credentials and has passed the Jersey bar. His partners have law degrees from Panama. Right now, I can't tell if Dickie is dumb or dirty."

"Did the bugs work?"

"The meeting was canceled. We listened until a little after ten and packed up when Dickie went to bed."

"So you weren't listening when shots were fired."

"No, but I was in his house after the police sealed it, and it looks to me like Dickie left the house wearing the same clothes he had on all day. We've tried scanning to pick up a bug, but haven't had any luck. Either he's out of range, or the bugs have been found and destroyed."

"Now what?"

Ranger took a little plastic bag from his pocket. It contained another bug. "Do you think you can plant this on Peter Smullen?"

I felt my jaw drop and my eyebrows shoot up into my forehead. "You're not serious."

Ranger took a file off the dashboard and handed it to me. "Smullen wasn't in the office yesterday. He had a dentist appointment. So he shouldn't recognize you.

Here are a couple pictures of Smullen, a short bio, plus our best guess at what his schedule will be like tomorrow. He divides his time between Trenton and Bogotá. When he's in town, he's a creature of habit, so running into him won't be a problem. Try to tag him tomorrow morning, so I can listen to him all day."

"And I'm going to do this, why?"

"I'll let you wrestle with that one," Ranger said. He looked through the Cayenne windshield at my car. "Is there a reason you're driving the Vic?"

"It was cheap."

"Babe, *free* wouldn't be cheap enough."

"You haven't asked me if I killed Dickie," I said to Ranger.

"I know you didn't kill Dickie. You never left your apartment."

There was a time when I considered Ranger's surveillance an invasion of privacy, but that time was long gone. There's not much point to worrying about things you can't control, and I had no control over Ranger.

"Where is it? On my car?" I asked him, doing a pretty decent job of not sounding completely pissed off.

Ranger's mouth didn't smile, but his eyes crinkled a little at the corners. "GPS unit in your bag. Please don't remove it."

I took the file and the bug-in-a-bag and got out of the Cayenne. "I imagine you'll be watching my every move."

"Just like always," Ranger said.

I got into the Crown Vic, cranked the engine over, and turned the heat on full blast. I looked in my rearview mirror. No Ranger.

I studied the pictures of Peter Smullen. He was an average-looking guy with receding brown hair and a beer belly. Heavy five o'clock shadow in all the photos. Lips like a flounder. His file put him at five feet eight inches. Forty-six years old. Married with two kids, ages twenty and twenty-two. Both kids and the wife were in Colombia. Smullen kept a bachelor apartment in Hamilton Township. When Smullen was in town, at precisely eight A.M., he'd roll into a parking garage that was a block from his office at the law firm and get a triple-shot Frappuccino at the Starbucks on the corner.

I'd get him at the Starbucks.

I closed the file, turned to lay it on the seat next to me, and the Vic's driver's side door was suddenly wrenched open. Joyce Barnhardt glared in at me and called me the "c" word.

Joyce was six feet tall in four-inch, spike-heeled black boots. She was wearing a black leather duster lined with fake fur, her eyes were enhanced with rhinestone-studded fake eyelashes, her red enameled nails were long and frightening. The package was topped with a lot of shoulder-length brilliant red hair arranged in curls and waves. Joyce had never moved beyond Farrah Fawcett.

I narrowed my eyes at her. "Is there a point to this conversation?"

"You killed him. You found out we were a couple, and you couldn't handle it. So you killed him."

"I didn't kill him."

"I was inches from marrying the little turd, and you ruined it all. Do you have any idea how much he's worth? A fucking fortune. And you killed him, and now I get nothing. I *hate* you."

I turned the key in the ignition and put the Vic into drive. "I have to go now," I said to Joyce. "Good talk."

"I'm not done," Joyce said. "I'm just beginning. I'm going to get even. I'm going to make your life a misery." Joyce pulled a gun out of her coat pocket and aimed it at me. "I'm going to shoot out your eye. And then I'm going to shoot you in the foot, and the knee, and the ass . . ."

I stomped on the gas pedal and rocketed off with my door still open. Joyce squeezed off two rounds, putting a hole in the rear window. I looked in my mirror and got a glimpse of her standing in the middle of the road, giving me the finger. Joyce Barnhardt was nuts.

I drove one block down Hamilton and turned into the Burg. I was thinking that after the traumatic Joyce experience, I needed something to calm myself . . . like a piece of the raspberry Entenmann's. Plus, my dad had all kinds of things stashed in his cellar, like electrician's tape, that I could use to patch my rear window. Wind was whistling through the bullet hole, creating a draft on the back of my neck. It would have been perfectly okay in July, but it was damn cold in February. I wound through the maze of Burg streets to my parents' house and parked in the driveway. I got out and examined the car. Hole in the rear window, and Joyce had taken out a taillight.

I hunched against the sleet and ran to the front door. I let myself in, dropped my bag on the sideboard in the foyer, and went to the kitchen. My mother was at the sink, washing vegetables. Grandma was at the little table with a cup of tea. The Entenmann's box was on the small kitchen table. I held my breath and approached the box. I flipped the lid. Two pieces left. I anxiously looked around. "Anyone want this Entenmann's?" I asked.

"Not me," Grandma said.

"Not me either," my mother said.

I shrugged out of my jacket, hung it on the back of the chair, and sat down.

"Anything new in the world of crime?" Grandma asked.

"Same ol', same ol'," I told her. "What's new with you?"

"I'm outta that glue stuff for my dentures. I was hoping you could run me out to the drugstore."

"Sure." I wolfed down the last of the cake and scraped back in my chair. "I can take you now, but then I need to get back to work."

"I'll just go upstairs to get my purse," Grandma said.

I leaned toward her and lowered my voice. "No gun."

Grandma Mazur carried a .45 long barrel named Elsie. It wasn't registered, and she didn't have a permit to carry concealed. Grandma thought being old gave her license to pack. She called it the equalizer. My mother kept taking the gun away, and the gun kept mysteriously returning.

"I don't know what you're talking about," Grandma said.

"I've got enough problems with the police right now. I can't afford to get pulled over for a broken taillight and have them discover you're armed and dangerous."

"I never go anywhere without Elsie," Grandma said.

"What's all the whispering about?" my mother wanted to know.

"We were trying to decide if I needed to put on some fresh lipstick," Grandma said.

I looked over at her. "You don't need lipstick."

"A woman always needs lipstick."

"Your lipstick is fine."

"You're getting to be just like your mother," Grandma said.

There was a time when that statement would have freaked me out, but now I was thinking maybe it wouldn't be so bad to have some of my mother's qualities. She was a stabilizing influence on the family. She was the representative of accepted social behavior. She was the guardian of our health and security. She was the bran muffin that allowed us to be jelly doughnuts.

Grandma and I were at the front door, and I remembered the hole in the windshield. "Duct tape," I called to my mother. "Where would I find it, the garage or the cellar?"

My mother came with a roll. "I keep some in the kitchen. Are you fixing something?"

"I have a hole in my back window."

Grandma Mazur squinted at the Vic. "Looks like a bullet hole."

"Dear God," my mother said. "It's *not* a bullet hole, is it?"

"No," I told her. "Absolutely not."

Grandma Mazur buttoned herself into her long royal blue wool coat. She buckled a little under the weight but managed to right herself and get to the car.

"Isn't this the kind of car the cops use?" she asked.

"Yes."

"Does it have one of them flashing lights?"

"No."

"Bummer," Grandma said.

THREE

I followed Grandma up and down the aisles, past personal products to Metamucil, hemorrhoid remedies, hair spray, Harlequin romances, greeting cards. She got her denture glue and moved to lipsticks.

A gap-toothed, redheaded kid rounded a corner and came to a stop in front of us.

"Hi!" he yelled.

He was followed by Cynthia Hawser. Cynthia and I had been classmates. She was married now to a gap-toothed, redheaded guy who'd fathered three gap-toothed, redheaded kids. They lived a block over from Morelli in a little duplex that had more toys than grass in the front yard.

"This is Jeremy," Cynthia said to Grandma and me.

Jeremy had trouble written all over him. Jeremy just about vibrated with energy.

"What a cute little boy," Grandma said. "I bet you're real smart."

"I'm too smart for my britches," Jeremy said. "That's what most people tell me."

An old man shuffled up and looked us over. He was wearing a wavy jet-black toupee that sat slightly askew on his bald dome. He had bushy, out-of-control eyebrows, a lot of ear hair, and even more slack skin than

Grandma. I thought he looked to be on the far side of eighty.

"What's going on here?" he asked.

"This is Uncle Elmer," Cynthia said. "There was a fire in his apartment at assisted living so he came to live with us."

"It wasn't my fault," Uncle Elmer said.

"You were smoking in bed," Jeremy said. "It's lucky you didn't cream yourself."

Cynthia grimaced. "You mean *cremate*."

Uncle Elmer grinned at Grandma. "Who's this sexy young thing?"

"Aren't you the one," Grandma said to Elmer.

Elmer winked at her. "The boys at the home would love you. You look hot."

"It's the coat," Grandma said. "It's wool."

Elmer fingered the coat. "Looks like good quality. I was in retail, you know. I can tell quality."

"I've had it for a while," Grandma said. "I was taller when I first bought it. I've shrunk up some."

Elmer gave his head a small shake, and the toupee slid over one ear. He reached up and righted it. "The golden years are a bitch," Elmer said.

"You don't look like you shrunk much," Grandma said. "You're a pretty big guy."

"Well, some of me's shrunk and some of me's swollen up," Elmer said. "When I was young, I got a lot of tattoos, and now they don't look so good. One time, I got drunk and got Eisenhower tattooed on my balls, but now he looks like Orville Redenbacher."

"He makes good popcorn," Grandma said.

"You bet. And don't worry, I still got it where it counts."

"Where's that?" Grandma asked.

"In the sack. Hangs a little lower than it used to, but the equipment still works, if you know what I mean."

"Uncle Elmer poops in a bag," Jeremy said.

"It's temporary," Elmer said. "Just 'til the bypass heals up. They put some pig intestine in me on an experimental basis."

"Gee," I said, "look at the time. We have to be running along now."

"Yeah, I can't be late for dinner tonight," Grandma said. "I want to make the early viewing at the funeral parlor. Milton Buzick is laid out, and I hear you wouldn't even recognize him."

"You got a good funeral parlor here?" Elmer asked Grandma.

"I go to the one on Hamilton Avenue. It's run by two real nice young men, and they serve homemade cookies."

"I wouldn't mind some homemade cookies," Elmer said. "I could meet you there tonight. I'm looking for a lady friend, you know. Do you put out?"

Cynthia smacked Uncle Elmer on the head. "Behave yourself."

"I haven't got time," Elmer said, readjusting his hair. "I gotta know these things."

"Now what?" I asked Grandma Mazur when we'd settled ourselves in the car.

"I gotta go home, so I can get ready for tonight. That Elmer is a frisky one. He'll get snapped up fast. Myra Witkowski would snap him up in an instant if I let her."

"Remember, I'm looking for Simon Diggery. Check out Milton's jewelry for me, and let me know if he's going in the ground with anything pricey enough to get Diggery out to the cemetery on a cold night."

Morelli and Bob strolled in a little after six. Morelli shucked his boots and jacket in the foyer and dumped a grocery bag and a six-pack onto the kitchen counter.

He grabbed me, and kissed me, and cracked open a beer from the six-pack.

"I'm starving," he said. "I didn't have time for lunch."

I pulled a bunch of chili dogs and a bucket of cheese fries out of the grocery bag. I put two dogs and some fries in a bowl for Bob and unwrapped a dog for myself.

"This is what I love about you," I said to Morelli. "No vegetables."

Morelli ate some hotdog and drank some more beer. "Is that all you love about me?"

"No, but it's high on the list."

"The Berringer murders are going into the toilet. The security company didn't have film in any of the surveillance cameras. Everyone hated the two people who were killed. It was cold and overcast and there was no exterior lighting in the back of the building. No one saw anything. No one heard anything. Forced entry. Nothing stolen."

"Maybe you should hire a psychic."

"I know you're being a wiseass, but I'm about at that point."

"What's happening with Dickie? Am I still a suspect?"

"Right now, Dickie is just a missing person who disappeared under suspicious circumstances. If his body floats in on the tide, you could be in trouble. Marty Gobel is still the primary investigator, and he wants to talk to you first thing tomorrow. I gave him your cell number."

"Do you think I should use the orgasm defense?"

"Yeah, my reputation could use a boost." Morelli finished off his second hotdog and ate some fries. "I'm not on the case, but I've been poking around on my own, and I don't like Dickie's partners. I'm probably going to regret saying this, but maybe you should bring Ranger in. He can do things I can't. Ranger doesn't mind bending the law to get information. Have him take a look at the partners."

"You're worried about me."

Morelli wiped his hands on his jeans and pulled me to him, wrapping his arms around me. "Dickie was a respected lawyer. And Joyce is making a lot of noise. This is going to go high profile, and the politicians will have to point a finger at someone. When the media gets hold of this case, unless new evidence is found, you're going to be in the spotlight." He rested his cheek on the top of my head. "I can manage the media attention. I couldn't manage having you taken away from me."

I tipped my head back and looked at him. He was serious. "Do you think I might be arrested and convicted?"

"I think the possibility is slim, but I'm not willing to take a chance on it. Ask Ranger for help and keep your head down. Don't do anything to bring more attention to yourself."

I was dragged awake by something ringing in the dark room. Morelli swore softly, and his arm reached across me to the nightstand, where he'd left his cell phone.

"What?" Morelli said into the phone.

Someone was talking on the other end, and I could feel Morelli coming awake.

"You're fucking kidding me," he said to the caller. "Why does this shit always happen in the middle of the night?"

I squinted at my bedside clock and grimaced. Three A.M.

Morelli was up and moving around the room, looking for his clothes. He still had the phone to his ear.

"Give me an address," he said, and a moment later he snapped his phone closed. He slipped his watch onto his wrist and pulled his jeans on. He sat on the edge of the bed and tugged on socks. He leaned over and kissed me. "I have to go, and I probably won't get back tonight. I'll take Bob with me."

"Is this about the Berringer murders?"

"Someone else was just found dead in the building."

He clipped his gun onto his belt and pulled a sweater over a T-shirt. "I'll call when I can."

I had a third of a jar of peanut butter in my pantry, no milk, no bread, no juice. Half a box of Cheerios. I dropped some Cheerios into Rex's food dish and mixed some up with the peanut butter for myself. I washed the Cheerios and peanut butter down with black coffee and grabbed my coat.

Marty Gobel, the cop who was in charge of Dickie's disappearance, was supposed to call to talk. If I wasn't Morelli's girlfriend, I'd probably be getting fingerprinted. Good thing I had something solid in my stomach because otherwise I might be inclined to throw up. I really didn't want to go to jail.

Peter Smullen was first on my list of hideous jobs. According to Ranger's research, Smullen would be rolling into Starbucks a little after eight. I arrived fifteen minutes in front of the hour and tried to look inconspicuous by studying the shelves of coffee mugs for sale. Not that inconspicuous was much of a problem. The place was packed, and anyone under seven feet tall wasn't going to stand out.

I saw Smullen push through the door at five of eight and realized I might have a problem. He was buttoned into a black cashmere overcoat. There was no way to drop a bug into his suit pocket. Fortunately, the store was warm and the line was long. If the line went slowly enough, he'd unbutton his coat. I watched from my spot at the front of the store. I had a plan. I was going to wait until he had his coffee, and then I'd approach him. My coat was open, and I was wearing a low-cut V-neck sweater with a push-up bra. I looked pretty good considering my boobs were real, but it was hard to compete with all the double-D silicone jobs.

Smullen finally got to the counter and put in his order. He unbuttoned his coat to get his wallet, and I almost collapsed with relief. I had access to his pockets. He shuffled to the pick-up counter, got his triple Frappuccino, and when he turned toward the door, he was flat against me. I had my boobs pressed into his chest and my leg between his.

"Whoops," I said, sliding my hand under his coat, dropping the bug into his pocket. "Sorry!"

Smullen didn't blink. He just hung on to his Frappuccino as if this happened every morning. And maybe it did. There were a *lot* of people in the store. I took one step back and one step to the side to let Smullen get past me, and he inched his way toward the door and disappeared.

I felt someone lean in to me from behind, and a coffee was placed in my hand.

"Nice," Ranger said, guiding me out to the sidewalk. "I couldn't have gotten that close. And he wouldn't have been distracted by my chest."

"I don't think he even noticed."

"A man would have to be dead not to notice," Ranger said.

"Morelli's worried I'll be involved in Dickie's disappearance. He said I should ask you for help."

"He's a good man," Ranger said.

"And you?"

"I'm better."

* * *

Lula was filing when I walked into the bonds office.

"What's with this?" I asked.

"Hunh," Lula said. "You act like I never do nothing. It's just I'm so efficient I get my work done before anyone notices. My name should be Flash. You ever see any files laying around?"

"I assumed you were throwing them away."

"Your ass," Lula said.

For a short time, we had a guy named Melvin Pickle doing our filing. Pickle was a filing dynamo. Unfortunately, he was so good he was able to get a better job. Les Sebring hired him to work in his bonds office, and Connie had to coerce Lula to take back filing responsibilities.

Connie was carefully adding a topcoat to her nails. "Having any luck with the new batch of FTAs?"

"No, but Milton Buzick is getting buried today. I'm waiting to get a jewelry report from Grandma."

"If he got a Rolex on, I don't want to know," Lula said. "Two things I'm not doing. I'm not going back to that trailer, and I'm not sitting in no cemetery. Dead people creep me out."

"What about Carl Coglin?" Connie asked. "He looks pretty straightforward. He has a small shop attached to his home."

"Who's Carl Coglin?" Lula wanted to know.

I pulled Carl's file out of my bag and flipped it open. "Sixty-four years old. Never married. Lives alone. His sister put up the bond. Accused of destruction of personal property. Doesn't go into detail. Lists his occupation as taxidermist."

"Taxidermist," Lula said. "We never busted a taxidermist before. It could be fun."

A half hour later, we were in North Trenton, standing in front of Coglin's house. This was a working-class neighborhood filled with people stretched too thin to plant flowers in the spring. Houses were neat but shabby. Cars were tired.

Coglin lived in a redbrick single-family house with mustard trim. The paint was blistered and the wood around the windows had some rot. The front porch had been enclosed as an afterthought, and a small sign on the door advertised Coglin's taxidermy business.

"Don't look to me like taxidermy pays real well," Lula said.

A scrawny little guy answered my knock, and I knew from the picture on file that it was Coglin. Hair the color and texture of steel wool. Wire-rimmed glasses.

"Carl Coglin?" I asked.

"Yes."

"I represent Vincent Plum Bail Bonds. You missed your court date last week, and I'd like to help you reschedule."

"That's nice of you," Coglin said, "but I don't want to inconvenience you."

"It's my job."

"Oh," Coglin said. "Well, what does this rescheduling involve?"

"You need to go to the courthouse and get rebonded."

We were standing in Coglin's front-porch showroom, and it was hard not to notice the animals lining his walls.

"Where's the mooseheads?" Lula asked Coglin. "I thought you taxidermy guys stuffed lions and tigers and shit. All I see is cats and dogs and pigeons."

"This is *urban* taxidermy," Coglin said. "I restore pets and found objects."

"What's a found object?" Lula wanted to know.

"Treasure found in nature. For instance, if you were walking through the park and you found a deceased pigeon, that would be a found object. And sometimes

I make performance pieces. The performance pieces are mechanicals. There's a growing market for the mechanicals."

Lula looked at a woodchuck posed on a piece of Astroturf. Some of its fur had been worn away, and it had what appeared to be part of a tire track imprinted on its back. "You're a sick man," Lula said.

"It's *art,*" Coglin said. "You don't understand art."

"I understand roadkill," Lula said.

"About that rescheduling," I said to Coglin.

"Maybe I could reschedule next week," Coglin said. "I can't leave now. I have to stay at the house. I have a fresh opossum on the table."

"Oh boy," Lula said.

"It's hard to get an opossum at this time of year," Coglin said. "I was lucky to find it. And it won't be good when it defrosts."

"This won't take long," I told him.

"You're not going to leave without me, are you?" he asked.

"No."

Coglin looked at his watch. "I suppose I could go with you if this doesn't take long. Let me get my coat and lock the back door. In the meantime, feel free to browse my showroom. All these items are for sale."

"I'm glad to hear that," Lula said. "I always wanted a stuffed dead dog."

Coglin disappeared into the house, and I tried not to look too hard at the critters. "These animals are creeping me out," I said to Lula. "It's like being in a whacked-out pet cemetery."

"Yeah," Lula said. "They've seen better days." She picked up a stuffed squirrel. "This guy's got three eyes. He must have lived next to the nuclear power plant."

I heard the back door slam and then a motor crank over.

"Car!" I said to Lula.

We ran to the back of the house and saw Coglin pull away in a green Isuzu SUV. We turned and sprinted through the house, out the door to the Vic.

"There he goes," Lula said, pointing to the corner. "South on Centerline."

I had the Vic in gear and moving. I took the corner on two wheels and put my foot to the floor. Coglin was a block ahead of me.

"He's turning," Lula said.

"I'm on it."

"He's got a light," Lula said. "He has to stop for the light."

I jumped on the brake, but Coglin ran it. He sailed through the light and was lost in traffic.

"Guess he didn't feel like going to jail," Lula said.

The light changed and I slowly moved forward. I looked over at Lula and saw she still had the squirrel.

"We were in such a rush to get out of the house, I forgot I was holding this here mutant rodent," Lula said.

"It doesn't look like a third eye," I said to her. "It looks like a switch. Maybe this is a mechanical rodent."

Lula pushed the switch and studied it. "It's making a noise. It's sort of ticking. It's . . ."

BANG. The squirrel exploded.

We both shrieked. I jumped the curb and sideswiped a streetlight.

"What the fuck?" Lula said.

"Are you okay?"

"No, I'm not okay. That squirrel just friggin' blew hisself apart on me. I got squirrel guts on me."

"Doesn't look like guts," I said, examining the hair and skin plastered to the dashboard. "Looks like he was stuffed with some kind of foam that melted when it exploded."

"This guy's building rodent bombs," Lula said. "We

should report him to someone. You can't just go around building rodent bombs, can you?"

I backed up and tried to open my door, but it wouldn't open. I rolled the window down, climbed out *Dukes of Hazzard* style, and examined the damage. Some of the door was bashed in where I'd hit the light. I climbed back into the car and drove off the sidewalk.

"I got foam and squirrel hair stuck to me," Lula said. "I probably need a rabies shot or something."

"Yeah," I said. "Problem is, I don't know whether to take you to a veterinarian or an upholsterer."

"Smells funky," Lula said, sniffing her finger. "What's it smell like?"

"Squirrel."

"I didn't know squirrels had a smell."

"This one does," I told her.

"I'm gonna need to take this coat to the dry cleaner, and I'm gonna send the bill to that Coglin freak. He got some nerve exploding a squirrel on me."

"You *took* the squirrel."

"Yeah, but it was entrapment. I think I got a case."

"Maybe we should go to lunch," I said to Lula. "Take your mind off the squirrel."

"I could use some lunch."

"Do you have any money?"

"No," Lula said. "Do you?"

"No."

"There's only one thing to do then. Senior buffet."

Ten minutes later, I pulled into the Costco parking lot.

"Where we gonna start?" Lula wanted to know, taking a shopping cart.

"I like to start in produce and then go to the deli and then frozen."

Costco is the all-American free lunch. If you can't afford to buy food, you can buy a minimum membership at Costco and get freebies from the give-away ladies. You just have to kick your way through the seniors who stand ten deep around them.

"Look over there," Lula said. "They got a give-away lady frying up them little bitty sausages. I love those little sausages."

We had some apple slices dipped in caramel, some carrots and raw broccoli dipped in ranch dressing, some goat cheese, some frozen pizza pieces, some tofu stir-fry, some brownie pieces from the bakery, and some of the sausages. We did a test-drive on Guatemalan coffee and sparkling apple cider. We used the ladies' room, and we left.

"Whoever invented Costco knew what they were doing," Lula said. "I don't know what I'd do without my Costco membership. Sometimes, I even buy shit there. Costco's got everything. You can buy a casket at Costco."

We got into the Vic, and I drove us back to Coglin's house. I idled at the curb for a couple minutes, watching to see if anything was going on, then I motored around the block and took the alley that led to Coglin's backyard. No car in his parking place, so I parked there.

"Gonna see if he's hiding in a closet?" Lula asked.

"Yep."

I knocked on Coglin's back door and yelled, "Bond enforcement!"

No answer.

I opened the door and yelled again. Still no answer. I stepped into the kitchen and looked around. It was just as we'd left it over an hour ago, except for the opossum on the kitchen table. The opossum looked like a balloon with feet. And it smelled worse than squirrel. A lot worse.

"Whoa," Lula said. "He wasn't kidding about this sucker defrosting."

"Maybe we should put it in the freezer for him."

Lula had her scarf over her nose. "I'm not touching it. Bad enough I got squirrel on me. I don't need no 'possum cooties. Anyways, it's not gonna fit in his freezer with the way it's all swelled up."

"Coglin isn't here," I said to Lula. "He would have done something with this animal if he'd returned."

"Fuckin' A," Lula said. "I'm outta here."

I parked in front of the office, behind Lula's Firebird, and Lula and I got out of the Vic and gaped at the telephone pole at the corner. It was plastered with posters of me. It was a candid photo, and the caption read WANTED FOR MURDER.

"What the heck?" I said. My first reaction was panic deep in my chest. The police were looking for me. That only lasted a moment. This wasn't any sort of official "wanted" poster. This was made on someone's home scanner and printer.

I tore the posters off the pole and looked down the street. I could see posters on a pole half a block away.

"There's posters all over the place," Lula said. "They're stuck to store windows, and they're stuck on parked cars." She unlocked her Firebird. "I'm going home. I gotta get this squirrel funk off me."

I went into the office and showed Connie the posters.

"It's Joyce," Connie said. "I saw her putting them up, but I didn't realize what they were."

"They're probably all over town. I should probably ride around and take them down, but I have better things to do with my time . . . like find out who killed Dickie."

"Anything I can do to help?"

"Yes. I need a background search. Joyce says he's worth lots of money."

Connie punched his name into one of the search programs and the screen filled with information. "He leased a $42,000 Audi a year ago. His house is appraised at $350,000. And it's mortgaged to the rafters. No litigation pending against him. Nothing derogatory in his file. He's part owner of the building housing his law firm. His partners are also listed as owners. Looks like the building was bought outright. No mortgage there."

Connie printed the report and passed it over to me.

"Any calls for me?" I asked her.

"No. Were you expecting calls?"

"I was supposed to talk to Marty Gobel this morning. I expected him to call my cell." Not that I wanted to talk to Marty Gobel, but it was better than having a warrant issued for my arrest.

I dialed Morelli. No answer.

Ranger was next up.

"Babe," Ranger said.

"Anything new on Dickie?"

"No, but the natives are restless. I can feel Smullen sweating on the bug."

I left the bonds office, climbed into the Vic, and drove to Dickie's house. It was easy to find since it was the only house on his block draped in yellow crime scene tape. It was a large cape with black shutters and a red door. Probably thirty years old but recently painted. Two-car garage. Nicely landscaped. Medium-size lot. Very respectable, if you overlooked the tape. I wasn't sure what I'd expected to find, but I'd felt compelled to do a drive-by. Morbid curiosity, I suppose, since Joyce had been impressed with his wealth. As it was, he seemed comfortable but not excessively rich.

I did a mental reenactment of the crime. I imagined the door to Dickie's house open, and Dickie getting dragged out by whoever shot him. There would have been a car in the driveway. Shots were fired a little before midnight, so it was dark. Overcast sky. No moonlight. Still, you'd think someone would have at least seen the car leave. If you hear shots fired, and you care enough to call the police, you care enough to look out the window.

I parked the Vic, crossed the street, and knocked on the door of the house across from Dickie's. The knock was answered by a woman in her fifties.

"I'm investigating the Orr incident," I told her. "I'd appreciate it if you could just answer a few questions for me."

"I suppose, but I've already spoken to the police. I don't have much more to say."

"You reported the shots?"

"Yes. I was getting ready for bed. I heard the shots, and I thought it was kids. They ride through and shoot at mailboxes. But then when I looked out the window, I saw the car pull out of the Orr driveway. And I saw that the front door to the house was left open."

"What did the car look like?"

"It looked a little like your police car. It was dark out, so I can't be certain, but I think it was that burgundy color. And the shape was similar. I'm not much of a car person. My husband would have known exactly, but he was already in bed. He didn't get to the window in time."

"Did you see any people in the car? Did you see the license plate?"

"No. I just saw the car. It pulled out of the driveway and went north, toward 18th Street."

I thanked her and went back to the Vic.

I had two means of exit from the Vic. I could crawl across the console and go out the passenger side door, or I could crawl out the driver's side window. It was easier to crawl out the window, but that meant the window stayed open, and it was freezing cold when I returned to the car. Although, since I had half a rotting squirrel stuck to my dashboard, there was some advantage to the open window.

I'd chosen to do the crawl over the console thing this time so as not to tip off the neighbors I wasn't really a cop. I returned to the Vic, got some heat going, and reviewed my choices. I could take a shot at finding one of the remaining skips. I could go on a poster hunt. I could head over to my parents' house and talk to Grandma about Milton Buzick. Or I could go home and take a nap.

I was leaning toward the nap when my phone buzzed.

"I need help," Grandma said. "I got a hot date tonight with Elmer. We're going to the Rozinski viewing, and I'm thinking I might have to show some skin to keep Elmer away from Loretta Flick. I figure I can open a couple buttons on my blue dress, but I can't get my boobs to stay up. I thought you might be able to get me one of them push-up bras."

Forty-five minutes later, I had Grandma in the Victoria's Secret dressing room, trying on push-up bras.

"Okay," Grandma said from the other side of the door. "I got them all lifted up, and they look pretty good except for the wrinkles."

"I wouldn't worry about the wrinkles," I told her. "It looked to me like Elmer has cataracts."

"Maybe I need one of them thongs to go with this bra," she said.

I didn't want to think about Grandma in a thong. "Some pretty panties might be better."

"As long as they're sexy. I might get lucky tonight."

If she got lucky, Elmer would drop dead before dinner. "I'll pick out something that will match while you're getting dressed," I told Grandma.

We were at the register with the bra and panties, and I heard something sizzle in my head, and the next thing I knew I was on the floor and my lips were tingling.

"Wha . . ." I said.

Grandma was bending over me. "You got zapped by Joyce Barnhardt. I heard you go over, and I turned around and saw Joyce standing there with a stun gun. We called the police, but she ran off. Dirty rotten coward."

I looked past Grandma and saw a mall rent-a-cop nervously looking down at me.

"Are you okay?" he asked. "We got a doctor coming."

"Get me up on my feet," I said.

"I don't know if I should," he said. "Maybe you should just lay there until help gets here."

"Get me up!" I yelled at him. "I don't need a doctor. I need a new car and a new job and ten minutes alone with Ranger. This is all his fault."

The rent-a-cop got me under my armpits and hoisted me up. I went down to my knees, grabbed hold of his shirt, and pulled myself up again.

"Jeez, lady," he said.

"Don't worry," I told him. "This happens to me a lot. I'm good at it."

Grandma led me through the mall, and we managed to get to the parking lot and the Vic without the doctor finding me. I was supposed to be keeping a low profile. I didn't want to find myself on the evening news. Local bounty hunter stun-gunned in mall. Details at eight.

Grandma stood back and looked at my car. "Was your car decorated like this when we left it? I don't remember all this writing on it."

Someone had spray-painted PIG CAR in black and white on the passenger side door and trunk lid.

"It's new," I said.

"I would have used brighter colors," Grandma said. "Gold would have looked good. You can't go wrong with gold."

"The black and white goes better with the squirrel hair stuck to the dash," I told her.

"I was wondering what that was," Grandma said. "I figured it was one of them new animal print decorator schemes."

"Lula helped me with it."

"Isn't she the one," Grandma said.

I got behind the wheel and motored out of the lot and onto the highway.

"Do you hear a grinding sound?" Grandma asked.

"All cars sound like that," I said. "You're just noticing it because I don't have the radio on loud enough. What about Milton? Did you notice if he was wearing jewelry?"

"Nothing worth anything. His lodge lapel pin. That was about it. I know you're looking for Simon Diggery. It'll take something good to get him out in this weather. I'll check out Harry Rozinski, but he probably won't have anything worth taking, and he's not Diggery's size."

"Do you need a ride tonight?"

"No. Elmer has a car. He's picking me up."

It was a little after four when I dropped Grandma off. Lights were on in Burg houses and tables were being set for dinner. This was a community where families still sat together for meals. I turned right onto Hamilton and ten minutes later, I was in my apartment building. I let myself in, and Bob rushed over to me.

"Where's Joe?" I asked him.

Not in the kitchen. Not in the dining room. Not in the living room. I went to the bedroom and found him asleep in my bed.

"Hey Goldilocks," I said.

Morelli came awake and rolled onto his back. "What time is it?"

"Four-thirty. Have you been here long?"

"Couple hours."

"I heard a news report on the Berringer murders

while I was in the car. They said the police were baffled."

"Baffled and tired. I need some sleep. I'm too old for this middle-of-the-night murder shit."

"There was a time when you did all sorts of things in the middle of the night."

"Come here and you can tell me about them."

"I thought you were tired."

"I just want to talk," Morelli said.

"That's a big fib. I *know* what you want to do."

Morelli smiled. "Hard for a man to keep a secret."

FOUR

Morelli was at my kitchen counter, drinking coffee, eating cereal. His hair was still damp from the shower, and he was clean-shaven. In ten minutes, he'd have a five o'clock shadow. He was wearing worn-out black jeans, a pale gray cable-knit sweater, and black motorcycle boots.

"You don't look like a cop," I told him. "All the other guys wear suits."

"I've been asked by the chief not to wear a suit. I look like a casino pit boss when I wear a suit. I don't inspire trust."

I poured myself a bowl of cereal and added milk. "It was nice of you to bring all this food."

"Your cupboards were empty. And your refrigerator. I'm guessing the bounty hunter business is slow."

"It comes and goes. Problem is, I only make enough money to live day by day. I can't make enough to get ahead."

"It would be easier if you moved in with me."

"We've tried that. It's always a disaster. Eventually, we drive each other nuts."

"It's your job," Morelli said.

"It's your expectations."

He put his cereal bowl in the sink and buckled his

gun onto his belt. "Yeah, my expectations are that you'll give up your job."

"Are we fighting?"

"Am I yelling and waving my arms?"

"No."

"Then we aren't fighting." He crooked an arm around my neck and kissed me. "I have to go. I'm working with Phil Panchek. He hates being baffled without me."

"Marty Gobel never called to talk to me. Does that mean I'm off the hook?"

"No. It means he's dreading talking to you for fear you don't have an alibi, and he's procrastinating as long as possible."

Bob was leaning against me. "Are you taking Bob?"

"Yeah, I'll drop him off at my house. He has a routine. He eats the couch. He takes a nap. He gnaws on a dining room table leg. He takes a nap. He spreads the garbage all over the kitchen floor. He takes a nap."

I fondled Bob's ear. "You're lucky you have a dog who can amuse himself while you're gone."

Morelli shrugged into his jacket and clipped Bob's leash on him. "Later."

I finished my coffee and cereal and hand-washed the dishes. I took a shower and put in the minimum effort on my hair. Truth is, the minimum effort isn't that far removed from the maximum effort, and my hair pretty much looks the same no matter what I do with it. I applied some mascara and looked myself in the eye in the mirror.

"Today is the day," I said to myself. "Time to get serious. If you don't catch someone soon, you'll get kicked out of your apartment."

I got dressed in my lucky jeans and my lucky black sweater. It was still cold, but it wasn't snowing or sleeting, so I traded my fake Uggs for running shoes . . . just in case I had to chase down Diggery. I had cuffs in my back jeans pocket. Pepper spray in my jacket pocket. A stun gun clipped to my belt. I went to the kitchen and took my gun out of my cookie jar. It was a little five-shot Smith & Wesson. I spun the barrel. No bullets. I looked in the jar. No bullets. I rummaged through kitchen drawers. No bullets. I put the gun back into the cookie jar. I didn't really want to shoot anyone today anyway.

I got bundled up in my parka and scarf and gloves, and went out to the Vic. I crawled in and plugged the key into the ignition. It took a while, but the engine finally caught. All right, so I didn't have a great car. No big deal, I told myself. At least it was running. And today was the day it was all going to turn around. I was going after Diggery first and then Coglin. And then I was going to plow through the rest of the cases.

I took Broad and headed for Bordentown. It was just past rush hour, and traffic was heavy but moving. The cloud cover had finally lifted and the sky was as blue as it gets in Jersey. I was on Route 206, cruising along, listening to the radio, when the grinding sound coming from under the hood turned into *BANG, BANG, BANG* and the car coasted to a stop at the side of the road. It wasn't entirely unexpected, but it left me breathless all the same. Another example that sugar isn't pixie dust, and wish as hard as you might, it won't make you invisible.

I was sitting there trying to keep from crying, running through my options, and Ranger called.

"Babe, you're stopped on Route 206. What's up?"

I remembered the gizmo in my bag. RangeMan was monitoring me. "My car died."

Fifteen minutes later, I looked in my rearview mirror and saw Ranger pull in behind me. He got out of his car and into mine. Ranger didn't smile a lot, but clearly he was amused.

"I don't know how you do it," Ranger said. "In a matter

of days, you've managed to turn a perfectly good piece-of-shit car into something so fucked up it's a work of art."

"It's a gift."

"The bullet hole in the rear window?"

"Joyce Barnhardt," I told him. "She's unhappy with me because she thinks I killed Dickie."

"And the crud on the dash?"

"Squirrel bomb."

He looked incredulous for a moment and then burst out laughing. In all the time I'd known Ranger, this was maybe the third time I'd seen him actually laugh out loud, so it turned out to be worth getting squirrel-bombed.

Ranger dropped back to a smile and tugged me out of the car. He kicked the door closed, slung an arm around my shoulders, and walked me back to his Porsche Cayenne. "Where were you going?" he asked.

"I'm looking for Simon Diggery," I said. "I stopped by his double-wide on Tuesday, but no one was home. I thought I'd try again."

Ranger opened the Cayenne door for me. "I'll go with you. If we're lucky, we might get to see his snake eat a cow."

I looked back at the Vic. "What about my car?"

"I'll have it picked up."

Ranger didn't bother parking out of sight of Diggery's trailer. He drove the Cayenne onto the blighted grass and pulled up between the trailer and the stand of hardwoods. We got out of the Porsche, and he gave me his gun.

"Stay here and shoot anyone who makes a run for it, including the snake."

"How do you know I don't have my own gun?"

"Do you?"

"No."

Ranger did another one of those almost sighing things and jogged around to Diggery's front door. I heard him rap on the door and call out. There was the sound of the rusted door opening and closing and then silence. I held my ground.

After a couple minutes, Ranger reappeared and motioned for me to join him.

"Simon is off somewhere, but the uncle is here. And stay away from the sink," Ranger said.

I gave him his gun back, followed him into the trailer, and immediately checked out the kitchen area. The snake was sprawled on the counter, its head in the sink. I guess it was thirsty. The uncle was at the small built-in table.

The uncle wasn't much older than Simon Diggery, and the family resemblance was there, blurred over a little by hard drinking and an extra fifty pounds. He was wearing black socks and ratty bedroom slippers and huge boxer shorts.

"Give you a quarter if you pull your shirt up," Bill Diggery said to me.

"I'll give *you* a quarter if you put your shirt *on,*" I told him.

Ranger was against the wall, watching Diggery. "Where's Simon?" Ranger asked.

"Don't know," Bill said.

"Think about it," Ranger told him.

"He might be at work."

"Where is he working?"

"Don't know."

Ranger's eyes flicked to the snake and back to Bill. "Has he been fed today?"

"He don't eat every day," Bill said. "He probably ain't hungry."

"Steph," Ranger said. "Wait outside so I can talk to Bill."

"You aren't going to feed him to the snake, are you?"

"Not all of him."

"As long as it's not all of him," I said. And I let myself out.

I closed the door and waited for a couple minutes. I didn't hear any screams of pain or terror. No gunshots. I hunkered down in my jacket and shoved my hands into my pockets to keep warm. A couple more minutes passed, and Ranger came out, closing the door behind him.

"Well?" I asked.

"Simon is working in the food court at Quaker Bridge Mall. Bill didn't know more than that."

"Did you feed Uncle Bill to the snake?"

"No. He was right . . . the snake wasn't hungry."

"Then how did you get him to talk?"

Ranger slid an arm around me, and I felt his lips brush my ear when he spoke. "I can be very persuasive."

No kidding.

Quaker Bridge is on Route One, northeast of Trenton. It seemed like a long way for Diggery to drive for an odd job in a food court, but what the heck, maybe Diggery was lucky to get it. And maybe he had a better car than I did. That thought brought me up to a sobering reality. Diggery for sure had a better car than I did because I had no car at all.

Ranger drove out of Diggery's neighborhood and headed north. We were on Route 206, and I was dreading the section of highway where I'd left the Vic. I didn't want to see the poor, sad, broken-down car. It was a reminder of what was wrong with my life. Crappy job, hand-to-mouth existence, no future I was willing to commit to. If it was June and the sun was shining, I might feel different, but it was cold and the clouds had returned and a mist had started to fall.

"I need macaroni and cheese," I said to Ranger, clapping my hands over my eyes. "I promised myself French fries, jelly doughnuts, birthday cake . . . and I never got them."

"I have a better way to make you happy," Ranger said. "Less fattening but more addicting."

"Pharmaceuticals?"

"Sex. And you can open your eyes. The Vic's gone."

"Gone where?"

"Car heaven."

Twenty minutes later, Ranger stopped at a light on Broad, and his cell buzzed. He answered on a Bluetooth earpiece and listened for a couple minutes, his mood somber, his expression not showing anything. He thanked the caller and disconnected.

"They found the accountant, Ziggy Zabar," Ranger said. "He washed ashore about a quarter mile south of the Ferry Street Bridge. He was identified by a credit card and a medic alert bracelet for a heart condition."

Ranger parked behind the medical examiner's truck, and we walked the distance to the crime scene. It was turning into a miserable day and the weather was holding the crowd down. Only a few hardy photographers and reporters. No gawkers. A handful of uniforms, a couple plainclothes guys. An EMS team that looked like they wanted to be somewhere else. No one I recognized. We ducked under the yellow tape and found Tank.

Tank is Ranger's next in command and his shadow. No need to describe him. His name says it all. He was dressed in RangeMan black, and he looked impervious to the weather.

Tank was with Ziggy Zabar's brother, Zip, also in RangeMan black, his face stoic, his posture rigid.

"We picked the call up from police dispatch," Tank said, stepping away from Zip. "He's been in the water awhile, and he's not in great shape, but I've looked at him, and even in his condition it's obvious it was an execution. Single bullet nice and clean in the forehead. He's wearing an ankle shackle, so I'm guessing he was attached to something heavy, and the tide broke him loose."

I sucked in some air. I didn't know Ziggy Zabar, but it was horrible all the same.

We stayed for a while, keeping Zip company while he watched over his dead brother. The police photographer left and the EMS guys came in with a body bag. I could hear the motor running on the ME truck at the top of the hill. The uniforms had their collars turned up and were shuffling their feet. The mist had turned into a drizzle.

Ranger was wearing his SEAL ball cap. He tucked my hair behind my ears and put his hat on my head to keep me dry. "You look like you need that birthday cake."

"I'd settle for a peanut butter sandwich and some dry socks."

"I want to talk to the ME, and then I have some things to do." He handed me the keys to the Cayenne. "Use my car. I can ride with Tank and Zip. I don't care if you destroy the car, but take care of the hat. I want it back."

I scrambled up the hill, hoisted myself into the Porsche, and turned the heat on full blast. As I pulled off the service road onto Broad, my cell phone buzzed. It was Marty Gobel.

"I need you to come in and make a statement," Marty said. "I know this isn't anything you want to do, but I can't put it off any longer."

"That's okay," I told him. "I understand. I'll be there in ten minutes."

The cop shop is on Perry Street. Half the building is the courthouse and half the police station. It's red-brick, and the architecture could best be categorized as utilitarian municipal. Money wasn't wasted on fancy columns or art. This is strictly a 60-watt building. Still, it serves its purpose, and it's in a neighborhood where it's convenient for the police to find crime.

I parked in the public lot across the street and stowed

the pepper spray, handcuffs, and stun gun in the console. I applied fresh lip gloss and went to talk to Marty.

I crossed the lobby to the cop-in-a-cage and gave him my name. Court was in session across the hall and people were milling around, waiting to pass through security.

Marty met me in the lobby. We got coffee and found an empty room where he could take my statement.

"So," Marty said when we were seated, "why did you kill Dickie Orr?"

I felt my mouth drop open and my eyes go wide.

Marty gave a bark of laughter. "I'm just fucking with you," he said. "The guys made me do it."

"Should I have an attorney present?" I asked him.

"Do you have one?"

"My brother-in-law."

"Oh jeez, are you talking about Albert Kloughn? He chases ambulances. He paid for his law degree with chickens. Got it somewhere in the islands, right?"

I did some mental knuckle cracking. "What do you want to know?"

"Do you have an alibi?"

Oh boy.

An hour later, I pushed my chair back. "I'm done," I told Gobel. "If you want any more, you'll have to feed me."

"The best I could do is a Snickers bar."

"How many?"

Gobel closed his notepad. "I'm done anyway. You and Morelli aren't planning on going out of the country any time soon, are you?"

I slanted my eyes at him. "What are you saying?"

"Well, you know, you're kind of a suspect. Actually, you're our *only* suspect."

"What's my motive?"

"You hated him."

"Everybody hated him."

"Not true. Not *everybody.* And you stand to inherit a lot of money. He had a will drawn up when you were married, and it never got changed. You get everything."

"What?" I said it on a whoosh of air because it literally knocked the wind out of me.

"You didn't know?"

"I don't believe it." This was the most contentious divorce in the history of the Burg. The shouting was heard for miles. We called each other names that didn't even exist.

"Believe it," Marty Gobel said.

"How do you know about the will? Aren't wills secret?"

"Not this one. His girlfriend has a copy. Joyce Barnhardt. He was in the process of changing it, so she would be his sole heir, but he never signed it."

"You're kidding again, right? This is another joke."

"Swear to God. If they ever find his body you'll be rich. Of course, you might not be in a good position to enjoy it."

I left Gobel, locked myself in the Cayenne, and called Morelli. "Did you know I was Dickie's sole heir?" I asked him.

"No. How did you find that out?"

"Gobel. Joyce told him. Apparently she has a copy of Dickie's will."

"So you talked to Marty. How'd it go?"

"By the time we were done, I was sort of feeling I might have killed Dickie."

There was a moment of silence. "You didn't, did you?"

"No! Yeesh. I'm going home. I'm all discombobulated."

"Look in the freezer when you get home. I got you happy food."

"How happy?"

"Stouffer's macaroni and cheese. The family size."

"I love you!"

I could feel Morelli smile at the other end. "I own you now. I know where all the buttons are."

I rushed home and went straight to the freezer. I yanked the door open and there it was—the family size. I almost fainted from joy. I popped it into the microwave and ran into the bedroom to get dry clothes. I was changing out of my socks, and I realized the room didn't feel exactly right. I'd left the bed unmade and rumpled, and now it was less rumpled, and the pillows were all lined up on the headboard. And my T-shirt drawer was partially open.

I moved to the chest beside the bed and got the cylinder of pepper spray from the top drawer. I looked under the bed and in every closet. Didn't find anyone. Whoever had been here was now gone.

I called Morelli.

"I've got it in the microwave," I told him. "When did you bring it over?"

"Yesterday. When I brought all the rest of the stuff. Why?"

"I think someone was in my apartment while I was gone this morning."

"Probably Ranger fingering your underwear."

"No. I was with Ranger. And if Ranger was here, I'd never know." And if Ranger wanted to finger my underwear, he'd do it while I was wearing it.

"If you're worried, you can move yourself over to my house. Bob loves company."

"How about you?"

"I'd like it too. Just kick the beer cans and pizza boxes out of your way and make yourself at home."

"Could it have been the police looking for evidence?"

"No. We couldn't use evidence obtained that way.

And besides, no one's that smart here. Only television cops do that sort of thing."

"Good to know. Gotta run. My mac and cheese just dinged."

"I've got some paperwork to finish, and then I'm heading out. Where will I find you?"

"I'm going to stay here. There weren't any death threats spray-painted on the walls, so maybe I'm just imagining things. I'm a little spooked, what with being accused of murder."

"You're not accused yet," Morelli said. "You're only under suspicion."

I hung up, stuffed my feet into the shearling boots, and pulled a hooded fleece sweatshirt over my head. I liked Morelli's house better than my apartment, but all my clothes and makeup and hair things were here. When Morelli spent the night with me, he borrowed my razor, used whatever soap was in the bathroom, and re-dressed in the clothes that had hit the floor the night before. He kept some underwear and socks here, and that was it. When I stayed with Morelli, it was a whole production.

I polished off the mac and cheese and washed it down with a beer. I was now warm inside and out, and no longer cared so much about the Dickie issue.

I'd dropped a cheesy macaroni into Rex's food cup, and he was busy stuffing it into his cheeks. His whiskers were whirring and his tiny black eyes were bright.

"Time to go get a Diggery," I said to Rex. "Now that I'm full of mac and cheese, I can do *anything*—leap tall buildings in a single bound, stop a speeding locomotive, get a bikini wax."

Rex flicked a glance at me and scurried into his soup can.

FIVE

It was mid-afternoon and still gray and drizzly, but the drizzle wasn't freezing on the roads. I thought that was a good sign. I was on my way to the mall in Ranger's car and hat, and I was feeling very kick-ass. I was armed with the pepper spray and the stun gun. I had my cuffs. I had my paperwork. I was ready to do a takedown.

I parked at the food court entrance and made a tour of the concessions. Pizza, burgers, ice cream, smoothies, Chinese, cookies, subs, Mexican, sandwiches. I didn't see Diggery. Then I did a fast scan of the tables and spotted him on the far side, against a wall. He was talking to someone, and there were papers spread across the table.

I got a diet soda and found an empty table just behind Diggery. He was busy talking and didn't notice me. He seemed to be filling out some sort of form. He finished the form, gave it to the woman across from him, and she gave him some money and left. A new person immediately sat down and gave Diggery a large yellow envelope.

I wasn't taking any chances with this. I wasn't going to give Diggery an opportunity to bolt and run. I quietly moved to Diggery and clapped a bracelet on his right wrist.

Diggery looked down at the cuff and then up at me. "Fuck," Diggery said.

"You need to get rebonded," I told him. "You missed your court date."

"I'm conducting business now," Diggery said. "A little respect, okay? I don't come barging into *your* office, do I?"

"This isn't an office. It's a food court. What the heck are you doing?"

"He's doing my taxes," the woman across from him said. "He does them every year."

I looked at the woman. "You let *him* do your taxes?"

"He's certifiable."

Couldn't argue with that. "He's also under arrest," I told her. "You're going to have to make other arrangements."

"What arrangements? I can't do these forms. I can't figure them out."

Four more people came forward. Three men and a woman.

"What's going on?" one of the men asked. "What's the holdup?"

"Simon has to leave now," I told him.

"No way. I've been waiting for an hour, and I'm next in line. You want a piece of Simon, take a number."

"Get up," I said to Diggery.

"It's gonna get ugly," he said. "You don't want to piss off Oscar over there. He don't got a lot of patience, and he's missing his afternoon TV shows to do this."

"I can't believe you're doing taxes."

"It was just one of them things that mushroomed. Not that it should be so surprising since I have a very strong entrepreneurial side to me."

I looked at my watch. "If we hustle, I can get you bonded out today, and you can be back here in a couple hours."

"I'm not waiting no more couple hours," Oscar said, giving me a shot to the shoulder that knocked me into the woman behind me.

I took the stun gun out of my coat pocket. "Back off," I said to Oscar. "Simon is in violation of his bond, and he needs to go with me."

"I've got one of those too," the woman behind me said. And *ZINNNNG*.

When I came around, I was on my back on the floor, and I was looking at the rent-a-cop from the lingerie trip with Grandma.

"Are you okay?" he said. "Did you have a spell? Can you get a flashback from a stun gun?"

"It's my life," I said to him. "It's complicated."

He dragged me up and set me in a chair. "Do you want water or something?"

"Yeah, water would be good."

By the time he came with the water, the clanging in my head had almost completely stopped. I sipped the water and looked around. No Diggery. His clients were gone too. No doubt moved on to a taco stand or gas station. I was missing my cuffs and stun gun. I was probably lucky they hadn't taken my shoes and my watch.

I retreated to the parking lot, and carefully maneuvered the car onto the highway. I drove on autopilot and suddenly realized I was stopped in front of my parents' house. I checked to make sure I was no longer drooling, then went into the house. My dad was in front of the television, sound asleep with the paper draped over his stomach. My mother and grandmother were in the kitchen cooking.

Grandma was wearing tight black spandex yoga pants and a pink T-shirt that said *I'm Sassy,* and she'd dyed her hair red. My mother was at the stove, but the ironing board was up, and the iron was plugged in. I suspected it was the red hair that got the iron out.

Since the iron was already out, I decided I'd just jump in. "So," I said to Grandma, "how'd the date go?"

"It was pretty good," Grandma said. "The funeral parlor had a new cookie. Chocolate with white chocolate chips. And they did a real good job with Harry Rozinski. You couldn't hardly tell half his nose was eaten away with the skin cancer."

"Was he wearing jewelry?"

"No. But Lorraine Birnbaum was next door in viewing room #4, and she was all decked out. She was wearing a real nice-looking watch, and they left her wedding band and diamond on her. The diamond was real big too. You probably don't remember Lorraine. She moved away when you were little. She came back to live with her daughter after her husband died last year, but she didn't last too long. Her memorial said she was being buried on Friday."

"Did Elmer behave himself?"

"Yeah. That was the only disappointment. I was ready to put out, but he got some acid reflux from the cookies and had to go home."

My mother was at the stove sautéing ground beef for stuffed peppers. She reached for the cupboard where she kept her liquor stash, paused, then pulled herself together and went on with the sautéing.

"Sissy Cramp and I went shopping today," Grandma said, "and I got these new clothes and went to the beauty parlor. I thought I should spruce up since Elmer has all that nice black hair. It's a marvel that at his age he hasn't got a gray hair on his head."

"He hasn't got *any* hair on his head," I told Grandma. "He wears a wig."

"That would explain a lot of things," Grandma said.

My mother and I looked at each other and shared a grimace.

"I read somewhere red is the hot color for hair this

year," Grandma said. "So I had Dolly do me red this time. What do you think?"

"I think it's fun," I told Grandma. "It brings out the color in your eyes."

I could see my mother bite into her lower lip, and I knew she was eyeing the liquor cabinet again.

"It makes me feel like a whole new person," Grandma said. "Sissy says I look just like Shirley MacLaine."

I zipped my jacket. "I just stopped in to say hello. I have to get back to the office."

I checked myself out in the hall mirror on my way to the door to make sure there were no leftover effects from the stun gun . . . like my tongue hanging out or my eyes rolling around in my head. I didn't notice anything, so I left my parents' house, buckled myself into the Cayenne, and called Lula.

"Un hunh," Lula said.

"I'm going to check on Carl Coglin. Want to ride along with me?"

"Sure. Maybe I can explode another squirrel on myself."

Five minutes later, I picked her up in front of the bonds office.

"Now this is what I call a car," Lula said, getting into the Cayenne. "Only one place you get a car like this."

"It's Ranger's."

"Don't I know it. I get a rush just sitting in it. I swear, that man is so hot and so fine it's like he isn't even human."

"Mmm," I said.

"Mmm. What's that supposed to mean? You think he isn't fine?"

"He involved me in a murder."

"He told you to choke Dickie in front of the whole law office staff?"

"Well, no. Not exactly."

"Not that Dickie don't deserve getting choked."

"Dickie's scum."

"Fuckin' A," Lula said.

"Although it would appear I'm the sole beneficiary in his will."

"Say what?"

"Apparently, he had a will drawn up when we were married, making me heir, and he never got around to changing it."

"How do you know that?"

"Joyce has a copy. She told the police about it, and they brought me in for questioning."

"Then it's Joyce that involved you in this murder."

"Yes!"

"Bitch," Lula said.

I drove up Hamilton and pointed the Porsche toward North Trenton. It was four o'clock, and another day was slipping by without a capture. If this continued, I'd have to scrounge around for another job. At least something part-time.

"What's the plan here?" Lula wanted to know.

"If he's home, we grab him and cuff him and drag him to the car. You have cuffs, right?"

"Not with me. You're the big-deal bounty hunter. You're supposed to have the cuffs."

"I lost my cuffs."

"Again? Honest to goodness, I've never seen anybody lose things like you."

"You usually have cuffs," I said to Lula.

"They're sort of attached to my bed. Tank was over, and we got playful."

Eeek. Either one of them in handcuffs attached to a bed wasn't a good picture. "I didn't realize you were a couple."

"We're one of them couples who don't see each other all the time. We just see each other some of the time. And sometimes it goes to once in a while."

"Okay, then we can grab Coglin and stun-gun him. Do you have your stun gun?"

"Sure I got my stun gun." Lula pulled her stun gun out of her big purse. "Uh-oh, low battery."

I knew she had her Glock. And I knew it was loaded. But I didn't especially want her to shoot Coglin.

"How about I grab him and sit on him until he gives up?" Lula said.

"I guess that would work."

I cruised down Coglin's street and idled in front of his house. Lights were off inside. I drove around the block and scoped out the back of the house. No car parked in the alley. I cut the engine and Lula and I got out and walked to Coglin's back door. I rapped on the door and announced myself. No answer.

Lula had her hand on the doorknob. "It's unlocked," she said, pushing the door open, stepping inside. "This guy's real trusting."

"Maybe he never came back."

We went room by room, flipping lights on, looking around. The stuffed animals were everywhere. He had an entire bedroom filled with pigeons.

"Who would want a stuffed pigeon?" Lula asked. "I mean, what sort of a market do you suppose there is for a dead pigeon?"

We went back downstairs, made our way out to the porch showroom, and Lula stopped in front of a beaver.

"Look at this bad boy," Lula said. "Now, this is what I'm talking about. This here's the biggest fuckin' rodent ever lived. This is practically prehistoric."

I'd never seen a beaver up close and personal, and I was surprised at the size. "Do you suppose they're always this big?"

"Maybe Crazy Coglin overstuffed it."

Lula picked up a remote that had been placed beside the beaver. The remote had two buttons. One of the buttons was labeled EYES and the other BANG!

Lula pressed the EYES button and the beaver's eyes glowed. She pressed it again and the eyes shut off.

"Probably I don't want to press the BANG! button," Lula said. "This here looks to me like a exploding beaver. And it's not like it's some second-rate squirrel. This mother's gonna make a mess. This is atomic. This is something you only give to the enemy."

I looked over at Lula and smiled.

"I know what you're thinking," Lula said. "You're thinking of Joyce and how she deserves this beaver. You're thinking we have a obligation to give this beaver to Joyce."

"She likes animals."

"Yeah, especially big trained dogs and ponies."

"Maybe the second button doesn't explode it. Maybe the beaver sings a song or something."

"The button says BANG!"

"It could be mislabeled."

"I see where you're going," Lula said. "You're thinking we have to say a lot of Hail Marys if we send this to Joyce and explode it on her. But it wouldn't be our fault if it exploded accidental. Or if there was a misunderstanding on our part."

"I wouldn't want to maim her."

"Of course not."

"Just because she shot at me, zapped me with a stun gun, and ratted me out to the police isn't any reason to do her bodily harm."

"Whatever."

"Still, it would be fun to send her a singing beaver."

Lula looked at her watch. "How long we gonna stand here doing this rationalizing shit? I got stuff to do."

I scrounged around in my purse and came up with eight dollars and forty cents. I left it on the table and pocketed the remote.

"What's that?" Lula wanted to know.

"It's for the beaver. I'm in enough trouble. I don't want to be accused of stealing a . . . singing beaver."

"And you think it's worth eight dollars and forty cents?"

"It's all I've got." I wrapped my arms around the beaver and hefted it off the table. "This weighs a ton!"

Lula got her hands under his butt and helped me to the door. We loaded the beaver into the Cayenne cargo area and drove it across town to Joyce's house.

Joyce lives in a big white colonial with fancy columns and a large yard. The house is the result of her last divorce. Joyce got the house, and her husband got a new lease on life. There was a red Jeep in the driveway, and lights were shining in the downstairs windows.

Lula and I dragged the beaver out of the back of the Cayenne and lugged it to Joyce's front porch. We set the beaver down, I rang the bell, and Lula and I ran for cover. We hunkered down behind the red Jeep and gulped air.

The front door opened, and Joyce said, "What on earth?"

I pushed the button to make the eyes glow, and I peeked around the car. Joyce was bent over looking at the beaver.

A man came up behind her. Not Dickie. A younger, chunkier guy in jeans and a thermal T-shirt. "What is it?" he asked.

"It's a beaver."

"Well, bring it inside," he said. "I like beaver."

Joyce pushed and pulled the beaver inside and closed the door. Lula and I scurried to a window on the side of the house where curtains hadn't been drawn and looked in at Joyce and the Jeep guy. The two of them were examining the beaver, patting it on the head, smiling at it.

"Think they've had a few drinkiepoos," Lula said. "Anyone in their right mind wouldn't bring the beaver from hell into their house."

After a minute or two, Joyce and the Jeep guy got tired of the beaver and walked away. I waited until they were a safe distance, and then I pushed the BANG! button. There was a moment's lag, and then *BLAM!* Beaver fur and beaver stuffing as far as the eye could see.

The fur and glop hung from couches, chairs, tables, and table lamps. It was in Joyce's hair and was stuck to the back of her shirt. Joyce froze for a beat, turned, and looked around with her eyes bugged out.

"Fuck!" Joyce shrieked. "Fuck, fuck, fuck!"

"Holy crap," Lula said.

We sprang from the window and ran through the neighbor's yard to where we'd parked the car. We jumped in, and I laid rubber out of there.

"Guess it wasn't a singing beaver after all," I said.

"Yeah, darn," Lula said. "I was looking forward to hearing some singing."

I was smiling so wide my cheeks ached. "It was worth my last eight dollars."

"That was awesome," Lula said. "That Coglin is a freakin' genius."

Lula had her Firebird parked in the small lot behind the office. I dropped her off at her car and motored home to my apartment.

Morelli was watching television when I came in.

"You look happy," he said. "You must have had a productive day."

"It started off slow, but it ended okay."

"There's a casserole in the refrigerator. It's from

my mom. It has vegetables in it and everything. And I could use another beer. The game's coming on."

Hours later, we were still in front of the television when Morelli's cell phone rang.

"I'm not answering it," Morelli said. "The guy who invented the cell phone should rot in hell."

The ringing stopped and a minute later, it started again.

Morelli shut the phone off.

We had three minutes of silence, and my phone rang in the kitchen.

"Persistent bastard," Morelli said.

The ringing didn't stop, and finally Morelli went to the kitchen and answered the phone. He was smiling when he came back.

"Good news?" I asked.

"Yes, but I'm going to have to go to work."

"The Berringer case?"

"No. Something else."

He went to the bedroom, rousted Bob off the bed, and snapped the leash on him. "I might have to go under for a while, but I'll call," Morelli said. "And don't worry about Dickie. I'm sure it'll work out okay." He grabbed his jacket and kissed me. "Later."

I closed and locked the door after him and stood for a moment taking the pulse of the apartment. It felt empty without Morelli. On the other hand, I could watch something sappy on television, wear my ratty, comfy flannel jammies, and hog the bed.

SIX

I got up late because there was no real good reason to get up early. I made coffee and ate junky cereal out of the box and pushed it down with a banana. My files were spread across the dining room table. Coglin, Diggery, and a third file I hadn't yet opened. Today was the day for the third file. I had the file in my hand when my phone rang.

"Are you all right?" my mother asked.

"Couldn't be better."

"Have you seen the paper this morning?"

"No."

"Don't look," she said.

"Now what?"

"It's all over the news that you killed Dickie."

"Tell her I'll visit her in the big house," Grandma yelled at my mother. "Tell her I'll bring cigarettes so she can pay off the butch guards."

"I'll call you back," I said to my mother.

I disconnected and looked out my peephole. Good deal. Mr. Molinowski's morning paper was still lying in front of his door. I tiptoed out, snatched it up, and scurried back into my apartment.

The headline read LOCAL BOUNTY HUNTER PRIME

SUSPECT IN ORR DISAPPEARANCE. Front page. And the article was accompanied by an unflattering picture of me taken while I was waiting for Gobel in the municipal building lobby. They'd interviewed Joyce, and Joyce was quoted as saying I'd always been jealous of her and had fits of violent behavior even as a child. There was a mention of the time Grandma and I accidentally burned down the funeral home. There was a second file photo of me with no eyebrows, the result of my car exploding into a fireball a while back. And then there were several statements by secretaries who'd witnessed me going postal on Dickie. One of the secretaries stated that I pointed a gun at Dickie and threatened to "put a big hole in his head."

"That was Lula," I said to the empty apartment.

I put the paper back on Mr. Molinowski's welcome mat, returned to my apartment, threw the bolt on the door, and called my mother.

"All a pack of lies," I said to my mother. "Ignore it. Everything's fine. I went downtown to have coffee with Marty Gobel and someone got the wrong idea."

There was a pause while my mother talked herself into halfway believing the story. "I'm having a roast chicken tonight. Are you and Joseph coming to dinner?"

It was Friday. Morelli and I always had dinner at my parents' house on Friday night.

"Sure," I said. "I'll be there. I don't know about Joe. He's on a case."

I drank coffee and read the third file. Stewart Hansen was charged with running a light and possession of a controlled substance. He was twenty-two years old, unemployed, and he lived in a house on Myrtle Street at the back end of the Burg. The house had been posted as collateral on the bond. It was owned by Stewart's cousin Trevor.

I heard a sharp rap on my door and went to look out the security peephole. It was Joyce.

"Open this door," she yelled. "I know you're in there." She tried to rattle the door, but it held tight.

"What do you want?" I called through the door.

"I want to talk to you."

"About what?"

"About Dickie, you moron. I want to know where he is. You found out about the money and you somehow managed to snatch him, didn't you?"

"Why do you want to know where he is?"

"None of your business. I just need to know," Joyce said.

"What's with the knit hat on your head?" I asked her. "I almost didn't recognize you. You never wear a hat."

Joyce fidgeted with the hat. "It's cold out. Everyone wears a hat in this weather."

Especially everyone who has beaver fur stuck to their hair.

"So where the frig is he?" Joyce asked.

"I told you, I don't know. I didn't kill him. I didn't kidnap him. I have no clue where he is."

"Great," Joyce said. "That's how you want to play it? Okay by me."

And she stomped away.

"What's wrong with this picture?" I asked Rex. "How did this happen?"

Rex was asleep in his soup can. Hard to have a meaningful conversation with a hamster in a can.

I thought that with the way my morning was running, it wouldn't hurt to have Lula along when I went to see Stewart. Lula wasn't much good as an apprehension agent, but she understood the need for a doughnut when a takedown went into the toilet.

* * *

"So what did this guy do?"

Lula was in the passenger seat of Ranger's Cayenne, looking through Stewart Hansen's file. "It just says controlled substance here. Who wrote this? It don't tell you anything."

I turned onto Myrtle and drove by the house. It looked benign. Small cottage. Small plot of land. Indistinguishable from every other house on the street. Christmas lights still up, outlining the front door. Not lit. I circled the block and parked one house down. Lula and I got out and walked up to Stewart Hansen's house.

"This house is closed up tight," Lula said. "It got blackout drapes on all the windows. Either they're trying to conserve energy, or else they're running around naked in there."

I had new cuffs and a stun gun from Connie. "Easier to stun-gun someone when he's naked."

"Yeah, you got a lot to choose from. You ready to do this?"

I gave her a thumbs-up, and she hauled out her gun and jogged around the house to secure the back door. I felt comfortable she wouldn't have to shoot anyone because Lula, holding her big Glock, dressed in her Sasquatch boots, poison-green tights, and matching spandex mini skirt, topped off with a shocking-pink rabbit fur jacket, was enough to make a strong man faint.

I had my cell phone on speaker, clipped to my jacket, the line open. "Are you in place?" I asked Lula.

"Yep," Lula said from the back of the house.

I rapped on the front door with my two-pound Maglite. No one answered, so I rapped again, and yelled, *"Bond enforcement!"*

"Shit," Lula said on speakerphone. "Turn your head when you do that. You just about busted my eardrum."

"I'm going in," I told her.

"Don't exert yourself breaking the door down. The back is open."

I heard a gunshot and had a moment of panic.

"Oops," Lula said. "Ignore that."

The front was locked, so I waited for Lula to open the door for me. She was smiling wide when she let me in.

"You're not gonna believe this," she said. "We hit the jackpot on this one. We must have died and gone to heaven, and no one told us."

I stepped into a small foyer constructed of raw wallboard. A door opened off the foyer, and beyond the door was cannabis. The house was a pot farm. Grow lights, silver reflective walls, fans and vents, and racks and more racks of shelves filled with plants in various stages of growth.

"Wait until you see the dining room," Lula said. "They got primo shit growing in the dining room."

I gave her a raised eyebrow.

"Not that I would know," Lula said.

"There's weed sticking out of the pockets of your jacket."

"I gathered some evidence on my way through the house."

"I assume you didn't see any Hansens?"

"No, but there's a car back there. And the back door to the house was open. I wouldn't be surprised there's someone hiding in here."

"Do we have to worry about them getting away in the car?"

"No. Someone shot a hole in the right front tire."

I locked and bolted the front door, and Lula and I began working our way through the house.

"You go first and open the doors, and I'll be behind you with my gun," Lula said. "I'd go first, but it's hard to hold a gun and open a door. I want to be able to concentrate on the gun. It's not like I'm afraid or anything."

"Just don't shoot me in the back."

"Have I ever shot you? Honest to goodness, you'd think I didn't know what I was doing."

We searched the living room, dining room, and kitchen.

"At least these boys are neat," Lula said. "They got their empty beer bottles all lined up. Guess that's so they have room in here for planting the little seedlings and weighing and bagging. And they got a nice digital scale here. You could see they put some thought to this."

I poked around in the collection of pots and pans and bottles and jars by the stove. "Looks like they have a science experiment going on. Alcohol, coffee filters, ether."

"These guys are nuts," Lula said. "They're making hash oil. You could turn yourself into a barbecue making that stuff."

We moved down the hall to the bedrooms. No need to search under beds because there weren't any. Two sleeping bags were thrown against a wall in one of the bedrooms. A television sat on the floor. The closet was filled with clothes. The rest of the room was cannabis.

"This is kind of cozy," Lula said. "I bet it's like sleeping in the jungle."

We checked out the bathroom and the second bedroom. Lots of weed drying out in the second bedroom, but no Hansens.

"We're missing something," I said to Lula, going back to the kitchen.

"We opened every door," Lula said. "We looked around all the racks. We looked behind the shower curtain, and we moved the clothes all around in the closet. There's no cellar and no garage and no attic."

"There's a cup of coffee sitting on the counter, and the coffee is still warm. Someone was in here, and I don't think they had time to leave. You were at the back door, and I was at the front door. We checked the windows. No one went out through a window."

Lula cut her eyes to the cupboard over the counter. "Maybe he left just before we got here. You know, lucky coincidence for him."

"Yeah," I said, cuffs in one hand, stun gun in the other, attention focused on the cupboard. "That could be it."

Lula stepped back and two-handed the Glock, aiming it at the cupboard. I reached up and opened one of the doors. And Stewart Hansen tumbled out, crashing onto the counter, sending the science experiment flying. He flopped off the counter onto the floor and scrambled like a cat on black ice—legs moving but no intelligent forward motion.

In the excitement of the moment, Lula squeezed off a shot that went wide of Hansen but knocked out the ether bottle. The liquid splashed onto the gas stove, and we were all paralyzed for a moment.

"Pilot light," Hansen said.

We all dove for the back door, and I think I was in the air when the explosion occurred. Or maybe it was the explosion that threw me out of the house.

"Holy crap," Hansen said.

He was on the ground next to me, and Lula was on her back, skirt up to her neck, next to him.

"Who shot that bottle?" Lula said. "It wasn't me, was it?"

I clapped the cuffs on Hansen, and we all took a bunch of steps backward.

"Anyone else in the house?" I asked Hansen.

"No. I was alone."

We watched the fire rush through the house. It was

like a brush fire, and almost instantly the whole house was burning, and clouds of pot smoke were billowing out over the Burg. Sirens were screaming in the distance, and the three of us leaned against Hansen's car and sucked it all in while tiny pieces of cannabis ash sifted down around us.

"This is good shit," Hansen said, taking a deep breath.

"Smells like you had some Hawaii 5-O," Lula said. "Not that I'd know."

I looked down to make sure my toes weren't smoking. "Maybe we should move back a little."

We all scurried to Hansen's rear boundary.

"This is pretty funny," Lula said. "We burned down a house." And Lula started laughing.

Hansen was laughing too. "Probably a million dollars' worth of grass in that house," Hansen said. "Up in smoke."

I was laughing so hard I tipped over and found myself on the ground. "Look at me," I said. "I can make snow angels."

"I'm getting wet," Lula said. "Is it raining?"

Sounds carried from the front of the house. The rumble of the fire truck engines and the crackle and squawk of police band radios.

"I am so fucking hungry," Lula said. "I need chips. I'd fucking kill for chips."

A black SUV slid to a stop behind Hansen's car. Tank left the car and walked toward us. "I've got her," he said into his walkie. "She's in the back with Lula."

Ranger's Cayenne pulled in behind the SUV. Ranger got out, scooped me up off the ground, and held me close.

"I was afraid you were in the house," Ranger said. "Are you all right?"

"I got blown out of it," I told him. "And then it started raining."

"It's not rain. It's from the fire hoses on the other side of the house." He pulled back a little and looked at me. "Babe, you're high as a kite."

"*Yes!* And you are *so cute.*"

Ranger put me in the Cayenne and handed Hansen and Lula over to Tank. We drove the length of the alley and turned onto Chambersburg Street.

"You're always so *quiet,*" I said to Ranger. "What's with that?"

Ranger didn't move, but I suspected he was rolling his eyes.

"Well?" I said.

"I like quiet."

"Quiet, quiet, quiet," I said. And I gave Ranger a shot to the arm.

"Don't do that," Ranger said.

I gave him another shot.

Ranger pulled to the curb and cuffed me to the sissy bar over the passenger side window.

"Are you going to have your way with me now that I'm handcuffed?" I asked.

"Would you like that?"

"Absolutely not."

Ranger smiled, put the Cayenne in gear, and pulled away from the curb.

"I saw that smile," I said.

On the one hand, I was feeling very flirty and clever. On the other hand, in a dark, back corner of my mind I suspected I was one of those people who gets obnoxious on wacky tobacky. No matter which was right, I couldn't seem to stop.

"So," I said, knowing I was pressing the issue. "Don't you want to have your way with me?"

"More than you could possibly imagine, but right now you're wet, and you smell like pot. You're lucky I let you in my car."

"Where are we going?"

"I'm taking you home, so you can take a hot shower and get dressed in dry clothes."

"And then?"

"We'll see."

Oh boy.

Ranger was in the kitchen making a sandwich when I straggled in. I'd steamed myself in the shower until the water ran cold, and then I'd slipped into jeans and a T-shirt, letting my hair dry on its own.

He looked over at me. "How are you feeling?"

"Hungry and tired."

"You had a full morning. You burned a house down to the ground."

I took two slices of bread, slathered them with mustard, and added ham and cheese.

"Technically, Lula started the fire. It was an accident. She winged a bottle of ether, and it spilled onto the gas stove."

"We're holding the kid in the cuffs. What do you want to do with him?"

"He's FTA. I need to turn him in."

"If you turn him in, you're going to be implicated in the fire. It's going to get you more publicity."

"I need the money."

Ranger got a bottle of water from the fridge. "I can give you a job if you need money."

"What would I do?"

"Fill my minority quota, for one thing. I only employ one woman, and she's my housekeeper."

"Besides that?"

"Odd jobs," Ranger said. "You can work part-time on an *as needed* basis."

"Do you need me now?"

Ranger smiled.

"You missed your chance," I told him.

"I'll get another one. You got a phone call while you were in the shower, and he left a message. You should listen to it."

The message was from Peter Smullen. He wanted to speak to me. Would I please call him back.

Ranger was leaning against the counter, arms crossed, watching me.

"Hard to believe my day could get any worse," I said to him.

"You underestimate yourself."

I dialed Smullen's number and waded through layers of secretaries. Finally, Smullen came on.

"I appreciate the callback," he said. "I imagine your days are complicated since Dickie's disappearance."

"It's been interesting."

"I was hoping we could get together for a chat."

"What do you want to chat about?" I asked him.

"Things."

"That narrows it down."

"I prefer not to discuss sensitive issues on the phone. I have a full schedule this afternoon, but I was hoping we might meet for a drink after hours. Perhaps the bar at the Marriott at eight?"

"Sure. See you at eight."

"I have a date," I said to Ranger. "It turns out I'm very in demand. Everyone wants to talk to me. The police, Joyce, Peter Smullen."

"Did Smullen say why he wanted to meet with you?"

"He said he wanted to talk about *things*." Like, maybe the fact that I planted a bug on him.

"And Joyce?"

"She was here this morning, demanding to know where I stashed Dickie."

"As in chopped-up body parts you fed to your neighbor's cat? Or alive and living in your closet?"

"I don't know."

"You should find out. Maybe she knows something we don't."

"Maybe *you* should talk to her," I said to Ranger. "She likes you."

"You'd throw me into the shark tank?"

That got me smiling. "Is big, bad Ranger afraid of Joyce Barnhardt?"

"I'd rather face the python."

"Joyce doesn't have a long attention span. I'm surprised she's still involved in this."

Ranger's phone buzzed, and he answered it on speaker mode.

"You have a meeting on the calendar for one o'clock," Tank said. "Do you need a ride?"

"Yes."

"I'm in the lot."

"I'll be right down."

Ranger took the Cayenne keys from his pocket and placed them on the counter. He counted out four hundred dollars and placed that on the counter as well. "Caesar is designing a system for a new client tomorrow morning, and a female point of view would be helpful. He'll pick you up at nine. I'll send a uniform with him. The money is an advance on salary for services you'll provide."

He backed me against the wall, leaned into me, and kissed me. His tongue touched mine, and I felt my fingers involuntarily curl into his shirt as heat rushed through my stomach and headed south. He broke from the kiss and looked down at me with a suggestion of a smile. Just a slight curve to the corners of his mouth.

"That's an advance on services *I* provide," he said.

He grabbed his jacket and left.

SEVEN

Since I was no longer desperate for money, I decided to spend the afternoon on activities designed to keep me out of jail. I heard what Morelli was saying . . . that Dickie was just a missing person and I shouldn't worry. But people had been sent to jail for less. I knew this for a fact. I helped put them there.

First up was the conversation with Joyce. I drove to her house and parked in her driveway behind a Pro Serve van and hatchback. Joyce's front door was open, and I could see a cleaning crew working inside. A couch and chair had been set curbside. Terminal victims of the beaver explosion.

I picked out a guy who looked like he might speak English and asked for Joyce.

"Not here," he said. "She let us in and split."

"That's okay, I'll just look around until she gets back. I'm her interior decorator. We had an appointment, but I'm early."

"Sure," he said. "Knock yourself out."

The house was elaborately decorated with a lot of velvet upholstery and gilt-framed mirrors. Rugs were plush. Marble in the kitchen and bathroom. Satin in the bedroom. Flat-screen televisions everywhere. Joyce had married well this last time around. She'd chosen more velvet and gilt than I could manage, but it looked expensive.

There was a designated office/library, the shelves filled with hardcover books that had probably belonged to her ex. A large carved mahogany desk floated in the middle of the room. The desktop was clean. Telephone but no scribble pad. No computer. I checked all the drawers. Telephone book. Nothing else.

I returned to the kitchen and sat at the little built-in workstation. The phone was attached to an answering machine. A Starbucks coffee mug held pens and markers. A couple sticky pads were stacked next to the phone.

I opened the top drawer and found a piece of paper with two nine-digit numbers and a phone number scrawled on it. I recognized one as Dickie's Social Security number. Odd how you remember things like that. I didn't recognize the second number or the phone number.

I dialed the phone number, and a programmed voice introduced itself as the Smith Barney automated Reserved Client Service Center and asked for an account number. That was as far as I was going to get, so I copied the three numbers on a sticky pad and put the paper in my pocket.

I didn't see anything else of interest on Joyce's desk. I scrolled through calls made and calls received on her phone, and copied the list, going back four days.

I packed up and ran into Joyce as I was leaving the kitchen.

"What the fuck?" Joyce said.

"I was looking for you," I told her.

"Well, you found me. What do you want?"

"I thought if we put our heads together we might be able to figure out what happened to Dickie."

"I know what happened to him. I just don't know where he is *now*."

"Why do you care?" I asked Joyce.

"I love him."

I burst out laughing, and Joyce cracked a smile.

"Okay, even *I* couldn't keep a straight face on that one," Joyce said.

"Do you think he's dead?"

"Hard to say one way or another until a body turns up. What I can tell you is this—stay out of my way. I've got an investment here, and I intend to collect. And I'll run over anyone who tries to stop me."

"Hard to believe Dickie had that much money. From what I could see, he wasn't that smart."

"You have no idea what's involved here. And I'm warning you again. Stay out of it."

Joyce was really starting to annoy me. Bad enough from time to time Morelli and Ranger tried to push me around, now Joyce was telling me to butt out.

"Looks like you're doing some redecorating," I said to Joyce. "Is that animal fur on your chandelier?"

We locked eyes, and I knew the thought was fluttering in her head . . . did Stephanie Plum mastermind the beaver bombing? And then the moment passed, and we both stepped back from it.

I walked to the Cayenne, got in, and powered out of the driveway. I drove to Coglin's house just for the heck of it and saw that the green SUV was parked in the alley, two tires on Coglin's property line. I angle-parked behind the SUV, blocking its exit, and approached Coglin's back door with stun gun in hand.

Coglin answered the door with a sawed-off shotgun in his. "Now what?" he asked.

"Same ol', same ol'," I told him.

"I'm not going with you. I can't. I gotta stay here. I'll go as soon as I can."

I looked down the barrel of the sawed-off. "All right,

then," I said. "Good conversation. Call me when you're ready to, uh, you know."

I got into the Cayenne and took off for the bonds office.

"If you're looking for Lula, she isn't here," Connie said when I walked in. "She went home to get dry clothes and never came back. Sounds like you had a busy morning. I hear people are driving from all over the state to breathe Burg air."

"I swear, I didn't have anything to do with that fire. I wasn't anywhere near that house."

"Sure," Connie said. "Did you get Hansen?"

"Yes and no. I came here to use the by–phone number program."

"Is this for Hansen?"

"No. I'm trying to make sense of the Dickie mess. Joyce is tied up in it. I don't exactly know how or why, but I got some numbers off her phone, and I want to run them down. One of them is for the Smith Barney automated Reserved Client Service Center."

"That's heavy," Connie said. "Reserved clients are those with at least ten million in assets. What else do you have on that list?"

I pulled a chair up to Connie's desk and gave her the list. "The three numbers on the sticky page came from a piece of paper in Joyce's desk. The rest came from her phone."

"Doing some breaking and entering?"

"Only entering. Her door was open. I'd like to get into that account, but it asks for an account number."

Connie looked at the sticky page. "Joyce isn't smart. If she had to write the phone number down, I'm guessing the rest of the information is there too."

"The top number is the phone number. The second

number I don't recognize, and the last number is Dickie's Social Security number."

"And they were written in this order on her pad?"

"Yep."

Connie punched the Smith Barney phone number in. The automated voice asked for the account number and Connie gave it the second nine-digit number. The voice asked for the access code and Connie punched in the Social Security number. Access denied. Connie went through the routine again and gave it just the last four digits of the social security number.

"I'm in," Connie said. "There's a zero balance. And the last transaction was a forty-million-dollar withdrawal. That was two weeks ago." Connie hung up and looked at me. "That's a shitload of money. Whose account is this?"

"I don't know."

"It can't be Joyce's," Connie said. "She'd be in the Bahamas buying men and goats. The access code is from Dickie's Social Security number, so the logical assumption would be that it's Dickie's account. But I don't know how Dickie would get that kind of money. That's a lot of billable hours."

No kidding. When Joyce said Dickie was worth money, I wasn't thinking *this* kind of money. "Maybe he stole it from the guys who snatched him, and they got cranky."

Connie took the list of numbers I'd lifted from the phone, typed them into her computer, and plugged them into the by–phone number program.

"After we get rid of the dupes, there are sixteen numbers," Connie said. "I'll run them and print them out for you."

I watched the information come in. Five calls from the law firm in the last two days. And Joyce got an incoming call at one in the morning from Peter Smullen right after Dickie disappeared.

"Isn't Smullen a partner?" Connie asked.

"Yes. That's kind of weird that he called Joyce at one in the morning."

"Maybe there's something going on with them."

Yuk. What would that mean for my meeting? I thought Smullen wanted to talk to me about kidnapping and murder. It would be horrible if it turned out he wanted to talk about sex. Maybe he didn't notice the bug. Maybe he noticed the cleavage.

The rest of the list looked benign. I took the printed copy from Connie and shoved it into my bag.

"Gotta go," I said to Connie.

Connie reached into her top drawer, took out a box of rounds for my Smith & Wesson, and tossed them to me. "Just in case."

I left the bonds office, settled myself in the Cayenne, and called Ranger.

"Yo," Ranger said.

"I took your advice and went to talk to Joyce, and I learned there's a Smith Barney account that has Dickie's Social Security number as an access code. It has a zero balance and the last withdrawal was forty million dollars."

"Joyce shared that with you?"

"More or less. When you went through Dickie's house, did you search his home office?"

"No. I wanted to see the crime scene, and I didn't have time for much else. I slid in between police investigations."

"Maybe it would be a good idea to poke around in Dickie's office and see what turns up. I'd like to prowl through his law office too, but that feels more complicated."

"Where are you now?"

"I'm at the bonds office."

"Pick me up at RangeMan."

RangeMan is located on a quiet side street in downtown Trenton. It's a relatively small, unobtrusive seven-story building sandwiched between other commercial properties. There's a number on the front door and a small brass plaque, but no sign announcing RangeMan. Parking is underground in a gated garage. Ranger's private apartment is located on the top floor. The whole operation is very high-tech and secure.

Ranger was waiting outside for me. I pulled to the curb and placed his hat on the console. He got in and put the hat on.

"Do you feel better now?" I asked him.

"A friend gave this hat to me just before he died. It's a reminder to stay alert."

I glanced over at him. "I thought you wore it because it looked hot."

That got a smile from him. "Do you think I look hot in this hat?"

I thought he looked hot in *everything.* "It's a pretty good hat," I told him.

When I reached Dickie's house, I did a slow drive-by. The crime scene tape had been taken down, and the house no longer felt ominous. No cars in the driveway. No lights shining from windows.

"Park in front of the house," Ranger said. "We're going in like we belong here."

We walked to the door, and Ranger tried the handle. Locked. He took a small tool from his jacket pocket, and in twenty seconds the door was open. I suspected the tool was for show, and if I hadn't been watching he'd say *abracadabra* and the door would unlock.

I followed Ranger in and the ominous feeling returned. There were still bloodstains on the floor, and the house had been tossed.

"Did it look like this when you were here?" I asked.

"No. Someone's been here looking for something, and they weren't subtle."

We went room by room, not disturbing the mess that had been made. Drawers were open, contents thrown onto the floor. Cushions were on the floor too, and some of them were slashed. Mattresses ditto. His office was more orderly only because it had clearly been carefully picked over. His computer was missing. His files were also missing. No way to know if they'd been taken by the police or by whoever ransacked the house. All messages on the answering machine were from Joyce.

"Time's up," Ranger said. "We need to get out of here."

We left the same way we came in. Ranger slid behind the wheel of the Cayenne, and we drove away. I checked my watch and realized I was due for dinner at my parents'.

I reached Morelli on his cell. "It's Friday," I said.

"And?"

"Dinner?"

"Oh crap," Morelli said. "I forgot. I can't make it. I'm tied up here."

I didn't say anything. I just sat on the phone.

"It's my job," Morelli said. "You can't get mad at me for doing my job."

And that was true, but I didn't want to go to dinner without Morelli. I was afraid I'd get relentlessly grilled about Dickie if I didn't have Morelli on board to distract my mother and grandmother.

"Is that Bob barking?"

"Yeah, Bob's with me."

"So what kind of job is this?"

"It's a secret job."

"And when is this secret job going to be done?"

"I don't know. Hopefully soon."

"I could swear I hear television."

"Bob's watching a movie."

I hung up and looked at Ranger.

"No," Ranger said.

"You don't even know what I was going to ask."

"You were going to ask me to fill in for Morelli at dinner."

"Roast chicken."

"You'll have to come up with something better than roast chicken."

"Do you have dinner plans?"

"Are you going to nag me on this?"

"Yes."

"What happened to the Stephanie who thought I was mysterious and scary?"

"Gone."

Actually, that wasn't entirely true. Ranger was still mysterious and scary at times—just not today, just not compared to my mother and grandmother.

Ranger parked in the driveway behind my father's Buick. "We need to be out of here at seven-thirty. If you tell Tank I did this, I'll chain you naked to the traffic light on Hamilton and Broad. And I'll shoot your grandmother if she grabs me."

I was pretty sure he was kidding about the traffic light.

"Isn't this something," Grandma said when she saw Ranger. "What a nice surprise. Is Joe coming too?"

"Nope," I said. "Just Ranger."

"Look here, Helen," Grandma called to my mother. "Stephanie's swapped out Joseph tonight."

My mother stuck her head out the kitchen door. "Where's Joseph?"

"Working," I told her.

"I'm just spooning out the gravy," my mother said. "Everyone sit down."

The doorbell rang and Grandma ran to get it. "It's him," she said to me. "It's my honey."

My father got out of his chair in the living room and took his seat at the table. "I don't care if he craps in a bag," he said to Ranger. "I'll give you a hundred bucks if you can scare him into marrying her and moving her into his room at the old people's home."

"They won't take him back," I said to my father. "He started a fire, and they kicked him out."

"Guess I look like I could still scare *somebody,*" Ranger said to me.

"You look like you could scare *anybody,*" my father said to him. "Don't you ever wear anything but black?"

"Sometimes white socks," Ranger said.

Ranger was smiling a little, and I was thinking he was getting into it, starting to enjoy himself.

"This is my honey, Elmer," Grandma said to everyone.

Elmer was dressed for the occasion in red plaid slacks and a white turtleneck that shoved his loose neck skin up so that it spilled over the top and looked like a turkey wattle.

"Howdy doody," Elmer said. "You have a peach of a home here. And just look at all these hot women I'm gonna get to have dinner with."

"Cripes," my father said.

My mother put the gravy boat on the table and poured herself a glass of wine.

"Elmer's taking me to the Benchley viewing tonight," Grandma said, taking her seat. "It's gonna be a beaut."

Elmer sat next to Grandma. "I read it was the pancreatic cancer that got him. He was a young guy too. Seventy-eight." Elmer reached for the potatoes and his toupee slid over his ear.

The small smile hovered at the corners of Ranger's mouth.

We were passing the chicken, gravy, mashed potatoes, green beans, cranberry sauce, dinner rolls, and pickled vegetable dish when the doorbell chimed. Before anyone could get out of their chair, the door opened and closed and Joyce Barnhardt swept into the house. Her red hair was cut super short and spiked out punk style. Her eyes were lined in black, shadowed in metallic gray. Her lips were inflated to maximum capacity, and her lips and nails were the color of my mother's wine. Joyce removed her leather duster, revealing a black leather bustier that showed a lot of cleavage, and black leather pants that displayed what had to be a painful camel toe. She draped the duster over my father's television chair on her way to the dining room.

"Hey, how's it going?" Joyce said. "I saw the car parked in the driveway, and I said to myself, I bet that's Stephanie's car. So I thought I'd come in and see how she was doing." Her eyes flicked to Ranger for a split second, and I was pretty sure I saw her nipples get hard behind the black leather.

My father was frozen in his chair with his fork halfway to his mouth. And Elmer looked like he'd just filled his bag.

"Give me your gun," I whispered to Ranger.

Ranger slid his arm across the back of my chair and leaned close. "Stay calm."

"Nice house you've got here, Mrs. P.," Joyce said. "You obviously have a talent for decorating. I could tell that by the fabric choice on the slipcovers in the living room."

Grandma beamed at Joyce. "I've always said that. She's got a real eye for picking out just the right thing."

"And you set an excellent table too."

"The secret is you gotta take the olives out of the jar and put them in a little bowl," Grandma said. "If you notice, we put everything in a bowl. That's what makes the difference."

"I'll try to remember that," Joyce said. "Put everything in a bowl."

Grandma turned to my mom. "Isn't it nice to see such a polite young person? Almost no one appreciates things today."

My mother tried to refill her wineglass, but the bottle was empty. "Darn," my mother said.

"We cooked up two big chickens," Grandma said to Joyce. "You could stay for dinner if you want. We have plenty."

Joyce wedged a chair between Grandma and Elmer so she could look across the table at Ranger. "I wouldn't want to impose."

"I'll get you a place setting," Grandma said, scraping back in her chair.

"Eddie Haskell," Ranger whispered against my ear, leaning in to me.

"What?"

"Joyce is doing Eddie Haskell from *Leave It to Beaver.* Eddie Haskell was the obnoxious kid who was always sucking up to the Cleavers."

"You watched *Leave It to Beaver*?"

"Hard to believe, but I didn't start out at age thirty. I actually had a childhood."

"Mind-boggling."

"Sometimes it boggles even *my* mind," Ranger said.

"What are you two whispering about?" Joyce asked. "And where's Morelli? I thought this was his gig."

"Joe's working," I told her. "Ranger volunteered to stand in."

Joyce opened her mouth to say something, thought better of it, and forked up some chicken.

"I'm going to the kitchen to get some hot gravy," I told everyone. "Joyce, why don't you help me?"

I closed the kitchen door behind us, nuked the gravy boat, and turned to Joyce. "What's going on?"

"I realized I was going about this wrong. We're both looking for Dickie, right? But you have Studman out there working with you. That gives you a real advantage over me. So instead of forcing you to butt out, I'm going to stick to you like glue. You and Studman will find Dickie for me."

"Ranger won't turn Dickie over to you."

"I'll worry about that when he finds him. Ranger's a man, and I know what to do with a man. You get them undressed, and they're all basically the same. Scrotum and ego. If you stroke them, they're happy. And I don't see you doing much stroking with Ranger. Looks to me like he's open season."

I took the gravy boat out of the microwave and carried it back to the table. Ranger's chair was empty.

"Where's Ranger?" I asked Grandma.

"He said he had business to take care of, but he left you the keys to the car. They're by your plate. He said he'd catch up with you later."

I put the keys in my pocket and wondered about Ranger's needs. It wasn't as if I was fulfilling them. And it wasn't as if he was a low-testosterone kind of guy.

"That's some outfit you got on," Elmer said to Joyce. "I bet you put out."

"Behave yourself," Joyce said.

"And you got a nice pair of melons there. Are they real?"

Joyce smacked Elmer on the head and his toupee flew off and landed on the table in front of my mother. She jumped in her seat and beat the toupee to death with the empty wine bottle.

"Omigod," my mother said, looking at the mangled hair. "It startled me. I thought it was a giant spider."

Elmer reached over, retrieved his hair, and settled it back onto his head. "This used to happen all the time at the home too."

I made it through the chicken and the chocolate cake. I helped my mom clear the table and do the dishes, and that brought me up to seven-thirty.

"Gotta go," I said to my mom. "Things to do."

"Me too," Joyce said, following me to the door.

I couldn't have Joyce tail me to my meeting at the Marriott, so as I saw it, I had two options. The first option would be to handcuff her at gunpoint to a dining room chair. The second would be to lose her on the road. I decided to go with option two. Mostly because I had the box of bullets in my purse, but no gun.

Joyce was driving a black Mercedes sedan, which I was pretty sure represented husband number two. She got behind the wheel and gave me a thumbs-up. I got into Ranger's Porsche and responded with a stiff middle finger.

I drove off, and after a block I realized Joyce wasn't following. I checked her out in my rearview mirror and saw that she was out of the car, looking under the hood. I turned around and pulled alongside her.

"What's up?" I asked.

"I don't know much about cars," Joyce said, "but I think someone took my engine."

EIGHT

I parked in the hotel garage and walked to the hotel. It was a few minutes before eight, and there was a corporate party going on in the ballroom. Lots of women in cocktail dresses and men in suits congregating in the public areas. Lots of drinking and laughing and flirting. I suspected some of it would get nasty in a couple of hours.

The bar was packed, but Smullen wasn't there. I found a chair in the lobby and waited. After half an hour, I did a tour of the bar and restaurant. Still no Smullen. I called Ranger at nine.

"I've been stood up," I told him.

"Lucky you," Ranger said.

"Did you take Joyce's engine?"

"My instructions were to disable the car, but one of my men bet Hal a burger he couldn't get the engine out. So Hal removed the engine."

I knew Hal. He'd been with RangeMan for a couple of years, and he was one of my favorite people. He looked like a stegosaurus, and he fainted at the sight of blood.

I left the hotel and walked past a few desperate souls hunkered in a corner by the entrance, trying to smoke without freezing their asses off. No one coming or going to the parking garage. Just me, my steps echoing on the cement floor. I approached the Cayenne, and Ranger moved out of a shadow.

"I'll drive," he said. "I want to make sure no one's waiting for you in your apartment."

"I appreciate the thought, but I wasn't going home. I was going to hang out in the cemetery and see if Diggery relieves Lorraine Birnbaum of her diamond."

"It's seventeen degrees," Ranger said. "If Diggery is desperate enough to rob graves in this weather, the least you can do is let him have the diamond."

Ranger crossed Broad and turned onto Hamilton. A dark figure scuttled from between parked cars, and quick as a flash it scooped something off the road with a shovel. The figure was momentarily caught wide-eyed in Ranger's headlights. And then the figure was gone, sucked back between the parked cars, lost in the night.

I gasped and did a whole body shiver.

"Someone you know?" Ranger asked.

"Crazy Carl Coglin. He's on my FTA list."

"Babe."

If I was any kind of bounty hunter, I would have chased Coglin down, but I really didn't want to see what was on the shovel. So I decided to go with Ranger's philosophy. If Coglin needed roadkill that badly, the least I could do was let him keep it.

Three traffic lights later, Ranger cut off Hamilton and parked in my lot. He looked up at my dark apartment windows, shut the Cayenne off, and turned to face me. "Tell me about your kitchen discussion with Joyce."

"She realized you would be helping me find Dickie and decided it was smarter to follow me around than to go off on her own. So she's my new best friend.

"I told her I didn't think it was likely you'd turn Dickie over to her, and she said she had a way with men. She said men were basically scrotum and ego, and they were happy when they got stroked."

Ranger reached across the console and traced a line down the side of my face. His fingertip was warm and his touch was gentle. "I'd like to think I'm more than just scrotum and ego, but she was right about the stroking."

An SUV crept into the lot and parked behind us.

Ranger looked back at it. "That's Tank. He's giving me a ride back to RangeMan after I check your apartment. I'll leave the Cayenne with you."

Caesar rang my bell precisely at nine A.M. He was dressed in RangeMan black, and he was slimmer than most of Ranger's men. Caesar wouldn't single-handedly haul an engine out of a Mercedes. I placed him in his late twenties. He handed a tote bag plus winter jacket over to me and politely stepped into my apartment.

"I'll just be a minute," I told him. "Make yourself at home."

He nodded, but he remained standing just inside the door, hands folded in front of him. Parade rest.

I'd worked for RangeMan once before, and Ranger's housekeeper, Ella, knew my size. She'd sent black leather cross-trainers, black cargo pants, a long-sleeved black T-shirt with the RangeMan logo in magenta, and a black webbed canvas belt. The black winter jacket was identical to the one Ranger wore with the logo in black.

I got dressed and looked at myself in the mirror. I was mini-Ranger. I said good-bye to Rex, locked the apartment, and followed Caesar to an immaculate black Ford Explorer. No logo.

Caesar drove to a large rambling colonial north of town. The grounds were perfectly landscaped even in winter, and the house had a sweeping view of the river.

We parked in the circular drive, Caesar took a clipboard from the backseat, and we went to work.

"The owners are off-site," Caesar said, keying us into the house. "A vacation in Naples. We're installing a new security system while they're away. The husband does a lot of travel, and the wife stays home with two school-age children. So we need to make the system meet the wife's needs. Ranger thought you would be helpful since you see things from a woman's perspective."

We did a fast tour of the house and then went through a second time more slowly, making notes. I didn't know anything about living in a house like this, and I didn't have experience as a mother, but I knew something about fear. And I've broken into enough houses to know what serves as a deterrent. In a house this size, I'd want to know if a door was opened. I'd want closed-circuit television on entrances. I'd want exterior security lighting. I'd want some mobile touchpads to give myself flcxibility. I'd want to make sure the children's rooms were protected against intrusion. That would mean the screens should be wired into the alarm system.

It was almost noon when Caesar dropped me at my apartment building. I ran upstairs, made myself a peanut butter and olive sandwich, and pawed through my junk drawer while I ate. My job as a bounty hunter heavily relies on my ability to stretch the truth and go into sneaky mode. I have patches and hats for almost any occasion, from pizza delivery to plumbing to security specialist.

I found a patch that advertised Richter Security and used double-sided sticky tape to plaster the patch over the RangeMan logo on the black jacket. I dropped a travel flash drive into my pocket so I could record computer data, and I grabbed a clipboard and pad.

It was Saturday, and I was guessing there would be a single security guard on front-desk duty at Petiak, Smullen, Gorvich, and Orr. I hadn't learned anything from Dickie's house. I was hoping his files were still intact at his office.

I parked the Cayenne in the small lot adjacent to the building, and sat there for a moment, gathering my courage. Truth is, I'm not all that brave. And I'm not all that good at what I do. And I was pretty close to getting nervous bowels. I was going to break into Dickie's office, and I was doing it because it wasn't nearly as frightening as the prospect of going to jail for a murder I didn't commit. Still, it was pretty damn frightening.

I talked myself into getting out of the Cayenne, walked to the front of the building, and let myself into the foyer. The large glass door leading to the law offices was locked and, just as I'd suspected, a security guard was behind the desk. I showed him my clipboard and pointed to my watch, and he came to the door.

"Richter Security," I told him, handing him a business card that went with the Richter Security logo on my jacket. "I'm scheduled to come in and work up an estimate on a new system."

"I don't know anything about that," he said. "The offices are closed."

"You were supposed to be notified. There must be someone you can call."

"I've only got emergency numbers."

"They specifically requested a Saturday so business wouldn't be disturbed. I moved a lot of jobs around so I could do this, and if I can't get in today, I don't have another Saturday opening until October."

Now, here's the good part. Men trust women. Even if I looked like a five-dollar hand-job hooker, this guy would think I was the real deal. Women grow up wary, and men grow up thinking they're immortal. Maybe that's overstated, but I'm in the ballpark.

"Just exactly what are you supposed to do?" he asked.

"I guess everyone got a little freaked over the disappearance of one of the partners, and they decided to upgrade the security system. My specialty is video surveillance. I'll be designing an enhanced video system for use throughout the building. Obviously, this isn't something that can be done during business hours. No one wants to think their every action is being monitored."

"Yeah, I guess I can see that. How long will this take?"

"An hour, tops. I just need to draw some room diagrams. Are the partners' offices open?"

"Yeah. No point locking them. They're hardly used. Only Mr. Orr came in every day. And sometimes Mr. Smullen when he's in town."

"That's weird. What kind of lawyer doesn't use his office?"

"Don't ask me. I'm just part-time. Maybe they're all a bunch of rich guys who don't need to work. They just like to have their names on the door—you know what I mean?"

"Yeah. Well, I'm not rich like that, so I'd better get to work."

"Holler if you need anything."

I started in Dickie's office. My original intent had been to get into his computer and search for a client list, but his computer was gone. That brought me to Plan B. Raid his file cabinet. I went through three drawers of files and understood nothing. Why can't lawyers write in English?

I gave up on the files and sat at his desk. I opened the top drawer and found two file folders. One was labeled NUTS AND STALKERS and the other was labeled

CURRENT. Hooray! Now I was getting somewhere. I shoved the folders into my pants, under the waistband, and buttoned my coat over them.

Smullen's office was similar in design to Dickie's. Same furniture, but Smullen's desk drawers were filled with candy bars. Mounds, Baby Ruths, M&Ms, Snickers, Reese's Peanut Butter Cups, Twizzlers. His computer was fresh out of the box. Software installed. Nothing else. No Rolodex. A pen and a pad, but nothing written. Coffee cup stains on his leather desktop. Nothing of interest in his file drawers.

I snitched a couple Snickers and a Reese's and moved on to Gorvich. His office was also unused. No candy bars in the drawers. Gorvich's drawers were empty.

Ditto Petiak.

C. J. SLOAN had been printed in small block letters on the door to the office next to Petiak's. I had no idea what Sloan did for the firm, but he obviously did it in his office because there were stacks of files on every flat surface. There were four in/out baskets on his desk, and they were all filled with papers. His computer monitor was extra wide. And while there was a lot of clutter in the office, it was all perfectly aligned. Sloan was a totally anal neat freak.

I went into Sloan's computer and struck gold. Sloan had client lists with billable hours, current and past. I plugged my flash drive into a USB port and downloaded a bunch of files.

In a last-ditch effort, when I left Sloan's office, I tried the secretary's desk. She had all the hardware but not much content. Multi-line phone, super-duper computer, and a drawer filled with take-out menus. There was a small wooden crate, two cardboard boxes, and an industrial staple gun by the desk. Someone was packing.

The elevator binged and before I had time to react, a huge guy stepped out. He was dressed in shirt and tie and a badly fitting dark blue suit. He was late twenties, early thirties, and he lifted. Probably did some 'roids. His hair was buzzed short and bleached blond. L.A. muscleman.

Muscleman approached the desk and looked down at me. "Whatchadoin'?"

I had the Pizza Hut menu in my hand. "Ordering out. Do you like pepperoni?"

"The loser downstairs said he let you up here to install televisions."

I was on my feet behind the desk. "I'm doing the prelim on some security monitors."

"No, you're not. I know who you are. I saw your picture in the paper. You're the nut who tried to choke Mr. Orr."

"You're mistaken. I work for Richter Security. I guess I have a double out there somewhere, eh?"

"I don't make mistakes like that, lady. I got an eye for the girls. I even remember your name. Stephanie Plum. I remember it 'cause it's a 'ho name. Stephanie Juicy. Stephanie Good-to-Eat. Stephanie I'm-Gonna-Sink-My-Teeth-into-You."

Yikes. "Sorry," I told him. "I'm not on the menu."

"I think you are. I think I'm gonna have some fun with you before I turn you over to Mr. Petiak."

"Is he your boss?"

"Yeah. And he don't like intruders. He's got things he does to them so they don't intrude anymore, but sometimes he lets me have fun with them first."

I had pepper spray and a stun gun in my bag. "Let me show you my identification—"

"The only identification I care about is between your legs, Stephanie Juicy."

He was around the desk in two strides, reaching out for me. I knocked his hand away, grabbed the staple gun, pressed it into his crotch, and *bam, bam, bam,*

bam . . . I stapled his nuts. At least, I thought it felt like nuts, but hell, what do I know? There's other equipment down there, and I guess it could have been most anything.

Muscleman's mouth dropped open and his face turned red. He froze for a moment, sucking air, and then he doubled over and crashed to the floor.

I was in love with the genius who'd invented the electric stapler.

I wasted no time getting out of there. I ran out of the office and flew down the stairs. I crossed the lobby and was out the front door before the guard at the desk was on his feet. I bolted for the lot and ran flat-out into Ranger when I turned the corner. He absorbed the impact without moving and wrapped his arms around me to keep me from falling.

"We need to get out of here," I told him.

Tank was idling behind the Cayenne. Ranger signaled that he could leave, and Ranger and I got into the Porsche. Ranger drove out of the lot, made a U-turn half a block away, and parked.

"What were you doing in the lot?" I asked him.

"Hal was working the remote monitors and suspected you were in the law office building. He was worried about you."

"How about you? Were you worried about me?"

"I always worry about you."

"We didn't get anything out of Dickie's house," I told Ranger, "so I decided to look at his office. Didn't think there'd be much activity on a Saturday. Figured I could fly under the radar."

Ranger peeled the Richter Security label off my jacket. "And?"

"Dickie's office is a normal, working office. It looked like everything was still intact . . . at least until

I got there." I unbuttoned my jacket, removed the files, and handed them to Ranger.

We were sitting there watching the building when the big blond goon stumbled out the front door. He was doubled over, holding himself. He inched his way to the lot, crawled into a silver Camry, and slowly drove down the street.

Ranger looked over at me, eyebrows raised in question.

"It turned out I wasn't entirely under the radar," I told Ranger. "And I had to staple his nuts."

"Babe."

"He said he worked for Petiak. I'm not sure what he was doing there on a Saturday because the desk guard said Petiak never comes into the office. And Petiak's office looked unused. For that matter, all the partners' offices looked unused, excluding Dickie's."

Ranger skimmed the CURRENT folder. "These are all one-page summaries for quick reference, and at first glance they all look like normal low-grade cases. A couple property damage cases. A criminal case against Norman Wolecky for assault. Litigation against a landscaper. More property damage. I could be missing something, but it doesn't look to me like any of these cases would bring in big money."

"So we have three partners with empty file cabinets, a fourth partner who chased ambulances, forty million dollars withdrawn from a Smith Barney account, a dead accountant, and a missing Dickie."

"I talked to Zip about his brother. He said Ziggy did high-volume accounts. He was under the impression Petiak, Smullen, Gorvich, and Orr represented power."

"Apparently not Dickie. Dickie represented Norman Wolecky."

Ranger looked at the second folder. "Nuts and

Stalkers." He flipped it open. "There are only two summaries in here."

"Am I one of them?"

"No. I imagine you would be filed under BITCH EX-WIFE. The first summary is for Harry Slesnik. According to this, Slesnik is a self-described separatist who seceded from the United States and declared his town house a sovereign country. He was arrested when he tried to annex his neighbor's garage. Dickie quit the case after being paid in Slesnik dollars. The last piece of paper attached to this is a formal declaration of war against Dickie.

"The second nut is Bernard Gross."

"I know him," I told Ranger. "He's a World's Strongest Man wannabe. Vinnie bonded him out on a domestic violence charge, and he went FTA. I found him in a gym, and when I got him outside he freaked and wrecked my car. He got his hands under the frame and flipped it over like a turtle."

"Dickie represented him in his divorce . . . at least initially," Ranger said. "While deposing Gross, the subject of gynecomastia came up. Dickie made the fatal mistake of referring to them as man boobs, and Gross destroyed the conference room in a fit of steroid-induced rage. Apparently, Gross is sensitive about his . . . gynecomastia."

"Something to remember. Do you think either of these guys is crazy enough to steal Dickie?"

Ranger handed the file back to me. "I can see them stealing him. I can't see them keeping him."

"The office next to Petiak was occupied by someone who actually did work there. Probably the firm's finance officer. I downloaded a bunch of files onto a flash drive, but I'm not sure I have the software on my computer to read them. Spreadsheets and things. I was hoping you could open it."

Ranger turned the key in the ignition and gave the Cayenne some gas. "What should we do with your hitchhiker? Do you want to let her tag along, or do you want me to get rid of her?"

I turned and looked out the rear window. Joyce was behind us in a white Taurus. No doubt a rental.

"She must have picked me up when I left my apartment. You can let her follow. It'll kill her when we drive into the RangeMan garage."

We were in Ranger's office, which was attached to the RangeMan control room. Ranger was relaxed in his chair with a stack of reports in front of him.

"When Ziggy Zabar went missing, I ran Dickie and his partners through the system," Ranger said. "Credit reports, real estate, personal history, litigation. They look clean on the surface, but you put them together and it feels off. Smullen spends a lot of time out of country. Gorvich is a Russian immigrant. Petiak was military. Did a couple tours and got out. Smullen, Gorvich, and Petiak all look like they bought their law degrees a couple years ago. And they all lived in Sheepshead Bay before moving here."

"So maybe they were getting together for *Monday Night Football* and decided they'd become lawyers and move to Trenton."

"Yeah," Ranger said. "That would work."

"Here's something weird. It's been four days since Dickie was dragged out of his house, leaving a trail of blood. Ordinarily, the chances of death increase with length of disappearance, but for some reason, the longer this goes on, the more I believe Dickie is alive. Probably just wishful thinking since I'm the prime murder suspect."

"I think Dickie and his partners were involved in bad business and something happened that made the deal start to unravel. Ziggy Zabar seems to be the first victim. Dickie appears to be the second. And now houses are getting tossed, and Smullen has contacted you and Joyce. We don't really know what happened at Dickie's house. We have gunshots fired and evidence indicating someone was dragged out of the house. DNA testing on the blood hasn't come back yet, so we aren't sure who got shot. It's possible Dickie is in the wind, and someone is scrambling to find him. It's also possible he's dead, and he had something that wasn't recovered before he died."

"Like the forty million," I said.

"Yes."

"What else do we know about the partners?"

"All three partners are in their early fifties. Petiak moved into the area five years ago, and Gorvich and Smullen followed. Petiak owns a modest house in Mercerville. Gorvich and Smullen are renting in a large apartment complex off Klockner Boulevard. Before moving to Trenton, Smullen owned a car wash in Sheepshead, Gorvich had part ownership in a restaurant, and Petiak owned a limo service consisting of one car. Somehow, the three men found Dickie, and between them they managed to buy an office building downtown, an apartment building that sits on the edge of public housing, and a warehouse on Stark Street. No litigation against any of them. Smullen is married, with a wife and children in South America. Gorvich is currently unmarried and has been divorced three times. And Petiak has never married."

Ranger plugged the flash drive into his computer, opened a spreadsheet, and broke into a smile. "You downloaded the firm's financial records. Clients. Fees for service. Services provided. There's a separate spreadsheet for each partner."

I dragged my chair next to his so I could see the screen as he scrolled down.

"Dickie has normal clients and is pulling in around two hundred thousand," Ranger said after a half hour of reading. "Smullen, Petiak, and Gorvich have client lists that read like Who's Who in Hell. South American drug lords, gunrunners, mercenaries, and some local thugs. And they're billing big money."

I'd been taking notes and doing a tally in my head as we moved from one partner to the next, and I had a grip on how much money we were talking about.

"Forty million and change," I said.

"Now we know who owned the Smith Barney money. We just don't know where it went." Ranger gathered the reports together, slid them into a large envelope, and handed them over to me. "This is your copy. I'll have my financial guy go over the material on the flash drive and summarize it for us." He looked at his watch. "I have to get to the airport. I'm flying to Miami to escort a high-bond FTA back to Jersey. I should be home tomorrow night. I'll call when I get in. Tank will be available if you have problems."

NINE

"Okay, so run this by me again," Lula said. "We're all dressed up like Handy Andy for why?"

"Dickie is part owner of an apartment building. On the odd chance that he isn't dead, I thought it might be a place he'd hole up. Or maybe a place someone would hold him hostage. It's on Jewel Street, right on the edge of public housing. I did a drive-by, and it looks like a candidate for urban renewal. There are ten units, and I'm sure they all have leaky faucets and broken toilets. I figure we go in looking like maintenance, and we won't have a problem poking around."

"I hope you realize I could be shopping right now. There's a big shoe sale at Macy's."

"Yes, but since you're with me, going on a crime-solving adventure, you get to wear this neat tool belt. It's got a hammer and a tape measure and a screwdriver."

"Where'd you get this thing anyway? It don't hardly fit a full-figure woman like me."

"Borrowed it from my building super, Dillon Rudick."

I parked the Cayenne next to a Dumpster in the alley behind the building. Joyce was still following me, but I didn't care a whole lot as long as she stayed in her rental car and didn't interfere.

"We'll start at the bottom and work our way to the top," I told Lula. "It shouldn't take long."

"Just suppose we find this dickhead, then what? It's not like he committed a crime. It's not like he's FTA and we can haul his bony ass off to jail."

"I guess we sit on him and call the *Trenton Times* to come over with a photographer."

"I would have worn something different if I'd known that. I got a sweatshirt and baggy-ass jeans on so I look handy. This isn't gonna show me off in a photograph. And look at my hair. Do I have time to change my hair color? I photograph much better when I'm blond."

I opened the back door to the building and peered into the dark interior. It was a three-story walk-up with a central stairway. Four apartments on the first floor, four on the second, and two on the third. It was late afternoon. Coming up to dinnertime. Most tenants would be at home.

I knocked on 1A and a Hispanic woman answered. I told her we were checking toilet seals.

"Toilet don't work," the woman said. "No toilet."

"What do you mean it don't work? You gotta have a toilet," Lula said.

"Don't work."

Lula elbowed her way in. "Maybe we could fix it. Let me have a look at this toilet. Sometimes you just gotta jiggle the handle."

The apartment consisted of one large room opening off a galley kitchen, plus a single bedroom and bathroom. Seven kids and six adults were watching a small television in the living room. A big pot of something vaguely smelling like chili bubbled on the stove.

Lula wedged herself into the little bathroom and stood in front of the toilet. "This toilet looks okay to me," Lula said. "What's wrong with it?"

"Don't work."

Lula flushed the toilet. Nothing. She picked the lid up and looked inside. "There's no water in this toilet," she said. "That's your problem." Lula reached around and turned the valve on the pipe leading to the toilet. "It's gonna work just fine now," she said. She flushed the toilet again and the bowl began to fill with water.

The Hispanic woman was waving her arms and talking rapid-fire Spanish.

"What's she saying?" Lula asked me.

I shrugged. "I don't speak Spanish."

"You're with Ranger all the time. Don't he ever speak Spanish?"

"Yes, but I don't know what he says."

The toilet bowl was now entirely filled with water and the water was still running.

"Uh-oh," Lula said. "Maybe I should shut the water off." She reached behind the toilet, turned the valve, and it came off in her hand. "Hunh," she said. "This ain't good."

"Don't work," the Hispanic woman said. "Don't work. Don't work."

The water was running over the side of the toilet bowl, splashing onto the floor.

"We gotta go now," Lula said to the woman, giving her the handle to the valve. "And don't worry, we're gonna put this on our report. You'll be hearing from someone." Lula closed the apartment door behind us and we headed for the stairs. "Maybe we should skip right to the second floor," she said.

"Don't offer to fix anything this time," I said. "And let me do the talking."

"I was just trying to be helpful is all. I saw right off her problem was she didn't have the water turned on."

"She didn't have it turned on because the valve was *broken*."

"She didn't communicate that to me," Lula said.

I knocked on the door to 2A and my knock was answered by a little black woman with short gray hair.

"We're checking to see if there are any maintenance issues with this building," I told her.

"I don't have any problems," the woman said. "Thank you for asking."

"How about your toilet?" Lula said. "Does your toilet work okay?"

"Yes. My toilet is fine."

I thanked the woman and pushed Lula away from the door, over to 2B.

"I know something's wrong here," Lula said, sniffing the air. "Smells like a gas leak. Good thing we're going around checking on these things."

"We're not checking on anything. We're looking for Dickie."

"Sure, I know that," Lula said. "That don't mean we can't detect a gas leak."

The door was answered by a fat guy wearing boxer shorts. "Waddaya want?" he asked.

"We been sent by the gas company," Lula said. "We smelled a leak." She stuck her head into his apartment. "Yeah, it's coming from in here all right."

"There's no gas in here," he said. "Everything's electric."

"I guess I know gas when I smell it," Lula said. "My partner and me are from the gas company. We know these things. How about the oven? Are you sure the oven isn't gas?"

"Waddaya think this is, the Hotel Ritz? The oven don't even work. The oven never worked. I gotta cook everything in the microwave."

Lula pushed past him. "Stephanie, you go walk around and make sure there's no gas leakin' out of anything."

I stepped in and gasped at the stench. I looked at the

fat guy and I was pretty sure I knew what was leaking gas, but I held my breath and did a fast run through the apartment to make sure Dickie's corpse wasn't rotting in the bathtub.

"This place reeks," Lula said to the fat guy. "What are you cooking in that microwave?"

"Bean burritos. It's all it cooks. It explodes everything else."

"Guess we found the gas source," Lula said. "And you should put a shirt on. It should be illegal for you to go without a shirt."

"What about my microwave? Are you gonna fix it? It explodes everything."

"We're from the gas company," Lula said. "We don't do microwaves."

"You got a tool belt on," the guy said. "You're supposed to fix things, and I want my microwave fixed."

"Okay, okay," Lula said. "Let me take a look here."

"Careful of the door," he said. "It sticks."

"That's probably your problem. It takes you too long to get the door open, and then you cook everything too long, and it explodes." Lula gave the door a good hard yank, a couple screws flew off into space, the hinges snapped, and the door came off in her hand. "Oops," Lula said.

I didn't waste any time getting out of there. I was halfway up the stairs to the third floor when I heard Lula slam the door on 2B and come pounding after me.

"Least he won't be stinking things up eating more of them microwave burritos," Lula said.

My cell phone rang. It was Tank.

"Are you okay?" he asked.

"Yep."

Tank disconnected.

"Who was that?" Lula wanted to know.

"Ranger's out of town, and Tank's in charge of my safety."

"I thought I was in charge of your safety."

I rapped on 3A. "I'll tell him next time he calls."

A tall black guy with red dreads answered the door.

"Holy cow," Lula said. "It's Uncle Mickey."

"Your uncle?"

"No. Uncle Mickey's Gently Used Cars! He's famous. He does those commercials on television. 'Come to Uncle Mickey's Gently Used Cars and we'll treat you right.' Everybody knows Uncle Mickey."

"What can I do for you girls?" Uncle Mickey asked. "Are you looking for a deal on a car?"

"No, we're the Fix-It Sisters," Lula said. "We're going around fixing things."

I did a mental eye roll. We were more like the Break-It Sisters.

"What are you doing in a dump like this?" Lula asked Uncle Mickey.

"Not as much profit margin as you'd expect in used cars," Mickey said. "Uncle Mickey's fallen on some hard times. Got a lot of overhead. Had a bad run with the ponies." He peeked out into the hall. "You aren't going to tell anyone Uncle Mickey lives here, are you?"

"You living here by yourself?"

"Yeah, just Uncle Mickey all by himself in the penthouse. I don't suppose you girls would like to come in and entertain Uncle Mickey?"

"We got work to do," Lula said. "You're gonna have to entertain yourself."

Uncle Mickey disappeared behind his door, and we moved to 3B.

"That was sort of depressing," Lula said. "He looks so sincere in those commercials. You just want to rush out and buy one of his cars."

A voluptuous, dark-haired, dark-eyed woman answered my knock at 3B. She was wearing a red sweater and jeans and had an expensive watch on her wrist and a diamond cocktail ring that went knuckle to knuckle. I put her age at forty with very good genes.

"Yes?" she said.

"We're working our way through college fixing things," Lula said. "You got anything broken?"

"I know who you are," the woman said to me. "I saw your picture in the paper. You're the woman who murdered Dickie Orr."

"I didn't murder him," I said. "I have an alibi."

"Yeah, right. Everyone's always got an alibi. You're in big trouble. Orr embezzled a shitload of money from the firm, and you killed the little worm before anybody could figure out where he put it."

"How do you know that?"

"The guy I'm living with is a partner. Peter Smullen. He tells me everything. We're getting married as soon as he gets a divorce from his bitch wife. Then we can buy a house and get out of this dump."

"Peter Smullen lives here?"

"Usually. When he's not traveling. Or screwing around. He didn't come home last night, and it's going to cost him big. I've had my eye on a bracelet at Tiffany's. I've been waiting for him to pull something like this."

"A woman's gotta plan ahead," Lula said. "Gotta take advantage of those opportunities."

"Fuckin' A," Smullen's girlfriend said.

"Okay then," I said. "Have a nice day. We'll be moving along."

Lula and I stopped on the second-floor landing to regroup.

"That was interesting," Lula said. "Do you want to try the other tenants? We missed a bunch on the first and second floors."

"I don't think Dickie is here, but we might as well finish the job we started. And for God's sake, don't offer to fix anything."

Joyce followed me to my apartment building and parked two rows back. I could be a good person and tell her I was done for the night, or I could be mean and let her sit there for a while before she figured it out. I decided to go with mean. She wouldn't believe me anyway. I took the elevator to the second floor and found a guy in RangeMan black waiting in front of my door.

"I'm supposed to make sure your apartment is safe before you go in," he said.

Good grief. I guess I appreciated the concern, but this was feeling a little over the top.

I unlocked the door and waited while he did his thing, looking under beds and checking out closets.

"Sorry," he said when he was done. "Tank made me do it. If something happens to you while Ranger's away, we're all out of a job."

"Ranger should get a grip."

"Yes, ma'am."

I closed the door and looked at him through the peephole. He was still standing there. I opened the door.

"Now what?" I said.

"I'm not allowed to leave until I hear you lock and bolt the door."

I closed the door, locked and bolted it. I looked through the peephole again. No RangeMan. I hung my coat and bag on the hook in the hall and gave Rex a cracker.

"I have a very strange life," I said to Rex.

I got a beer out of the fridge and called Morelli's cell phone.

"What?" Morelli said.

"I just wanted to say hello."

"I can't talk now. I'll call you later."

"Sure."

"He won't call," I said to Rex. "Men are like that."

I tried Ranger's cell and got his answering service. "You're a nut," I told him.

I took the envelope filled with reports into the living room and began reading through the material. There was nothing in any of the reports to link Smullen, Gorvich, and Petiak together, other than their previous addresses. And that connection was vague. They were all from different neighborhoods in Sheepshead. Ranger had checked not just Smullen, Gorvich, and Petiak, but their parents as well. All families seemed to be hardworking and clean. No criminal records anywhere. No indication of mob connections. Gorvich was Russian-born but immigrated with his parents when he was twelve. There was also nothing to link Smullen, Gorvich, and Petiak to Dickie prior to their entering into business together.

TEN

I woke up on the couch with Petiak's credit report clutched in my hand and sun streaming in through the two living room windows. The bad part was I had a crick in my neck from sleeping on the couch all night. The good part was I was already dressed.

I went to the kitchen and started brewing coffee. I poured out a bowl of cereal and added milk, saying a silent thank-you to Morelli. It had been thoughtful of him to bring food, and I was sure he would have called back last night if it had been at all possible. I felt my eyes narrow and my blood pressure rise a little thinking about the phone call I never got and made an effort at composure. He was busy. He was working. He was Italian. Yada yada yada.

I finished the cereal, poured myself a cup of coffee, and took it to the living room window. I looked down into the parking lot. No white Taurus.

Mr. Warnick walked out of the building and got into his vintage Cadillac. He was wearing a sports jacket and tie. All dressed up for church. He didn't look cold. The sky was blue. The sun was shining. Birds were chirping. Spring had sneaked in while I was asleep on the couch.

My head was filled with miscellaneous facts about

Smullen, Gorvich, and Petiak. They were all mediocre students in high school. Petiak went to a state college on a military scholarship. Smullen and Gorvich went to colleges that were unfamiliar to me. None of the men had been involved in varsity sports. Smullen had a sweet tooth. Gorvich collected wives but didn't keep them. Smullen had a wife in South America and a girlfriend in a slum in Trenton.

Smullen had arranged a meeting with me, but didn't show. He'd also done a no-show on his girlfriend. I had bad vibes about Smullen. I was afraid something had gone down, and it hadn't been good for Smullen.

Next up was a visit to Grandma.

Unfortunately, all RangeMan vehicles are equipped with a tracking device. Between the bug in my purse and the transmitter in the Porsche, RangeMan knew my every move. And the guys were on high Stephanie alert until Ranger returned. I wanted to take a look at the warehouse this morning, and I didn't want to attract a lot of attention. I didn't want five guys in RangeMan black hovering around the structure, wondering if they should break in SWAT-style. So I was going to leave my purse and Ranger's Porsche at my parents' house and take Uncle Sandor's Buick.

Uncle Sandor gave Grandma his '53 powder blue and white Roadmaster Buick when he went into the nursing home. It's a classic car in cherry condition, and it's eerily indestructible. Men think it's a very cool car, but if I had my choice, I'd go with a red Ferrari.

I drove the Cayenne to my parents' house and popped inside.

"I'm going to borrow the Buick," I told Grandma. "I'll bring it back in a couple of hours."

"You could drive it all you want. It almost never gets used."

I got behind the wheel of the monstrous Buick and

cranked the V-eight over. I put it into reverse and backed it out of the garage and onto the street. The car rumbled under me, sucking gas and spewing toxins. I shoved it into drive and muscled it out of the Burg, took Hamilton to Broad, and cut through the center of town.

The warehouse Dickie partly owns is on Stark Street. Stark Street starts bad and gets worse. The early blocks are marginal businesses mixed with slum housing. Shady entrepreneurial private enterprise flourishes on this part of Stark. You can buy everything from shoplifted Banana Republic T-shirts to the drug of your choice to a backseat BJ. It's a long street, and the farther you travel, the more the street gives over to anger and despair. Squatters live in the graffiti-riddled, condemned buildings of middle Stark. And finally, Stark turns to scrub fields and the skeletal remains of factories that are too wasted to draw even gang interest. Beyond this moonscape of scorched brick rubble, at the very end of Stark, just past the salvage graveyard, is a light industrial park. The rent is cheap and the access to Route One is excellent. Dickie's warehouse was in this industrial park.

I turned onto Stark and had the road to myself. Sunday morning and everyone was sleeping off Saturday night. Good thing too, because I would have attracted attention in the Buick. I drove past the junkyard and into the small industrial park. It was dead quiet.

The warehouse was next to an automotive paint and body shop. No cars were parked in the warehouse lot, but there were a couple cars in the body shop lot. I docked the Buick next to one of the cars in the body shop. Just in case someone happened by, I didn't want to make it obvious I was in the warehouse.

The body shop was closed up tight, but I could hear a power tool being used inside. The diode on a security camera over a door blinked from red to green. I was being filmed. Probably worked on a motion sensor.

I was debating moving the Buick when the door opened and a huge, tattooed, wild-haired guy stepped out.

"Now what?" he said. "I'm clean."

It was Randy Sklar. He'd gotten busted for possession about six months ago. Vinnie had bonded him out, and he'd failed to appear. I'd found him in a bar drunk off his ass, and Lula and I had literally dragged him back to the police station.

Only one reason for Randy Sklar to be up and working on a Sunday morning. This was a chop shop and Randy was taking a car apart. You don't let a hot car sit. You take a torch to it and in a couple of hours, the evidence is gone.

I smiled at Randy because before he passed out and I slapped the cuffs on him, he'd been fun at the bar. And I was also smiling because this was a stroke of luck. Randy wasn't going to call the police if I broke into the warehouse. He was going to keep his bay doors down and locked and hope no one wanted to talk to him.

"I'm not looking for you," I told him. "I heard you managed to wiggle out of the possession charge."

"Yeah, there were some problems with police procedure. Are you looking to get rid of the Buick?"

"No. I just want to park here while I go next door."

"Not much over there," Randy said. "Looked to me like they cleaned house."

"I'm looking for the guy who owns it."

"Don't know nothing about that. Just know trucks come in and out at night while we're working. Figured it was the mob running a hijacking op, so we stayed away. Like to keep a low profile anyway. Then, a couple days ago, there's nonstop activity, and from what I could see through the open bays, the place got emptied out. And no one's been there since. At least no trucks."

"Cars?"

"Haven't seen any, but they could park on the side. There's a door over there. Looks like there are offices on the second floor."

"So how's life?"

"Life's okay. You should come back to the bar. I'll buy you a drink."

"That's a deal."

I crossed a small patch of blighted grass and circled the warehouse. Four loading docks in the back. Windows at the upper level. A locked front door. And a locked side door. If I were with Ranger this wouldn't be a problem. There was a frosted window and vent on a back corner. Bathroom. I could break the window and climb in. Probably set off a security alarm, but I'd have at least twenty minutes before anyone would respond to this location. And chances were decent no one would come at all.

I went back to the Buick and got a tire iron out of the trunk. I whacked the window with the tire iron and cleaned out the glass as best I could. I carefully crawled through the window with minimum damage. A scrape on my arm and a tear in my jeans.

I was in a bathroom that was best used in the dark. I held my breath and tiptoed out. I'd soak my shoes in Clorox when I got home. I flipped a switch, and overhead fluorescents blinked on.

Randy was right. The warehouse had been swept clean. Not a scrap of garbage anywhere . . . other than in the bathroom. Lots of empty shelves. A couple long folding tables. Some folding chairs neatly stacked against a wall. No hint as to the use other than a lingering odor of something chemical. Gasoline or kerosene.

There was a freight elevator and an enclosed stairwell servicing the second floor. I very quietly took the stairs. The door at the top was closed. I opened the door and found another empty storage area. An office with a large, smudged, frosted window looked out at the storeroom. I looked more closely and realized the window was dark with soot. This got my heart to flop around a little in my chest. I tried the door. Locked. I took a deep breath and used the tire iron on the office window.

I looked inside the office, and it took a moment to figure it out. Sometimes things are so ghastly it takes time for your mind to catch up with your eyes. I was looking at a cadaver sitting in a chair behind a desk. The desk, the chair, the body, and the wall behind it were scorched black. All burned to a crisp. It was so terrible, so far removed from reality, that at first I had no emotional reaction other than disbelief. I was at the broken window, looking into the room, and the room smelled of smoke and charred flesh.

I'd like to think I am good in an emergency, but the truth is, instinct takes over, and it doesn't always lead to intelligent action. The moment I smelled the smoke, I went completely spastic. My only thought was to get as far away as possible as fast as possible. I tumbled through the door, all flailing arms and frantic legs, and slid down five stairs before getting my footing. I was about to open the ground-floor door when there was a sound like a giant pilot light igniting. *Phunnnnf!*

I opened the stairwell door to a wall of flame and more spastic horror. I slammed the door shut and ran back up the stairs. There were no windows in the storeroom, only windows in the torched office. I scrambled over broken glass into the office, opened a window on the outside wall, and looked down. I was at least thirty feet from the ground.

So here was a choice. I could dive headfirst and splatter like Humpty Dumpty, or I could stay in the building and burn like the guy at the desk.

Randy came running from the body shop. "Jump!" he yelled at me.

"It's too far."

A second guy came running. "Holy shit," he said. "What's she doing up there?"

"Get the truck," Randy said to the guy. "Hurry!"

Flames were starting to lick up the side of the building, and the floor was hot under my feet. An eighteen-wheeler rolled out of the body shop, over the grass, and idled at the front of the warehouse.

"He's going to drive it under you, and you need to jump fast before it catches fire," Randy yelled at me.

Okay, so it was a little Hollywood. Doesn't mean it wouldn't work. And it's not like I had a lot of options.

I straddled the open window, the truck moved in, I swung my other leg over, sucked in some air, and jumped. I hit the metal roof feetfirst and lost my balance. I went to my hands and knees, looking for something to grip, clawing at air. I slid over the side of the trailer and grabbed a strut as the truck drove away from the building. I hung like that, flopping around and swearing, for just a couple of seconds before my fingers released and I crashed to the ground.

I was spread-eagled on my back with all the air knocked out of me. I had cobweb vision. The truck engine chugged in my ear, and Randy bent over me. His face was inches from mine, the sun framing his Wild Man of Borneo hair in a glorious corona.

I couldn't speak. The air hadn't yet returned to my lungs. "Un," I said.

"What should I do?" he asked. "Should I feel for broken bones? Maybe around your rib cage. Loosen your clothes."

"Un!"

"It was worth a try," he said. "A guy's gotta try, right?"

"I'm assuming I'm not dead."

"No. You're just a little scratched up and . . ."

"And what?"

"And nothing."

"You're looking at my hair. What's wrong with my hair?"

"It's a little . . . singed."

I closed my eyes. "Shit."

"You're not gonna cry, are you? My girlfriend always cries if I say the wrong thing about her hair. I *hate* that."

I made an effort to get up, but I was in pain everywhere and not making much vertical progress. Finally, Randy got me under the armpits and dragged me to my feet.

"I don't suppose you found the guy you were looking for," Randy said.

"Hard to tell."

"Are you waiting around for the police and the fire trucks?"

"Do you think they'll come?"

"Not unless we call them."

"I'm not inclined to do that."

"Me either."

"Thanks for getting me out of there," I said to Randy. "That was a really big truck."

"It's a double-decker car hauler. We use it to . . . uh, haul cars."

The warehouse was an inferno, completely engulfed in flames, the heat stinging my skin. Black smoke billowed about a quarter mile into the sky.

"It's a decent fire," Randy said, looking up at the smoke. "We might get some action on this one."

I limped to the Buick, managed to get behind the wheel, and did some slow breathing. I sat for a couple of minutes, collecting myself. A bay door to the body shop opened, and the car hauler rolled out. The shop had cleaned up for visitors.

I got the Buick started and followed the hauler to Route One. Sirens screamed in the distance, but we were traveling away from them. When we reached Route One, the hauler went north and I went south. I took the Broad Street exit and drove back to my apartment. Ranger's Porsche and my purse were still at my parents' house, but I wasn't going to retrieve them looking like this. I'd lost about an inch of hair, and the ends were scorched black and frizzed. I was cut and scraped and blistered and sore. I was going to take a shower and crawl into bed and stay there until my hair grew back.

I stepped out of the elevator and slowly propelled myself down the hall, leaving smudges of soot and blood. Before the day was over, Dillon would be working on the carpet with his rug shampooer. Mental note: Get a six-pack for Dillon.

I opened my door, trudged inside, and almost keeled over when I saw Ranger. He was sitting in my living room, in my only good chair, his elbows on the arms, his fingers steepled together in front of him. His face showed no emotion, but he was radiating anger. I could have popped corn on the invisible energy Ranger was throwing.

"Don't start," I said to him.

"Do you need a doctor?"

"I need a shower."

His eyebrows raised ever so slightly.

"No," I said.

I limped into the bathroom and whimpered when I saw my reflection in the mirror. I closed the door and dropped my clothes onto the floor. Lucky for me, the weather was still cool, and I'd been wearing a heavy sweatshirt and jeans. The clothes had saved most of my skin from the broken glass. I washed away the grime and a lot of the blood. I slapped some Band-Aids over the deeper gashes, got dressed in clean clothes, and went out to face Ranger.

"You got home early," I said.

"I had to fly charter. Couldn't get on a commercial plane with my man."

"How did you know I wasn't visiting my mom?"

"Your visits are never that long. Hal got suspicious and called your cell and talked to your grandmother."

"I wanted to take a look at the warehouse, and I was afraid I'd be followed by a RangeMan caravan."

He didn't say anything to that. If you didn't know Ranger, you would think he looked relaxed in the chair, one long leg extended, one bent at the knee, arms on the upholstered armrests. If you knew him at all, you would be extremely wary.

I sat across from him, on the couch, easing myself down. I leaned my head back and closed my eyes for a moment, struggling with composure, not wanting to burst into tears in front of Ranger. I opened my eyes and blew out a sigh because he was still there, watching me.

"I assume you burned the warehouse down," Ranger finally said.

"It wasn't my bad. I think someone set a bomb, and I got caught."

"Anyone else in there?"

"A dead guy. He was sitting behind a desk on the second floor. Looked like he'd been toasted with a flamethrower. I only know flamethrowers from movies and the six o'clock news, but that's what it looked like to me. The body was burned beyond recognition.

It was awful. Both Dickie and Smullen are missing. I suppose it could have been one of them. No way to know for sure.

"I was leaving when the building caught. I was in the stairwell. Something went *phunnnnf* and then there was fire everywhere. I had to go back up to the office and jump out the window. That's the short version."

"Did anyone see you there?"

"No one we need to worry about."

"You should pass this on to Morelli so they know to look for the body."

"I'll pass it on, but trust me, there's no body left."

"What kind of shape are you in?" Ranger asked. "Are you functioning? We've still got Stewart Hansen on ice at RangeMan. You can bring him in now, and no one will associate you with the cannabis farmhouse fire."

"He won't tell anyone?"

"I don't think he'll remember," Ranger said. "And if he does say something, I doubt anyone will believe him. We've been keeping him very happy."

"Do you have him drugged?"

"Quality weed, Ella's cooking, and nonstop television on a fifty-inch plasma." Ranger stood and pulled me to my feet. "Would you rather do this tomorrow?"

"No. I'll be okay."

"You don't look okay. You've got blood soaking through your jeans."

I looked down at my leg. "I should have used a bigger Band-Aid."

"Do you need stitches?"

"No. It's just a cut. I had to go through a smashed window to get out of the building."

"I'm going to ask you again. Do you need stitches?"

I didn't know. I hoped not.

"Let me see it," Ranger said.

I bit into my lower lip. This was embarrassing.

"Babe, I've seen it all," Ranger said.

"Yes, but you haven't seen it lately."

"Has it changed?" he asked.

That got me smiling. "No."

I popped the snap to my jeans and slid them down. I was wearing a lime green lace thong, which was a lot like wearing nothing.

Ranger looked and smiled. "Pretty," he said. Then his attention moved to the gash in my leg. "I know you don't want to hear this, but it'll heal faster and neater if you get some sutures in it."

We put a washcloth against the cut and wrapped my leg with surgical tape.

"Do you have any other injuries that are this serious?" he asked.

"No," I said. "This was the worst."

We went to St. Frances emergency and had a minimal wait. The kids with colds and the after-lunch heart attack victims had all been cleared out. There'd been only one Sunday afternoon gang shooting, and he'd been D.O.A. And it was still early in the day for domestic violence.

My leg was pumped full of local anesthesia and stitched. I got salve for the burns on my neck and face, and antiseptic ointment for my other scrapes and cuts.

Louise Malinowski was working emergency. I'd gone to school with Louise. She was now divorced with two kids and back home living with her mom.

"Who's the hot guy out there?" she asked, helping me get my jeans up over my numb leg and new stitches.

"Carlos Manoso. He owns a security agency downtown."

"Is he married?"

"He's as unmarried as a man can get."

* * *

Ranger watched me buckle myself in. We'd left the Buick in my lot and taken his Porsche Turbo. It was black and new and fast, just like all his other cars, but even more so.

"Where do all these new black cars come from?" I asked him.

"I have a deal. I provide services for cars."

"What sort of services?"

"Whatever is required." He put the car in gear and pulled away from the hospital. "I'm going to take you to your parents' house so you can get your purse, and I want you to call Morelli."

Not something I was looking forward to. This wasn't going to make Morelli happy.

"What?" Morelli said when he answered the phone. Not sounding especially mellow.

"How's it going?"

"It's going not fast enough. What's up?"

"Did you hear about the fire at the warehouse on Stark?"

"No. I don't hear about anything. I'm locked away, babysitting a moron, and I'm looking at an episode of *Raymond* that I've seen forty-two times."

"Dickie and his partners owned a warehouse on Stark and—"

"Oh, Christ," Morelli said. "Don't tell me."

"It burned down . . . just now."

"Are you okay?"

"Yeah. Ranger took me to get stitches."

There was silence on the other end, and I imagined Morelli was staring down at his shoe with his lips pressed tightly together.

"Anyway, I'm fine," I told him. "I just got cut on some glass when I had to break a window to get out. Is it okay to talk on your cell phone like this? I mean, no one can listen, can they?"

"Everyone can listen," Morelli said. "Don't let that stop you. Is this conversation going to get worse?"

"If you're going to give me attitude about this, I'm not going to talk to you."

I looked over at Ranger, caught him smiling, and punched him in the arm.

"No one saw me," I said to Morelli. "I left before the fire trucks arrived. And it wasn't my fault. I'm pretty sure someone set a bomb. The thing is, there was a guy sitting behind a desk on the second floor, and I think he'd been toasted with a flamethrower. I doubt there's much left of him after the second fire, but Ranger wanted me to tell you."

This created a lot more silence.

"Hello?" I said.

"Give me a moment," Morelli said. "I've almost got myself under control."

"How much longer are you going to be on this assignment?" I asked Morelli.

"At least two more days. Let me talk to Ranger."

I gave Ranger my phone. "Morelli wants to talk to you."

"Yo," Ranger said. He did some listening, and he cut his eyes to me. "Understood," he said to Morelli. "Don't expect miracles. She's an accident waiting to happen." Ranger disconnected and handed the phone back to me. "I'm in charge of your well-being."

"Morelli should mind his own business."

"That's exactly what he's doing. You're a couple. You *are* his business."

"I don't feel like his business. I feel like my own business."

"No shit," Ranger said.

What was worse, I was caught off guard by the couple status. "Do you think Morelli and I are a couple?"

"He has his clothes in your closet."

"Only socks and underwear."

Ranger parked in my parents' driveway and turned to face me. "You want to be careful what you tell me. My moral code stops short of 'Do not covet someone else's woman.' You've been holding me at arm's length, and I respect that, but I'll move in if I feel that barrier relax."

I already knew this, but having it said out loud was disconcerting. I didn't want to make more of it than was necessary, so I tried being playful. "Are you telling me socks and underwear are borderline in terms of couple qualifications?"

"I'm telling you to be careful."

When Ranger issued a warning, he didn't do playful.

"That's just great," I said. "I'm so *not good* at being careful."

"I've noticed," Ranger said.

My grandmother opened the front door and waved.

Ranger and I waved back, and I eased myself out of the car and went to retrieve my bag.

"Is that blood on your pants leg?" my grandmother asked when I stepped into the foyer.

"Kitchen accident," I said. "It's fine. Gotta go. Just came in to get my bag. I'll bring the Buick back later."

I hurried to the Porsche and angled in.

"Barnhardt is two houses down and across the street," Ranger said. "She was here when we drove up. She must have spotted the Cayenne."

Ranger rolled out of the driveway and down the street. Joyce rolled with us, staying a couple car lengths back.

"I'm taking you home with me," Ranger said. "I have to catch up on paperwork and meet with Tank, and I don't want to worry about you. You can spend the night and turn Hansen in when the court opens in the morning."

"I can't spend the night at RangeMan."

"Morelli said I should keep you safe."

"Yes, but no one's after me. I've just had some unfortunate luck."

"Babe, you've destroyed a car, burned down two buildings, stapled a guy's nuts, and you have sixteen stitches in your leg. Take a night off. Have a glass of wine, watch some television, and go to bed early."

ELEVEN

Ranger's apartment occupies the seventh floor of the RangeMan building. It's professionally decorated in neutral earth tones and classic comfortable furniture. It's cool. It's calm. It's inviting in a mildly masculine way. The carved mahogany front door opens to a long narrow foyer. Coat closet and powder room on one side. Cherry wood credenza on the other. Ranger's housekeeper, Ella, keeps fresh flowers on the credenza, plus a silver tray for keys and mail. Modern kitchen with stainless appliances and granite countertops to the right at the end of the hall. Breakfast bar. Small dining room. Small living room. The master bedroom suite consists of a den, a bedroom with king bed and smooth, white, thousand-thread-count sheets, a dressing room with all black clothes, and a weapons cabinet, and a luxurious bathroom with walk-in shower that smells like Ranger's Bulgari Green Tea shower gel.

Ranger electronically unlocked his apartment door and I followed him inside. He took an identical lock fob from a drawer in the credenza and gave it to me.

"If you decide to leave, take the GPS monitor with you. Hal's bringing the Cayenne back. It'll be parked downstairs with the key on the seat. It's yours for as long as you need it. I'm sure Ella has dinner in the kitchen. Help yourself. I've got a lot to do. I'm going to grab a sandwich downstairs." He curled his fingers into my sweatshirt, dragged me to him, and kissed me. "If you want to stay up for me, I'll make it worth the wait," he said, his lips barely touching mine when he spoke. And he was gone.

I've lived in Ranger's apartment once before for a short time when my life was in danger. And for a short time, I worked in the RangeMan office. The building felt very safe back then, but after a while, claustrophobic.

I prowled through the kitchen and found a chicken stew with rice and vegetables. I scarfed down the stew with a glass of wine, and took a second glass into the den to watch television. I sunk into Ranger's big, comfy couch and remoted the plasma.

Morelli's house was comfortable ground for me. It was filled with hand-me-down furniture left to him by his Aunt Ruth. It looked a lot like my parents' house, and in a strange, unexpected way, the house fit Morelli. When Morelli had time, the house was kept neat and orderly. When Morelli was overworked, the house became cluttered with abandoned shoes and empty beer bottles.

Ranger's apartment felt exotic. The furniture was expensive and chosen for Ranger. Very comfortable but a little sterile. No family photos. No dog-eared books. This was a place where Ranger slept and worked and ate but didn't live.

Morelli's house was a destination for him. Ranger's apartment felt like part of his journey.

I probably should have gone home, but the truth is I love visiting Ranger's apartment. It smells great . . . like Ranger. His television is bigger and better than mine. He has better water pressure in his shower. His towels are softer and fluffier. And his bed is wonderful, even when he isn't in it. Ella irons his sheets and plumps his pillows. If there's a woman out there who could make me turn, it would be Ella.

I fell asleep in front of the television. I woke up at eleven and again at eleven-thirty. I forced myself away from the television and into the bedroom, shucked most of my clothes, and crawled into Ranger's fabulous bed.

The alarm jolted me awake, and I had a moment of utter confusion before realizing I was at RangeMan. The room was dark, but I could see Ranger outlined against his dressing room light. He crossed the room and stood at the bedside to turn the alarm off.

"I have an early meeting with a client this morning," Ranger said. "And I want to talk to you before I get involved in RangeMan business. Ella has breakfast on the table." His cell phone rang, and he left the bedroom.

I painfully rolled out of bed, my whole body aching from the fall off the car hauler. I flipped the light on, limped across the room to Ranger's closet, and shrugged into a robe that had been bought for Ranger, but I was sure had never been worn. I couldn't imagine Ranger lounging around in a robe.

Ella was a small, slim woman with intelligent, dark eyes, short black hair, and contained energy. Ella's husband managed the property, and Ella managed the men of RangeMan. She cooked and cleaned and did whatever was necessary to get Ranger out of his apartment each morning in presentable condition. She bought his shower gel, did his laundry, ironed his orgasmic sheets, and set out fresh flowers.

The breakfast tray she brought to his door was almost always the same. Coffee, fresh fruit, whole-grain bagels, lox, fat-free cream cheese. An egg-white frittata with vegetables. Very pretty. Very healthy. This morning, Ella had set the dining room table for two.

Ranger ended his call and joined me at the table. He was in corporate attire. Black dress slacks, black dress shirt, black-on-black striped tie, black gun and holster. He draped a black cashmere sports coat on an empty dining room chair, then poured coffee while still standing, and sat across from me.

"Holy cow," I said to him. But I was thinking *Holy Cow!*

"I wasn't trying for holy cow," Ranger said. "I was shooting for respectable."

"Good luck with that one," I told him.

Ranger was strong inside and out. He was intelligent. He was brave. He was physically and emotionally agile. He was incredibly sexy. He was deceptively playful. But more than anything else, Ranger reeked of bad boy. It would take a lot more than a cashmere sports coat and an Armani tie to offset the testosterone and male pheromones that leaked out of him. I doubted Ranger would ever be entirely respectable.

"Okay," Ranger said. "I admit respectable was a stretch. How about successful?"

"Yes," I said. "You look very successful."

He helped himself to fruit and a slice of the frittata. "I'm going to make a deal with you. The deal is that you work with me on the Dickie thing, and you don't go off on your own."

"That's the deal?"

"The alternative is that I lock you in my bathroom until I get this mess figured out."

"What about you? Are you going off on your own, without me?"

"No. I'll include you in everything."

"Deal."

"Gorvich, Petiak, and Smullen all have legitimate addresses, but none of them spend any time at them. And they don't spend a lot of time at the office downtown. I had someone search the three residences, and he found nothing. No computers. No clothes in the closets. Nothing in the refrigerators. We've been calling their phones and only get a message service. Never a callback."

"Lula and I went through the law firm's apartment building on Jewel Street and discovered Smullen was keeping a woman on the top floor. The woman said Smullen lived there when he was in the country. He was missing in action when we got there, and his girlfriend was angry. I should check to see if he's still missing." I took a bagel and loaded it up with cream cheese. "Why don't these guys live in their houses?"

"Maybe they're worried an unhappy client might come calling. I've been looking at the material you lifted from the law office. Rufus Caine paid the firm a little over a million dollars last year for legal services. I thought we might want to talk to him."

You couldn't be associated with crime in Trenton and not have heard of Rufus Caine. Vinnie had never bonded him out, so everything I knew was secondhand. And what I knew mostly was that he wasn't a nice guy. "Rufus Caine is middle-management pharmaceuticals. Will he talk to us?"

"I have a relationship with Rufus. He lives and works out of a slum apartment building behind the train station. I thought we'd pay him a visit this afternoon. In the meantime, I have your FTA, Stewart Hansen, ready to go. Call the control room when you want him brought down to the garage. I'll send one of my men with you, but you probably don't want to involve RangeMan in the delivery." Ranger finished his coffee and pushed back from the table. "I have to run."

Hansen was in the backseat of a Ford Explorer, physically ankle-chained to the floor, mentally floating in La La

Land. Ranger hadn't been kidding when he said they'd been keeping Hansen happy. Hard to tell if Hansen was in this euphoric state from too many episodes of *Scooby Doo* or too much wacky tobacky.

I parked the Explorer in the public lot across from the courthouse and unlocked Hansen's ankle shackles. His hands were still cuffed behind his back, and I had to help him out of the SUV. Ranger's guy was in the front passenger seat, looking nervous, not sure how much help he was supposed to give me and still stay politically correct.

"I'll be back," I told the RangeMan guy. "Don't go anywhere."

I maneuvered Hansen into the building, stood him in front of the docket lieutenant, and Hansen started giggling.

"Shit," the docket lieutenant said. "Last time I was that happy, I was in charge of the evidence room and we'd just busted a gangbanger carrying a suitcase full of medicinal weed."

I completed the paperwork, got a body receipt, and called Connie and told her Hansen was in the lockup in case someone wanted to spring him again.

Ranger had said he'd be busy until noon, and it was still early, so I jogged to the SUV, got behind the wheel, and drove to Coglin's house. Ranger had made me promise to work with him on the Dickie thing. He hadn't said anything about my FTAs.

"Small detour," I said to the RangeMan guy. "What's your name?"

"Brett."

He didn't look like a Brett. Guys named Brett were supposed to have a neck. This guy looked like he should be named Grunt.

I parked at the curb and had Brett follow me to the door. Brett was wearing a full utility belt with gun, stun gun, a can of pepper spray that could take down a grizzly, and cuffs. He was dressed in RangeMan SWAT, and he was scary-looking as hell. My intent was that Coglin would see Brett with me and keel over in a dead faint before he got to fire off the shotgun.

I knew Coglin was home. I'd seen him moving in the glassed-in front porch just before I'd parked. I hadn't heard the car leave from the backyard, so I rang the bell and listened for the car. If I heard the car engine catch, I'd take off and run him down at the cross street. I rang the bell again.

Brett was close behind me at the ready. "Should I break the door down?"

"No," I said. "It's probably not locked."

Brett stepped in front of me and tried the door handle. He pushed the door open, stepped inside, and *bang!* Brett was covered in funk and short mousy brown hairs. Hard to tell what the creature had been. I was guessing sixty-pound rat.

"What the—" Brett said.

"It's getting old," I yelled into Coglin's house. "I'll be back."

I led Brett to the Explorer and drove him back to RangeMan.

"What is this stuff on me?" he asked. "What happened?"

"I think you might have been beavered, but there's no way to know without DNA testing."

I walked him upstairs to the control room and turned him over to Hal. Down the hall, Ranger stepped out of his meeting and glanced my way.

"It wasn't my fault," I said to Ranger.

Ranger smiled and returned to his meeting.

Ella brought salad and sandwiches up at noon and Ranger strolled in minutes behind her.

"How'd the meeting go?" I asked him.

"Good."

He selected a sandwich and ate it standing up in the kitchen. I did the same.

"I notice you're dressed in RangeMan colors," Ranger said to me.

"Turns out I have clothes in your closet."

"More than just underwear and socks," Ranger said. "They were left from the last time you stayed here."

"Does that make us a couple?"

"Spend another night with me, and I'll explain couple to you," Ranger said.

I was tempted to ask him how we'd spent *last* night, but thought maybe it was best not to know. I'd gone to bed alone, and he was up and dressed when the alarm went off. I was telling myself he'd slept on the couch. That was my story and I was going to go with it.

He removed his tie and unbuttoned his dress shirt, and I managed to keep myself from dragging my tongue down his chest to his belt buckle. I conjured the image of Morelli in my kitchen and told myself it wouldn't be a good idea to spend another night here.

Ranger disappeared into his dressing room, and when he returned, he was in cargo pants, T-shirt, and cross-trainers. His gun was clipped to his belt. He grabbed our jackets and hats from the coat closet. His hat said SEAL and mine said RANGEMAN.

"Let's roll," Ranger said.

We were in Ranger's turbo, parked on Ellery, looking out at the pathetic apartment building where Rufus Caine conducted his business. Other buildings on the block were graffiti-decorated, but Caine's building was unscathed. It was four floors of eroded redbrick and peeling paint trim. And the front door was missing.

"Are you sure you want to leave the Porsche here?" I

asked Ranger. "What are the chances it'll be here when we come back?"

"Chances are good. Only a dealer would leave a turbo sitting out here in front of Caine's building. And no one wants to steal that car. No one wants that kind of trouble."

We left the car and stopped at the building's stoop. The tiny foyer was littered with used condoms and syringes and what I hoped was *dog* poo.

Ranger scooped me up and carried me to the stairs. "This way we only have one pair of shoes to throw away," he said.

We hiked to the fourth floor and Ranger knocked on the door.

"Yeah?" came through the closed door to us. "Who's there?"

"Ranger."

The door opened and a toady looked out at us. "Who's she?" he asked Ranger.

Ranger didn't say anything, and the toady backed up and opened the door.

There were four people in the room. Three goons and Rufus Caine. Easy to tell Rufus. He was the two-hundred-pound, five-foot-five guy having a midlife crisis, all decked out in jewelry and hair plugs. He was on the couch with a napkin daintily perched on his knee and a glass of champagne in his hand. There was a mound of sandwiches on a large plastic take-out platter on the coffee table in front of him.

"I was having lunch," Rufus said to Ranger. "Help yourself."

"I just ate," Ranger said. "But thanks."

Rufus eyeballed me like I was dessert. "Who's your bitch?"

"This is Stephanie," Ranger said. "She's running relief for Tank."

"I didn't know you and Tank had that kind of relationship," Rufus said.

Ranger didn't smile.

"So wassup?" Rufus asked.

Ranger didn't say anything. He just stared at Rufus. Rufus made a little flick with his hand and the three idiots left the apartment.

"Sit," Rufus said to Ranger.

Ranger sat, and I stood. I was the muscle in the room.

"I'm thinking about retaining some counsel," Ranger said. "I'm looking at Petiak, Smullen, Gorvich, and Orr."

"Good firm," Rufus said.

"Why is it good?"

"Discreet. Got a good business ethic."

"And?"

"Understands the barter system. You sure you don't want a sandwich?"

"I want to know more about the barter system," Ranger said.

"Why?"

Ranger didn't say anything. He didn't blink. He didn't smile. He didn't sigh. He just silently stared at Rufus.

"Good thing I like you," Rufus said to Ranger, "because you could improve on your social skills. You're not exactly a fun guy. Anyone ever tell you that?"

Ranger cut his eyes to me and then back to Rufus.

"The barter system is where you trade some shit for other shit," Rufus said. "Wait a minute. Maybe I don't mean the barter system. What is it when you say you're paying for legal advice, but you're really paying for inventory?"

"Lying," Ranger said.

"Yeah, that's what those assholes understand . . . lying."

Ranger reached forward and took the bottle of champagne off the coffee table and refilled Caine's glass. "Anything else you want to tell me?"

"What's your angle?"

"No angle," Ranger said. "Like I told you, I'm looking to retain counsel and I like the firm. I'm just having a hard time finding someone to talk to. No one's answering the phone."

"Do you have something to . . . barter?"

"You want to stay away from Jimmy Monster. He's wearing a wire."

"Ow."

"And?" Ranger said.

"I'm meeting Victor Gorvich tonight. He has a package for me. We used to make the drop at a warehouse, but the warehouse burned down, so I'm seeing him at ten at Domino's."

"The strip club on Third Street?"

"That's the one. Just make sure my business is concluded before you move in."

Ranger stood. "Be careful," he said to Rufus.

"Fuck that," Rufus said.

We were a couple blocks away from the apartment building when my cell phone rang.

"I can't talk long," Morelli said. "I just wanted to pass some information on to you. The guy in the warehouse was identified by his wedding band and key ring. It was Peter Smullen."

"Holy crap.

"The guy in the warehouse was Peter Smullen," I said to Ranger.

"Who are you talking to?" Morelli asked.

"Ranger."

"You're with Ranger?"

"You told him to take care of me."

"Yeah, but I didn't mean—"

"I'm getting static," I said to Morelli. "Hello? Hello?" And I disconnected. "He needed a moment to collect himself," I said to Ranger.

"Understandable."

"Let's recap," I said to Ranger. "First the law firm's accountant goes swimming with the fishes. Then Dickie gets dragged out of his house. And now Peter Smullen is dead."

My cell phone rang again.

"We got cut off," Morelli said.

"Cell phones," I said. "Go figure."

"I wanted to tell you Marty Gobel might want to talk to you again. Smullen's secretary said Smullen was supposed to meet with you the night he disappeared."

"Are you suggesting I might be under suspicion for Smullen's murder?"

"You have an alibi, right?"

I hung up and slouched in my seat. "Smullen's secretary told the police I was supposed to meet with Smullen the night he disappeared."

Ranger hooked a U-turn on Broad. "Let's see what Smullen's girlfriend has to say about all this."

We passed Joyce, who was now going in the wrong direction in her rented white Taurus.

"I used to be such a badass," Ranger said. "Everyone was afraid of me. Everyone wanted to kill me. I needed Tank walking behind me to keep the paid assassins under control. And now look at me. I'm followed by a woman in a rented Taurus." He made a vague gesture with his hand. "And I can't remember the last time someone tried to kill me."

"It wasn't that long ago," I said. "It was in my apartment, and you got shot a bunch of times, and it wasn't all that much fun.

"Not to change the subject, but if I understood the

conversation back there, Victor Gorvich is supplying Rufus with drugs."

Ranger turned off Broad and drove toward the projects. "Not only is he supplying drugs, he's laundering the money through the firm. He's billing Rufus for legal advice when Rufus is actually paying him for inventory. If you look at the client list you lifted, it's a shopping cart filled with the World's Most Wanted. Not just drug dealers, but gunrunners and agents for dictators. One or more of the partners is shuffling drugs around and washing the money as billable hours."

"Gorvich, for sure."

"Looks that way."

Ranger parked curbside at the law firm's slum apartment building, and we both got out. Ranger took a remote gizmo, aimed it at the Porsche, and the Porsche chirped.

We hoofed it up to the top floor and rang the bell. No answer. We rang it again, and Uncle Mickey stuck his head out his door.

"She isn't there," Uncle Mickey said. "She went shopping." He looked at Ranger and retreated into his apartment.

Ranger took his little tool out of a pocket on his cargo pants and opened the apartment door.

Smullen's apartment had been freshly painted and carpeted. The furniture was new. The kitchen appliances were new. The countertop was Corian. The building was a slum, but Smullen's apartment was not. Smullen's toilet worked.

Smullen's clothes were hanging in the closet and neatly folded in bureau drawers. His toiletries were still in the bathroom. I checked pants pockets for the bug, but didn't find it.

I walked out of the bedroom and caught Ranger at

the living room window, looking down. He was standing hands on hips, watching two men direct a flatbed tow truck up to the Porsche. His car alarm was wailing away, and the men were ignoring it.

Ranger unlocked and raised the window, unholstered his gun, took aim, and shot one of the men in the leg. The guy crumpled onto the pavement and rolled around, holding his leg. The flatbed driver jumped out and helped drag the wounded guy into the truck, and they drove away. Ranger aimed his gizmo at his car and silenced the alarm.

"Do you feel better now?" I asked. "You got to shoot someone today."

"I've still got the touch," Ranger said.

"Smullen's clothes are here, but I didn't find the bug. Did you come up with anything interesting?"

"No. He doesn't have a home office. Not even a laptop squirreled away somewhere."

The lock tumbled on the front door, and Smullen's girlfriend pushed into the apartment. She had a brown grocery bag in the crook of her arm, and she was out of breath from the stairs.

"What the fuck is this?" she said to Ranger and me.

"We came to visit, but you weren't home," I said to her.

She cut her eyes to Ranger. "Who's the hot guy? Is he a cop?"

"No. He's Ranger."

"Why's he dressed like a cop? What is this, Halloween and no one told me?"

I glanced back at Ranger. "You aren't going to shoot her, are you?"

"Thinking about it."

"Was Peter involved in anything shady at work?" I asked her.

"Sure. He was a lawyer."

"I mean *really* shady. Like illegal. Trafficking in drugs, for instance."

She set the bag on the kitchen counter. "I don't think so. Why would he do something like that? He was making a fortune just being a lawyer."

"Did he have another office somewhere? I noticed he doesn't have a home office here."

"He works at the law office. What's the deal, anyway? I'm calling the cops. You jerk-offs broke into my apartment. Hey, wait a minute. You aren't going to kidnap me, are you? Omigod, you've got Peter, right? That's why he hasn't come home. You've got Peter! Help!" she yelled. "Help! Police!"

"Go ahead," I said to Ranger. "Shoot her."

"We aren't going to kidnap you," Ranger said. "And we didn't kidnap Peter Smullen. In fact, we have some very bad news for you."

"Help!" she yelled. "Help! Help!"

Ranger looked at me. "You have any ideas besides *shoot her*?"

"I love your boots," I said to her. "Vuitton, right?"

She looked down at the boots. Knee-high, black leather, stacked heel. "Yeah," she said. "They cost a fortune, but I *had* to have them. I got a bag to match. You want to see the bag?"

"Sure."

She went into the bedroom and came back with the bag. "This is the shit, right?" she said.

"It looks great on you. You can carry a big bag like that," I told her. "It's a to-die-for bag. And speaking of dying . . . Peter Smullen is dead."

"Waddaya mean, he's dead?"

"He was caught in a fire in a warehouse last night and he died. I'm so sorry," I told her.

"How do you know?"

"It was made public this morning."

She was deer-in-the-headlights for a moment. "Are you sure?"

"He was identified by his wedding band and his key ring."

"Sonovabitch. All that money and I was so close to getting my hands on it, and the jackass had to get himself toasted in a fucking warehouse. Life is so unfair." Her eyes darted around the room. "This apartment belongs to the law firm," she said. "I need a truck! Do you have a truck?"

"No."

"We'll have to rent one."

"Uh, actually, we have to be moving along," I said. "Like to stay, but . . ."

Ranger was at the door.

"Uncle Mickey lives across the hall," I told her. "He can get you a truck."

I followed Ranger down the stairs and out of the building. I was about to get into the Porsche when I spotted Joyce half a block away.

"Be right back," I said to Ranger.

I jogged down to Joyce and leaned in her car window. "Peter Smullen is dead," I said. "He was killed in a warehouse fire last night. His girlfriend lives in that building we just left. She's on the top floor. We couldn't get any information out of her, but you might want to try."

"Are you shitting me?"

"No. Swear to God." I jogged back to Ranger and slid into the passenger seat. "I think I got rid of Joyce for a while."

TWELVE

Ranger and I were in his den watching a basketball game.

"How's your leg?" he asked.

"It's a little sore."

"I need to leave for Domino's. Do you want to come with me or would you rather stay here?"

"I'll go with you."

He looked at my V-neck sweater with the Range-Man logo embroidered in purple. "Do you have something to wear that doesn't say RangeMan?"

"No. Even my underwear has your name on it."

"It's Ella. She got a machine that stitches the logo, and she can't control herself. She puts it on everything." He stood. "I'm going to change. I'll be ready to go in a minute."

I'd been to Domino's once before. Lula and I made an apprehension there last spring. It was a typical titty bar with a raised stage and pole dancers. I was told it had a back room for lap dances, but Lula and I didn't get back there. Our man was at the bar, stuffing money into G-strings.

Ranger had changed into black jeans and a long-sleeved, collared black shirt that he wore out to hide his gun.

"Do you have money for the girls?" I asked him.

"I try not to hand money out at strip bars. It's like feeding stray cats. Once you feed them, they never go away."

"Yes, but I'll be there to protect you this time."

Ranger held my jacket for me. "I usually rely on Tank, but tonight the job is yours."

We took the elevator to the garage, and Ranger chose a black Explorer over one of his private cars. Easier to blend. Domino's was just ten minutes away from RangeMan. For that matter, everything was ten minutes from RangeMan. Ranger had placed his security company in a good location. If an alarm went off anywhere in Trenton, RangeMan was there in ten minutes or less.

On weekends, Domino's rocked. It was filled to capacity with bachelor parties and couples out for fun. On a Monday night, it was half empty, and there was no problem getting a table. Ranger steered us to a dark corner where he could put his back to the wall. Most of the men were at the bar that surrounded the dance platform. A bunch of sad regulars and some out-of-town businessmen who'd straggled in from the hotels on Route One. Tonight, I was the only woman.

The music was loud. Disco. The two women onstage were in four-inch stilettos and dental floss. They looked like they wouldn't mind getting out of the shoes.

A waitress stopped by, all smiley face. "Hey, handsome," she said to Ranger. "What'll it be?"

"Vodka rocks," Ranger said. "Two of them."

I raised an eyebrow at him when the waitress left. "You drink vodka rocks?"

"Less to dump on the floor," he said.

We didn't want to make an entrance and have Gorvich spot us, so we'd arrived early. The disadvantage to this soon became apparent. Ranger was a bimbo magnet.

The dancers finished their set, and one immediately strolled over to our table and straddled Ranger.

"Want a private party?" she asked.

"Not tonight," Ranger said. He handed her a twenty, and she left.

"What about the cat-feeding theory?" I asked him.

"Out the window."

Our drinks were delivered and a new dancer popped up in front of Ranger. "Hey, sweetie," she said. "How's it going?" And before Ranger had a chance to answer, she had her huge breasts in his face and her leg over his lap.

"Not tonight," Ranger said. He handed her a twenty, and she left.

"I'm seeing a pattern here," I said to Ranger. "How often do you come here?"

"Too often. I thought you were going to run interference."

"It's like they come out of nowhere. Before I know it, they're on top of you."

A woman in rhinestone pasties and a rhinestone G-string stopped by, and Ranger handed her a twenty before she got her leg over him.

"You could go through a lot of money fast this way," I said to Ranger.

"All for you, babe. Small price to pay to keep you out of jail."

He dumped his vodka onto the floor behind him. The waitress swooped in, took his glass, and gave him a fresh vodka.

Rufus rolled in at five minutes to ten. He took a seat at a table by the bar and ordered a drink. One of the girls approached him and was allowed to do her thing. Guess the room in the back was closed on Monday, and the action came out front.

Ranger and I watched her gyrate and bounce and rub against Rufus.

"I know men like this sort of thing," I said to Ranger, "but personally, I prefer a shoe sale at Macy's. On the plus side, we'll be in good shape if we have to follow him. She's shedding so much body glitter, he's going to glow in the dark."

The dancer slithered up Rufus, and his entire face got smushed into her breasts.

"She's going to kill him," I said to Ranger. "He's going to suffocate. Do something."

"He's okay. His color still looks good," Ranger said.

"His color is terrible. He's purple."

"It's the lights."

"Do men have . . . you know, reactions to this rubbing and writhing stuff in public?" I asked Ranger.

"I guess, but this is the first time I've seen someone turn purple."

At ten after ten, the big blond muscle guy with the stapled nuts came into the bar and sat across from Rufus. He said something to the dancer, and she abruptly got up and left. Rufus called for the check and finished his drink. He paid his bill and left with the muscle guy.

"Give them time to get out of the building," Ranger said. "We don't want to ruin this by getting recognized."

"Aren't you afraid of losing them?"

"Tank is in the lot, and Hal is on the street."

Ranger took a call from Tank.

"They're moving," Ranger said, snapping his phone closed.

He signaled the waitress and dropped a hundred dollars on the table. We left the club and followed Tank's directions through town. We turned into the projects, and I guessed where we were headed. The law firm's apartment building.

There was only on-street parking on Jewel Street, and at this time of the night, every parking place was taken.

"Rufus went in the car with the muscle," Tank said over speakerphone. "He got dropped off in front of the building and the muscle kept driving. Hal followed the car to Stark Street and lost it in traffic. I'm double-parked across the street from the building. Rufus went in and hasn't come out. No one else has gone in since I've been here. Only a few minutes."

Ranger called Hal. "Look at the back of the building and make sure it's secure."

"Yessir," Hal said. "I'm a couple blocks away. I'll get right to it."

Ranger circled the block and found a parking place on a side street. We left the car and walked to where Tank was idling. We stood on the sidewalk and looked up at the building. Lights were on in units 1A and 3A. Curtains were drawn in 3A.

"It has to be the third floor," I said. "I was in every apartment, and I can't see any of the others as a possibility."

"I told Rufus I'd wait for him to clear before I made a move, but this feels off," Ranger said.

"What do you want to do with Gorvich when you find him?" I asked.

"I want to talk to him."

A car careened onto Jewel half a block away and screamed past us, going in the opposite direction. Two men in the car. The passenger in shadow. The driver was the blond muscle guy.

Hal was half a block behind with his foot to the floor. Tank jerked away from the curb, hooked a U-turn, and Tank and Hal disappeared down the street in pursuit.

Ranger and I ran to the building and took the stairs two at a time to the third floor. I smelled the gasoline before we even reached the top of the stairs. It was mingled with cooked meat and forest fire.

Ranger didn't bother with the locksmith tool. He

put his foot to the door and crashed it open. Smullen's girlfriend had moved fast. The apartment looked completely cleaned out, with the exception of a large upholstered couch. Probably too awkward to get down the stairs on short notice. Either end of the couch was intact. The middle of the couch was charred. And the two bodies sitting on the couch were charred. The wall behind the couch was burned black.

"This is just like the warehouse," I said. "Someone's doused this apartment with gasoline. There's probably a bomb in here somewhere."

Ranger grabbed me and shoved me out of the apartment. "Go to the second floor and get everyone out of the building."

I flew down the stairs and started banging on doors. I had two apartments empty and was on the third when Uncle Mickey hustled down the stairs with Ranger behind him.

"Go to the first floor," Ranger said to me. "I'll finish up here."

We had everyone on the street and sirens were wailing in the distance when flames shot out of the windows to 3A. The fire raced through the structure, and Ranger and I ran to the neighboring building and made sure everyone evacuated.

The police cars were the first on the scene and then the fire trucks and paramedics. I was relieved to give the disaster over to the professionals and fade away into the crowd of bystanders. I was sweating from horror and exertion and the heat of the fire, and I was shivering with nervous energy.

Ranger pulled me into a shadow and wrapped his arms around me. I held tight to his open jacket and tucked my face into him, trying to get my teeth to stop chattering. Ranger wasn't trembling, and he wasn't sweating. His breathing was measured and normal.

"Breathe," Ranger said, his voice soft against my ear. "Try to breathe deeper."

His calm washed into me, the shivering and chattering stopped, and tears rolled down my cheeks and soaked into his shirt.

"I f-f-feel like an idiot," I said to him.

"It's just a letdown from the adrenaline rush."

"Why aren't you letting down?"

"My body is more efficient at producing and using adrenaline."

We stood like that, locked together, for a couple more minutes, until I stopped crying.

Finally, Ranger looked down at me. "How are you doing?"

"I'm good."

"I want to talk to Tank," Ranger said. "Stay with me."

"I'm pooped. I thought I'd go sit in one of the cars."

Ranger took my hand. "Not yet. I don't want you out of my sight."

"Afraid I'll burn down another building?"

"Afraid you'll get arrested."

Five men in RangeMan black stood shoulder-to-shoulder in front of us. Tank and Hal were among them. Ranger dismissed all but Tank.

"Hal got to the back of the building just as the car was leaving," Tank said. "Hal saw a rope hanging from a third-floor window. Looked like someone might have rappelled out. Hal had to turn around to follow the car, and we were both too far behind to catch him. He was really moving."

"Did Hal get a plate?"

"He got a plate the first time he followed him. We've already traced it."

"Stolen?" Ranger asked.

"Yes."

"I'm taking Stephanie home. Stay here a while longer and let me know if anything weird goes down."

Ranger opened his apartment door for me and walked me to the kitchen.

"Are you hungry?" he asked.

"Famished. And tired."

"I can call Ella. She'll make whatever you want. Or you can prowl through the kitchen. There's still peanut butter from the last time you were here."

"Peanut butter sounds perfect."

I shucked my coat and assembled a peanut butter and olive sandwich while Ranger leaned against the kitchen counter and punched a number into his phone.

"Who are you calling?" I asked.

"Morelli. Do you want him on speakerphone?"

"No. I haven't the energy."

"We need to talk," Ranger said to Morelli. "There was a second fire tonight. Two people toasted by a flamethrower. I saw them just before the building exploded. Same drill as the warehouse. Both times there were victims already burned, accelerant in the area, and there must have been an incendiary device on a timer. I'd like to see the reports. And it would be good to get a fast ID on the bodies in the apartment building tonight."

Morelli said something, and Ranger looked over at me.

"No, she wasn't directly involved," Ranger said. "She was with me the whole time. She's fine. Her hair didn't even catch fire."

I rolled my eyes and gave Morelli and Ranger the finger.

"I wanted to bring this to you first," Ranger said. "If you're unavailable, I can go to your captain. This probably could benefit from a task force."

Ranger flipped his phone closed and uncorked a bottle of red wine. He poured me a glass and ate an olive from the bottle.

"Is Morelli going to run with this?" I asked.

"He's going to make a phone call."

I had my sandwich made, but I was so exhausted I could hardly chew. I washed a chunk down with wine and felt all my bones dissolve.

"I'm going downstairs to research flamethrowers," Ranger said. "I'll be up later."

I finished the sandwich and wine and fell asleep wearing one of Ranger's T-shirts. It was big and comfy, and it was the first thing I laid hands on in the dressing room.

Sleep is very strange stuff. One minute you don't know anything, and then you're awake and life starts over. I opened my eyes to Ranger, fully dressed, standing over me, coffee cup in his hand.

"I let you sleep as long as possible," he said. "We have a meeting at the station in a half hour. You have ten minutes to shower and get dressed. I'm putting your coffee in the bathroom."

"Meeting?"

"Fire marshal—that would be Ken Roiker—Morelli, Captain Targa, Marty Gobel. Don't know who else. We're going to give information, and we're going to get information." He looked down at me. "If I leave, you'll get up, right?"

"Yeah."

"You won't go back to sleep?"

"No."

"I don't believe you. You have that go-back-to-sleep look."

He ripped the covers off and dragged me into the bathroom. He turned the shower on and shoved me in still wearing his T-shirt.

"You are such an asshole," I yelled at him.

"Ten minutes," he said. And he left the bathroom, closing the door behind him.

I was at the sink, wearing his robe with the hair dryer in my hand, when he rapped on the door. "Ten minutes are up."

"Bite me," I said.

"I've got clothes for you."

I stuck my head out. "You picked out my clothes?"

"It wasn't hard. They're all the same."

I took the clothes, closed the door, and got dressed. Only the bra didn't have RangeMan embroidered on it.

I gave up on the hair drying and skipped makeup. I'd take care of that in the car.

Ranger was waiting in the kitchen. He had coffee in a travel mug and a bagel with cream cheese in a Styrofoam box. Ranger hated being late for a meeting. Only death or dismemberment or the opportunity for morning sex were considered acceptable reasons for Ranger to be late to a meeting.

I took the coffee and bagel and trotted after Ranger out of the apartment and into the elevator.

"Do we know any more about last night?" I asked.

"Tank saw Joyce at the fire scene, and it sounded like she had Smullen's girlfriend with her. Other than that, no."

We got into the Turbo and Ranger drove out of the garage. I had my coffee in the Turbo's cup holder, the bagel in one hand and a mascara wand in the other.

"Don't jerk around," I said to Ranger. "I could go blind doing this."

"Wouldn't it be safer to do without?"

"Yeah, but I hide behind it. I put it on when I need to feel brave."

"You don't need to feel brave today. Nothing bad is going to happen at this meeting."

"I've been sleeping in your bed, and I've got your name embroidered on my underpants, and now I'm going into a meeting where your air space is going to intersect with Morelli's."

"Babe, nothing's been happening in my bed, and no one's going to see your underpants in this meeting unless you go goofy."

We parked in the public lot and crossed the street to the municipal building. Ranger had meeting instructions, so we ignored the cop-in-a-cage and went directly to a conference room. There were six men already seated. Ranger and I took our seats, and that left one chair empty. Morelli. Morelli's chair was directly opposite mine. Ranger was to my right. Already I was sweating the seating arrangement.

The conference room door opened, and Morelli entered. He nodded to everyone and claimed his place at the table. He looked across at me and smiled. The smile was small and intimate, and his brown eyes softened just a little for just a moment. He was in jeans and a cream sweater with the sleeves pushed to his elbows.

I had no idea what was going on inside Morelli or Ranger. They looked perfectly at ease and in control. Both of them were good at hiding emotion. Both were good at compartmentalizing. I wasn't good at any of that stuff. I was a wreck inside.

"Sorry I'm late," Morelli said. "I had to wait for the babysitter."

Everyone knew Morelli had someone locked down.

"You called this," Targa said to Morelli. "You want to run it?"

"Stephanie and Ranger have information they want to share with us," Morelli said. "And they're hoping we have information to share with them." His eyes went first to me and then to Ranger. The eyes didn't say anything. Morelli was in cop mode.

"For reasons that are obvious, Stephanie and I have been looking for Dickie Orr," Ranger said. "Stephanie was looking for him in the warehouse when the fire started. And we were in the apartment building last night when that fire occurred. We know that all three fire victims were dead before the fire. We know there was an accelerant in the apartment. I called 911 and did a fast search, but I didn't find anything that looked like a bomb. And for that matter, in both instances, there was no explosion of any significance."

"You saw the victims before the fire?" Targa asked.

"Stephanie saw Smullen. We both saw the two bodies in the apartment building. All three had been burned beyond recognition. The scorch trail suggested flame-thrower."

"The accelerant was gasoline," Roiker said. "We found the cans."

"Do you know how it was ignited?" Ranger asked.

"Both times it started in a kitchen. In the case of the warehouse, it was a corner set aside for a cooler and a microwave and a toaster. The lab guys are still working, but it looks like someone rammed something that would burn into the toaster. . . . Hell, it could have been one of those breakfast tart things. The pop-up mechanism was disabled and the toaster was wired with an interior timer. We suspect the toaster was fitted with a fuse to make sure the flames reached the accelerant, but there was no evidence of it."

"The flaming toaster bomb," Marty Gobel said. "We see a lot of them."

Morelli cracked a smile and Ranger nudged my knee with his.

"Have you identified the victims from the apartment fire?" Ranger asked.

"Working on it. Not a lot left of them. The explosion was set closer and the fire burned hotter."

"We saw Rufus Caine enter the building. And we believe he was meeting Victor Gorvich," Ranger said. "Tank was watching, and he didn't see either man come out the front of the building. Someone rappelled out a back window."

Ranger didn't share information on the drug connection or the missing $40 million, and no one mentioned Dickie Orr.

Five minutes before the meeting closed, Morelli's phone buzzed and he went outside to take the call and never returned. At eleven o'clock, Ranger and I left the building and buckled ourselves into the Porsche.

"Do you think he was pulling our leg on the toaster?" I asked Ranger.

"No. He's not that clever. I did a fast run through the apartment, looking for an incendiary, and didn't see anything. Smullen's girlfriend had taken everything except the couch and the toaster. I saw the toaster and didn't give it a second look."

"Next time we enter a building soaked in gasoline, we'll think to unplug the toaster."

Ranger glanced in his rearview mirror when we were a block from RangeMan. "It looks like Joyce got her Mercedes running."

I turned and looked out the back window. Joyce was a car length behind us.

"I have to give her credit," I said. "She's good."

"She's too good," Ranger said. "She's finding us on the road."

He keyed himself into the underground garage and parked in his space in front of the elevator.

"Do you have plans for today?" he asked me. "I can give you paperwork if you haven't anything better to do."

"I have two skips I'm working on. I thought I'd check on them."

"If you're going to leave your bag anywhere, please take the monitor with you. Put it in your pocket."

"Is it okay if I only take one?"

"How many do you have?"

"Three."

Ranger sat there for a beat. "I only planted one."

"Shit."

We rode the elevator to Ranger's apartment, went inside, and I emptied my bag onto the kitchen counter.

Ranger picked a pen out of the mess. "This is mine."

I took it from him and put it into my pocket.

"This lipstick is another one," I said, handing him the tube.

"I'm guessing this is from Joyce," Ranger said. "You can buy these in The Spy Store."

"And the third." I gave him what looked like a menthol cough drop in a paper wrapper.

"This is good," Ranger said, examining the cough drop. "Super small. Well disguised. How did you discover it?"

"I tried to eat it."

"That's the flaw. You can write with my pen."

"This is so creepy. Three people planted a transmitter on me, and I never knew they were doing it. What else am I missing? We know one of the transmitters belongs to you, and you planted it on me to protect me. We suspect the second belongs to Joyce, and she wanted me to lead her to Dickie. So what does this third one represent?"

"It could be as simple as one more person with the same agenda as Joyce. One of the partners who thought you might lead him to Dickie and the money. Maybe someone was casting a wide net. Maybe Joyce is walking around with a transmitter in her bag too."

"You don't want me to freak over this."

"I don't want you to get bogged down in negative

emotion. And the truth is, we aren't sure what these toys do. I'm going to take them downstairs and give them to one of my tech guys."

"Omigod, I just had a thought. I killed Rufus Caine! If the cough drop is a transmitter, the owner would have known we visited Rufus. He would have known we were at the club. And he would have known we followed Rufus to the apartment."

"You didn't kill Rufus. And even if you did, it wouldn't be much of a loss."

"Death by flamethrower is gruesome."

"That's the appeal. The threat is demoralizing. It instills fear. And fear can be a controlling, paralyzing emotion. There are paramilitary groups that make good use of flamethrowers. It's not an especially effective way to kill a man, but it sends a message."

"You think someone is sending a message here?"

"No. I think this killer is a freak. He has a reason for killing these people, but he's also getting off on the experience. He torches them, and then he sets a fire to hide his thrill kill. Problem is, both times you screwed things up. You saw the torched bodies before the fire. His secret is out."

"He might not know that."

"If he's the owner of the cough drop, he knows."

"What about not wanting to scare me?"

"You asked," Ranger said. "Are you scared?"

"Big time."

"You're safe here."

"Yes, but I can't stay here forever. In fact, I can't stay here tonight. I think my free pass has expired."

"I don't want to force you to leave and put you in harm's way," Ranger said, "but I have limits."

"You need a larger apartment," I told him. "You need a guest room."

"I don't know why I put up with you," Ranger said. "You're a real pain in the ass."

"You put up with me because I'm amusing, and you love me, and I pose no threat to your lifestyle because I'm involved with Morelli."

"That's all true," Ranger said. "But it doesn't make you any less of a pain in the ass."

I shoved my stuff back into my bag. "I'm heading out. I need to check on Rex, and then I'm going to the office."

"I need to stay here, but I can give you one of my men."

"Not necessary. I'm okay."

"I thought you were scared."

"It's a way of life."

"What the heck is this?" Lula asked when I walked into the office. "You're all in RangeMan black. Are you working for RangeMan again?"

"I ran out of clean clothes, and this was available. I'm going to try to talk to Coglin. Want to ride along?"

"Sure. Maybe we could stop at the video store. Tank's coming over tonight, and I'm gonna rent a movie. I need something to put him in the mood. I was thinking one of them *Lethal Weapon* movies. Or maybe *Transporter*."

"What kind of mood were you aiming for?"

"Man mood. In all my years of being a 'ho, I learned blood is better than sex if you want to get a man stirred up for action. You let a man watch someone getting his face mashed in, and you got a horny guy. It's the beast thing."

Something to keep in mind if I ever want to do it with a beast.

"We have all the *Lethal Weapon* movies at Morelli's house. You can borrow them if you want."

"You sure he won't mind?"

"He isn't home. He's locked down with a witness. And even if he was home, he wouldn't mind."

"That'd be great since I was going to have to kite a check to get movie money."

THIRTEEN

Morelli's house is officially outside the Burg, but not by much. It was a five-minute drive from the bonds office. I parked the Cayenne and fished Morelli's house key out of my bag.

"I'll be right out," I said to Lula. "Stay here."

Morelli lives in a narrow two-story house configured a lot like my parents'. Rooms are shotgunned with living room going to dining room going to kitchen. Front door. Back door. Downstairs powder room. Small, barren backyard leading to an alley. Three small bedrooms and old-fashioned bath upstairs. Morelli inherited the house from his Aunt Rose and little by little has been making it his own.

I unlocked the front door and stepped into the short hallway that serves as foyer and also leads to the stairs. I'd expected the house would be silent and empty, but the television was on in the living room. My first reaction was confusion, fast followed by a rush of embarrassment. Someone was living here in Morelli's absence. Maybe an out-of-town relative or a down-on-his-luck cop. And I'd barged in unannounced.

I was about to quietly sneak out when Dickie Orr walked in from the kitchen. He was eating ice cream out of the tub, his hair was a mess, as if he'd just rolled out of bed, and he was in his underwear—a white undershirt with a chocolate ice cream stain dribbling down the front and baggy striped boxers.

Time stood still. The earth stopped rotating. My heart stuttered in my chest.

"Wha . . ." I said. "Wha . . ."

Dickie rolled his eyes and shoved his spoon into the ice cream. "Joe!" he yelled. "You've got company."

I could hear Morelli's sneakered feet on the stairs and then he was in the room.

"Oh, shit," Morelli said when he saw me.

I gave him a little finger wave. "Hi."

I was feeling awkward. Embarrassed that I had stumbled into this, and angry that it had been kept from me.

"I can explain," Morelli said.

"Uh-hunh."

"Good luck on that one," Dickie said. "There's no explaining to her. You make one slipup and that's it. Sayonara."

"Shut up, Dick breath," I said. "And anyway, it wasn't one slipup. In the fifteen minutes we were married, you screwed half the women in Trenton."

"I have a high libido," Dickie said to Morelli.

"It had nothing to do with your libido. It had to do with the fact that you're a pathological liar and a worm."

"You have control issues," Dickie said. "Men aren't designed for monogamy, and you can't handle that."

I narrowed my eyes at Morelli. "Hit him."

"I can't hit him," Morelli said. "He's in my protective custody."

"And you!" I said to Morelli.

"I had no choice," Morelli said. "He had to get squirreled away somewhere, and I had the house, so he got dropped in my lap."

"You could have told me!"

"I couldn't tell you. You would have acted differently."

"I thought I was going to jail for murder!"

"I told you not to worry," Morelli said.

"How was I supposed to know that actually meant something? People say that all the time."

"What about me?" Morelli said. "Where's the sympathy for me? I've been trapped in my house with this idiot."

"Boy, that hurts," Dickie said. "I thought we were bonding."

"What about the shooting at your house the night you disappeared?" I asked Dickie. "And what about the blood on your floor?"

Morelli was hands in pockets, rocked back on his heels. "Dickie shot one of the hired help in the knee. And then he ran like hell out his back door, right, Dickie?"

"I ran like the wind."

"And why is Dickie here in protective custody?"

"They wanted him on ice while they investigated the law firm's client list. The original thought was we needed him to testify against his partners, but his partners have disappeared in one way or another. One is confirmed dead and another presumed dead. And the third dropped off the face of the earth when Dickie went missing."

"You can't find Petiak?"

"Vanished. We know he's still around because from time to time one of his goon squad surfaces."

"So I'm off the hook."

"Yep," Morelli said.

"What about Gorvich? I thought I was a suspect there."

"I wanted you to dredge up an alibi in case the press came to you." His attention fixed on my RangeMan jacket. "What are you doing in RangeMan clothes? You were head-to-toe RangeMan this morning."

"I ran out of clean clothes and these were available."

"Available? Where were they available?"

"In Ranger's closet."

"Are you fucking kidding me? I'm holed up here with the witness from hell and you've moved in with Ranger?"

"You told him to take care of me."

"Not *that* way!"

"There's no *that* way going on. It's no different from what you've got here. You've got Dick-head in protective custody. Does that mean you're sleeping with him?"

The color was rising in Morelli's face. "I'll kill him."

"You will *not* kill him. Read my lips . . . nothing has happened between us." At least, not the main event. I chose to believe the prelims didn't count in this case. "And I'm not moved in with him. I'm going home and I'm going to get on with my life now that I know I'm not a murder suspect."

"Maybe you should move in here," Morelli said. "There's a lunatic out there with a flamethrower, and you're mixed up in it somehow."

"No thanks. I already did time with Dickie. I'll take my chances with the flamethrower." I went to the television and looked through the DVDs stacked alongside. "I just stopped around to borrow the *Lethal Weapon* collection." I found the boxed set and looked over at Morelli. "You don't mind?"

"What's mine is yours," Morelli said.

I let myself out and jogged to the Porsche.

"I thought you decided to take a nap in there," Lula said.

I handed the DVDs over to her and pulled the car out of Morelli's driveway. "It took a while to find them."

In a half hour, we were in front of Coglin's house. I paged through his file, found his phone number, and called him.

"I'm in front of your house," I said. "I want to talk to you, and I don't want to end up with squirrel guts in my hair. Can we call a truce for ten minutes?"

"Yeah, I guess that would be okay," Coglin said. "If you promise you won't try to take me in now."

"Promise."

Lula followed me to the door. "He better not go back on his word. I don't want to smell like rodent when Tank comes over tonight."

I opened the door and took a step back. "Is it okay to come in?" I yelled into the house.

Coglin appeared in the hall. "I disconnected the booby trap. It's safe to come in."

"Someday you're gonna hurt someone with those beaver bombs," Lula said.

"I only use stuffing that's soft," Coglin said.

"Yeah, but what about them button eyes? Suppose you got hit with one of them eyes? That would leave a bruise."

Coglin had an apron on. "I'm kind of busy," he said. "What did you want?"

"Are you stuffing up some roadkill?" Lula asked.

"No. I'm making a meatloaf for supper."

"I wanted to talk to you about your court appearance," I said to Coglin. "When you didn't show up, you became a felon. And the original charge didn't look that bad. Destruction of property. The details aren't on the bond application. What sort of property did you destroy?"

"I went nuts and exploded an opossum in a cable company truck."

"Uh oh," Lula said. "The cable police will get you for that one."

Coglin turned white. "Omigod, there are cable police?"

"She's kidding," I told him. "You're kidding, right?" I said to Lula.

"Probably," Lula said.

"It all started when the city put in new water pipes," Coglin said. "They cut through my cable line when they dug a trench through my front yard to lay the new pipe. So I called the cable company and left my name, but they never called me back."

"Those fuckers," Lula said. "They never call anyone back."

"I called them and left my name every day for three weeks, and no one ever called me back. Then after three weeks someone actually answered a phone at the cable company. A real person."

"Get out," Lula said. "They don't have real people working there. Everyone knows that."

"No. I swear, it's true. Someone answered the phone. So after they had me on hold for an hour, I explained the problem and they said they would send someone out in two weeks, and they gave me the day. So I stayed home all that day, and the next day, and the next day. And on the third day, someone came to fix my cable problem. Except they were told the problem was inside my house, and it was really outside, so they couldn't fix it.

"It's not like I just have television, you know. I sell my animals on the Internet, and I didn't have any Internet connection all this time. So I gave the guy twenty dollars, and he ran a line from the junction box across the street to my house. Only it's like a plastic cable kind of thing, so right away, with all the cars rolling over it, the cable started breaking. So I wrapped it in electrician's tape. And I do that twice a day to hold the cable together."

"How long you been doing this?" Lula asked.

"Three months. I keep calling them back and telling them, and they keep saying they're going to send the first available crew out to me, but I have to be home or I'll get put at the end of the line. So that's why I can't go downtown with you. I never leave for more than five minutes unless it's real late at night. Even when it looks like my car is gone and I'm not in the house, I'm watching from somewhere. I can't take a chance on missing the cable repairman."

"And the opossum in the truck?"

"The cable repairman stopped at my neighbor's house three weeks ago and swapped out his broken box, and I went postal and threw a performance piece through the driver's side window."

"And you think they're still gonna give you cable service after you bombed their truck?"

"They send me a bill every month, and I always pay on time. I figure that means something. And twice I got an automated message that said a crew was scheduled, but they never showed up."

"Well, I can understand why you can't go to the police station and get rebonded," Lula said. "There's extenuating circumstances."

"They might *never* show up," I told Coglin.

"My friend Marty lives on the next block, and he had the exact same thing happen, and they showed up one day and fixed his cable."

"How long did he wait?"

"It was almost five months."

"And he stayed home for five months?" I asked Coglin.

"Yes, you have to. It's the rule. He lost his job, but he got his cable fixed."

"I hate those fuckers," Lula said.

"So as soon as the cable guy shows up and fixes your cable, you'll call me?"

"Yes."

Lula and I walked back to the Cayenne and stopped to look at the cable running across the road. It was thick with electrician's tape, and in places had been wrapped in foam and then overwrapped with the tape."

"So what's going on with you and Tank?" I asked Lula. "Is it serious?"

"Yeah, but only for about twelve minutes at a time."

"Twelve minutes is good."

"We've been working up to it. And then, if you add all the twelve minutes together, you get a whole hour. You want an hour with Morelli, you just get him watching one of them *Lethal Weapon* movies."

I wasn't sure I wanted an hour. My egg timer was set on twenty-two minutes. Eighteen, if Morelli was on his game. An hour sounded like a lot of work. And if it was divided up into five twelve-minute sessions, I suspected I'd need mechanical devices. Although there was no doubt in my mind Morelli could manage it.

I drove Lula back to the office and dropped her at her car.

"Looks like Joyce is parked across the street," Lula said. "And she's got Smullen's girlfriend with her."

I waved at them. "Hi," I said.

"Fuck you," Joyce yelled.

"She's in a mood," Lula said.

Most likely because it was a lot harder to pick up my trail now that I wasn't broadcasting.

"Have fun tonight," I said to Lula. "See you tomorrow."

I drove to my apartment with Joyce tagging along. No threat there. I wasn't going to lead her to anything. It was late afternoon, and I was going to have a peaceful evening at home. I'd call Ranger and tell him I was home with Rex and that everything was right with my world. Then I'd shove something frozen into the microwave, crack open a beer, and watch television. And Joyce could sit in my lot until her ass fell asleep. The $40 million was out there somewhere, but I didn't care anymore. Joyce's problem, not mine. I was off the hook. I wasn't wanted for murder. Hooray.

I parked, ran upstairs, and waltzed into my apartment. Nice and quiet. Not as luxurious as Ranger's apartment, but it was mine, and it felt like home. I gave Rex fresh water and dropped a small chunk of cheese into his cage.

Something banged against my front door. I went to the peephole to look out, but before I reached the door, there was a wrenching noise and another loud thud, and the door flew open and crashed against the wall.

It was the big, bleached-blond, muscle-bound moron with the stapled balls. He rushed inside and grabbed me. I shrieked, and he clamped a hand to my mouth.

"Shut up," he said, "or I'll hit you. I'd like to do that anyway, except my boss wants you in one piece."

"Why?"

"I don't know. That's just his way."

"No, I mean why does he want me?"

"My boss doesn't like people who get too nosy. And you've got a knack for being in places you don't belong. My boss thinks you know something."

"Who, me? No way. I don't know anything. You could fill a room with what I don't know."

"You can tell it to my boss. He wants to talk to you. You can cooperate and walk out with me. Or I can stun-gun you and carry you out. Which is it?"

One more stun gun and I was going to permanently forget half the alphabet.

"I'll walk out."

He turned and Joyce was standing there with a gun in her hand.

"No way, José," Joyce said. "*I'm* following her. I saw her first. You want the money? Find it yourself."

"Fuck off. And my name isn't José. It's Dave."

"I'm counting to three, Dave. If you aren't hauling ass by three, I'm going to shoot you in the nuts."

"What is it with my nuts? Why's everybody picking on my nuts?"

"One," Joyce said.

"You're getting on my nerves."

"Two."

"Screw this," Dave said.

He grabbed the barrel of the gun, the gun discharged, and Joyce shot off the top of his pinkie finger.

Dead silence. We were all surprised.

Dave looked at his shortened pinkie, his eyes rolled back in his head, and he crashed face-first to the floor.

"Shit, Joyce," I said to her. "There's blood all over the hall and Dillon just did the floors."

Joyce put her boot to Dave and rolled him onto his back. "Was his nose always flat like that?"

"No. And he didn't used to have blood coming out of it either. He broke it when he fell on his face."

Joyce took his hand and shoved it into his pants so he wouldn't get any more blood on the floor. "What do you want to do with him? We could call 911. Or we can put him in the elevator and push the button."

"Was he alone?"

"No. He has a partner waiting in a black BMW."

"We'll turn him over to the partner."

We dragged him to the elevator and rode him down to the ground level. Then we dragged him out to the parking lot, and Joyce whistled through her teeth to get the partner's attention.

The BMW drove up and the partner got out and

squinted down at Dave. Dave still had his hand rammed into his pants, and his crotch had a big bloodstain.

"Jesus, lady," Dave's partner said. "Goddamn."

"It's not as bad as it looks. Joyce wanted to shoot him in the nuts, but the gun discharged prematurely. Probably that happens a lot with you guys, right?"

"What?"

"Anyway, she just shot his pinkie finger off. We put his hand in his pants so he wouldn't bleed on the carpet."

"Man, that's cold."

"Do you need help getting him into the car?"

Dave's partner reached inside and popped the trunk.

"He's not dead," I said to the partner.

"This is a new BMW with real leather seats. I don't want him bleeding all over everything. He'll be fine in the trunk."

Joyce had her gun drawn, presumably protecting her investment, which was me. Go figure, saved by Joyce Barnhardt.

"Don't try anything stupid," Joyce said to Dave's partner. "It was disappointing to have to settle for a pinkie finger. I wouldn't mind getting a second chance to shoot someone's nuts off."

I grabbed Dave's leg and helped wrangle him into the trunk. We closed the lid, and the BMW sped out of the lot.

"So what's the deal for the rest of the day?" Joyce said. "Are you staying here?"

That was the original plan, but I had a feeling Dave might come back after he got his nose straightened and his finger stitched up.

"I'm going to spend the night at RangeMan," I told Joyce.

"Give him a tug for me," Joyce said. And she walked to her car and took off.

I ran upstairs, hung my bag on my shoulder, and wrapped my arms around Rex's aquarium. I carted Rex out to the Porsche. Then I ran down to the basement and told Dillon about the door and the carpet. Dillon didn't look all that surprised. It wasn't the first time he'd had to fix my door.

FOURTEEN

At seven o'clock, I heard the keys get tossed onto the silver tray in the hall, and seconds later, Ranger walked into the kitchen.

"I thought you were staying in your apartment tonight," Ranger said.

"Change of plans."

He glanced at Rex on the kitchen counter. "This looks serious."

"Remember the guy who got his boys stapled? He came visiting. He wanted me to go for a ride with him, but I declined."

Ranger took two wineglasses out of the cabinet and uncorked a bottle of red. He poured two glasses and gave one to me. "What did it take to discourage him?"

"Joyce Barnhardt with a gun. She tailed me to my apartment and saw Dave follow me into the building. That's the guy's name, Dave. She came up to check things out and decided Dave was a threat to her future earnings. So she shot the top of his pinkie finger clear off his hand. Then Dave's partner came and loaded him into the trunk of their Beemer and drove him away. That's the short version."

"Go figure," Ranger said.

"Exactly."

We both sipped some wine.

"That's not even the best part of the day," I said to Ranger. "I stopped at Morelli's house to get some DVDs for Lula, and I walked in on Dickie."

"Dickie Orr?"

"Yep. It wasn't Dickie's blood in his house. The goon squad was sent to roust him, and he shot one of them in the knee and fled. Morelli has him in protective custody. He's locked away so he can live to testify against his partners, but his partners are disappearing. Smullen is confirmed dead. The police are presuming Gorvich is dead. And they can't find Petiak."

The doorbell buzzed and Ranger opened the door to Ella and dinner. He took the tray from her and carried it into the kitchen.

"Have you eaten?" he asked.

"A peanut butter sandwich at five."

Ella had sent grilled vegetables, pork tenderloin, and saffron rice for two.

"Ella knew I was here?"

"Everyone knows you're here. There aren't a lot of secrets in this building. Only the private apartments and the lavatories aren't monitored."

"Do they know anything about our relationship?"

"No. And they won't ask."

"Not even Tank?"

"Not even Tank."

"So they think we're sleeping together."

"Probably." Ranger set two place settings at the breakfast bar. "Did Morelli or Dickie say anything about the money?"

"No. Morelli said the police were investigating the law firm's client list, but he didn't say more than that. It wasn't a long visit. Lula was outside, waiting in the car."

We both dug into the food.

"Did Dave say anything interesting?"

"He said I was nosy, that I had a knack for being in places I didn't belong, and his boss didn't like it."

"So they were going to do what to you?"

"Dave didn't say, but I don't think it was anything good."

I cleaned my plate and looked over at the tray. No dessert. Ranger never ate dessert. Another reason I couldn't marry Ranger. That and the fact he didn't see marriage as an option.

We loaded the dishwasher, put the leftover food in the fridge, and migrated into the den to watch television.

"Do you watch television a lot?" I asked him.

"Almost never." He remoted his way through the guide. "No games on tonight. Only boxing."

I thought about Lula's theory on bringing out the beast in a man. So far, Ranger had the beast under control. Best not to disturb that balance.

"No boxing," I said.

"Okay, let's roll through the movies. *The Terminator, Pulp Fiction, Braveheart, The Transporter, Deliverance.* Any of those turn you on?"

Where was *Terms of Endearment* when you needed it? "They're all sort of violent," I said.

"And?"

"There must be other movies."

Ranger clicked through more of the guide. "Bruce Lee?"

"Keep going."

"I'm not watching *Jane Eyre.*"

"Okay, great, go with Bruce Lee."

"Maybe you'll learn something," Ranger said.

"Just don't get any ideas."

"About what?"

"About anything."

Ten minutes into Bruce Lee, I sucked in some air. "Uh oh," I said.

The *uh oh* had been an inadvertent exclamation. Nature had struck at an inopportune time, placing me in an awkward position.

Ranger looked over at me. "What?"

"Nothing." At least nothing I wanted to share with Ranger.

"It's something. What is it?"

"Cramps."

"Babe."

"I need . . . you know," I said to him.

"You don't have anything with you?"

"I was planning on staying in my apartment. And then I left in a hurry. And I forgot until just now."

"Do you want me to send one of my men out for something?"

"Would they do that?"

"I'd have to pay him extra."

"Maybe Ella can help me."

I ran downstairs to see Ella, and ten minutes later, I was back on the couch.

"Everything okay?" Ranger asked.

"Yes. Ella had some."

Bruce Lee was kicking ass on the screen, and God knows what this was doing to Ranger's libido, but I now realized nature had come through for me. What had at first seemed like an embarrassing disaster was in actuality a blessing. This was my lucky week. First Joyce, and now nature.

Ranger slid an arm around me and nuzzled my neck. Bruce Lee was getting to him.

"Lula has a theory that violent movies put a man in the mood," I said to Ranger.

"Everything puts a man in the mood," Ranger said.

"Good thing I got cramps, eh? I'm safe."

"Not from me," Ranger said.

Eek. "Guess again," I told him.

Ranger changed channels to *Jane Eyre*. "The two toys we found in your bag were simple transmitters. With the exception of my device, you're supposed to be clean. How did Joyce find you this afternoon?"

"She picked me up at the bonds office."

I opened my eyes and looked at the clock. Almost eight A.M. No Ranger. I checked under the covers. I was still wearing all the clothes I'd started with when I went to bed. Another night of successfully dodging the bullet. I scrambled out of bed and into the shower.

I'd had a brilliant idea halfway through *Jane Eyre*. I knew how I was going to get Coglin to court to re-register. I'd have Grandma babysit his house. I got dressed in more RangeMan black and went to the kitchen to forage for breakfast. I called Ranger with a fast message while I finished my coffee.

"I'm heading out," I said. "I'm going to get Grandma and take her to Coglin's house. I've got the pen transmitter with me. See you later."

Morelli was up next.

"What's new?" I said.

"Unfortunately, nothing. What's new with you?"

I told him about Dave and Joyce.

"So I'm back at RangeMan," I said.

"I'm going to try to put a positive spin on this," Morelli said. "At least I know you're safe."

"This morning I'm doing bounty hunter stuff," I said. "I'm going to get Grandma to help me."

"So much for safe."

Connie was last on the list. "If I can get Coglin to the courthouse, can you get him rebonded right away?" I asked her. I can catch people, but I can't write bond. Only Connie and Vinnie can do that.

"As long as the judge will grant bond. Lula is here. She can answer the phones. How are you going to get Coglin to the courthouse? I thought he was beaver-bombing everyone."

"It turns out he can't leave his house because he's waiting for the cable company."

"Those fuckers," Connie said.

"Yeah, well I'm going to have Grandma house sit for him."

I took the elevator to the garage and powered up the Cayenne. As I rolled out, I kept my eyes open. I was pretty sure Dave and his partner would surface at some point in the day. Without the help of a transmitter, they were going to have to make a pickup choice based on my history as they knew it. They knew I'd spent nights at RangeMan, but I was thinking between the broken nose, the stapled nuts, and the amputated pinkie finger, Dave wasn't moving so fast this morning. I probably had time to get Grandma and drop her off at Coglin's house before the bad guys were on the hunt.

I drove three blocks, adjusted my rearview mirror, and saw the black SUV two cars back. I called Ranger.

"Who's with me today?" I asked him.

"Hang on. I have to talk to control." A couple minutes later, he returned. "It's Binkie. He's new. And he's riding solo. I'm short today. Don't give him a hard time. And if you go back to your apartment, don't get undressed in your foyer or living room. I've installed monitored security cameras."

"Roger and out."

Truth is, I didn't want to give Binkie a hard time. I was grateful to have someone watching my back. I circled my parents' block before parking. I didn't see anything out of the ordinary, so I pulled into the driveway behind my dad's Buick.

Grandma was watching morning television when

I walked in. "Look at you," she said. "You look like Ranger. And look at the shirt with RangeMan written on it. Ain't that a pip."

"I have to take someone downtown to get rebonded, and he needs someone to house sit. He's expecting the cable company."

"Those fuckers," Grandma said. "Excuse the language. Just let me get my purse."

I went to the kitchen to tell my mom.

"It'll be good for her to get out and do something," my mother said. "She's been feeling down because Elmer got shipped off to an assisted-living complex in Lakewood."

Grandma was wearing her favorite lavender-and-white running suit. Her hair had faded to orange, and she had her big black patent leather purse in the crook of her arm. I wasn't going to ask what she had in the purse.

"I'm all ready," she said, getting her coat out of the hall closet. "Where are we going?"

"North Trenton. Hopefully this won't take long."

Binkie stuck close to me all the way to Coglin's. When I parked in front of Coglin's house, Binkie parked half a block away. I got out and waved to him, and he waved back.

Grandma followed me up the sidewalk and waited while I rang the doorbell.

Coglin stuck his head out. "I'm still waiting," he said.

"I brought you a house sitter," I told him. "This is my Grandma Mazur. She's going to stay here while you go with me to get bonded out again. She'll wait for the cable company."

"I guess that would be okay," Coglin said. He looked Grandma over. "Are you up to the cable company?"

"Bring 'em on," Grandma said.

"Don't let them leave without fixing my cable."

Grandma patted her purse. "Don't worry about it." She stepped inside and looked around. "What the heck's going on here?"

"Carl is a taxidermist," I told Grandma.

"The best in the city," Coglin said. "I'm an artiste."

"I never seen anything like this," Grandma said. "You should go on the shopping channel. I bet you could clean up."

"I've thought of that," Coglin said. "I even wrote a letter to Suzanne Somers once. I think my performance pieces would be especially popular."

"Everything's real lifelike. You expect them to just start walking around."

"Sometimes when pets die, people bring them here to get restored, so they can take them home and put them on display," Coglin said.

Grandma was standing wide-eyed in front of a dog with big glass eyes and a tooth missing. "Isn't that something. That's a pip of an idea. I'm surprised they haven't thought to do that with people." Grandma looked to me. "I could have brought your grandfather home and set him in his favorite chair." She slid her dentures around and gave it more thought. "Would have been hard when I moved into your mother's house. It's already jammed full of furniture. I would have had to get rid of Harry."

"Sometimes my pieces get sold on eBay," Coglin said.

"I love eBay," Grandma said. "Harry probably wouldn't have fetched much, but the chair was worth something."

I put a call in to Connie and told her I was leaving for the courthouse with Coglin in tow.

"Just be careful not to touch any of the performance pieces," Coglin told Grandma.

"Don't worry about me. I won't break anything," Grandma said.

"And don't shoot anyone," I said to Grandma. "Especially the cable people."

"Those fuckers," Grandma said.

"That wasn't so bad," Coglin said when we turned onto his street. "I didn't have to wait in jail or anything." He was sitting forward, straining against his seatbelt. "I don't see a cable truck."

"It's still early," I told him.

I parked in front of his house and Binkie parked behind me. Coglin got out and checked the cable stretching across his street for breaks. It looked intact, so we went to the house to spring Grandma.

Grandma had the door open before we reached the porch. "Good thing I was here," she said. "The cable man showed up almost as soon as you left. He ran a new cable under the road, and I stood out there and watched him to make sure he wasn't fibbing about the new cable. And then I wouldn't let him leave until he came in and tried the television. And it looks to me like everything's good now. And he's sending someone to remove the old cable that's running across the road. Probably won't happen for another six months, but it don't really matter."

"Oh gosh," Coglin said. "I can't believe it. The nightmare is over. I can leave the house during the day. I can fill e-mail orders and pay my online accounts." He swiped at a tear. "I feel real stupid getting all emotional like this, but it's been terrible. Just terrible."

"That's okay," Grandma said. "We all get like that over the cable company."

"I can't thank you enough. This was so nice of you to stay here."

"I've been having a good time looking at all the animals," Grandma said. "It's like being in a museum or something. My favorite is this big groundhog because he has three eyes. Imagine that, a groundhog with three eyes."

Grandma reached out and touched an eye and *bang!* Grandma was head-to-toe groundhog. There was groundhog hair stuck everywhere.

"Son of a bee's wax," Grandma said.

"That's okay," Coglin said. "I've got a bunch of groundhogs."

I led Grandma down the sidewalk to the car and got her strapped in.

"He must have overstuffed it," Grandma said.

"It happens all the time," I said to Grandma. "Don't worry about it. I'm going to take you home, and we'll get you cleaned up and you'll be good as new."

I called my mother from the road to warn her.

"Grandma had a little accident," I said to my mother, "but she's fine. She's just got some groundhog stuck to her. I think if you scrub her down with Goo Gone, she'll be okay. And maybe you could call Dolly and see if she's got an opening at the hair salon for a wash and set . . . maybe a cut."

There was a silent pause and I could imagine my mother making the sign of the cross and looking over at the liquor cabinet. I disconnected and turned into the Burg.

"I hear Elmer got shipped off to Lakewood," I said to Grandma.

"Yeah, he was a dud anyway. I'm thinking about taking up bowling. Lucy Grabek joined one of them leagues, and she got a pink bowling ball with her name on it. I wouldn't mind having one of those."

I parked in front of my parents' house and my mother came out to collect Grandma.

"Is this really groundhog?" my mother asked.

"The little brown hairs and patches of hide are groundhog. I don't know about the white stuff. I think it's some kind of synthetic foam," I said.

Binkie and I waved good-bye to Grandma and my mom, and then we drove to the bonds office.

Connie had reached the office ahead of me and was writing out my capture check. "Good work," she said. "That was clever of you to have Grandma babysit. How'd she do?"

"She got woodchucked."

"I bet it was the third eye that got her," Lula said. "You can't hardly resist the third eye."

"How'd last night go?" I asked Lula. "Did the movies work?"

"We never got to the movies. Turns out he don't need no mood enhancement. I'm telling you, I think I'm in love. I might even learn to cook for him."

Connie and I did raised eyebrows.

"Okay," Lula said. "Learning to cook probably isn't gonna happen, but I could learn something."

My phone buzzed and I picked up to Morelli.

"He's gone," Morelli said.

"Who?"

"Dickie."

"Where'd he go?"

"I don't know. I was working upstairs, and when I came down, he was gone. Television on. Back door unlocked."

"Is anything missing?"

"Not that I can tell. My car is still here. His clothes are all here. No signs of struggle. No blood on the floor."

"Maybe he went for a walk."

"He's not supposed to go for a walk. He's not supposed to leave the house. That was the deal. I've been out driving around, and I don't see him."

"Do you think someone took him?"

"I don't know."

"Maybe he went to find Joyce for a nooner."

"Joyce. That's a good idea. Is she still following you?"

I looked out the big plate-glass window in the front of the office. "Yeah. She's sitting across the street. Do you want me to talk to her?"

"Yes, but you can't let her know anything about Dickie."

"What was that about?" Lula wanted to know.

"Morelli thought Bob was missing, but he found him. I'll be right back. I want to say hello to Joyce."

I crossed the street, the Mercedes's driver's side window slid down, and Joyce looked out at me.

"Hey," I said. "How's it going?"

"It's not. Why don't you get off your ass and do something? You think I have nothing better to do than follow you around?"

Smullen's girlfriend was in the seat next to Joyce.

"I never caught your name," I said to her.

"Rita."

"Going tag team?" I asked Joyce.

"If I keep her next to me, I don't have to worry about her sneaking up and stabbing me in the back."

"Fuck you," Rita said to Joyce.

"All right then," I said. "Guess I'll be moving along."

Joyce glanced at the black SUV parked behind Ranger's Cayenne. "Do you have a permit for a parade?"

"That's Binkie. He's practicing surveillance techniques."

I went back to the office and dialed Morelli. "Nothing there," I said.

"I can't believe this happened. I lost my witness. I'll probably get busted back to uniform patrol."

"He was a witness, not a prisoner. It's not like you could chain him to the toilet."

"I don't suppose you'd want to come over and cheer me up," Morelli said.

"You lost a witness and that's the first activity that comes to mind?"

"That's *always* the first activity that comes to mind."

"Sorry, but here's the second bad news of the day. It's that time."

"So?"

"Yeesh."

"Okay, let's table my love life for a couple hours. I need to find either Dickie or Petiak," Morelli said.

"Petiak is easy. We just set me out on the curb and wait for him to kidnap me."

"I'm not excited about that plan."

"Just for giggles, let's suppose Dickie didn't get snatched. Let's suppose he went after the money."

"What money?" Morelli asked.

"The forty million dollars."

"I don't know anything about forty million dollars."

"The forty million Dickie withdrew from the firm's Smith Barney account. The forty million everyone wants, including Joyce and Rita, Smullen's girlfriend. Didn't Dickie tell you about the forty million?"

"That little prick better hope I don't find him because I'm going to kill him."

"You're going to have to take a ticket on that one."

"How do you know about this?"

"Joyce left her front door open one day and I happened to wander in and sit down at her kitchen desk and the drawer sort of opened and I found a bunch of numbers—"

"Stop. I don't want to know," Morelli said.

"I just got a capture check. Suppose I treat to lunch."

"That would be great, but I'm afraid to leave the house in case our boy returns."

"You're in luck. I deliver."

I left the bonds office and was about to plug the key into the Porsche's ignition when Ranger called.

"I'm looking at a monitor, and I'm not believing what I'm seeing," Ranger said. "Dickie Orr just broke into your apartment. Isn't he supposed to be holding hands with Morelli?"

"Morelli just called and said Dickie disappeared."

"Looks like we found him. Tank's on his way. Stay away from the area until I give you an all clear."

Yeah, right. Douchebag Dickie just broke into my apartment, and I'm going to stay clear. Not. I put the car in gear and wheeled around into the Burg. First thing, I had to lose Joyce. I cut through the alley behind Angie Kroeger's house, hung a fast right, ripped through the parking lot for the Colonial Bar and Grille, and came out on Broad. I drove Broad for two blocks, hit Hamilton, and zipped past the bonds office. Joyce was nowhere in sight. Neither was Binkie. I was pretty sure Binkie had his Bluetooth working, calling the control room to see where the devil I was. The control room would be tuned to the GPS transmitter in the Cayenne and my purse, but I'd be in my lot by the time Binkie caught up with me.

I came up on my building and saw the black Range-Man SUV parked close to the back door. Tank was inside, doing his thing, so I hung back by the Dumpster, sitting at idle, trying to keep as low a profile as possible. Not easy in a Porsche Cayenne.

After a few minutes, the door to the building opened and Tank and Dickie emerged. A shot was fired and Tank went down. A black BMW whipped out of a parking space and slid to a stop in front of Dickie. Two men in the car. Dave was one. And his partner was driving. Dave jumped out of the car, grabbed Dickie, and shoved him into the backseat. Dave had two black eyes, a Band-Aid across his nose, and a huge bandage on his pinkie finger. He turned and drew his gun on Tank and fired.

I mashed my foot down hard on the gas and put my hand to the horn. Dave looked up in surprise but didn't move fast enough. Possibly the result of having had his nuts stapled. I bounced him off my left fender and took the side door off the BMW. I stopped and put the Cayenne into reverse. I wasn't entirely rational at that point, but I'm pretty sure my intent was to run over Dave a second time and finish the job. Fortunately for Dave, he was able to drag his ass into the Beemer before I got to him. The Beemer took off, laying rubber on the asphalt, squealing out of the lot as it passed Binkie on the way in.

Binkie and I ran to Tank. He was hit in the chest and leg. He was conscious and swearing and bleeding a lot, so we didn't wait for help. We loaded Tank into the back of the Explorer and took off for St. Frances Hospital. I was driving and Binkie was in back, applying pressure, trying to slow the bleeding. I called 911 so emergency would be waiting for us. Then I called RangeMan and Morelli.

We off-loaded Tank at emergency, and he was whisked away. We were still in the drop zone when Ranger arrived in his turbo, followed by a RangeMan SUV. Morelli was behind the SUV with his Kojak roof light flashing.

We all got out and stood in a clump, five guys and me. If adrenaline was electricity, we were turning out enough to light up Manhattan.

"How bad is it?" Ranger asked.

"He should be okay," Binkie said. "He was hit in the

thigh and right side of the chest. Didn't sound like he had a lung problem. Maybe cracked a rib."

"Dave shot him once from a distance and then again at pretty close range," I told Ranger. "Fortunately, his aim wasn't great with the big bandage wrapped around his pinkie finger."

Ranger went inside to complete the paperwork. When he was done, he joined Morelli and me in the ER waiting room. Binkie waited outside.

"I don't think Dickie was with Dave," I said. "Dickie seemed surprised to see Dave. I think Dave and his partner were waiting for me, and they hit the jackpot."

We all looked over when the waiting-room door slid open and Lula burst in and stormed across the floor, arms waving, hair standing on end.

"What the heck happened here?" Lula shouted.

"Tank was investigating a break-in and he got shot," I told her.

Lula turned on Ranger. She was in his face, hands on hips, eyes looking like a raging bull's. "Did you send that man out all by hisself? What the Sam Hill were you thinking? You got him shot. And I'm here telling you, he better be okay with all his parts in working order, or you're gonna answer to me. I don't fucking believe this." She looked around, searching the room for someone who looked official. "What's happening here? I want to see the doctor. I want to get some answers. He better not be fucking dead is all I'm saying. I'm holding all you accountable."

Ranger was showing nothing. He was in his zone, listening and thinking. Only his eyes moved and focused on Lula. She finished her tirade and Ranger redirected his attention to Morelli and me.

"Hey!" Lula yelled, back in Ranger's face. "You look at me when I'm having a breakdown. And don't you pull that mysterio silent shit on me. I don't take that bus, you see what I'm saying? You're just a little pipsqueak compared to that man you got shot. And nobody even called me. I had to hear it on the police band. What's with that? Holy shit. Holy fuck. Goddamn."

And then it was like she was a big balloon and someone let all the air out. Lula sat down hard on the floor, eyes unfocused.

Jean Newman was the nurse working the desk. She came over and eyeballed Lula. "Looks to me like she hyperventilated," Jean said, getting Lula on her feet. "I'll take her in the back and put a pressure cuff on her and give her some juice."

We sat there for a moment, absorbing the silence that filled the void left by Lula.

Ranger's mouth wasn't smiling much, but his eyes were flat-out laughing. "It's been a long time since I was called a pipsqueak," he said.

Morelli grinned. "That wasn't even the best part. She called you on the mysterio silent shit. You're hanging out there naked."

"Not the first time," Ranger said.

"Where do we go from here?" I asked.

"Maybe not far," Morelli said. "You told me the guy who grabbed Dickie had a broken nose and heavily bandaged finger. He might have come here to get patched. And if he did, he would leave a paper trail. Medical insurance, address, whatever. Plus, you just bounced him off your fender. If he was hurt, he'd have to go somewhere for an X-ray. If not here, Helen Fuld."

"You are so smart," I said to Morelli. "I guess that's why they pay you the big bucks."

Morelli stood. "You two stay here and worry about Tank, and I'll go do my cop thing."

He didn't have to badge Jean. She was from the neighborhood. She knew Morelli and his entire family. She knew he was a cop. And even if Morelli hadn't been a cop, she probably would have answered his questions because the Burg doesn't have a sense of secret. The Burg is gossip central. And more important, women seldom said *no* to Morelli . . . for anything.

"Do you have any idea why Dickie went to your apartment?" Ranger asked me.

"No. It's not like we're friends."

"He was looking for something."

"Money? A gun?"

"If I was Dickie, I'd be looking for the forty million," Ranger said.

"I can guarantee you, I haven't got it in my apartment."

"Still, someone broke into your apartment right after Dickie went missing. And now Dickie walked out of his safe house and went straight to your apartment. It feels like there should be a connection. Maybe Dickie was the first intruder, and maybe he wasn't looking for something. Maybe he was hiding something. And maybe he came back to get it."

"Why would he hide something in *my* apartment?"

"You'd just had a confrontation. You would be on his mind. And you weren't someone anyone would think he'd go to with his treasure. You would feel safe."

"If he hid something, wouldn't he know exactly where it was? Wouldn't he have gone directly to that spot when he broke into my apartment?"

"Maybe it was originally in plain sight, and it got moved. I don't know. I'm just thinking out loud. I'm sure there are other possibilities."

Morelli returned with his notepad in hand. "His full name is Dave Mueller. He didn't use insurance. Paid in cash. He came in on Jean's shift for his pinkie, and she copied his address from his driver's license. According to his license, he's living in the same apartment complex where Smullen and Gorvich kept apartments."

"I'll check it out," Ranger said.

Morelli tore a page out of his notepad and handed it to Ranger. "This is the address. Jean called around. None of the clinics have a record for Mueller, so I'm guessing either Stephanie killed him, or else he has no broken bones or internal bleeding."

"I almost never kill people," I said to no one in particular.

We sat for another half hour in our own thoughts, until an aide came to find us.

"Pierre is out of surgery and awake," she said. "You can see him now."

I looked at Ranger. "Pierre?"

"If you want to live, you'll forget you heard that," Ranger said. "Tank isn't overly fond of being named Pierre."

Lula was already in the room when we got there.

"How's it going?" I asked her.

"I'm better now," she said. "I just had a moment, but I had a glass of juice and a pill, and now I'm back to my old self."

"I thought that *was* your old self," I said to Lula.

"Hunh," Lula said.

Tank had his eyes open, but there wasn't much going on behind them, and he looked like he was down a quart of blood.

"I talked to the doctor, and he said Tank's in good shape," Lula said. "He's just still dopey from the anesthetic. He might even be able to go home tomorrow."

"Yo," Tank said.

"Yo," we all answered.

"I'm gonna stay with him awhile," Lula said. "Make sure he don't rip no tubes out chasing nurses down the hall."

Ranger and Tank did one of those male bonding hand

things, and Ranger and Morelli and I filed out of the room and into the hall.

"I'm going back to my apartment," I said. "Maybe I can find whatever it was Dickie was looking for."

"If you'll take over my Stephanie watch, I can visit Dave," Ranger said to Morelli.

"Done," Morelli said.

I felt my blood pressure raise just a tic. "Excuse me. Time out. Nice to know you're concerned about my welfare, but I'm not excited about getting passed around like luggage."

Morelli and Ranger looked at each other.

"The ball's in your court," Ranger said to Morelli.

"I have nothing," Morelli said.

"Terrific," I told him. "You have exactly one minute to come up with something. And while you're at it, you can explain this buddy-buddy routine. What happened to the rivalry, the animosity? You used to think Ranger was a nut. What about that?"

They stood, hands on hips, counting down.

"It's her time of the month," Morelli finally said.

"Dude," Ranger said.

I huffed out of the hospital to the parking garage and realized I had no car. The Porsche was still in my lot.

Morelli was behind me, smiling. "Need a ride?"

FIFTEEN

I plugged the key into my front door lock, and Morelli drew his gun.

"The apartment is monitored," I told Morelli. "RangeMan would call if someone entered."

"Humor me," Morelli said. "Ranger handed you over to me, remember? It'd be embarrassing if you got kidnapped on my watch."

"Admit it. This is weird."

"Beyond weird, but if Ranger and I draw a line in the sand that can't be crossed right now, everyone will lose."

Forty minutes later, there was nothing left to be searched. We'd covered every square inch and found nothing.

"Let's run through this one more time," Morelli said. "Dickie's got forty million dollars stashed somewhere, and everyone but the Easter Bunny is looking for it. Dickie leaves the safe house and comes straight here and starts searching. He thinks something is here, but it looks like he doesn't know where. The conclusion we've reached is that he hid something out in the open, and it got moved."

"Except I don't remember moving anything. And nothing seems to be missing."

We went to the kitchen and hauled out cold cuts and bread and made sandwiches.

Morelli looked over at the small security camera in my foyer. "Sharing you with Ranger doesn't even rate high on my 'hate this' list compared to being beamed into his control room while I make a sandwich."

"Did you report Dickie's kidnapping?"

"Yes. There's a bulletin out on him."

My kitchen phone rang and I answered it on speaker.

"Stephanie?" the voice said. "I'm surprised you returned home."

"Who is this?"

"I've been wanting to speak to you, but you've been very uncooperative."

"Well, here I am. What did you want to speak to me about?"

"You have something I need. You have the key."

"I have a bunch of keys. Which one are you interested in?"

"I'm not amused. You know which key."

"The key to the forty million dollars?"

"Yes. Now listen closely. If you give me the key, I'll allow you to live. If you choose to be difficult, I'll make sure you have a horrific death. You've already seen some of my work. The next victim will be your ex-husband. He's served his purpose. And as you know, I like to keep things tidy."

"How am I supposed to get the key to you?"

"I think it would be nice if you brought it in person."

"Not going to happen," I told him.

"Do you think I'm scary?"

"Yes."

"You have no idea. You haven't even seen my best work."

"Back to the key . . ."

"I'll think of something. Do you like surprises?"

And he hung up.

Morelli didn't look happy. "You're getting too good at this," he said. "You've been scared and threatened so many times, you're starting to think it's normal. You were so cool with that guy. And he was insane. Genuine psychopath. And you played him."

"Isn't that what I was supposed to do?"

"Yes, but that isn't what I want the woman I love to do. You should have freaked. You should be shaking and crying. Look at you. You're smiling."

"I did a good job."

Morelli pulled me into him and wrapped his arms around me. "You did a great job. I'm proud of you, but I wish your life was different. I don't want you involved in this garbage."

"He thinks I have a key."

"We looked everywhere, and we didn't see a key."

"A key might be easy to miss."

"I didn't miss a key. It's not here," Morelli said.

"Then what the heck's he talking about?"

"The more disturbing question is why would he think you have a key?"

"Dickie."

"That's my best guess," Morelli said. "Dickie told him you have the key."

Morelli's hand had managed to get under my shirt and was starting to head north.

"We're on television," I said to him.

"Shit," Morelli said, removing his hand, stepping back from me. "I forgot."

My cell phone buzzed, and I tuned in to Grandma Mazur.

"I'm at the beauty parlor, and I'm all done," she said. "I was hoping you could give me a ride. Your mother's car is still on the blink."

"Sure," I said. "I need to go to the office anyway."

Ten minutes later, I picked Grandma up at the salon.

"I didn't expect to see Joseph," Grandma said, getting into Morelli's SUV.

"I can't get rid of him," I told her.

Grandma looked pretty good, considering she'd just been groundhogged. As far as I could see, she didn't have any gunk clinging to her. And her hair was newly washed and curled and had faded to apricot.

"I even got my nails done," Grandma said. "I got them to match my hair, and I got a new lipstick too. Dolly said I couldn't wear red with my hair this color, so I got a lipstick named Orgasm. It's gotta be good with a name like that."

Morelli almost ran up on the curb at the thought of Grandma wearing a lipstick named Orgasm.

"Are you still looking for Diggery?" Grandma wanted to know.

"Yes."

"They buried Stanley Berg today, and I heard at the beauty parlor that he went in the ground wearing a diamond pinkie ring and a new Brooks Brothers suit that would fit Simon Diggery. And the weather is nice and mild. We're supposed to get some rain later, but I don't think a little rain would stop Diggery if he needed a new suit."

We dropped Grandma off, then went to Morelli's house to get Bob. Morelli parked in the alley behind his house, took the key out of the ignition, and dropped it into his pocket.

"Wait here," Morelli said. "I'll be right out."

I gave him a raised eyebrow. "You took the key?"

"You wouldn't be here when I came out if I left the key."

"I still might not be here."

"Yeah, but at least I'll have my car."

Morelli jogged to his back door, disappeared inside

the house for a few seconds, and reappeared with Bob. Bob bounded out of the house, tethered to his leash, doing his happy dance. He tinkled on a small patch of dead grass, then rushed to the back of the SUV, anxious to go for a ride. Morelli loaded Bob into the car and got behind the wheel.

"Now what?" he asked.

"I was going to stop in at the office."

"Okay," he said, putting the SUV in gear. "To the office."

"This is ridiculous. Are you going to stick with me all day?"

"Like stink on a monkey, Cupcake."

Connie was putting together files when I walked in.

"I have some new guys for you," she said. "Nothing big. Possession, domestic violence, and grand theft auto. All FTA." She put the paperwork in a folder and handed it to me. "How's Tank? I understand he was shot."

"He's going to be okay. I saw him when he came out of surgery."

"Lula flew out of here when she heard."

"We met her at the hospital. She decided to stay with Tank for a while. Make sure he behaves himself."

The front door banged open and Lula swung in. "They wouldn't let me stay. They said I was a disruptive influence. Do you believe that? Hell, I wasn't disrupting nothing."

"Imagine, someone thinking you're disruptive," Connie said.

"Yeah, they got a bunch of stick-up-their-ass nurses in that place," Lula said. "It was okay, anyways, because they gave Tank some happy juice in his IV and he fell asleep." She looked through the front window. "What's Morelli doing out there?"

"Waiting for me," I said.

"Why?"

"I don't want to talk about it."

"He's babysitting you, isn't he?" Lula said. "It's got something to do with Tank getting shot, right?"

"Do you want the long version or the short version?" I asked them.

"I want the long version," Connie said. "I want all the details."

"Yeah," Lula said. "I don't want to miss nothing. I got a feeling this is gonna be good."

It took a little over ten minutes for me to get through the long version, mostly because Lula went on a rant that Morelli didn't tell me about Dickie.

"What do you mean he didn't tell you?" Lula said. "After all you do for him?"

"Yeah," Connie said. She looked over at Lula. "What do you mean?"

"I'm talking about the nasty," Lula said.

We all thought about that for a moment.

"Okay, maybe that's not a good example," Lula said. "Everybody wants to do the nasty with Morelli."

"There must be other things you do," Connie said.

Connie and Lula waited to hear what I did for Morelli.

"Sometimes I babysit Bob," I said.

"See that?" Lula said. "She babysits Bob. Right there he should have told her. He didn't tell me, and I'd slap him a good one."

"You'd slap Morelli?" Connie said. "Joe Morelli?"

"Okay, maybe not Morelli," Lula said. "But most men."

"Seems to me he was just doing his job," Connie said.

"Yeah, and it don't look like Stephanie does a whole

lot for him," Lula said. "Maybe you should do more for Morelli," she said to me.

"Like what?"

"Well, we wouldn't expect you to cook or clean or anything, but you could pick his undies up off the floor and fold them. I bet he'd like that."

"I'll keep that in mind," I told Lula.

"Boy, you get into a lot of trouble," Lula said to me. "Trouble finds you. Good thing you got Morelli riding shotgun for you, even if it is sort of humiliating and demeaning."

"Yeah," I said. "Good thing."

I took the FTA folder from Connie, left the office, and got into Morelli's SUV.

"What's new?" he asked.

"I have some new FTAs. And Lula said I should pick your undies up off the floor and fold them. She said you'd like that."

"I'd hate that. I leave them on the floor so I can find them if I have to leave in a hurry."

Grandma Mazur called on my cell phone.

"You'll never guess," she said. "That nice Mr. Coglin just called to thank me again. And we got to talking, and one thing led to another, and he's coming for dinner."

"Get out."

"Good thing I got my hair and my nails done. I guess he's a little young for me, but I'm pretty sure I can handle it. I thought you and Joseph might want to come to dinner too."

I'd sooner poke myself in the eye with a sharp stick.

"Gee," I said. "I think we have plans."

"That's a shame. Your mother made lasagna. And she's got chocolate cake for dessert. And I was sort of hoping you could come in case your father don't like taxidermists. It's always good to have a police officer at the table in case things get cranky."

I looked at my watch. Almost five o'clock. Dinner would be at six. Morelli and I would have an hour to take Bob to the park for a walk.

SIXTEEN

Grandma was waiting at the door when we got to the house.

"Mr. Coglin isn't here yet," she said.

Morelli let Bob off the leash, and Bob ran into the kitchen to say hello to my mother. I heard my mother shriek and then all was quiet.

"He must have eaten something," Grandma said. "I hope it wasn't the cake."

The house smelled good, like Italian spices in marinara sauce and garlic bread in the oven. The dining room was set for six. Two bottles of red wine on the table, a bowl of grated Parmigiano-Reggiano. My father was asleep in front of the television, and I could hear my mother working in the kitchen, talking to Bob.

"Be a good boy, and I'll give you a little lasagna," she said to Bob.

I followed Grandma into the kitchen and looked around for Bob damage. "What did he eat?" I asked my mother.

"It was almost the cake, but I caught him in time."

I went to the stove and stirred the extra sauce cooking in the pan. I love being in my mother's kitchen. It is always warm and steamy and filled with activity. In my mind, I have a kitchen like this. The cabinets are filled with dishes that actually get used. The pots sit out on the stove, waiting for the day's sauces and soups and stews. The cookbook on the counter is dog-eared and splattered with grease and gravy and icing smudges.

This is a fantasy kitchen, of course. My actual kitchen has dishes, but I eat standing over the sink, paper towel in hand. I have a single pot that is only used to boil water for tea when I have a cold. And I don't own a cookbook.

Sometimes, I wanted to marry Morelli so I'd have a kitchen like my mom's. Then, other times, I worried that I couldn't pull it off, and I'd have a husband and three kids, and we'd all be eating take-out standing over the sink. I guess there are worse things in the world than take-out, but in my mother's kitchen, take-out feels a little like failure.

The doorbell chimed and Grandma took off like a shot.

"I've got it!" she yelled. "I've got the door."

My mother had the hot lasagna resting on the counter. The bread was still in the oven. It was three minutes to six. If the food wasn't on the table in eight minutes, my mother would consider everything to be ruined. My mother operates on a tight schedule. There is a small window of opportunity for perfection in my mother's kitchen.

We all went into the living room to greet Carl Coglin.

"This here's Carl Coglin," Grandma announced. "He's a taxidermist, and he got the best of the cable company."

"Those fuckers," my father said.

"I brought you a present for being so nice and watching my house," Coglin said to Grandma. And he handed her a big box.

Grandma opened the box and hauled out a stuffed cat. It was standing on four stiff legs, and its tail looked like a bottlebrush. Like maybe the cat had been electrocuted while standing in the rain.

"Ain't that a pip!" Grandma said. "I always wanted a cat."

My mother turned white and clapped a hand over her mouth.

"Holy crap," my father said. "Is that son of a bitch dead?"

"His name is Blackie," Coglin said.

"He won't explode, will he?" Grandma asked.

"No," Coglin said. "He's a pet."

"Isn't this something," Grandma said. "This is about the best present I ever got."

Bob came in, took one look at Blackie, and ran off to hide under the dining room table.

"Goodness," my mother said, "look at the time. Let's eat. Everyone take a seat. Here, let me pour the wine." My mother poured herself a tumbler and chugged it down. It took a couple beats to hit her stomach, and then the color started to come back into her face.

Grandma dragged an extra chair to the table so Blackie could eat with us. Blackie had close-set eyes, one higher in his head than the other, giving him a pissed-off, slightly deranged expression. He peered over the edge of the table, one eye focused on Morelli and one eye on his water glass.

Morelli burst out laughing, I gave him an elbow, and he bowed his head and sunk his teeth into his lower lip to gain some self-control. His face turned red, and he started to sweat with the effort.

Bob growled low in his throat and pressed himself against my leg.

"I'm not eating with a dead cat at the table," my father said.

Grandma put her hands over Blackie's ears. "You'll hurt his feelings," she said to my father.

"Just shoot me," my father said. "Morelli, give me your gun."

My mother was on her third glass of wine. "Honestly, Frank," she said. "You're such a drama queen."

Morelli's phone buzzed, and he excused himself to take the call.

I grabbed his shirt when he stood. "If you don't come back, I'll find you, and it won't be pretty."

Minutes later, he returned, leaning close to me. "That was Ranger. He has Dickie, and he's drugged but okay. He was being held in Dave's apartment. I don't know any more details. Ranger's taking Dickie to RangeMan. I said we'd be over when we were done here."

"Carl said he would teach me taxidermy," Grandma said. "I was gonna take up bowling, but now I'm thinking taxidermy might be the way to go. Carl said I could do my taxidermy right here in the kitchen."

My mother's fork fell out of her hand and clattered onto her plate.

Dickie was in a holding cell at RangeMan. He was stretched out on a cot with an ice bag on his face. We were looking at him through a one-way window in the door.

"I didn't know you had holding cells," I said to Ranger.

"We like to think of them as private rooms," Ranger said.

"Why's he got the ice bag?"

"To keep the swelling down on his broken nose. It's not a bad break. We put a Band-Aid on it and gave him some Advil. Apparently, they had to encourage him to talk."

"Anything else wrong with him?"

"Yeah, lots of things," Ranger said, "but not from

the time spent with Dave. They gave him something to keep him quiet. We won't get much information out of him until it works its way through his system. We can keep him here until he comes around, but we can't keep him against his will beyond that."

"You might as well unload him on me now," Morelli said. "I'm going to get stuck with him eventually anyway."

"I'll have him brought to your house. We'll bring him in through the back."

"What about Dave?" I asked Ranger.

"Never saw Dave. Dickie was alone in the apartment. They had him chained up in the bathroom. We set an alarm off when we went in, so it's likely Dave won't return. I left a man in the area just in case. I did a fast search of the apartment, but didn't find anything that would tell us where Petiak is hiding. We didn't wait for the police."

Ranger walked us down to the parking garage.

"What do you want to do about Stephanie?" Ranger asked Morelli. "She can't go back to her apartment. Do you want to leave her here, or do you want her with you?"

"I don't see her living in the same house as Dickie," Morelli said to Ranger. "Can you be trusted with her?"

"No," Ranger said. "Not for a second."

"Good grief," I said. "I won't stay with either of you. I'll stay with Lula or my parents. I need to go after Diggery tonight anyway."

"So tell me again what's going on," Lula said.

We were in her Firebird in front of RangeMan, and Binkie was at idle behind us.

"We're going after Diggery," I said. "Stanley Berg was buried this morning in a nice new suit and a diamond pinkie ring."

"I'll drive you to the cemetery, but I'm not walking around with you. I'm staying in my car. There's a full moon out tonight. That cemetery is probably full of werewolves and all kinds of shit."

I looked out the windshield. "I don't see a moon."

"It's behind the clouds. Just 'cause you can't see it don't mean it isn't there. The werewolves know it's there."

"Okay, fine. Wait in the car. Leave the window cracked so you can call the police if you hear me screaming."

"Sounds like a plan to me," Lula said. "I swear, you're a crazy person. You go around up to your eyeballs in snakes and dead people and exploding beavers. It's just not normal. Even when I was a 'ho, my life wasn't that freaky. Only thing normal about you is your hot boyfriend, and you don't know what the heck to do with him. To make matters worse, you got that spook Ranger sniffing after you. Not that anyone wouldn't want him sniffing after them. I mean, he is finer than fine. But he's not normal."

"Sometimes he seems normal."

"Girl, you aren't paying attention. He is way better than normal."

Lula pulled up to the gate leading in to the cemetery and stopped. "I can't go no further," Lula said. "This sucker's closed to traffic at night."

"I'll go the rest of the way on foot," I told her.

"You got a flashlight?"

"I can't use a flashlight. I can't take a chance on Diggery seeing me."

"This is nuts," Lula said. "I can't let you go out there by yourself. You don't even got a gun."

"Binkie will go with me."

"Binkie don't look like the sharpest tack on the corkboard. I can't turn you over to Binkie. Honest to goodness, we should all be at home watching television, working our way through a bag of chips, but no, we're out in a boneyard. The way things are going, we probably find Diggery, and he got his snake with him."

I got out of the Firebird and walked back to Binkie.

"I'm after an FTA who sidelines as a grave robber," I said to Binkie. "I have reason to believe he'll be here tonight."

Binkie looked at the pitch-black cemetery. "Oh jeez."

I understood Binkie's reluctance to traipse through the cemetery. At first glance, it was kind of creepy, but I'd chased Diggery through this cemetery before at night and lived to tell about it. What I've discovered with my job is that there's a difference between being brave and being stupid. In my mind, bungee jumping is stupid. Stalking an FTA in a cemetery at night doesn't seem to me to be all that stupid, but the creep factor is moderate to high, so it requires some bravery. And I've found I can sometimes force myself to be brave. Usually, the bravery is accompanied by nausea, but hell, it's not a perfect world, right?

"You can wait here," I said to Binkie.

Binkie opened his door and stepped out. "No way. Ranger'll kill me if anything happens to you. I'm not supposed to let you out of my sight."

Lula came over and checked Binkie out. He was in RangeMan SWAT black with a loaded utility belt, and he stood a full foot taller than Lula.

"You got silver bullets in that Glock you're carrying?" Lula asked.

"No, ma'am."

"Too bad, on account of this place is probably full of werewolves tonight, and you need silver bullets to get rid of those bad boys. And we should probably have garlic and crosses and shit. You got any of those?"

"No, ma'am."

"Hunh," Lula said.

I set out, walking down the private road that led into the cemetery. It was an old cemetery that sprawled over maybe fifty acres of low, rolling hills. It was laced with paths leading to family plots that held generations of hardworking people laid to rest. Some of the headstones were elaborately carved and worn by time and weather, and some were flat pieces of recently polished granite.

"Where are we going?" Lula wanted to know. "I can't hardly see anything."

"The Bergs are just ahead on the left. They're halfway up the hill."

"How far on the left? It all looks the same."

"They're behind the Kellners. Myra Kellner has an angel carved at the top of her marker."

"I don't know how you remember these things," Lula said. "Half the time, you get lost in Quaker Bridge parking lot, but you know where the Kellners and Bergs live in this graveyard."

"When I was little, I used to come here with my mother and grandmother. My relatives are buried here."

I used to love the cemetery excursions. The family plot, like my mother's kitchen, is tended by women.

"This is your Great-Aunt Ethel," Grandma Mazur would say to my sister, Valerie, and me. "Ethel was ninety-eight years old when she died. She was a pip. She loved a good cigar after dinner. And Ethel played the accordion. She could play 'Lady of Spain' by heart. Her sister Baby Jane is buried next to her. Baby Jane died young. She was only seventy-six when she died. She choked on a kielbasa. She didn't have no teeth. Used to gum all her food, but I guess you can't gum kielbasa so good. They didn't know the Heimlich in those days. And here's your Uncle Andy. He was the smart one. He could have gone to college, but there was no money for it. He died a bachelor. His brother Christian is next to him. Nobody really knows how Christian died. He just woke up dead one day. Probably, it was his heart."

Valerie and I had every square inch of our plot committed to memory, but it was part of the experience to have Grandma point out Great-Aunt Ethel. Just as it was part of the experience to go exploring in the tombstone forest while my mother and grandmother planted the flowers. Val and I visited the Hansens and the Krizinskis and the Andersons on the top of the hill. We knew them almost as well as Great-Aunt Ethel and Baby Jane. We planted lilies for Easter and geraniums for the Fourth of July. In the fall, we'd visit just to clean things up and make sure all was right with the family.

I stopped going to the cemetery when I was in junior high. Now I only go for a funeral or to chase down Simon Diggery. My mother and grandmother still go to plant the lilies and geraniums. And now that my sister has moved back to the Burg with her three girls, I'm sure they'll help plant the lilies this year and listen to Grandma talk about Ethel.

"Here's an angel," Lula said, stepping off the path, heading uphill. "Excuse me," she said, walking on graves. "Sorry. Excuse me."

Binkie was silent behind me. I turned and looked at him, and he had his hand on his gun. I wasn't sure what he thought he might have to shoot.

"Simon Diggery isn't usually armed with anything other than a shovel," I told Binkie. "Lula and I have done this before. We'll get to the grave site and find a place to hide. Then we'll let Simon dig himself into a hole. It makes the apprehension easier."

"Yes, ma'am," Binkie said.

"I hate being ma'am," I told him. "Call me Stephanie."

"Yes, ma'am, Stephanie."

"I'm at the top of the hill, and I don't see no fresh-dug grave," Lula said.

"Are you sure you turned at Kellner?"

"I turned at the angel. I don't know about Kellner."

I squinted into the darkness. Nothing looked familiar.

"Is that rain I feel?" Lula asked. "It wasn't supposed to rain, was it?"

"Chance of showers," I told her.

"That's it," she said. "I'm going home. I'm not being out here in the rain. I'm wearing suede." Lula looked around. "Which way's home?"

I didn't know. It was pitch black, and I was all turned around.

"We can't go wrong if we go downhill," Lula said, taking off. "Oops, excuse me. So sorry. Excuse me."

It was raining harder and the ground was getting slick underfoot.

"Slow down," I said to Lula. "You can't see where you're going."

"I got X-ray vision. I'm like a cat. Don't worry about me. I just gotta get this coat out of the rain. I can see there's a tent ahead."

A tent? And then I saw it. The grounds crew had erected a tarp over a hole dug for a morning burial.

"I'm just waiting under this tent until the rain lets up," Lula said, rushing forward.

"No!"

Too late.

"Whoops," Lula said, disappearing from view, landing with a loud *whump.*

"Help!" she yelled. "The mummy got me."

I looked down at her. "Are you okay?"

"I think I broke my ass."

She was about six feet down in a coffin-sized hole. The sides were steep and the surrounding dirt was fast turning into mud.

"We have to get her out of here," I said to Binkie.

"Yes, ma'am. How?"

"Do you have anything in the car? Rope?"

Binkie looked around. "Where's the car?"

I had no idea.

I flipped my cell phone open and called Ranger.

"We're in the cemetery and we're lost," I said to him. "It's raining and it's dark and I'm cramping. I've got the transmitter thingy in my pocket. Can you get a bead on us?" There were a couple beats of silence. "Are you laughing?" I asked him. "You'd better not be laughing."

"I'll be right there," Ranger said.

"Bring a ladder."

We were a ragtag group, standing in the rain at the cemetery gates. Ranger and two of his men fading into the night in their black rain gear, Lula head-to-toe mud, and Binkie and me soaked to the skin.

"I feel funky," Lula said. "I got graveyard mud on me." She had her car keys in her hand. "Do you need a ride somewhere?" she asked me.

"I'm good," I said to her.

Lula got into her car and drove off. Binkie left and Ranger's men got into their SUV and left.

"Just you and me," Ranger said. "What's the plan?"

"I want to go to Morelli's house. I want to be there when Dickie starts talking."

Thirty minutes later, Ranger walked me to Morelli's back door and handed me over.

"Good luck," Ranger said to Morelli. "You might want to hide your gun."

And Ranger left.

Morelli brought me into the kitchen. "Diggery?" he asked.

"Never saw him. We got lost in the cemetery and had to get Ranger to track us down. I need a shower."

I slogged upstairs to the bathroom, locked myself in, and stripped. I stood in the shower until I was all warmed up and squeaky clean. I ran a comb through my hair, wrapped a towel around myself, and shuffled into Morelli's bedroom.

Morelli was in the middle of the room looking like he wanted to do something but wasn't sure where to begin. Bed linens and clothes were in a crumpled mess on the floor, and there were empty beer bottles, plates, and silverware on all surfaces.

"This isn't good," I said to him.

"You have no idea what this has been like. I hate this guy. I hide in my room. I'd like to hit him, but it isn't allowed. He eats all my food. He controls the television. And he's always talking, talking, talking. He's everywhere. If I don't lock my door, he just walks in."

"Is he still drugged?"

"Yeah. I'd like to keep him that way."

"Do I have any clothes here?"

"Some underwear. I think it's mixed in with mine."

I found the underwear and borrowed a T-shirt. I located some clean sheets and made the bed.

"This is nice," Morelli said. "I knew the room needed something, but I couldn't figure out what. It was sheets."

"Stick a fork in me," I said, crawling into bed.

SEVENTEEN

I woke up to someone banging on the bedroom door and Morelli in bed next to me with the pillow over his face. I took the pillow off Morelli. "What's going on?"

"If I go out there, I'll kill him," Morelli said.

I crawled out of bed, toed through the clothes on the floor, and located a pair of sweatpants that looked fairly clean. I stepped into the sweats and rolled them at the waist. I was still in Morelli's T-shirt. Didn't bother to brush my hair. I opened the door and looked out at Dickie. He had two black eyes and a Band-Aid on his nose.

"Yeah?" I said.

"Jesus," he said. "What are you doing here? The nightmare never ends."

Good thing for him I didn't have a staple gun.

"How did I get here? Last thing I remember I was kidnapped," Dickie said.

"Go downstairs and look for breakfast. We'll be right down."

I turned and bumped into Morelli, who was standing behind me, naked. What is it with men that they can walk around like that? I could barely get naked to take a shower.

"No clothes?" I asked him.

"You're wearing my last almost-clean sweats."

"Underwear?"

"None. I need to do laundry. Dickie's been wearing my clothes."

"I'm not going downstairs with you naked."

Morelli kicked through the clothes and came up with a pair of jeans. I watched him put the jeans on commando, and my nipples got hard.

"I could have these pants off in record time," Morelli said, eyes on my T-shirt.

"No way. Dickie might hear."

"We could be quiet."

"I couldn't concentrate. I'd be imagining Dickie with his ear to the door."

"You have to concentrate?" Morelli asked.

"Hey!" Dickie yelled from the foot of the stairs. "There's no milk."

I followed Morelli down the stairs to the kitchen, where Dickie was eating cereal out of the box.

"There's no milk," Dickie said. "And there's no more orange juice."

"There was orange juice last night," Morelli said.

"Yeah, but I drank it."

Morelli fed Bob and got the coffee going. I looked for something to eat that might not be contaminated with Dickie cooties. I didn't mind sharing a cereal box with Morelli, but I wasn't going to eat from something Dickie had just stuck his hand in. God knows where that hand was last.

"Tell me about the key," I said to Dickie.

"What key?"

I glanced at Morelli. "I'm going to hit him."

"I'll close my eyes," Morelli said. "Tell me when it's over."

"You can't do that," Dickie said. "You're supposed to protect me. Especially from her. You do one little thing wrong with her and the Italian temper comes out. And God forbid you come home late for dinner."

"Four hours!" I said. "You'd come home four hours late for dinner, and you'd have grass stains on your knees and your shirt caught in your zipper."

"I don't remember that part," Dickie said. "Did I used to do that?"

"Yes."

Dickie started laughing. "I wasn't making a lot of money back then. I couldn't afford a hotel room."

"It's not funny!" I said.

"Sure it is. Grass stains and rug burns are always funny." He looked over at Morelli. "She didn't like to do doggy."

Morelli slid a look at me and smiled. There wasn't much I didn't like to do with Morelli. Okay, a few things, but they involved animals and other women and body parts that weren't designed for fun.

"What?" Dickie said. "What's that smile? Oh man, are you telling me she does doggy with you?"

"Leave it alone," Morelli said.

"Is it good? Does she bark? Do you make her bark like a dog?"

"You need to stop," Morelli said. "If you don't stop, I'm going to *make* you stop."

"Arf, arf, arf!" Dickie said.

Morelli gave his head a small shake, like he didn't fucking believe he had Dickie in his kitchen. And then he grabbed Dickie by his T-shirt and threw him halfway across the room. Dickie hit the wall spread-eagle like Wile E. Coyote in a Road Runner cartoon, and the cereal flew out of the box. Bob came running from the living room and snarfed up the cereal.

"What's that about?" Dickie asked, struggling to get to his feet.

"Trying to get your attention."

I handed Morelli a cup of coffee. "Ask him about the key."

"I'm telling you I don't know anything about a key," Dickie said.

"Let me refresh your memory," I said to him. "You left the safety of this house and went straight to my apartment, where you were caught on camera breaking in and searching for something. Later that day, I got a call from a guy who wanted the key."

"So?"

"So I know there's forty million dollars out there. I know everyone wants it. And I know someone thinks I have the key. And unless I can figure this out, I'm going to get barbecued like Smullen and Gorvich."

"Let's start from the beginning and build up to the key," Morelli said. "How did you meet Smullen and Gorvich and Petiak?"

"I met Petiak at a financial-planning conference. We got to be friends, and he introduced me to Smullen and Gorvich. I'd just been passed over for partnership, and I could see the handwriting on the wall. Office politics weren't in my favor. So I was looking at options. Petiak had money and clients but no ability to litigate if the need should arise. He suggested we go into business together, and I agreed. I knew his client list was questionable, but I thought I could live with it."

"Smullen and Gorvich?"

"We needed more money to buy the building, and Petiak knew Smullen and Gorvich from a previous life, and he knew they were looking for a place to practice. It was all a con, of course. They were always the unholy triad. At some level, I suspected this, but I had no idea how unholy they actually were. I was desperate to be a partner somewhere and get my own business established, so I didn't look at anything too closely."

Dickie shook the cereal box and turned it upside

down. Empty. "I'm hungry," he said. "This was the last of the cereal. And I want coffee."

"Help yourself to the coffee," Morelli said.

"I need cream. I can't drink black coffee."

Morelli looked like he was going to throw him against the wall again.

"I'll go to the store," I said.

Not so much as a favor to Dickie. More because I needed cream for my coffee too.

"I want to go with you," Dickie said. "I'm tired of being cooped up in this house."

"I can't take a chance on having you recognized," Morelli said. "If Petiak or one of his idiots spots you in my car, we'll blow our cover."

"I can wear a hat," Dickie said.

"Put him in a hooded sweatshirt," I told Morelli. "He can put the hood up and slouch down. I need food."

Morelli got a hooded sweatshirt off the living room floor and tossed it to Dickie. "I'm going with you," Morelli said. "Give me a minute to find clothes."

My socks had dried, but my shoes were still wet. I grabbed a jacket from Morelli's hall closet and put a ball cap on my head.

We all skulked out to the SUV parked in the back of the house. Dickie rode shotgun, and I got in behind him. Morelli walked Bob down the alley until Bob did everything he had to do, and then Morelli ran Bob back and put him in the cargo area.

Morelli went south to Liberty Street and pulled into a strip mall that was anchored by a 7-Eleven. I took everyone's order, Morelli gave me a wad of cash, and I went shopping. I was on my way out with a bag of food when I spotted Diggery at the other end of the mall, doing taxes out of the back of a beat-up Pontiac Bonneville. He had the trunk lid up, and he had a little folding table and two stools set out. There were seven people in line. I handed the bag over to Morelli and walked down to Diggery.

"Oh jeez," he said when he saw me.

"You're up early," I said to him, checking out his fingernails for signs of fresh dirt.

"This here's convenience taxes," Diggery said. "You can pull your pickup in and get your fresh coffee and then come get your taxes done and go off to work."

"I was next," a woman said to me. "You gotta get to the rear of the line."

"Chill," I told her. "I'm wanted for murder, and I'm not in a good mood."

"Here's the thing," Diggery said to me. "I know it's not a big deal to go get bonded out again, but it's gonna cost me more money, and I don't have it. I had to buy winter coats for the kids and rats for the snake. If you let me finish my tax business, I'll come with you. I'll have money from the taxes. Tell you what, you cut me some slack here, and I'll do your taxes. No charge."

"How much longer do you need?"

"Two weeks."

"I really could use some help with my taxes."

"Just put your pertinent information in a shoe box and bring it all to me. I'll be able to fit you in next Monday. I'll be at Cluck-in-a-Bucket on Hamilton Avenue between ten and twelve at night."

"What was that about?" Morelli asked when I got back to the SUV.

"Simon Diggery doing taxes. He said he needed the money to buy rats for the snake, so I let him go."

"That's my girl," Morelli said. He flipped a bagel back to Bob and took us home.

I'd gotten bagels, doughnuts, cream cheese, milk, orange juice, bread, and a jar of peanut butter. Dickie chose a bagel and loaded it up with cream cheese. Morelli and I ate doughnuts.

"Talk while you eat," Morelli said to Dickie. "You went into business with Smullen, Gorvich, and Petiak. Then what?"

"It was all looking good. We bought the building, and then we were doing well, so we made some other real estate investments. Petiak and Gorvich both had home offices and I only saw them at the off-site Monday meetings. Fine by me. I always thought Petiak was a little creepy. He has this quiet way of talking, choosing his words as if English is his second language. And there's something about his eyes. Like light goes in but doesn't come out. And Smullen had ties to South America, so I saw him sporadically. It was a little like having my own firm. I had my own clients and my own staff. There were four names on the stationery, but I was usually the only partner in the building."

Morelli refilled his coffee and topped off my coffee and Dickie's. "What went wrong?"

"It was Ziggy Zabar, the accountant. He figured out what was really going on, and he wanted to get paid off."

"And what was really going on?" Morelli asked.

"It's actually very clever," Dickie said. "They were using the law firm to launder money. Petiak was a military guy until he got booted out for something . . . probably insanity. Anyway, he was a supply officer. Worked in a depot and had access to all the munitions. And he saw a way to tap into these depots all across the country and move munitions out of the depots into his private warehouse."

"The warehouse on Stark Street?"

"Yes. Next comes Peter Smullen. Smullen is married to a woman from a cartel family. Smullen has contacts all over South America. These contacts have dope but need guns, so Smullen takes the dope, and Petiak delivers the guns. The last piece to the puzzle is Gorvich. Gorvich is the drug dealer. He gets the stuff from Smullen and packages it up and distributes it. Now comes the good part. The money Gorvich takes in for drug sales is recorded as payment for legal services. It gets deposited in the firm's account and is sanitized."

Morelli took another doughnut. "So Petiak smuggles guns off government property, stores them in your warehouse, and then ships them off to South America. The cartel pays for the guns with drugs. The drugs gets shipped to Trenton, probably to the warehouse, where they're packaged and sold to local dealers. And the dealers pay for the dope in billable hours."

"Yep," Dickie said. "Genius, right?"

"Not exactly. Zabar figured it out."

"Well, it was good in theory," Dickie said. "It would make a good movie."

"Where do you fit in all this?"

"I was the token real lawyer in the firm. I was supposed to give them some legitimacy. The only reason I know anything is because Smullen made a phone call from his office and I happened to be in the hall. He was on speakerphone talking to Petiak, and they were making plans to pull all the money out of the firm and disappear. Petiak said there was no rush. He said Zabar was taken care of and wasn't going to make any more problems. This was Tuesday morning, after the Monday partners' meeting that Zabar was supposed to attend. Smullen said if Zabar could figure it out, there were others in the accounting firm that could do the same thing. Petiak agreed but said they had to give Gorvich two weeks to transact business."

Bob came in and sat at Morelli's feet.

"You ate your bagel in the car," Morelli said to Bob. "You'll get fat if you eat another bagel."

Bob heaved himself to his feet and padded back to the living room.

"Was this when you cleaned out the Smith Barney account?" Morelli asked.

"Not right away. I didn't know what to make of it. My worst fear had always been that one of Gorvich's drug dealers would walk in and shoot up the office. I knew our client list was scary. A conspiracy never occurred to me."

"You must have known they were all from Sheepshead."

"Everyone has a circle of professionals they tap into when the need arises."

"They bought their degrees on the Internet," I said to Dickie.

"At the time, I didn't care. I didn't have the resources to make a success on my own, so I was willing to do some denial to get a partnership."

"Why didn't you go to the police when they killed Ziggy Zabar?"

"I didn't know they killed Zabar. Petiak said he took care of him. That could have meant anything. Later in the week, the police came asking if Zabar had attended the meeting, but even then I still thought he was just missing. Petiak could have paid him off, and Zabar could have gone to Rio. Anyway, have you seen Petiak? He's not a guy you could walk up to and ask if he killed your accountant." Dickie pushed back in his chair. "You need a television in here. How can you have a kitchen without a television?"

"I manage," Morelli said. "So what I'm supposed to believe is that you heard a phone conversation suggesting your partners were going to take your money and run, and you didn't do anything?"

"I didn't confront them, if that's what you mean. These are guys who have professional hit men on their client list. I represent Norman Wolecky. I backed out of the hall without making a sound, and when the building emptied out for the night, I went through all the financial records, and I found out how much money we had at Smith Barney. I knew from the phone conversation that something illegal had gone down, but I couldn't figure out what it was. I thought it was probably something like tax evasion. If it was tax evasion, I knew I was fucked. I signed the returns just like everybody else. What was pissing me off was that they were going to take the money and leave me behind to take the fall. I was sitting on this information, waiting for someone to come to me, and no one did. So Friday afternoon, I went to Joyce's house so no one would hear me, and I cleaned out the Smith Barney account. It was easy. All four of us have our own password to access the account. My plan was to wait for the Monday meeting. If they didn't say anything to me at the Monday meeting, I was going to leave the country and enjoy my forty million. Screw Smullen, Gorvich, and Petiak. My mistake was that I didn't leave soon enough. Smullen found out about the withdrawal and sent the goon patrol to my house Monday night."

"You still could have fled," I said to him. "Why did you hang around?"

"To begin with, I didn't have a passport. It was in my house, and my house was filled with cops. And then when I went back to my house, my passport was missing. I know there are ways to get a fake passport, but I'm not James Bond. I don't know how to go about getting a fake passport, and the thought of using one scares the crap out of me. I get nervous when I have to take my shoes off at the airport. I'm innocent and I feel guilty. What am I going to do when I'm actually guilty?

"So I put myself in a cheap motel in Bordentown until I could come up with a plan. I'm not talking to anyone. Not even Joyce. Okay, maybe phone sex, but that was it. And then I'm watching television, and the local news comes on, and they're talking about how Zabar, the accountant, washed up on the banks of the Delaware. Now I know Petiak killed Zabar. This is serious shit. This isn't just income tax evasion, this is also murder.

"Time to get out of Dodge, I tell myself. If I can't go to an island and lose myself, I can at least go to Scottsdale. Unfortunately, it turns out I can't get to the money. Now I'm really in a bind. I have no more cash in my pocket, and I'm afraid to use a credit card and have it traced. I get to thinking about the warehouse and the apartment building the firm owns, and I wonder if I can hang out there for just a couple days until I can locate the money. I go to the apartment building, and it's in use. Full. No empty apartments. Then I go to the warehouse, and I see Gorvich in the parking lot talking to Eddie Aurelio. Two of Aurelio's soldiers are standing watch at parade rest by Aurelio's Lincoln. It's like a scene out of *The Godfather*. I don't know a whole lot about the Trenton drug scene, but I know Aurelio is big-time mob.

"I drove past the warehouse and got on Route One and kept going until Princeton. I stopped at a Starbucks and tried to get my heart rate down over a latté. Decaf. I didn't know what the hell was going on, but I was running out of options until I could get the money. So I called the police and told them about Gorvich and Aurelio and Gorvich's client list, and about Smullen and Petiak taking care of Zabar the accountant. I told them I'd testify to all this, but they had to put me someplace safe. And I told them I only trusted Morelli. So here I am."

"Why Morelli?"

"Because you have the key," Morelli said to me. "He needed to be close to the key. He knew we were seeing each other, and he thought he might catch some stray information. He's been sitting here waiting for another opportunity to retrieve the key. What he didn't realize was that Petiak was staking out your apartment for entirely different reasons."

"Petiak is doing cleanup," Dickie said. "He's getting rid of anyone who looks like a threat. At least, that's the way he tells it. After spending some very scary time with him, my feeling is he's gone gonzo. I think Stephanie popped up on his radar screen and he just wanted to enjoy the experience of taking his flamethrower to her."

"And you gave him more reason, didn't you?" Morelli said.

"He hit me! First that RangeMan gorilla attacked me in the apartment, and then I got kidnapped on the way out of the building. It was traumatic. I was handcuffed, and they rammed me down onto the floor of the car so I couldn't see anything. And then when they dragged me out, I still didn't know where we were. I only knew I was in a two-car garage. No windows. No other cars. There was just the light from the garage-door opener.

"Petiak was there with his spooky eyes. He didn't say anything to me. I still had my hands locked behind my back, and he hit me in the face. Just like that . . . *bam!* 'What the fuck was that?' I said to him. 'That was to let you know I'm serious,' he said. Then he asked me where the forty million was and I said I didn't know. So he hit me again, except that time it wasn't in the face, and I decided to tell him whatever he wanted to know."

"You told him Stephanie had the key."

"I told you. He *hit* me!"

I saw Morelli's eyes turn black, and I felt the air pressure change in the room. I stepped between Morelli and Dickie and put a hand to Morelli's chest.

"You don't want to kill him," I said to Morelli.

"Get out of my way."

"This is complicated enough. And we might need him for something. And you'd have to go before a review board if you kill him."

"I don't get it," Dickie said to Morelli. "What's the big deal here? He already wanted to kill her. It's not like he could kill her twice. Man, you two are a pair. You have anger-management issues. I hope you're not planning on reproducing. Hate to see a kid with her hair anyway."

I turned to Dickie. "What's wrong with my hair?"

"It's always a mess. You should get Joyce to help you with it. She has great hair. If you'd been more like Joyce, things might have worked out differently."

After that, things happened pretty fast, and when Morelli pulled me off Dickie, his nose was bleeding again. Someone had knocked Dickie off his chair and gone after him like Wild Woman. I guess that was me. Morelli had me at the waist with my feet two inches off the floor.

"I don't know why I always feel like I have to take care of you," Morelli said to me. "You do such a good job of it all by yourself."

There was blood splattered across the floor, soaking into Dickie's shirt.

"Crap," I said. "Am I responsible for all that blood?"

"No, he cracked his nose on the table when he panicked and tried to get away from you. If I put you down, do you promise not to go after him again?"

"Forever?"

"No. Just in the next ten minutes."

"Sure."

Morelli got some ice out of the freezer, wrapped it in a towel, and handed it to Dickie. "Do you suppose you could try being a little less obnoxious?" he asked him.

"What'd I do? I'm sitting here minding my own

business, trying to be cooperative. Talk to Bitchzilla over there."

I looked at my watch. "Nine minutes," I said to Morelli.

"I've got blood all over my shirt," Dickie said.

Morelli mopped the blood up off the floor with some wadded paper towels. "First of all, it's *my* shirt. And second, it's still the cleanest shirt we've got until we do laundry."

"Well, for cripes sakes, do the laundry," Dickie said.

"I don't have a washer or dryer, and I can't leave you in the house alone."

"I can take the laundry to my mom's house," I said. "Gather it up for me."

"I want to know the rest of the story first," Morelli said.

Dickie had his head tipped back with the ice pack over his nose. "I'm not talking anymore. I have a headache."

Morelli went to the powder room and got a bottle of Advil. "From what I've heard so far, you didn't know a whole lot about the drugs-for-arms business. How did you find out about all that?"

"Petiak told me after he hit me. He's on a big nutso ego trip. Had to tell me all the details of his master plan. Even demonstrated his flamethrower. Almost burned the fucking garage down. I gotta admit, the flamethrower is pretty cool. He says he sells a lot of them to the South American drug lords. Apparently scares the bejeezus out of the locals. And I have to tell you, I almost messed myself at the thought of getting it turned on me."

"Why didn't he turn it on you?"

"I imagine he wanted to make sure I was telling the truth about the key. I got stun-gunned, and I guess injected with something, and next thing I knew, I was back here."

"And the key?" Morelli asked.

"It's actually a key card. It allows the cardholder to access a high-security account in Holland from a satellite location here in the States. I have the account numbers memorized and a second set in a safety deposit box, but they aren't any good without the card. Without the card, I have to go to Holland to appear in person and pass a retinal and fingerprint scan. Not an option without a passport."

"Stephanie seems like an odd choice for the key keeper."

"I didn't choose her. She took the key with her when she left my office. The key's in the clock. I wasn't too worried about it because I knew she'd take care of the clock. I figured in some ways it was probably safer than if I'd left it at the office."

"What clock?" Morelli asked.

"Her Aunt Tootsie gave us a desk clock as a wedding present. I was using it in my office, and Sticky Fingers took it on her way out. I went to her apartment twice to look for it and couldn't find it. It's not here either, so I'm assuming it's at her parents' house."

I'd entirely forgotten about the clock. I was mentally scrambling, tracing backward. When did I last see the clock? It was in my bag. Then I stopped at the food store. Put the bags in the back of the car. Put the clock with the bags. Took the bags into the house. Could I have left the clock in the car? I couldn't remember bringing the clock into my apartment.

"You're looking pale," Morelli said. "Like all the blood just drained out of your face. You're not going to faint, are you?"

"I think I left the clock in the car."

"What car?"

"The Crown Vic."

"Where is it now?" Morelli asked.

"I don't know. It broke down on Route 206 and Ranger had one of his men take care of it."

Dickie took the ice pack off his face. "You lost Aunt Tootsie's clock?"

"It's not your money anyway," Morelli said to Dickie. "It's drug money. It belongs to the government. It'll be confiscated."

I called Ranger and asked him about the Crown Vic. He called back three minutes later.

"Binkie had it towed to the salvage yard," Ranger said.

"Which one?"

"Rosolli's off Stark."

"How's Tank?"

"Tank's good. He was discharged this morning. Anything I need to know?"

"Yes, but it's too complicated to tell you on the phone. I'll be around later. Did you feed Rex breakfast and give him fresh water?"

"That's part of Ella's job description."

I flipped my phone closed. "It's at Rosolli's."

Dickie's eyes got wide. "The junkyard? My God, they'll compress it to the size of a lunchbox."

"I'll call it in," Morelli said. "They'll send someone out to locate the car."

"What about me?" Dickie said. "Do I stay here?"

"Your status hasn't changed," Morelli said. "Until I hear otherwise, you're in protective custody."

"Get me your laundry basket," I said to Morelli. "I need clean clothes. I think I'm starting to mold."

EIGHTEEN

Grandma Mazur had Blackie under her arm when she opened the door.

"What are you doing with Blackie?" I asked her.

"I've been trying to find just the right place to set him out. I want him to look natural."

At the risk of being unkind, Blackie would need to be in Frankenstein's lab to look natural.

"I have Morelli's laundry. I thought I'd throw it in the washer, and then I have to get back to Morelli," I told Grandma.

"Blackie and me will take care of it for you. We haven't got anything better to do."

I left the laundry with Grandma and ran back to Morelli's SUV. I thought maybe Lula was right and I didn't do much for Morelli. It wouldn't kill me to pitch in and clean his house today. It was only a matter of time before my life would be back to normal, although I was beginning to think weird might be normal for me. The police would get the car and the clock and the money. They'd find Petiak and lock him up. And I wasn't sure what would happen to Dickie.

Morelli's house was less than a quarter of a mile from my parents' house. I drove two blocks and was T-boned by a Hummer coming out of an alley that ran behind a row of houses. The impact rammed me into a parked car and left me breathless. Before I had a chance to collect myself, my door was wrenched open, and I was yanked from behind the wheel. It was Dave with a broken nose, bandaged finger, and brace on his knee.

"Haw," Dave said, jamming the barrel of a gun into my ribs. "We figured you'd come to see your mom. We've been waiting for you."

I recognized the garage from Dickie's description. No windows. Room for two cars. Large charred area where Petiak had demonstrated the flamethrower.

"We finally meet," Petiak said. "I hope you brought the key."

"Here's the thing about the key. I don't have it."

"Wrong answer. That's not at all what I wanted to hear. That answer's making me angry."

"Yes, but I know where it is."

"Why can nothing ever be simple?" Petiak asked, sounding a lot like my mother.

"As Dickie probably told you, I didn't realize I had the key. He hid the key in a clock. I took the clock. I didn't know there was a key in it. I left the clock in the trunk of a car. And the car was towed to a salvage yard."

"Dickie didn't tell me any of this."

"What did he tell you?"

"He told me you had the key."

"Yes. I *had* the key. But technically I don't have the key anymore."

"Well, at least I can have the pleasure of killing you," Petiak said.

"You're not listening to me. I know where the key is. We just have to go get it. But here's the thing . . ."

"I knew there would be another thing," Petiak said.

"You have to promise not to kill me. And I want a reward. A finder's fee."

"And if I don't agree?"

"I won't help you find the key. I mean, what's the incentive to finding the key if you're going to kill me no matter what?"

"How much of a reward do you want?"

"Ten thousand dollars."

"Five."

"Okay, five."

I didn't for a minute think Petiak wouldn't kill me. I was trying to make him feel more comfortable, maybe not keep me on such a short leash. I had the transmitter pen in my pocket. Ranger would wonder why I was at the salvage yard. He'd call Morelli. Morelli or Ranger would discover the car. If I stalled a little, there was a good chance I might not die a hideous flamethrower death. Plus, Morelli had called the Vic into the station. If I was lucky, the police would also show up. And if I kept thinking like this, I might not pass out and throw up from terror. Just focus, I kept saying to myself. Don't panic. Too late. Inside there was panic. A lot of it.

"Where is this salvage yard?" Petiak wanted to know.

"It's at the far end of Stark Street. Rosolli's Salvage."

We all piled into a black Beemer. Probably not the same one that was in my parking lot because this one had four doors. Dave's partner and Petiak were in front and I was in back with Dave. The flamethrower was in the trunk.

Dave didn't look happy to be sitting next to me.

"So how's it going?" I said to him.

"Shut up," Dave said.

"What's with the knee brace?"

"You fucking ran over me with your fucking car."

"Nothing personal," I said to him.

"Yeah," Dave said, "and it's not gonna be personal when we barbecue you."

The salvage yard was surrounded by nine-foot-high steel-mesh fencing. The entrance was gated and locked. I was guessing this was necessary because so many people wanted to steal cars that were squashed until they were only two feet high and had no working parts.

The Beemer pulled up to the gate and stopped.

"How do we get in?" Petiak asked.

"I don't know," I said to him. "I've never tried to get into a salvage yard before."

"Rudy," Petiak said to Dave's partner, "take a look."

Dave's partner was named Rudy. Grade school must have been hell with a name like that.

Rudy got out and looked through the gate to the other side. "Hey!" he yelled. He turned back to us and shrugged. "Don't see anyone."

"It's pretty big," I said. "Maybe there's another entrance."

Rudy got back behind the wheel and drove down Stark. He followed a side road that curved around the salvage yard and did a complete loop. We didn't see any other entrances.

"This is perplexing," Petiak said.

"Maybe you don't need the key," I said. I knew he needed the key. He'd gotten the codes off Dickie and now he needed the key to electronically transfer the $40 million. If he went to Holland to make a personal pickup, he couldn't pass the retinal and hand scan.

"Are you sure the key is in there?" he asked.

"Yep. This is where they took the car."

"Can you climb the fence?" Petiak asked Rudy.

"Yeah, but there's three feet of razor wire at the top. I'll get torn to shreds. I'll never get over the razor wire."

"Go back and try the gate. Maybe it's open. Maybe there's a call box."

Rudy went back and rattled the gate and looked around. He returned to the car. "I don't see anything. It's locked up tight with a padlock. I could get in if I had bolt cutters."

"Home Depot," I said.

Petiak cut his eyes to me. "You know where there's a Home Depot?"

Thirty-five minutes later, we were in the Home Depot parking lot, and I was imagining an elaborate rescue scenario. Ranger had tracked us down at Home Depot, and he was organizing an army to storm the salvage yard once we returned to break in with our newly purchased bolt cutters. Petiak and Dave and I were in the car, waiting for Rudy. No one was saying anything.

Finally, Rudy appeared, striding back to the car. No bolt cutters.

"Now what?" Petiak said.

"They didn't have any bolt cutters," Rudy told him, angling himself behind the wheel.

"I know where there's a Lowe's," I said.

Twenty minutes later, we were at Lowe's. I was loving this. More setup time for Ranger and Morelli. Probably the entire police department and the National Guard were at the salvage yard by now.

Rudy ran into Lowe's and fifteen minutes later came out. No bolt cutters.

"I'm losing patience," Petiak said. "Go back to the salvage yard."

We were now forty minutes away from the salvage yard, and I was thinking it would be good if we could resolve this hostage thing soon because before long I was going to need a bathroom. I'd had a lot of coffee with the doughnuts.

I concentrated on sending Rudy mental messages.

Drive faster. Drive faster. Unfortunately, Rudy was having none of it. Rudy wasn't taking a chance on getting stopped by a cop. Rudy was obeying all the rules. After what seemed like hours, we eased up to the salvage yard gate. Still locked. Still no one in sight.

"Ram it," Petiak said.

"Excuse me?" Rudy said.

"Ram the fucker," Petiak said. "Back up and floor it and ram the gate open."

"It's pretty sturdy," Rudy said.

Dave was stoic beside me, but I could smell him sweating. Dave was nervous.

"Maybe we should all get out and let Rudy ram the gate by himself," I said. "Then we can walk in if it works."

"We're in this together," Petiak said. "Rudy, ram the gate."

Rudy backed up and idled for a moment. We all sucked in air and held our breath. And Rudy floored it and rammed the gate.

Bang! The gate flew off its hinges, and the front-seat air bags exploded. Dave hadn't been buckled in and was thrown forward, hitting the front seat with a good solid thud. Rudy and Petiak were fighting the air bags. I unbuckled my seat belt, opened my door, and took off.

I ran into the salvage yard, where I imagined the Marines were waiting. I didn't see any Marines, so I ran as far and as fast as I could. I passed the crusher machine and took the stairs to a grid of catwalks that led to what looked like a boxcar on stilts. I forced the door and went inside and locked the door behind me. I was in the control room for the crusher machine. I looked out, and I could see Petiak and Dave and Rudy walking my way. Petiak was holding the flamethrower and Rudy and Dave had guns drawn.

My heart was beating so hard, it was knocking against my rib cage. No one was here. There weren't even distant sirens. Somehow, the system hadn't worked. The pen wasn't sending a signal. Someone was asleep at the switch at RangeMan. Whatever. I was on my own. I frantically looked for a phone, but I was in the throes of blind fear, and I wasn't seeing much of anything. I was trapped in a box. No way to escape. It was only a matter of time.

They were on the stairs—Petiak first, then Rudy, and Dave bringing up the rear. I was pushing buttons and flipping switches, looking for something that would make noise, call the fire department, jettison me out of harm's way.

I was so scared, my nose was running and my eyes were brimming with tears. It was the flamethrower. I'd seen its work. I could still recall the smell of burned flesh. I could see the horrible charred cadavers.

Petiak was on a catwalk, maybe thirty feet off the ground and level with my boxcar control room. I hit a red button and the hydraulics began moving the crusher walls below me. Rudy and Dave were on the stairs approaching the catwalk, and they stopped dead in their tracks, but Petiak was relentless in his mission. I could see him coming. He reached the control room door and tried the knob. The lock held. He stepped back and gave it a blast from the flamethrower. Nothing. It was a steel fire door. For that matter, the entire control room was steel. I was looking at Petiak through a small window in the door, and I could see the rage in his face. He leveled the flamethrower at me and pumped it. Flames shot toward me, flattened on the steel door, and curled back. Black smoke clouded the window. The door wasn't sealed tight, and heat and smoke crept into the room.

I stepped back and looked out the large window facing the crusher. Dave and Rudy were off the stairs and on the ground, running to the salvage yard entrance. I couldn't see Petiak. He wasn't on the stairs. I went back to the door. Smoke was no longer seeping in. There was no more heat. I squinted through the sooty pane of glass. I didn't see Petiak. I went back to the window over the crusher and saw him.

He'd inadvertently set himself on fire, and in his confusion and horror he'd fallen off the catwalk into the crusher. I hit the red button and the crusher stopped. Not that it mattered. Petiak was clearly dead. And I suspected the crusher would have stopped before it compacted him. It was designed for cars, not maniacs.

I took a moment to get myself under control and then I looked for a phone again. I found the phone and called Morelli.

"I'm in the salvage yard," I told him.

"I thought you were doing laundry," he said.

"Just c-c-come get me, okay?"

"Where's the car?"

"Forget the car. Find some other way to get here."

Then I called Ranger.

"Where the heck are you?" I asked him.

"I'm at RangeMan. What are you doing at your mother's?"

"I'm not at my mother's. I'm at the salvage yard."

I glanced down. I was wearing Morelli's sweats. The pen was in my jeans pocket, and the jeans were getting washed. Good thing I was so dumb. If I'd thought I'd been kidnapped without the pen, I would have died of fright an hour ago.

"Babe," Ranger said.

"You'll want to see this," I told him.

I called Connie.

"I'm at your cousin Manny's salvage yard," I told her. "Where is everybody? The gate was locked and no one's here."

"Manny's mother-in-law died. They had the funeral today. I didn't go. I only knew her in passing."

"The short version is that Roland Petiak set himself on fire and fell into your cousin's squashing machine. I thought your cousin would want to know. And also, I'm looking for my Crown Vic. It's somewhere in the salvage yard."

There was a stool in the control room where the operator sat when he was working the compactor. I sat on the stool and looked out the window, eager for someone to come rescue me. I didn't want to leave the safety of the little room until Morelli or Ranger was at my door. I avoided looking down into the squashing machine. I didn't want to see Roland Petiak.

I sat there for ten minutes and everyone arrived at once. Morelli and Dickie, Ranger, Connie and Lula and Connie's cousin Manny. And Joyce and Smullen's girlfriend. I couldn't remember her name.

I called Morelli's cell.

"I'm in the control room by the squasher machine," I said. "I'm not coming out until someone comes up here to get me."

Everyone looked up at me, and I waved down to them and wiped my nose on my sleeve.

Morelli took the stairs two at a time and crossed the grate to get to me. I opened the door and almost collapsed. My teeth were chattering, and my legs were rubber.

"I was afraid I'd fall off the catwalk if I didn't have someone to hang on to," I told Morelli.

Morelli wrapped an arm around me and peered into the compactor at what was left of Petiak. "That's not good."

"It's Petiak."

"Are you okay?"

"So far as I can tell." And I went down on one knee. "Whoops," I said. "Guess I'm a little wobbly."

Ranger was on the catwalk too, and between Ranger and Morelli, they were able to get me down the stairs.

"What the heck's going on here?" Lula wanted to know when I set my feet on the ground. "Nobody tells me anything."

"Yeah," Joyce said. "What the heck's going on?"

Dickie was still in the hooded sweatshirt, standing to one side, oogling Joyce and Smullen's girlfriend. "Hey, Sex Monkey," Dickie said to Joyce.

"Do you have it?" Joyce said.

"What?"

"You know . . . *it*."

"Do you mean the forty million? Nope. Government's going to confiscate it."

"You are such a turd," Joyce said. "I can't believe I wasted my time with you. How could you have lost that money?"

"It was all Stephanie's fault," Dickie said.

"Asshole," Joyce said. And she turned on her heel and stormed off, with Smullen's girlfriend matching her, stride for stride.

Morelli called the dispatcher and reported the death and gave a description of Dave and Rudy.

"I forgot to take the pen," I told Ranger.

"Sometimes it's better to be lucky than good," Ranger said.

"You were right about the drugs and guns and money laundering," I told Ranger. "The law firm was stealing guns, trading them for drugs, and then selling the drugs. Then they billed the drug dealers for legal services and washed the money through a legitimate business . . . Dickie's law firm. Dickie found out, cleaned out the firm's bank account, and transferred the money to his own account. The key to Dickie's account was in the clock."

"Aunt Tootsie's clock?" Lula asked. "What are the chances?"

"I forgot about the clock and left it in the Crown Vic's trunk. The Vic broke down, and it got towed here."

"When was this?" Connie's cousin Manny asked.

"Last week. It was an old cop car with 'Pig Car' written on the side and it had a couple bullet holes in it and rodent fur on the inside," I told him.

"I know just where that is," Manny said. "I remember it coming in. A couple SWAT guys, right?"

"Right."

Ranger's cell phone buzzed, and he took a short call. "I'm heading out," he said to Morelli. "She's on your watch. Next week she's mine."

I was pretty sure he was kidding, but then, maybe not.

"Come on," Manny said. "I'll take you to the Vic."

There were mountains of wheel covers and acres of scrap metal stacked together like lasagna in the salvage yard. We wound our way through a maze of cars in various stages of mutilation and finally Manny stopped at a seven-foot-tall block of multicolored metal and pointed about a third of the way up.

"See that burgundy layer? That's the Vic."

It was twelve inches thick.

"Your Aunt Tootsie's not gonna be happy about this," Lula said.

We retraced our steps, and watched the emergency vehicles pour into the salvage yard. EMS trucks, fire trucks, cop cars. A couple uniforms secured the area around the compactor with tape and the medical examiner and a crime scene photographer climbed the stairs to the catwalk. Marty Gobel followed.

"This is going to take a while to sort out," Morelli

said to me. "What would you like to do? I can have someone take you to your mother's or to my house."

I didn't want to do either of those things. I was still rattled, and I wanted to be near Morelli.

"I'd rather stay here," I said. "I'll find a place to hang out until you're done, and we can go home together."

It was dark when we rolled into Morelli's house. We'd stopped for a take-out pizza, and we'd picked up the laundry. I was still in Morelli's sweats and he was still commando in his recycled jeans. I clipped Bob to the long leash in the backyard, and Morelli and I leaned against the kitchen counter and ate pizza.

"This has been a very strange day," I said.

"Yeah, but it's over and Dickie is out of my house." Morelli helped himself to another piece of pizza. "Why on earth did you marry him?"

"In the beginning, before we were married, he was charming. He was probably fooling around, but I didn't see it. I was impressed with the law degree. I thought it showed intelligence and ambition. My parents loved him. They were ecstatic I wasn't marrying *you*."

"Those were my wild oats–sowing days."

"Dickie looked like a saint compared to you."

Bob scratched at the door, and we let him in and gave him some Bob food and a couple pieces of pizza.

"What do you suppose will happen to Dickie?" I asked Morelli.

"There's the irony. Dickie could end up being a very rich guy. As far as I can tell, he's guilty of being stupid and devious, but I'm not sure he ever got around to committing a crime."

"What about the drug sales?"

"Word at the station is that the books were kept clean. Everyone knows the firm's dirty, but no one's been able to prove anything. Now that Petiak, Smullen, and Gorvich are dead, Dickie might end up being the sole owner of the real estate and the forty million. At the very least, he'll keep his fourth. I guess that's the bad news. But the good news is Joyce blew Dickie off big-time at the salvage yard. At least Joyce won't see any of the money."

"I hate to see Dickie get that money. It's so wrong."

"Justice has a way of prevailing," Morelli said. "Dickie hasn't got the money yet."

I fed Bob the last chunk of my pizza. "I'm stuffed. I want to take a hot shower and get into some clean clothes."

Morelli locked the back door and tucked the laundry basket under his arm. "I have a better idea. Let's take a hot shower and get into *no* clothes." He looked at the neatly folded clothes in the basket. "Although I am looking forward to test-driving my underwear. Your mother ironed everything. My boxers have a crease."

And somewhere under those boxers I had a single pair of little black panties embroidered with Ranger's name that had all the potential of the toaster bomb.

"You can test-drive them tomorrow," I said to Morelli. "I like the no clothes idea for tonight."